"I'M GONNA MAKE LOVE TO YOU, WILDCAT. DO YOU STILL WANNA FIGHT ME?"

His kiss was not a gentleman's kiss, but one that seemed to go on forever as his hands roamed freely, memorizing the smooth texture of Ariel's skin and tempting contours of her body. If Ariel intended to stop this, now was the time. But she wanted this man.

His mouth was hot and demanding. He growled deep in his throat, his hands going to her shirt, stripping buttons from their holes, searching for and finding smooth, silken flesh beneath her thin chemise.

"Damnation, I can't remember when I've wanted a woman as fiercely as I want you," he murmured raggedly against her lips. "May my soul rot in Hell for what I'm gonna do. I can't stop now."

Love Me With Fury

CARA MILES

AVON BOOKS ◆ NEW YORK

LOVE ME WITH FURY is an original publication of Avon Books. This work has never before appeared in book form. This work is a novel. Any similarity to actual persons or events is purely coincidental.

AVON BOOKS
A division of
The Hearst Corporation
1350 Avenue of the Americas
New York, New York 10019

Copyright © 1991 by Connie Mason
Published by arrangement with the author
Library of Congress Catalog Card Number: 91-91796
ISBN: 0-380-76450-4

First Avon Books Printing: September 1991

AVON TRADEMARK REG. U.S. PAT. OFF. AND IN OTHER COUNTRIES, MARCA REGISTRADA, HECHO EN U.S.A.

Printed in the U.S.A.

RA 10 9 8 7 6 5 4 3 2 1

To Natasha Kern
who has made a difference in my life and career
and
To Maggie Lichota
for allowing me the pleasure of working with her.

Chapter 1

Texas—July 1875

T he door of the overturned coach was flung
open with a crash.

"Come out of there, you bastard, and bring
your doxy with you!"

Ariel groaned, barely conscious yet aware of the
commanding voice booming down at her, issuing
orders that didn't make sense. Was it one of the
two desperadoes who had been chasing the stage
when it overturned? she wondered groggily as
she shoved at the weight pressing down against
her. What was wrong with her arms—why
couldn't she seem to move them? Slowly gathering her wits, Ariel glanced down and saw that
one of the passengers had fallen on top of her
when the stage overturned. It was the lawman
who had boarded the stage at Texarkana with two
prisoners in tow. The prisoners, a man and
woman, had been shackled and remained so the
entire time since they left Texarkana.

"Do you hear me? Come out of there, Dillon!"

Slowly Ariel raised her eyes to the man who
had flung aside the door just moments ago, posing a new threat on this wild trip she had under-
taken without her mother's consent. Squinting
into the blazing sun, Ariel saw a pair of legs straddle the opening. And what legs! Denim clad, they

1

seemed to stretch to forever and back, his booted feet planted sturdily on either side of the opening. From what Ariel could see the man was tall, and if his powerful calves and thighs were any indication, the rest of him was a mass of muscle and brawn. Who was he? An outlaw? A desperado? Why was he referring to her as a "doxy"?

"Climb out—it's all over, Dillon. I've trailed you from one end of Texas to the other and I don't aim to let you two escape me now. I heard you were captured in Texarkana and being transported to Fort Worth. It's a good thing I moseyed this way to make sure you both got there safe and sound."

Squatting, the man peered inside the overturned coach. What he saw must have displeased him for he spit out a vile curse. "Where is he? What in blazes happened to Dillon?"

Ariel blinked, hoping she'd awaken and find this was just a horrible nightmare. She had encountered nothing but trouble from the moment she left her home in St. Louis several weeks ago. Since her mother and stepfather had forbidden her to travel to Texas and claim the ranch left to her by her father, she'd had to make all her own travel arrangements in secret and leave without their knowledge. She hated sneaking behind their backs but nothing was going to stop her from fulfilling her late father's wish that she live on his spread near Waco, Texas.

She'd only experienced routine traveling problems such as bad weather and awfully bumpy roads until she'd reached the border town of Texarkana. While waiting for a connecting stage to Fort Worth she'd learned that her fellow passengers were to be a lawman and the two prisoners he was transporting to Fort Worth for trial. At first Ariel thought to wait for another stage, but the depot master assured her that Sheriff Gore was perfectly capable of handling the two prisoners, particularly since they were both shackled and unlikely to cause trouble. Leery but anxious to reach her destination, Ariel had boarded the stage against her better judgment.

The crowning irony came when the stage was pursued by two desperadoes somewhere between Texarkana and Fort Worth. In a desperate effort to escape the would-be robbers the driver had whipped the horses into a froth. Then they had hit a chuckhole and lost a wheel. The stage bounced, spun wildly, and Ariel knew no more until she awoke to a rough voice rudely ordering her out of the stage.

Above Ariel, the man hunkered down on his haunches, staring into the coach as if stunned by what he saw. The man's huge frame blotted out the sun, shielding his features from her. The air around Ariel turned blue as he let loose a string of curses that burned her ears.

"The yellow-bellied son of a bitch is gone! You can bet your sweet ass you're not getting away from me, Tilly. Makes no nevermind who I turn in, you're both guilty as sin. I sure as hell would like to know where Bart Dillon disappeared to in this wilderness. Too bad about Sheriff Gore, he was a good man."

As he spoke he shoved the lifeless body of the sheriff aside. Ariel sighed, dragging in a welcome breath as the dead weight was lifted off her. Though her head still spun dizzily she could have sworn the man had called her Tilly. Who was Tilly?

"Are you hurt?" The hard edge to his voice left little doubt in Ariel's mind that her state of health was the least of his concerns.

"I—I don't think so—but I'm not . . ."

"Give me your hand, I'll pull you outta there."

Ariel balked. The notion of placing herself at this harsh stranger's mercy sent chills racing down her spine. But the choice was taken from her when she was hauled roughly through the door of the upturned stage and plopped down on the edge, her feet still dangling inside. Not until that moment did Ariel realize that her wrists were shackled. She stared at them stupidly, then at the man.

"I—don't understand. Why am I shackled? Who are you?"

The man crouched beside her, balanced on the balls of his feet, and Ariel got her first good look at him.

Her initial impression was that he was big. He hovered over her diminutive form like a huge vulture ready to gobble her alive. He looked lean, dangerous, and as tough as a two-bit steak. His very appearance suggested tempest and passion; his silver-gray eyes portrayed intelligence and fire. His features were bold and strong, his tanned cheekbones were high, his chin firm and squared. His mouth was full and wide. He wore a battered, flat-brimmed leather hat shoved to the back of his head, and a leather jerkin, plaid shirt, and denim pants so tight they could have been painted on.

Jet-black hair scraped the collar of his shirt and a gun belt clung to his narrow hips. There was an air about him that hinted of extraordinary conviction of purpose, of restive energy and power. Then the realization struck Ariel that he was handsome. And the most physically attractive man she'd ever seen. She exhaled raggedly, suddenly unable to breathe, overwhelmed by the raw masculine appeal of the man and her uncharacteristic response to him.

"Who are you?"

A lazy smile hung on one corner of his full lips though his voice expressed no amusement. "Jess Wilder. Do you recognize the name?"

"No, should I?"

"Perhaps you will recognize my brother's

name. It's Judd Wilder. You should, you and Bart Dillon killed him.''

Ariel gasped in disbelief. ''What! You're crazy. Who is Bart Dillon?''

''Go ahead and pretend innocence, you'll still hang. Where is your partner in crime?'' His sharp eyes searched the vast emptiness surrounding them. ''He couldn't have gone far. Did he kill Sheriff Gore? I'll find the bastard no matter where he's hiding. I always knew he was a skunk but leaving you behind showed his true colors.''

''Who are you? *What* are you?''

''Jess Wilder—didn't you hear me the first time? I'm taking you to Fort Worth to stand trial for robbery and murder. There are wanted posters floating all over Texas for your arrest. I've been trailing you and Dillon for quite a spell and I'm damn lucky to catch up to you before another bounty hunter beat me to it.''

''You're a bounty hunter?'' Shock and disgust colored her words. Ariel had heard of that relentless breed of men who fed off the misfortune of others.

''Among other things,'' Jess admitted cryptically. ''I doubt my past would interest you.''

Ariel's green eyes widened with apprehension when Jess uncoiled his long legs, rose to his full six foot three, and leaped to the dusty ground with the agile grace of a jungle cat.

''Wha—what are you going to do?''

''Get you down from there and bury the dead. Come on, Tilly, jump, I'll catch you.''

There it was, that name again! Obviously Jess Wilder had her confused with someone named Tilly. She intended to set this brash bounty hunter straight.

''You've made a serious mistake, Mr. Wilder. I'm not this person named Tilly. I'm Ariel Leland, from St. Louis.''

"Sure, Tilly, and I'm Jesus H. Christ. Come on, lady, move your butt."

Ariel's mouth tightened in outrage. Never had she been spoken to in such a vile manner. This man was crude, rude, and impossibly arrogant. Didn't he know a lady when he saw one? She had attended the best finishing school for young ladies in St. Louis, associated with only the city's elite, and traveled in the best circles. She had been gently raised by her mother and stepfather though her real father had provided generously for her support.

"You're despicable!" Ariel shouted furiously. "Obviously you've never met a lady before. I insist you treat me with respect and courtesy. You may call me Miss Leland."

Jess shoved his hat even further back on his head, squinting up at the disheveled beauty with mute amazement, and a certain amount of admiration. He wanted to laugh aloud but something in the set of her shoulders and stubborn tilt of her chin prevented him. If he didn't know for a fact that the woman was a cold-blooded killer he would almost have believed her. He'd never expected Tilly Cowles to be so damn beautiful. Or so young.

Had he made a mistake? he wondered. Was this ravishing, irate creature really Ariel Leland as she claimed? Or was she merely a good actress? He had to admit she was a fetching little thing, all female with her sweet curves, shiny ebony tresses, and fiery green eyes that promised pleasures that made a man burn. Jess was shocked at the jolt of lust that hardened his loins, and tried to remember that Tilly Cowles and Bart Dillon had killed his brother in a single act of violence that had taken away his only living relative.

Driven by revenge, Jess had quit a job he loved in order to become a bounty hunter. He had rented out the house he and Judd had shared in

Fort Worth, left his job as U.S. marshal, and taken his search for Judd's killers into the vast emptiness of Texas. Judd had been Jess' deputy, and only a twist of fate had placed Judd in the bank at the time of the robbery instead of Jess. Now Judd was gone and Jess had sworn to devote the rest of his life, if necessary, to bringing Judd's killers, identified as Bart Dillon and Tilly Cowles, to justice. Jess had spent the last two years carrying out his pledge.

"I'm sorry if my language offends you, Tilly. Now get down," Jess ordered roughly. For some reason this petite beauty completely unnerved him. She wasn't at all what he'd expected.

Jess followed his words with action, reaching up, grasping her arms, and dragging her over the side of the upturned vehicle. Clutching desperately at the broad width of his shoulders, Ariel slid down his hard body, the contact exciting her senses and making her blush. Her mouth dropped open. "Oh."

Jess felt it too and his dark brows arched upward, puzzled by his spontaneous reaction to a woman who robbed and killed for a living. Placing his hands on her waist, he set her aside.

"None of your tricks, Tilly," he warned ominously. "I can't be swayed by your womanly wiles. Your body, fascinating as it is, holds no interest for me. Flaunt your charms all you want, it will do you no good."

Ariel's face turned red. "You low-down, contemptible snake! You—you—" Words failed her. Instead, she raised her manacled hands and let them fly, straight into Jess' face.

Jess jerked backward, but not in time. The explosive sound of the blow and the red welt blooming across his left cheek provided Ariel with a measure of satisfaction. A smug smile lit her features.

Jess' reaction was swift and brutal as he grasped

her shoulders and jerked her so close their bodies touched.

"Don't ever do that again," he bit out from between clenched teeth so white they dazzled. "One mistake is all you're allowed."

His face was hard with implied menace and instinctively Ariel shrank from his fury.

"I can only be pushed so far, Tilly, and you've already tried my patience to the limit."

"How many times must I tell you I'm not Tilly Cowles?" Ariel shouted, her own anger matching his. "I'm Ariel Leland. I'm traveling to Waco to claim a ranch left to me by my father."

"It makes no nevermind what I call you, Tilly, I know who and what you are," Jess said with disgust. "If you want me to call you Ariel, fine, but it changes nothing." He flung her away. She stumbled, then righted herself, her bound wrists making it difficult to maintain her balance.

"You brute, why won't you listen to me? What makes you so damn certain I'm Tilly Cowles?"

"I know Tilly Cowles and Bart Dillon boarded the Fort Worth stage in Texarkana with Sheriff Gore. Sheriff Gore is dead, Dillon is missing, but you're here, so you can cut the crap about going to Waco to collect an inheritance. Do you know where Dillon disappeared to? Why did he leave you behind?"

"There were a man and a woman on the stage with the lawman," Ariel admitted slowly, "but I didn't know their names. They spoke little, and the sheriff and I only exchanged pleasantries. I—I don't know what happened to them. I was rendered unconscious when the stage overturned. When I awoke you were there ordering me out and they were gone. Was Tilly Cowles small with dark hair?"

"Nice try, Tilly, or Ariel, or whatever your alias. You know damn well Tilly is small with dark hair just like yours. What happened to the stage? Why did it overturn?''

Ariel's brow puckered. ''We were being chased by desperadoes. The coach speeded up, hit something, then overturned. The last thing I remember was being thrown against the side. Will you please remove these shackles? They're chaffing my wrists. How did they get from Tilly Cowles' wrists to mine?''

''You tell me. Why would Ariel Leland be wearing shackles?''

''Where is the driver? He could tell you I'm not lying.''

''Dead. So's the guard. Both crushed beneath the stage.''

''I have identification!'' Ariel suddenly recalled. ''There are letters and papers addressed to me inside the coach in my traveling bag and money in my reticule.''

Jess prided himself on being a fair man. The least he could do was give her the benefit of the doubt, no matter how small. Throwing Ariel an oblique look, he hauled himself atop the stage and disappeared through the open door. Ariel heard him moving around inside and after a short time he poked his head through the opening.

''You must take me for a fool. I found nothing inside but the body of Sheriff Gore. No traveling bag, no reticule. Not only that but Gore didn't die in the accident. He was shot in the back. Did you do it?''

Ariel gulped, offering a silent prayer for the dead sheriff. How could she convince this rough bounty hunter that she was innocent?

''I—certainly didn't kill the sheriff. I told you, I'm not Tilly Cowles. My bag and reticule have to be inside the stage. Look again.''

Jess ducked his head back inside. When he emerged a few minutes later he was scowling darkly.

"Damn sneaky female," he muttered. "Don't lie to me again."

"They were there, I swear it!" Ariel cried, growing frantic. "If you couldn't find them they must have been stolen by the man and woman you're looking for."

"Try again, Tilly, your excuse doesn't hold water. Too bad Dillon didn't take you with him when he took off, but I'll get him. I don't care how long it takes, I'll find the bastard and see him hang. He killed the only person in the world I truly cared about. Sit down over there in the shade." He pointed to a clump of mesquite. "I've work to do."

"What are you going to do?"

"Bury the dead."

"Don't leave me like this. Find the key and release my wrists."

"I don't trust you, lady. As long as you're bound you won't be looking for a weapon or shooting me in the back while I bury the sheriff, driver, and guard."

Ariel searched her brain for all the cuss words she'd ever heard. Unfortunately they were woefully lacking.

"Wait!" she cried. Jess hesitated, turning back to face her. "Why won't you believe me?" The desperate note in her voice nearly undid him until he forced himself to remember that this was a woman who robbed and killed for a living.

Eyeing her shrewdly, he pulled a much-creased and -perused sheet of paper from his vest pocket, carefully unfolded it, and shoved it under her nose.

"See for yourself. The picture isn't very clear but the description fits you to a tee."

The heat emanating from his silver-gray eyes mesmerized Ariel as she slowly lowered her gaze to stare at the poster. She saw immediately that the picture of Tilly Cowles obviously came from a bad photograph. It was so blurred that it could have been anyone—even her. The description that followed, however, provided detailed information about Tilly Cowles. She was described as being small, five feet two inches, with long black hair and green eyes.

"No," Ariel whispered, stunned. The description fit her, but so could it fit many other women, including the woman who had boarded the stage in Texarkana.

"Are you satisfied, Tilly?"

"Ariel," she insisted with quiet dignity.

"Of course, how stupid of me. Are you satisfied, Ariel?"

"That's not me."

"Your sister, maybe?" Jess challenged, one corner of his mouth curling in derision. He turned away.

"Mr. Wilder, I'm innocent. You've made a grave error."

"Sure I did. So did my brother when he entered the bank the day you and Dillon decided to rob it. Don't go away, Ariel," he mocked, "I'll get back to you." He kept on walking despite Ariel's gasp of outrage.

"My name is Ariel."

"You sure are one stubborn woman," he threw over his shoulder.

"And you're one callous bastard."

"Careful," Jess warned, "you're showing your true colors."

Ariel fumed in impotent rage as Jess disappeared inside the stage. Within a few moments he hauled the sheriff's body out and dragged him a short distance from the stage.

Jess located the bodies of the driver and guard crushed beneath the stagecoach. Reconstructing the accident, he surmised that the left wheels had hit a deep rut left by runoff from a recent deluge, causing the stage to skid a short distance then

overturn. Was the stage being pursued by desperadoes as Ariel claimed, he wondered, unaware that his mind had already accepted the
name she had given him. It certainly would explain how Bart Dillon got away. But why did he
leave Tilly behind? Unless she was unconscious
and Dillon didn't want to bother with her. Dillon
couldn't help but know he was being trailed by
bounty hunters. Had been for a long time. Perhaps he didn't want to wait around long enough
for one of them to find him.

The guard and driver were unlucky enough to
fall and become trapped beneath the lumbering
vehicle. But despite Jess' considerable strength he
was unable to move the coach and extract the
bodies.

Ariel's anger simmered as she watched Jess try
to move the stagecoach. The muscles in his thighs
and shoulders bulged obscenely as he strained to
his impossible task. Deliberately she looked away,
suddenly embarrassed by the way his tight den-
ims cradled and defined the taut mounds of his
buttocks when he bent. He looked strong enough
to crush her with one hand, Ariel thought, suppressing a shudder.

Everything about the man suggested power and
strength, and Ariel was astute enough to realize
he presented a danger to her she had never before encountered. He was too big, too powerful—
too damn attractive.

Jess finally abandoned his efforts to free the two
dead men from beneath the coach. Instead he retrieved a shovel attached to the back of the stage
and dug a shallow grave. The sunbaked earth was
hard and Jess was sweating profusely by the time
the grave was deep enough. Ariel looked away as
Jess searched the sheriff's pockets, removed his
badge, and rolled him into the hole, covering him
with dirt. Jess glanced in her direction and saw
that she had turned from the sight.

"You were lucky, Tilly—er—Ariel. You could have been thrown from the coach and crushed like the driver and guard. Too bad it wasn't your lover I buried."

"Lover! How dare you!"

Yes, lover, Jess thought in silent derision, wondering how she could let that bastard touch her. Until he reminded himself that she was as despicable as he was. For some strange reason Jess found it difficult to believe that Ariel was a killer wanted by the law. She appeared so young, so innocent, so—so untouched!

Keep your mind above your belt, Jess Wilder, he warned himself. A woman as beautiful and sexually tempting as Tilly Cowles was far from innocent. He reckoned she'd use every trick at her disposal to persuade him to let her go, and the Lord knew he never aspired to sainthood. Nor was he made of stone. He'd have to keep reminding himself that Tilly Cowles might not have pulled the trigger of the gun that killed his brother but she was just as responsible for Judd's senseless death as Bart Dillon.

"That man wasn't my lover," Ariel persisted stubbornly. "I never saw him until he got on the stage at Texarkana. Now I wish I had followed my first instinct and waited for another stage." She was beginning to sound like a magpie, repeating the same words over and over. For all the good it did her.

Jess glanced at her in exasperation. Undaunted, Ariel glared back.

"You're a bold little baggage," Jess observed, walking back to where Ariel sat in the shade. "If you're thinking what I think you are, forget it. It won't work."

"What I'm thinking can't be repeated by a lady," Ariel returned tartly.

Jess tilted his head back and roared with laughter. "A lady? No lady would be traveling with Bart Dillon."

"I told you, I don't know—"

"—Bart Dillon," Jess snorted, completing her sentence. Then he reached out and pulled her to her feet.

Ariel stiffened her spine and held out her wrists. "Release me."

Jess eyed her in silent speculation. "How do I know you won't bolt? Or try to shoot me when my back is turned?"

"Where would I go? I don't even have a horse. Or a gun. Besides," she said, measuring him with her eyes, "you're twice my size." Then she flung him a challenge Jess couldn't ignore. "Are you afraid of me?"

"No, but you sure as hell better be afraid of *me*, lady."

"You're going to look mighty foolish when you learn I'm not Tilly Cowles."

"I'll cross that bridge when I come to it."

It's going to be a long trek to Fort Worth, Jess sighed to himself as Ariel's soft bottom nudged his manhood. He had hoped to salvage one of the horses from the wreck but those that weren't killed outright had been too badly injured to ride. He was forced to put the poor creatures out of their misery and take Ariel on his own horse, placing her before him on his saddle.

While he had been occupied with the horses and after removing the manacles from Ariel's wrists using the key he had found in the sheriff's pocket, Ariel had rummaged in her trunk for a change of clothing. She rolled them along with a comb and a bar of soap into a petticoat and insisted that Jess stuff them in his saddlebag. Not entirely heartless, Jess allowed her the small comfort of her possessions. He even found her bonnet inside the stage and handed it to her, realizing that her ivory complexion would suffer dreadfully beneath the fierce Texas sun.

"Did you happen to find some identification in your trunk?" Jess asked in an effort to keep his mind from dwelling on her cloud of black hair whipping against his face and her soft body trying so hard not to touch his.

Ariel shook her head obstinately. "I told you my identification and money were in my reticule, which is missing. All I have left is the small amount pinned to my—never mind."

Jess made a disparaging sound deep in his throat. He had given her every opportunity to prove her identity but so far had been shown nothing to change his mind. Tilly Cowles was smart, he'd give her that much, and the best damn actress he'd seen in a hell of a long time. She almost had him convinced that she was Ariel Leland—almost, but not quite. For one thing, a lady wouldn't be traveling alone across the wilds of Texas. Desperadoes rode freely between towns and the Kiowa and Comanche still raided upon occasion.

"Where are you taking me?" Ariel asked.

She hoped it was someplace where she could wire St. Louis for proper identification. Her mother and stepfather would be horrified to learn she'd been mistaken for a common criminal. They had been against this trip from the beginning and had forbidden her to leave St. Louis. But Ariel was determined to prove everyone wrong and take over the reins of Leland Ranch. If her father had had enough faith in her ability to run his beloved ranch, she could not sell it as her mother insisted she do.

Mama considered Texas to be an uncivilized territory populated by Indians and desperadoes, and her stepfather, Tom Brady, agreed with her. That's why Mama had left her husband, Buck Leland, in Texas years ago when Ariel was still a

child. Eventually she'd divorced him and married
Tom Brady. Since Ariel hadn't yet turned twenty-
one she was forced to act on her own, discreetly
securing passage by stage to Texas. As much as
she hated doing so, she left without telling Mama,
leaving a note to explain her actions.

"There's a jail cell in Fort Worth with your
name on it," Jess said after a long pause.

He was deliberately slow in answering Ariel's
question, finding it extremely difficult to concentrate with her soft little bottom bouncing provocatively against the hardness of his thighs. He
shifted uncomfortably.

Damnation! he thought sourly. It had been too
damn long since he'd had a woman. The first order of business after he dumped Tilly at the jail
was to visit Miss Jolene's bawdy house. Any one
of Jolene's girls could take the sap right out of
him. Yes sirree, that's what he needed, a romp
between the sheets with a respectable whore. He
had no damn business lusting after a woman like
Tilly—or Ariel—or whatever she called herself. He
had to draw the line somewhere, and to his
knowledge he had never bedded a woman
wanted for murder and bank robbery.

Ariel had fallen silent after Jess' curt reply.
What could she say that hadn't already been said?
Obviously the big, hardheaded Texan was too
damn obstinate to listen. But she was stubborn
too. Hadn't she proved it by leaving St. Louis on
her own? Jess Wilder had met his match, Ariel
fumed in silent rage. And once he found out his
mistake she wasn't going to let him get away with
it. He'd pay for treating her like a common criminal and—and whore!

"I'm thirsty," Ariel complained, "and hungry."

"There's a stagecoach relay station ahead, we
can stop there for a bite to eat and to refresh ourselves," Jess said. "I need to report the accident

and deaths anyway. If I don't they'll wonder what happened when the stage fails to arrive on time."

Ariel's hopes soared. A relay station meant people and people meant help. Someone had to persuade this crude bounty hunter that he had the wrong woman.

"How long before we get there?"

"Three, four hours," Jess calculated, squinting off into the distance. "I'll be able to rent you a horse so we won't have to ride double. Although Soldier isn't complaining, riding double like this slows us down too dang much for my liking."

"Anxious to get rid of me?" Ariel taunted.

"Darn tootin' I am. The sooner you're behind bars the sooner I collect my money."

Ariel exhaled sharply. "You're despicable! Does human life mean so little to you?"

"I could ask you the same question," Jess returned, impaling her with the intensity of his silver eyes. "How many men have you and your lover killed? At least six that I know of, one of them my brother."

"Do I look capable of killing anyone?" Ariel challenged.

"Looks are deceiving," Jess said evenly.

The hard edge to his voice sent shivers down Ariel's spine. She pitied anyone unlucky enough to be called enemy by Jess Wilder. He was tough, tenacious, and impossibly difficult to dissuade once an idea took root in his brain. Yet—yet—she couldn't deny the powerful magnetism about the man, or fail to recognize his pure animal appeal.

Ariel had been courted by several men but so far had resisted marriage. At twenty years of age she was still looking for that special man, one who recognized her worth as a woman in her own right, not as an extension of himself. But Jess Wilder certainly wasn't that man, she thought derisively. He was crude, overbearing, argumentative, and too damn hotheaded to listen to the voice of reason. She hated the man for what he was doing to her.

Jess gritted his teeth and focused his attention on anything but the way his body was responding to the woman pressing so intimately against him. He just knew she was trying her damnedest to provoke a response in him, but he wasn't about to be hoodwinked by her shenanigans. After the first few miles Ariel had slumped against him, overcome by exhaustion. Tiny as she was, she had survived an accident that could easily have killed her.

Suddenly Jess became aware that Ariel was sleeping, and he shifted in the saddle to allow her to settle more comfortably against his chest. Her lips were slightly parted, her face flushed from the sun, and Jess was stunned by her beauty. He had expected Tilly Cowles to be jaded and coarse, her face hardened from the unorthodox life she led. The life of a desperado could hardly be conducive to maintaining one's beauty and youth. Yet Tilly Cowles' fresh-faced loveliness was a mockery, concealing a soul as black as Hades. What really rankled was the way he tingled and burned everywhere her body touched his. It was going to be a long rough trip to Fort Worth. He sighed, raising his eyes heavenward. He fervently hoped his comfort would improve once he got his hands on a second horse.

Chapter 2

Ariel stirred, then jerked awake. Reflexively Jess' arms tightened around her and she felt his muscles tense. In contrast to the usual free and easy manner in which he sat his horse, his big body grew rigid, every sense alert and watchful.

"What is it?" Ariel asked, alarmed.

"Shots," Jess muttered ominously.

Then Ariel heard them for herself, the staccato report of gunfire reverberating off the sunbaked hills and echoing through the plains.

"What does it mean?"

Except for today Ariel had experienced little of the violence Texas and the West were famous for. She'd been warned about desperadoes and Indians who roamed the desolate expanses of Texas, and once she'd begun her journey she'd lived in fear of meeting up with either or both.

"I don't know, but I reckon we'll find out soon enough." Jess frowned. "The stagecoach way station is just ahead—sounds like the shots are coming from that direction."

Twenty minutes later they approached the way station. Jess was cautious, his hand hovering above his gun. Nothing stirred but the leaves blowing across the yard in lazy, swirling abandon. Jess' attention was diverted to the corral, and a string of oaths slipped past his lips. The corral

19

gate gaped open; not one animal remained inside.

"Raiding party," Jess muttered. "Took all the stock. Sure as hell hope they left the Bartows alive."

"The Bartows?"

"The couple who sees to the needs of the passengers riding the Butterfield stage. Olga cooks the meals and keeps the sleeping rooms in order while Joe sees to the animals and the repair of the vehicles. They're good people, I know them well."

Just then the couple under discussion came walking out of the station, each clutching a rifle.

"Thank God you're both safe," Jess said. "What happened?"

"Injuns," Joe returned sourly. "Stole our stock. There'll be another stage here soon and they'll be wantin' a change of horses." His eyes settled on Ariel. "Who's the little lady, Jess?"

"This is Tilly Cowles. She was riding the Texarkana–Fort Worth stage."

"Somethin' happen to the stage, Jess?" Olga asked sharply.

During the past two years Jess had become well-acquainted with the Bartows. His pursuit of desperadoes took him across the breadth and width of Texas. He knew just about every stagecoach stop in the state.

"Howdy, Olga," Jess greeted her, removing his hat and swiping his sleeve across his face. "The Texarkana–Fort Worth stage had an accident. Driver's dead—the guard too."

"What about the other passengers?" Joe asked, concerned. In his late thirties, Joe was a tall, lanky man whose leanness belied his strength. Leather-faced and wiry, he looked like a man who had spent nearly all his adult years out in the open, in all kinds of weather.

"I'm not sure. Can't seem to make heads or

tails out of Tilly's story. I know for sure, though, that one of the passengers is dead, 'cause I buried him.''

"You're a lucky little lady, Miss Cowles," Joe said, turning to Ariel.

"My name is Ariel, Ariel Leland," she corrected him. Olga looked from Jess to Ariel, puzzled.

Jess snorted but said nothing.

"Come on inside, folks, I'll rustle you up some food. I'll bet you're hungry," Olga finally said, deciding she'd learn the truth in good time.

Jess dismounted and lifted Ariel to the ground. "You go with Olga," he said, "I'll be along directly. I want to talk to Joe."

Ariel followed the tall, rawboned woman inside. Olga was as lean and wiry as her husband; her chestnut hair and brown eyes softened her otherwise sharp features.

"Can I help?" Ariel offered.

"Naw, rest yerself, honey, I'm used to cookin'. Why don't you tell me what happened to the stage."

Ariel explained the accident to the best of her knowledge. It had all happened so quickly she still wasn't certain what caused it.

"What happened to the desperadoes?"

"I—I don't know. They were gone when I woke up. I'm glad you were able to scare off the Indians," she added.

"All them thievin' varmints wanted was the livestock." Olga snorted disgustedly. "About a dozen of 'em hit sudden-like and vamoosed fast."

"Does it happen often?" Ariel was wide-eyed with horror.

"Often enough," Olga allowed.

"Oh, dear," Ariel said. Forcing herself not to dwell on the threat of marauding Indians, she added, "Is there someplace I can wash?" She was anxious to rid herself of the layers of sweat, dust, and grime.

"There's a well and bucket out back, help yerself. There's an outhouse back there too, if you've a need. Supper will be dished up by the time yer finished."

Ariel lingered at the well, having used the outhouse and thoroughly refreshed herself with the cool well water. She would have liked to remove all her clothes and submerge herself in a hot tub but of course that was out of the question. Texas was hardly St. Louis. Abruptly she became aware that Jess had entered the station with Joe, leaving his horse tethered nearby. No one was watching her, no one was around to prevent her from leaping aboard Jess' horse and escaping from that madman who thought her a killer and a bank robber.

Cautiously Ariel edged over to where the big bay stallion was contentedly munching hay provided by Joe. She eyed him with a certain amount of apprehension. The bay was big, she observed, just like his owner. How in the devil was she going to mount him unaided? Ever resourceful, Ariel quickly found a solution to her problem. She spied a bucket filled with water beside the hay, evidently left for the horse's use. With an efficiency of motion she dumped the water, upended the bucket, and used it as a stool to hoist herself astride the horse's broad back.

So far so good, Ariel thought, hardly daring to breathe as she grasped the reins and gently slapped the horse's withers. She had no idea where she was going, only that she had to escape this intolerable situation. She'd head for Fort Worth, she decided, and wire her mother for confirmation of her identity. Since the Indian raid had emptied the corral no horses remained at the way station for Jess to give chase. At least something was going her way, Ariel thought smugly as she dug her heels into the bay's sides. She wouldn't feel safe until she put considerable distance between her and Jess Wilder.

The bay broke into a gallop, his long legs stretching across the sun-seared turf. Ariel threw back her head and laughed; the sheer pleasure of besting Jess Wilder tasted sweet on her tongue. Suddenly a shrill, piercing whistle interrupted the pounding of hooves and the horse responded so quickly that Ariel was caught unprepared. The bay skidded to a complete and abrupt halt, but Ariel kept right on going over the animal's head, smacking into the ground and rolling like a rag doll before coming to a stop. Then darkness surrounded her and she knew no more.

"She sure don't look like a killer or desperado."

"Looks are deceiving, Olga. Tilly and her lover have robbed more banks than you've ever been in."

"Why does she call herself Ariel Leland?" Compassion filled Olga's soft brown eyes as she gazed down at the petite young woman stretched out on the bed.

"An alias," Jess returned. "Believe me, Olga, whatever her name she's one tough woman."

Olga shook her head doubtfully. "Don't hardly seem possible."

"How soon will she come around?" Jess said.

"She oughtta be wakin' up soon. Couldn't find no broken bones—she's a mite shook up, is all."

"Much obliged, Olga. You go on about your work now, I'll see to Ariel." For some unexplained reason Jess preferred to think of Tilly as Ariel. Somehow the name seemed to fit her.

"I'll have supper on the table soon, come down when yer ready." After another quick glance at Ariel, Olga turned and left the room, closing the door quietly behind her.

"I'm not a tough woman."

Ariel had been awake long enough to hear most of the conversation between Jess and Olga. Every bone in her body ached; her head hurt, and besides that she was madder than a wet hen. Jess Wilder was an absolute crazy man.

"What happened?" she asked, groaning as she raised herself to a sitting position.

"What happened is that you tried to steal my horse," Jess replied sourly. He kept his eyes focused on anything but the entrancing way Ariel's breasts filled out her bodice. "Soldier is trained to my command. A signal from me is all it takes to stop him." His lips quirked upward in a semblance of a grin.

"I could have been killed," Ariel charged, her green eyes flashing angrily.

"How did I know you'd go flying over Soldier's head? You should have held on."

"Bastard," Ariel muttered darkly, unable to stop the word from tumbling past her lips.

Jess' silver eyes sparkled with mirth. "Careful, Tilly, you're showing your true colors again. Ariel Leland wouldn't use that kind of language."

"A gentleman wouldn't treat a lady the way you're treating me," Ariel returned hotly.

"Who said I was a gentleman? I might have been one once but experience taught me to suppress my gentle nature."

"Gentle nature!" Ariel snorted derisively. "There's not a gentle bone in your body."

"Now that we're through name-bashing, let's go eat. Can you manage on your own?"

"Of course. I'm stronger than I look."

Jess glanced at her doubtfully. She looked fragile enough to break in two with one of his big hands. Her features were soft and sweetly beguiling, and if he didn't watch his step he'd find himself falling under her witch's spell. Thank God he knew her for what she was.

Ariel slid her feet to the floor and took a hesitant step, faltered, then did a slow spiral downward. Big as he was, Jess moved agilely toward her, scooping her into his arms before she hit the floor.

"Little fool, why didn't you say you needed help?"

"I—didn't think I did. Not from you anyway. You can put me down, I'm sure I can manage now."

Despite his firm resolve, Jess felt his arms tighten around his luscious bundle. Her warm, scented flesh and cloud of dark hair smelled delicious, the aroma reminiscent of crushed violets. Her red lips were parted temptingly and her eyes were as clear and beguiling as precious emeralds.

"Put me down, Mr. Wilder."

Ariel's body vibrated with an emotion she couldn't identify. She literally shook from it. Never had she felt such overwhelming sensations. Never had a man's touch sent her senses into a tailspin. What manner of man was Jess Wilder?

Jess appeared dazed as he stared at Ariel's moist, parted lips. They taunted him outrageously, tempted him beyond redemption, and teased him with bold invitation. Say what you wanted about Jess Wilder, he was an honest-to-God flesh-and-blood man with honest-to-God flesh-and-blood needs.

Ariel realized Jess was going to kiss her too late to voice a protest. She struggled in his arms, but his lips came down on hers with such force, such insistence, she was stunned into unwilling compliance. But the moment she caught her breath her fists pounded at his chest with indignant fury.

The kiss seemed to go on forever as he held Ariel prisoner in his arms. The roughness of his tongue examined the soft contour of her lips then plunged inside when she gasped in stunned protest. Never had Ariel experienced anything so devastating or overwhelmingly sexual. Despite her shock she somehow managed to break free of the kiss.

"How dare you! What do you think you're doing?"

"Damned if I know," Jess said softly, setting her on her feet. "Best we go down to supper before I do something I'll regret."

Supper, though delicious, was a nightmare for Ariel. Olga and Joe stared at her throughout the entire meal, as if expecting her to produce a derringer from her clothing and kill them while they ate. Meanwhile, Jess devoured his food with such obvious gusto it was disgusting. Afterward he escorted her back to the room without so much as a by-your-leave.

"Now what?" Ariel asked, placing her hands on her hips.

"Soldier needs a rest, so we'll start for Fort Worth at daybreak. Get some sleep, we've a long trip ahead of us."

"What about the Indians?"

"Let's hope they got what they came for and left the area."

With casual indifference Jess sat on the bed and calmly began to unbutton his shirt.

"What are you doing?" Ariel asked, panic making her voice quiver.

"What does it look like? I'm getting ready for bed."

"Not in this room."

"Look, Til—er—Ariel, just lie down and go to sleep. I'm not going to let you out of my sight. You're worth one thousand dollars dead or alive and it makes no nevermind to me how I bring you in. After that little stunt you pulled today with Soldier I don't put anything past you."

Jess had yet to harm a woman but he'd be damned if he'd tell that to Ariel. Perhaps, he reflected, if she thought he might do her bodily harm in order to collect the reward it would render her docile.

Ariel didn't know what to think. She'd heard that bounty hunters were notoriously hard-bitten, cold-blooded, and vicious. His outrageous notion that she had killed his brother made him even more dangerous. Sooner or later he was bound to learn the truth about her and until he did she couldn't afford to rile him. Her day would come, she thought with smug satisfaction, and when it did she'd make Jess Wilder sorry he'd ever tangled with Ariel Leland.

"I'll sleep in the chair," Ariel said, stripping one of the blankets from the bed.

"Don't worry," Jess said with a hint of amusement, "I'm too tired to do you justice. I don't cotton to being compared unfavorably to Bart Dillon." He removed his boots, placed his guns beneath the pillow, and stretched out on the bed. "I'm a light sleeper," he warned. Then he rolled over and closed his eyes. Within minutes his breathing was soft and even, indicating that he had already fallen asleep.

Ariel remained in the chair until her head drooped and she caught herself falling sideways off the uncomfortable seat.

Muttering words a lady had no business knowing, let alone saying, Ariel rose and cautiously approached the bed. Jess did not stir. Gingerly she sat on the edge, but the only response from Jess was a soft expulsion of air past his lips. Dragging in a ragged breath, Ariel lay down, keeping as close to the edge as possible. Then the terrible events of the day caught up with her as she slowly slipped into slumber.

Sometime during the night Ariel sought the comforting warmth of Jess' big body. Still asleep, Jess responded by wrapping his arms around her and pulling her more deeply into the curve of his body. He awoke before dawn, startled to find Ariel curled contentedly against him, one of his big hands cradling a surprisingly full breast. For several long minutes Jess didn't move. A silly smile spread across his face as he savored fully the feel of soft pliant flesh filling his palm. He nuzzled her neck, the smell of violets driving him wild. His face assumed an arrested look. He was twice Ariel's size, he could awaken her and be deep inside her before she knew what was happening. A woman like that probably had had so many men one more couldn't possibly matter.

Jess grinned with slow relish, imagining what it would be like to make love to so exquisite a creature. Not just a quick lay but to make love to her with slow and easy passion, branding every inch of her sweet flesh with his mouth and hands. Jesus H. Christ, was he loco? Jess railed at himself. He must be out of his mind to want a woman like Tilly Cowles. With deliberate slowness he removed his hand from the soft mound of Ariel's breast and eased himself from the bed.

Ariel awoke as Jess was strapping on his gun belt. She yawned, rousing slowly from a wonderful dream. She felt warm and tingly all over. A secret smile curved her lips and she rolled over to continue her dream. But it was not to be. She squealed indignantly when Jess reached over and swatted her behind.

"Get your sweet little butt out of bed, Tilly, it's time to go."

"Ariel."

Jess didn't look amused. "Move it, *Ariel*, we haven't got all day."

Though very early, Olga and Joe were already up preparing breakfast. To Ariel's chagrin Olga refused to meet her eyes. It rankled to think that Jess had convinced the woman that she was a desperado. After the meal Olga prepared a package of food to eat on the trail and shyly presented

Ariel with a blanket. Jess already had his own bedroll.

"I'll stop by the stage office in Fort Worth and report the raid," Jess promised as he boosted Ariel aboard Soldier. "I reckon they'll send out replacements for your stock right soon since there'll be another stage through before long."

"You're welcome to wait fer the next stage, Jess, and ride in comfort to Fort Worth," Joe offered.

"Much obliged, Joe, but the sooner I get rid of this little baggage the happier I'll be. Bart Dillon is still walking free out there somewhere and I aim to find him. My life isn't my own until he's behind bars."

The going was rough. Riding a stage was sheer comfort compared to bouncing in the saddle in front of Jess Wilder. Sweat rolled down Ariel's back and soaked her armpits. The bonnet she wore offered scant protection against the relentless onslaught of the brutal July sun. Jess stopped once for a brief nooning then pushed on. The pace he set was deliberately slow and easy so as not to tire Soldier who carried a double burden. Too slow as far as Ariel was concerned.

She hated the way her body responded to the touch of Jess' hard thighs, heartily disliked the tingling sensation that made her all too aware of his powerful form pressed so intimately against hers. Most of all she despised the smug smile that clung to his lips as she sought to prevent their bodies from touching. When she felt herself drifting off to sleep she immediately jerked upright, Jess' amused chuckle drifting past her ears.

"Relax, Ariel, we've a heap of riding to do before we see Fort Worth. I don't like this any better than you do but the Indian raid on the way station gave us little choice. If you behave yourself we'll reach Fort Worth in a couple of days and be rid of one another.''

''It can't be too soon for me,'' Ariel retorted curtly.

They camped the first night beside a narrow stream that still boasted a trickle of water running down its center. It was coming on dusk and Jess saw to Soldier while Ariel walked to the stream, gazing wistfully into the shallow water. Suddenly making up her mind, she whirled and approached Jess.

''I want to bathe.''

Jess looked at her, then at the water, and shrugged. ''Go ahead.''

''I—want some privacy.''

''No way, lady. If you want to bathe I'll not stop you, but don't expect me to leave. Just pretend I'm not here. Somehow I can't picture you cooking over a campfire so if you wanna eat I reckon it's up to me to fix our grub.''

Ariel's face turned a dull red. ''Why must you be so obnoxious? I'm not going to bathe with you watching me. Will it change your mind if I promise not to try to escape?''

''Nope.''

''Mr. Wilder, please!''

''Just plain Jess will do. How do I know I can trust you? You haven't proved reliable so far.''

''You have my word. Besides, where can I go? I don't dare take your horse again.''

Jess pretended to mull over her words but in truth had already decided to grant her request. Though for the life of him he couldn't figure out why a woman like Tilly ''Ariel'' Cowles should be shy. But he reckoned even bangtails needed privacy now and again.

''Go ahead and bathe, Ariel,'' Jess allowed. ''I reckon I can use a bath myself. Don't know when we'll find another stream with water in it.''

Thinking he meant to bathe with her, Ariel

opened her mouth in vigorous protest, but Jess forestalled her. "You bathe here and I'll amble on downstream to that little bend. There's soap in my saddlebag. I'll give you fifteen minutes."

"Thank you," Ariel said with quiet dignity.

Jess stared at her, a puzzled expression furrowing his brow. Then he turned abruptly and walked downstream until he disappeared around the bend. Once he was out of sight Areil acted swiftly. She found the soap and her clean clothes, quickly stripped, and waded out to the middle of the shallow stream. She washed and rinsed her hair then soaped her body, splashing herself with clear water when she was finished.

Drying herself with her soiled clothes, Ariel decided at the last minute to wash those too. But first she donned her clean shift and bloomers. Hiking her shift up past her knees and fastening it to her waist, Ariel reckoned she had plenty of time as she scrubbed her soiled clothes in the stream. She splashed out of the water a short time later with the dripping clothes in her hand, shocked to find Jess watching her. His silver gaze raked her from head to toe.

Never had Jess seen a more arresting sight than Ariel walking out of the stream, her legs bare from the knees down and her shift clinging enticingly to her damp skin. Tiny as she was, her breasts were full and womanly, the nipples protruding prominently beneath the sheer fabric. Her flesh was as pale and smooth as ivory. Jess felt his loins swell and cursed his lack of control. It rankled him to think that he was attracted to the little wildcat, and no amount of self-flagellation could talk him out of it. He wanted her. Christ, how he wanted her! *He wanted his brother's killer!* Even as his mind utterly rejected her his feet moved him toward her.

Ariel froze. How long had Jess been standing there? Why hadn't she heard him return? "Stay where you are," she warned. "Don't come any closer. You said fifteen minutes, why didn't you keep your word?"

"I did," Jess said, impatiently. "I returned only moments ago. You were so engrossed in washing your clothes you didn't hear me. I didn't wanna startle you so I kept quiet."

"Likely story." Ariel sniffed.

"Are you gonna come out of there? As much as I enjoy seeing you like that I reckon we ought to eat and get some shut-eye."

"Turn your back." With a flip of her wrist Ariel released the skirt of her shift so that it dropped down to cover her legs.

Ignoring her request, Jess halted at the edge of the stream, bent, and picked up Ariel's clean dress from where she had placed it earlier. He held it out before him, his gaze boldly challenging.

Ariel was no fool. She was glaringly aware of how she must look standing there with her nearly transparent shift molded against her damp flesh. Her green eyes blazed with fury and she gnashed her teeth in mute frustration.

"Spawn of Satan!"

Tilting her chin at a defiant angle, Ariel was determined to remain aloof. She'd be damned if she'd let Jess Wilder goad her into doing or saying something she'd later regret. Soon this polecat would learn the truth about her and she'd have the last laugh. All she had to do was bide her time, grit her teeth, and survive. If only the bounty hunter didn't affect her in strange ways. Ariel sighed as she walked from the stream.

Jess had no idea what provoked him into teasing Ariel so outrageously. It wasn't the way he normally operated. Usually he took his business seriously, but for some vague reason this little wildcat made him forget that she was wanted for murder and bank robbery.

His silver eyes narrowed with desire as he watched Ariel walk toward him. She was so close now he could see the pulse at her throat beating with ardent fury. She was so angry that Jess knew that if she had a gun she would shoot him and never feel a smidgeon of guilt. She reached out to snatch her dress from Jess' hands, misjudged the distance, and stumbled into his arms. If he was honest with himself he'd admit it was exactly where he'd wanted her from the very first moment they met.

Outraged astonishment was plain on Ariel's face. How in the world had she ended up in the arms of a man she despised? She shuddered, and was shocked to discover it wasn't from revulsion. Jess' silver eyes bore into her green ones, a hint of suppressed savagery behind them. It was enough to frighten any well-bred, educated young lady. What did he mean to do to her? Whatever it was she intended to fight him tooth and nail.

Jess cursed the demon that possessed him as something inside him drove his mouth to claim hers. At first the hot tip of his tongue only flirted with the inside of her lower lip before he thrust it into the sweet cavern of her mouth. That alone was cause enough to anger Ariel, but when Jess filled his hand with the soft roundness of her breast, she erupted into a frenzy of wild fury.

How dare he touch her in such a vile manner! What he was doing with his tongue was—was—God, she loved it—hated it—couldn't think. Her mind went blank. His touch aroused her to a humiliating level. His lips enclosed her in a world that extended no farther than the powerful strength of his hard body and encircling arms. The urgent thrust of his loins against her soft mound brought a measure of sanity back to her spinning world. Ariel was too much of a lady to act the whore. It would serve only to bolster Jess' low opinion of her. She wasn't stupid. Her mother had taken her aside and warned her about men and what they expected from women. Especially women with loose morals.

Jess was so caught up in the moment and his stampeding ardor that he didn't feel Ariel stiffen. He howled in rage when she bit down on his tongue, releasing her so abruptly she stumbled and nearly fell before righting herself.

"You damn little wildcat!" He spat blood and Ariel ventured a smug smile.

"Serves you right," she said sweetly. "Next time keep your hands to yourself."

With amazing aplomb she picked up her dress from where it had fallen and stalked away. "I may be your prisoner but I'll never be your—your—doxy!"

Jess let fly a string of curses. Ariel had bitten him hard enough to draw blood. Fortunately it also brought him abruptly to his senses. What in tarnation had gotten into him?

"The only thing I want from you is the reward for your capture," he called to her departing back. "If you expect me to behave quit trying to entice me."

Ariel kept a wise silence though inwardly she seethed with anger and resentment—and a certain amount of satisfaction for having bested the arrogant bounty hunter.

Chapter 3

An uneasy silence existed between Jess and Ariel as they ate supper. Wary of the dark, powerful man who affected her in strange ways, Ariel said little. She withdrew into the protective shell of silence as she tried without success to analyze her odd behavior in regard to Jess Wilder. How could she detest the man yet tingle with excitement the moment he touched her? She didn't delude herself into thinking he cared a fig about what happened to her. Obviously the man was driven by lust and greed; her feelings meant nothing to him. No matter how often or emphatically she proclaimed her innocence, Jess Wilder refused to believe her.

Abruptly Jess uncoiled his long legs, stretched, and yawned. "Take one of the blankets," he growled, still angry with Ariel. His tongue was still swollen where she had bitten it. After he stomped out the fire, he retrieved his own blanket, rolled up in it beside the fire, and closed his eyes.

Ariel took the other blanket, settling herself several feet away. It took her a long time to go to sleep. And from the way Jess was tossing and turning Ariel suspected he was experiencing the same difficulty. She had no way of knowing Jess was as confused and disturbed by her as she was by him. Not only did Ariel get his dander up but she titillated and excited him until his loins were on fire for her. With at least four days yet between here and Fort Worth Jess wondered if it would get any better.

It didn't.

It got worse.

Much worse.

It got so bad that the slightest brush of their bodies as Ariel bounced in the saddle before him was sheer torture. He'd rather burn in hell than go through many more days of this, he told himself. The entire day he thought of nothing but Ariel, warm and willing beneath him, taking him deep into her body, Christ, was he crazy? The Texas sun must be getting to him.

That night visitors made an appearance at their campsite. Jess heard them approach long before the two horsemen appeared in the circle of light given off by the campfire. He reached for his pistol, and his big body grew taut, every sense alert.

"What is it?" Ariel asked.

"Visitors," Jess said tightly. "Two, maybe three riders. Keep your head down and don't say anything until we know who they are."

"I—don't hear anything." How could Jess hear something she couldn't? Her thoughts stuttered to a halt when two horsemen suddenly materialized from out of the blackness. They halted just inside the circle of light, greeted by the business end of Jess' Smith and Wesson.

"Evenin', friend," one of the men said. He slid his eyes from Jess to Ariel where they paused, then slid reluctantly back to Jess.

"I'm not your friend," Jess bit out.

"Me and Luke smelled yer coffee. Could ya spare a cup fer a couple of travelers? The name is Blackie, Blackie Rowe. This here is Luke Wilkes."

Jess studied the two men through narrowed lids. He didn't like what he saw. Rowe was big, burly, and unkempt. His battered hat hid much of his face but something in the man's voice set Jess' teeth on edge. Rowe's friend was even shabbier, his clothing worn and dirty. He wasn't as brawny as Rowe, nor as tall. He was as small and wiry as a fox. Jess trusted neither of them.

"I reckon we can spare you a cup of coffee," Jess allowed. "Then you'd best be on your way."

Ariel wondered why Jess was acting so unfriendly when obviously the men posed no threat.

"Much obliged, mister," Rowe said, dismounting. "What did you say yer name was?"

"I didn't."

Both men hunkered down beside the small campfire. Luke held out two cups and Blackie filled them from the pot sitting beside the fire. Blackie sipped at the hot brew thoughtfully, glanced at Ariel, and asked, "That yer woman? Don't say much, does she?"

Jess grunted. "Just drink your coffee and move on."

"It's a mite uncomfortable drinkin' coffee with that gun wavin' under my nose. We don't mean ya no harm, mister."

When Jess still refused to divulge his name, Blackie shrugged, turned to Ariel, and asked, "What's yer name, little lady?"

"My—wife's name is no concern of yours."

"Yer wife," Blackie repeated skeptically. "Yer a long way from civilization, ain't ya?"

Ariel shifted uneasily beneath Blackie's intense scrutiny. She began to share some of the same doubts about these men that plagued Jess.

"I could say the same for you," Jess replied, giving away nothing.

They drank their coffee, Blackie and Luke becoming bolder as they openly stared at Ariel.

Abruptly Blackie rose. "Well, friend, much obliged fer the coffee. Reckon me and Luke will mosey on."

Startled, Luke looked at Blackie in disbelief. "What! I thought . . ."

Blackie nudged Luke with his foot. "I said come on, I don't figure to sit here jawin' all night. These good people wanna get to bed." His gaze lingered on Ariel, a knowing smirk on his face.

Then he strutted over to his horse and mounted. Luke followed. Ariel drew her first calm breath since the men arrived as she watched them disappear into the darkness. Her sigh of relief echoed loudly in the sudden stillness of the night.

"Don't relax yet," Jess warned as he squatted down beside the fire and poured himself a cup of coffee.

"What do you mean?"

"We haven't seen the last of those varmints. Did you see the way they looked at you?"

"I—noticed. But perhaps you misread their interest. They seemed friendly enough. Maybe you're overreacting."

"I was born in Texas, lady, I know what to expect from men like that and what they're capable of. Can you say the same?"

"No, but I'm learning fast," Ariel said pointedly. "Now if you don't mind I'm going to bed."

Ariel was sound asleep when Jess rose from his place beside the fire and prepared his bedroll.

The campfire had burnt to smoldering embers, illuminating only two shadowy sleeping forms when two stealthy figures crept out from the mesquite.

"They're sleepin'," Luke whispered.

"Can ya make out which one is the woman?" Blackie asked, his voice a hoarse whisper.

Both men squinted through the darkness at the two forms hunched beneath their blankets. They waited until the moon slid out from behind a cloud and were rewarded for their patience when they noted that the figure sleeping closest to the fire sported long black hair. Due to the warm

night Ariel had thrown the blanket aside and a
cloud of dark hair cascaded over her shoulders.

"Kill the man," Blackie whispered, "but don't
hurt the girl. I got plans fer her. What do ya think
of havin' our own private whore, Luke?"

"I'd like it jest fine." Luke chortled.

"Let's go."

They burst into the crude campsite, guns blazing, all aimed at the place where Jess slept. The
first shot jolted Ariel into a rude awakening. It
took her a few seconds to gather her wits before
she knew what was happening. And even then
she wasn't sure, until she saw bullets slam into
Jess' bedroll. A scream left her throat, a long
drawn-out wail that adequately conveyed her de-
spair. Blackie smiled nastily.

"Shut up, lady, we ain't gonna hurt ya. Me
and Luke got other plans fer ya."

"No-o-o, you killed Jess!" Ariel sobbed hyster-
ically as she tried to run to Jess' aid. But to her
horror Blackie caught her in his massive arms,
holding her captive.

"Ya ain't goin' nowhere."

"I've got to help him!" Jess couldn't be dead,
he couldn't!

"Yer lover is beyond help now. Ain't nobody
could live through that barrage of bullets. Now
be good, honey, and give us a little kiss."

"Bastard! Bastard! Bastard!" Ariel screeched,
pounding him with her fists.

By now Luke had joined them, watching the
struggle with avid anticipation. "Maybe if I knock
her around some it might calm her down."

"Touch her and you're dead," came a deep,
menacing voice.

"No, it ain't possible. I drilled six rounds into
the son of a bitch!" Blackie gasped in disbelief.
"And he ain't even bleedin'."

"Let's see if he's a ghost," Luke growled,
palming his pistol and aiming. The shot never left

the chamber. Jess acted spontaneously, squeezing off a bullet that slammed into Luke so hard it spun him around before he dropped to the ground. He was dead before he hit the dirt.

When Jess looked over at Blackie, his gun was pressed against Ariel's temple, his free arm snaked around her neck. A nasty sneer contorted his ugly features. ''Move and yer woman's dead.''

''Let her go, Blackie.''

''I ain't dumb, mister. The woman is my ticket outta here.''

He began walking backward, dragging Ariel with him. Ariel fought for breath; Blackie's arm felt like a band of steel across her throat. She dug her heels in the ground, but it served only to make Blackie angry as he jerked her along like a rag doll. She had no idea where he was taking her, nor was she likely to stop him.

''Toss yer gun as far as ya can throw it and saddle yer horse fer me. My nag is worn out,'' Blackie ordered Jess.

Jess stared at him for the space of a heartbeat then moved to comply. He sent his gun sailing into a clump of mesquite and bent to retrieve his saddle from the ground. After he saddled Soldier he stepped aside.

With his gun still pressed to Ariel's head, Blackie hoisted her into the saddle then mounted behind her. Jess merely stood by, his face inscrutable, his silver eyes as cold as death. It wasn't until she was seated on Soldier that Ariel realized what Jess intended for Blackie. She searched her mind desperately for a way to help Jess and came up blank. But as Blackie reached around her for the reins Ariel suddenly found a solution. Acting swiftly, she sank her small sharp teeth into the sensitive skin of Blackie's wrist. Grinding her teeth together she was gratified to hear Blackie's yowl of pain.

"Bitch!" he spat, his hold on her momentarily broken.

Ariel was ready. Taking a deep breath, she gathered her strength and threw herself from Soldier's back. She hit the ground with a thud and rolled until she was clear of the huge horse's hooves. Blackie let loose a string of oaths but wasted little time on Ariel. Instead, he spurred Soldier cruelly, and hung on as the big animal bolted forward. Jess was in motion before Ariel hit the ground. Ignoring Blackie for the moment, he rushed to Ariel's side, dropping to his knees beside her.

"Are you hurt?"

"N-no, I don't think so. Are you going to let him get away?"

Jess rose to his feet, turned, and let out a piercing whistle. Neither could see what happened next but Ariel knew from experience that Soldier would obey his master's signal without question. She heard a shout and a thud, then nothing more. A few minutes later Soldier came trotting calmly back to Jess' side, Blackie conspicuously missing.

"Stay here," Jess ordered.

Ariel nodded, still too shaken to reply as Jess plucked his rifle from his saddlebag and sprinted in the direction Blackie had taken only moments before. Ariel remained on the ground where she had fallen, shivering with apprehension and fear for Jess' safety. What if Blackie was waiting out there somewhere to ambush Jess? Jess might be a hard, obstinate man but he wasn't cruel, not even when he thought she was partly responsible for his brother's death. On the other hand, she would suffer untold indignities if left to Blackie's dubiously tender mercies.

Her worries were unfounded for Jess returned several minutes later—alone. "Did he get away?" Ariel asked, her voice trembling. "Will he come back?"

"Blackie Rowe won't bother us again," Jess said tightly. He saw Ariel's eyes widen and added, "He's dead. The fall broke his neck. He had whipped Soldier up to a pretty good gallop by the time my signal stopped him. He was a big man and fell hard."

"Is it over, truly over?" Ariel asked in a small voice.

Jess frowned. For a woman accustomed to violence he thought Ariel more shaken than he would have suspected. A niggling suspicion took root in his brain but he stubbornly ignored it. The woman was clever; she had just proved it by using her brain and escaping Blackie virtually without his help. It occurred to Jess that the real Tilly Cowles might have preferred the company of a man like Blackie Rowe rather than end up behind bars. The notion bore thinking about, but not now. Not when Ariel was shaking like a leaf and in need of comforting.

"It's really over. Both Blackie and Luke are dead."

Jess helped Ariel to her feet, steadying her when her legs refused to support her. "I'm sorry," Ariel said, sheepishly. "I don't usually frighten so easily."

Something deep inside Jess compelled him to wrap his arms around Ariel and draw her close. She felt so tiny and fragile against his own hard sturdiness he was suddenly consumed by an overwhelming need to cosset and protect her.

"You were brave and wonderful," Jess said soothingly as he caressed her from shoulder to waist. "That could have been you lying there with your neck broken if you hadn't found a way to leave Soldier's back when you did. Very resourceful, but then I reckon you're accustomed to handling yourself in tight situations."

Ariel barely heard Jess' thinly veiled remark. His arms were too warm, too comforting, too damn stimulating for her to worry about his words. When his lips nuzzled her neck she snuggled closer, her arms creeping around his neck with a will of their own.

"Christ! This is no good!" The curse shot past his lips like a groan.

Suddenly Ariel felt herself floating as Jess scooped her up in his arms and carried her to her bedroll. He followed her down, pressing against her with an urgency that shocked him.

"You and I are gonna settle this thing between us once and for all. I've been hot for you since I laid eyes on you and I think you feel the same. You're driving me crazy, lady, I won't be able to ride tomorrow if we don't get on with it."

His hand slipped beneath her skirt, skimming past her knees. She found the roughness of his palm arousing as it touched the tender skin of her thigh.

"No, don't." The plea came from her in a ragged gasp.

Jess ignored her feeble protest, finding the silky softness of her skin utterly beguiling. Who would have thought Tilly Cowles would turn out to be so damn alluring, so youthful and innocent? He had no idea why but he wanted her with a need that couldn't be rationally explained. Somehow Tilly "Ariel" Cowles had gotten under his skin faster than any other woman he'd ever known.

"Don't play games with me, Ariel," Jess moaned against her lips. When had she become an obsession with him? "I won't hurt you. I've been told I'm a generous lover, I'll be good to you."

His mouth moved over hers with bold insistence, his tongue licking at the moist corners then slipping inside when she gasped in outrage. She squirmed and struggled and pounded at his chest, but it seemed only to fan the flames driving him. His loins swelled, their fullness pressing urgently

against Ariel's softness. Now he had her bodice
unfastened and toyed with the erect nipple of one
breast. He was tugging on her pantaloons when
Ariel found her tongue.

"You insensitive jackass! How can you want
this after—after what just happened? What kind
of man are you? Have you no feelings?"

"For those two bastards? Sorry, Ariel, I feel
nothing for them, but I'm feeling plenty for you
right now."

"And I feel *nothing* for you. Now get off me,
you big lummox."

Dragging in a ragged breath, Jess realized that
Ariel spoke the truth. She had been badly frightened and needed time to recover from the shock.
Obviously she was in no mood to make love and
he'd be a heartless bastard to force her when she
was still distraught. His hands trembled as he reluctantly reached over and pulled her skirt down
over her legs then fastened her bodice.

"It's a damn shame to cover those beauties but
you're right. I need to bury Luke and Blackie and
find their horses. There's still a few hours left till
dawn, so get some sleep."

Suddenly the thought of Jess leaving her alone
made Ariel panic. She didn't want to be alone,
not tonight. She needed Jess' solid presence. She
wanted him, but not in the same way he wanted
her. And since he no longer presented a threat to
her she didn't want him to go.

"Jess, don't leave me, I—don't want to be alone
right now. Just sit beside me till daylight."

Jess frowned. Ariel was asking something of
him he wasn't certain he could do. Sitting beside
her, touching her—how much torture could one
man take? Yet she looked so appealing, so utterly
lost, Jess hadn't the heart to refuse. With unaccustomed tenderness he gathered Ariel in his
arms, cradling her against the curve of his body.

"Go to sleep, Ariel, you're safe from me to-

night, and from anyone else who would harm
you. We'll call a truce. For a few hours I'll forget
who and what you are and you do the same.''

Though she left him aching in every conceiv-
able way he vowed he would not touch her. Not
tonight.

''First tell me how you escaped being shot by
Blackie and Luke. I saw them firing into your bedroll.''

''You don't think I trusted those desperadoes,
do you? I knew they'd be back. I made my bedroll
look as if I was in it and waited in the mesquite
for them to appear. I've lived this long by being
cautious and I'm not about to change now.''

''I . . . I'm glad they didn't kill you,'' Ariel said
sleepily.

Jess could think of no reply. ''Go to sleep, Ariel.''

Groggily, Ariel nodded her head, already half-
asleep. During the past several weeks she'd been
through more adversity and upheaval than other
sheltered young ladies might encounter in their
whole lifetimes.

Sunlight drew bright patterns across Ariel's face
as she blinked awake. She had slept so soundly,
so peacefully, she hadn't been aware of Jess leaving her side. She felt as if her faith in mankind
had been restored. Jess had been so tender, so
amazingly caring last night that she was certain
he now realized his mistake and no longer
thought her to be Tilly Cowles. By some miracle
the obstinate bounty hunter recognized the fact
that she was incapable of committing all those
horrible crimes. While she lay contemplating these
new developments, Jess ambled into her line of
vision. He was leading two horses from the grove
of mesquite surrounding their campsite. It was
then that Ariel noticed that Luke's body was

gone. She was grateful that Jess had arisen early and buried both bodies before she had awakened.

"I'm glad you're awake," Jess said, aware that Ariel was staring at him. "Thanks to Luke and Blackie you'll have a horse of your own to ride. And I'll have two more rewards to claim. I'm dead certain there's a price on the heads of those two desperadoes."

"At least you'll not come away from this empty-handed," Ariel said complacently.

"What in the hell are you jawing about?" Jess asked sharply.

"Why—why, surely you still don't think I'm Tilly Cowles?" Ariel gasped in disbelief.

"I've seen nothing to disprove it," Jess answered guardedly.

"But—I don't understand. Last night . . ."

"Last night only proved you were a badly frightened female. It didn't change my mind. I'm still turning you in to the law. I can't forget how your partner gunned down my brother. He was all the family I had. If you're not Tilly Cowles then let the sheriff settle the issue. Get a move on, we've got a lot of ground to cover."

Ariel's green eyes flared with sudden fury. This man was so obtuse he failed to recognize innocence when it stared him in the face. She hated him. She couldn't recall when she'd despised anyone as thoroughly as she did Jess Wilder. For a brief time last night she'd discovered a softness beneath his hard-bitten exterior, but this morning she learned just how wrong she was. Jess Wilder was a cruel, vindictive man who hadn't a sympathetic bone in his big body. If there was anything decent or caring in him he kept it well-hidden.

Ariel fumed in silent indignation as Jess began breaking camp, gathering up their gear and packing it on the back of the spare horse.

"The two extra horses will allow us to travel in

comfort," Jess remarked, glancing at Ariel. "You hungry?"

Ariel shook her head; she was too angry to eat. Food would surely stick in her craw and choke her.

"Suit yourself." Jess shrugged. "I don't have much of an appetite either. Soon as you're ready we'll leave."

Using a bit of water from her canteen, Ariel washed her hands and face, rinsed out her mouth, and discreetly disappeared into the bushes. She seriously entertained thoughts of fleeing Jess Wilder. It shouldn't be too difficult to melt into the mesquite and hide in the sagebrush and ridges surrounding them. But common sense prevailed. Ariel realized she was ill-equipped to fend for herself in such hostile country. She had no food, water, weapon, or horse. Besides, as cunning as Jess Wilder was, he'd soon track her down. When she returned to the campsite, Jess was waiting, his lips twitching in secret amusement. It was as if he'd read her thoughts and knew she'd opted to return rather than attempt to survive on her own in so hostile a land.

It certainly was less stressful riding her own horse, Ariel thought as she rode slightly behind Jess who sat Soldier as if he'd been born in the saddle. It was a great relief not to fight her own body's strange response to that impossible man. Unbidden, her eyes were drawn to that part of his anatomy that slapped with enticing regularity against the saddle. The taut, perfectly symmetrical mounds of his buttocks rose upward to slim hips and a narrow waist, then widened to the incredible width of broad shoulders. His body an erotic extension of the superb animal beneath his lean-muscled thighs.

My God! Ariel thought, aghast. What was happening? Her mind was taking her on a forbidden journey, one that could only lead to trouble.

By the time they halted for nooning and to rest the horses, Ariel was eager to accept the stringy piece of jerky and hard biscuit Jess offered her. She ate in sullen silence, unaware that Jess was studying her from beneath the black fringe of his long lashes.

Jess knew what and who Ariel was, so why did she keep up this ridiculous pretense? At first it had amused him to humor her, to call her Ariel when he knew her name was really Tilly. But now there was nothing remotely amusing about the way he reacted to her presence. Lordy, he wasn't a green kid who couldn't control his urges. He was a grown man who'd had his share of women in his twenty-eight years. Hell, a lot of living and hell-raising had gone into those years, so why did a beautiful liar like Tilly Cowles, alias Ariel Leland, cause him so much damn confusion?

Ariel flushed as she glanced up and found Jess looking at her with an enigmatic expression on his face.

"I've done nothing," Ariel insisted, tilting her chin at a defiant angle. "Don't stare at me as if I'm some kind of—of—unsavory character. I hope you choke on your presumptuous accusations when you learn the truth."

"Strange as it may seem, I'm beginning to feel the same," Jess muttered beneath his breath.

"What did you say?" Ariel asked, unable to catch his words.

"Nothing," Jess said brusquely, pulling himself together. "Mount up. I don't aim for this trip to last any longer than necessary. I won't rest easy until Bart Dillon is brought to justice for his crimes. Maybe I can get on with my life once Dillon joins you behind bars."

"Is there a woman waiting for you somewhere?" Now why did she ask that? Ariel chided herself. She couldn't care less if Jess Wilder was married or had a special woman in his life.

"I reckon you could say that," Jess admitted with a slow grin.

It was true—well, almost true, anyway. He'd thought a lot about Ellie Lu Dodge these past two years. She lived in Fort Worth, where he'd once been a U.S. marshal, and she'd vowed to wait for him for as long as needed to bring in Judd's killers. But that was two years ago and Jess had seen little of Ellie Lu during that time. She was tall, curvaceous, blonde, with skin as white as an Easter lily; it had occurred to Jess that Ellie Lu would make him a fine wife. If he felt no surge of overwhelming passion for the lovely, spoiled Ellie Lu, he blamed the weakness of his desire on his preoccupation with Judd's killers. If Ellie Lu was still available Jess intended to make her his wife one day soon and settle down.

Riding beside Jess, Ariel mulled over his answer, wondering about the kind of woman who loved a rough, hard-bitten Texan who was cold as ice and deadly as a rattler. Probably someone as crude and insensitive as he was, she decided.

Never had Ariel experienced such searing heat during the following days. The scorching sun beat down with unrelenting ferocity. Before the first few hours had passed Ariel felt certain her brains were fried. St. Louis summers were hot but nothing compared to this sunbaked Texas July. She felt all the moisture being siphoned out of her body until nothing was left but a dried-up shell. She could feel her skin blistering and her nose peeling.

They rode that day until the inside of Ariel's thighs were inflamed and raw. Until her back was a mass of aches and pains and her head pounded. She drooped in the saddle and would have fallen in another minute if Jess hadn't seen her sway and plucked her from the saddle, mounting her before him on Soldier.

"Go ahead and sleep if you want," he urged,

his voice losing some of its earlier gruffness. "I won't let you fall." His arm came around her waist as he tightened his grip on the reins.

"Damnation, you're wearing a corset in this heat!" he swore. Abruptly he sawed on the reins, halting Soldier. "Have you lost all the sense God gave you?" He slid her from Soldier's back until her feet touched the ground. "Take it off. And one or two of those infernal petticoats. You ought to know Texas well enough by now to realize a woman's trappings are of little use in this climate. Move your butt, Til—Ariel."

"How dare you! I certainly will not."

Deliberately Jess dismounted, towering over Ariel like an irate giant. His feet were planted wide apart, his arms crossed over the width of his massive chest. The cords in his neck bulged as he glared at her. "Do it now, Ariel! I intend to bring you back alive and well, not shriveled up from the heat. If you don't do it yourself I'll help you." He stalked her mercilessly, placing his big hands at the neckline of her dress.

Ariel felt the pressure of his fingers and realized that Jess meant to undress her if she didn't do it herself. "Wait! I'll do it. Turn your back."

Jess looked confused for a moment, then tilted his head back and laughed. "Lady, you sure as hell are something! How many men have you played whore for before joining up with Dillon? Don't act the innocent with me. Are you gonna take off that corset or not?"

Ariel angrily slapped Jess' hands aside and turned her back on him. Her hands shook as she unfastened the buttons of her bodice and removed her arms from the sleeves. When she reached around to loosen her corset strings, Jess was there before she could touch them. His long tan fingers were deft and sure as they untied the strings. When his hands brushed her soft skin, Jess was shocked by the way her flesh made him tingle and burn. Ariel must have felt it too for she stiffened and inhaled sharply. Suddenly Jess' hands tightened on the garment and he yanked viciously. Ariel gasped as the corset left her body and sailed over her head, landing in the dirt several yards away.

Angrily Ariel pulled up her bodice then turned to glare at Jess. "Was that necessary?"

"Yep. I'll never understand why women find it necessary to truss themselves up in a contraption that can only cause pain. You sure as hell don't need it. I can span your waist with my hands, with plenty of room to spare. Now the petticoats."

When Ariel hesitated too long he ran his hands insinuatingly under her skirt and undid the tape fastening on her petticoats. Two of the garments promptly fluttered down to settle in a froth at her feet. She had no choice but to step out of them. When Jess would have tossed them the way of the corset, Ariel protested vigorously.

"No! I—I'll need them."

"In jail?" Jess scoffed. Still, he granted her request, picking up the petticoats and stuffing them in his saddlebag. Then he lifted her and placed her back atop his horse, vaulting up behind her.

"I have my own mount," Ariel insisted.

"You can ride him again later, but not now. You nearly fell off and broke your fool neck a few minutes ago."

"Why should you care?"

"Damned if I know," Jess grumbled. "Go back to sleep. Once you're rested you can have your mount back."

Perversely, Ariel stiffened her spine, refusing to touch even one part of his hard frame. But to her chagrin her resolve quickly dissolved as sheer exhaustion, combined with the searing heat and the monotony of the landscape, caused her to slump against Jess.

Jess felt Ariel relax against him and his arms automatically tightened around her. What began next was a fierce struggle with his conscience as he reminded himself that Ariel's soft feminine allure was misleading. Beneath her innocent facade lurked a heart as black as pitch. She had robbed more banks than he could count and was involved in the killings of several men. It rankled to think he wanted her despite her lurid past and notorious reputation. All Jess had to do was remember how Judd had bled to death in the bank after being shot by Bart Dillon and his hot blood lusted for vengeance. Even knowing all that Jess found it difficult to come to grips with the fact that he wanted this woman in his arms no matter what she had done. Jess almost wished she *was* Ariel Leland, an innocent victim of mistaken identity.

Damnation! he thought with a snort of self-derision. He was growing soft with age. He couldn't wait until he rid himself of the little baggage so he could continue his search for Bart Dillon. Until then, until the day the slimy bastard was dead or behind bars, Jess promised himself again, he'd devote his life to finding Judd's killer. Indeed, he had no life as long as Dillon roamed Texas a free man.

Ariel wasn't asleep. She was hopelessly aware of Jess' body—the hard wall of his chest, his muscular arms as they circled her waist to hold the reins. But instead of feeling threatened, a sense of peace surrounded her. Soon she was slumbering, knowing that as long as Jess was nearby nothing bad would happen to her. It was a contradiction she was too exhausted to delve into more fully.

Chapter 4

Ariel was weary. Weary of traveling, weary of heat, dust, and mesquite. Weary of Jess Wilder. He was arrogant, insolent, and downright infuriating. She quit trying to convince him she wasn't Tilly Cowles; she was wasting her breath. She hoped the marshal at Fort Worth had sense enough to check out her story before jailing her for crimes she didn't commit. Ariel couldn't fault Jess for mourning his dead brother, but it still didn't excuse his deplorable behavior where she was concerned.

They stopped that night beside a small creek nearly devoid of water. Ariel had difficulty gathering enough water for a good wash. When Jess went off to hunt meat for their supper, she made good use of the time. When Jess returned with a pair of scrawny rabbits she had already washed, combed her hair, and changed into the one clean dress she'd brought along.

They ate in silence. Afterward Ariel placed her blanket beside the fire and lay down. She saw Jess watching her, always watching her, and shivered.

"We'll be in Fort Worth tomorrow," Jess said as he carefully placed his bedroll on the opposite side of the fire.

"That should make you happy," Ariel bit out sharply.

"I won't deny it," Jess admitted slowly. "You affect me in strange ways, Ariel. As you've no doubt discovered, I'm not a man easily influenced nor swayed by feminine wiles. But damn if I don't find myself wanting you something fierce. And I think you feel the same way. I've a good notion to satisfy both our cravings."

"You come near me, Jess Wilder, and you'll be sorry," Ariel said in frosty affront.

One dark brow lifted into a challenging arch. "I could make you change your mind."

"No, thank you. Whatever it is you're proposing is highly immoral and downright humiliating. Fortunately I'll only have to put up with you another day. Good night, Mr. Wilder."

Jess flashed a wicked grin. "Are you afraid that you'll like what I do to you? Does it frighten you that I might be a better lover than Bart Dillon?"

"I'm not afraid of anything you do or say," Ariel shot back quickly—too quickly.

Suddenly Jess was kneeling at her side, grasping her shoulders and bringing her to within inches of him. Ariel could feel his heat, and was stunned by the wild savagery behind his silver gaze. God, he was too much . . . too massive, too hard, too hot, too filled with lust—too wonderfully male. Too damn sure of himself.

"You tempt me, lady, you sorely tempt me."

Mesmerized, Ariel merely watched as his mouth covered hers, moist, hot, fiercely demanding. His tongue probed ruthlessly until Ariel's lips parted. In eager response, Jess moaned deep in his throat and plundered the sweet warmth of her mouth. Ariel detected no tenderness in the kiss, no real passion. Indeed, the emotion that drove him was a great outpouring of anger. Whether directed at her or himself was difficult to judge.

Ariel stiffened in shock when Jess ground his hips against her and she felt the full length of his arousal. Then his hand was on her breast, his strong fingers kneading the softness with bold insistence. Shoving against his chest, Ariel managed to free her mouth.

"Take your hands off me," she said on a note of rising panic.

With gut-wrenching dismay, Jess abruptly realized how close he was to making love to a woman involved in his brother's death. There was an arrested expression on his bold features as he released her—so suddenly Ariel fell back, stunned.

"I don't know what it is about you, lady, but you sure as hell light a fire in my britches. Go to sleep before I change my mind and douse the flames in that sweet little body of yours."

Gasping in outrage, Ariel glared at Jess with a look of profound disgust. Never had she known a man so outrageously unpredictable, so vile, so—so—damn infuriatingly male! The first thing she was going to do when she reached Fort Worth and cleared her name was to buy a gun and shoot the bounder. That's how mad she was. Somehow she managed to calm her temper, turn her back to Jess, and eventually fall into a fitful doze.

Fort Worth was the last major populated area between the Brazos and Kaw Rivers, and it appealed to cowboys as a place where they could get a "square deal" from the merchants and could have a "high ole time."

"Well, we're here," Jess said as they rode into town. "Cowtown. It's also known as 'Where the West Begins.' Actually, it's named for Major General Worth, commander of the federal troops who fought the Comanche."

"It doesn't look like much to me," Ariel complained as they rode through the dusty center of town.

She noted the usual number of stores and saloons lining both sides of the main thoroughfare.

The street was crowded, the stores enjoying a lively trade from cowboys and townspeople alike.

"It's a busy place and a good town," Jess told her. "I was born in Fort Worth and was U.S. marshal here for nearly four years. My brother was deputy. You ought a be well-acquainted with Fort Worth yourself—you and Dillon seemed to know the best route outta town after the bank robbery. Too bad Dillon left you high and dry to shoulder the blame."

"You're going to look mighty silly, Jess Wilder, when you find out I'm not Tilly Cowles."

"We'll learn soon enough, won't we?" Jess said tightly. "The story you've been telling me won't hold water once the marshal identifies you."

"If you expect the marshal to identify me from that terrible picture on the poster you're going to be disappointed."

"We'll let the marshal decide that," Jess said as he reined in outside the marshal's office.

He dismounted, then swung Ariel out of the saddle before she could slide down herself. He let his hands linger on her waist, strangely reluctant to let Ariel walk out of his life. He knew she was a thief, a killer, and a liar, yet she affected him in ways totally new to him. Ways that puzzled and frightened him. Abruptly his hands fell away. Grasping her elbow, he pulled her none too gently onto the wooden sidewalk and through the open door of the marshal's office.

The man sitting behind the desk was over forty, burly rather than fat, with thick graying hair and shaggy brows. He looked big enough to handle the meanest desperado and as tough as boot leather. He glanced up as they entered and his intelligent blue eyes lit up when he spied Jess.

"Jess! Jess Wilder, you old cuss! Where in tarnation have you been? Haven't seen you around Cowtown lately."

They clasped hands, obviously old friends. Ariel nearly groaned aloud. How could she expect fair treatment from a man friendly with Jess Wilder?

"Howdy, Caleb." Jess grinned. "Is Cowtown giving you any trouble?"

"None I can't handle," Caleb returned, "but if you're hankerin' to get your old job back you sure as hell can have it. Addie's been wantin' to go back East to visit our daughter and I'm thinkin' it's not such a bad idea."

"How is Addie?" Jess asked, recalling Caleb's wife with fondness.

"Feisty as ever." Caleb chuckled.

All the while Caleb spoke to Jess his eyes kept finding their way to Ariel. Finally Jess pulled Ariel forward and asked, "Do you recognize her, Caleb?"

Caleb's eyes narrowed shrewdly as they swept Ariel from head to toe. Then they widened as he seemed to recognize her. "If that don't beat all. She's the spittin' image of Tilly Cowles."

"She *is* Tilly Cowles."

For a moment Caleb looked startled. "Can't be. Received word two days ago that Tilly Cowles helped rob a bank in Nacogdoches. Funny thing, though, Bart Dillon wasn't with her. Witnesses swore the man with her was Frank Kells. There's a wanted poster out on him too."

"I told you," Ariel said with smug satisfaction.

"The witnesses were mistaken, Caleb," Jess persisted with grim determination. He had been so certain—so absolutely positive. "I found Tilly here in an overturned stage handcuffed to the lawman who was bringing her and Dillon to Fort Worth to stand trial. The lawman was shot in the head."

"I heard Dillon and Cowles had been apprehended and wondered why they were on the loose again. Last I heard they were expected on the Fort Worth stage from Texarkana."

"Forget about the stage. No one is alive to tell the tale but Tilly here. When I heard both Dillon and Tilly had been caught trying to cross into Arkansas from Texarkana, I thought my long search for the pair was finally ended. You can imagine my disappointment to find that half the team is still at large."

"I don't know, Jess," Caleb said, scratching his head. "Why would Dillon leave Tilly behind?"

"My name is Ariel Leland," Ariel interjected, unable to hold her tongue a moment longer. "I can't seem to get through to this stubborn mule."

Jess let out a snort of disgust. "Tilly was unconscious when I found her, handcuffed to the dead sheriff. I have no idea why Dillon left her behind."

"Why did the stage overturn?"

"We were being chased by desperadoes," Ariel said, anxious to clear up matters and get on with her life. This was like some horrible nightmare that went on and on.

"Desperadoes?" Caleb asked sharply. He and Jess exchanged looks, the meaning of which escaped Ariel. "Are you thinkin' the same thing I'm thinkin', Jess?"

"Yup. 'Pears like some of Dillon's friends got wind of his arrest and set out to intercept the stage. It's purely mystifying why they left Tilly behind but I reckon they had their reasons. My personal opinion is that the little baggage is more trouble than she's worth."

"They didn't leave Tilly behind," Ariel bit out angrily. "When that sheriff got on the stage the man was shackled to him and the woman's wrists were schackled together. I have no idea how I ended up shackled." She stared at Jess, chin tilted at a stubborn angle, eyes darkly defiant, daring him to prove her guilty of any crime.

They stood nearly toe-to-toe, glaring at one another, each unwilling to give an inch, unbending, unyielding, yet each aware of the other in ways that had nothing to do with Bart Dillon or Jess' brother.

"She could be right, Jess," Caleb allowed.

Astutely Caleb sensed an undercurrent pass between Jess and Ariel that spoke silently of their attraction for one another, and quite frankly it amused him. He'd known Jess Wilder a long time, watched him use then discard various women who threw themselves at him, and he thought it was about time someone came along and shook him up some. Caleb didn't believe for a minute that Jess would marry Ellie Lu, a spoiled, featherheaded bit of fluff if he ever saw one. He and Addie felt certain Jess didn't love Ellie Lu; but Jess was hardheaded and would have offered marriage merely because he was tired of wandering and wanted a little stability in his life.

"Don't tell me the little witch has you hoodwinked too?" Jess said disgustedly. "Any fool can see this is Tilly Cowles. Look." He reached in his vest pocket and drew forth the much-creased and well-worn poster he had been carrying around for two years. "Look at this picture and tell me the woman standing before you isn't Tilly Cowles."

"I'm familiar with the poster, Jess, and I admit the lady here fits the description, but if Tilly Cowles was spotted in Nacogdoches I have no reason to believe otherwise."

"Thank you, Marshal," Ariel said, smiling smugly at Jess. "At least someone here has the sense God gave him. I've told Mr. Wilder countless times in the last several days that I am not Tilly Cowles. I am Ariel Leland."

Caleb held out his hand. "Howdy, Miss Leland, I'm Marshal Hawks."

"You're not falling for her story, are you, Caleb?" Jess asked, dismayed.

"You have any identification, Miss Leland?" Caleb asked, sending Jess a quelling look.

"N-no, my identification and valuables were stolen from the stage. But you can wire my mother and stepfather in St. Louis; they'll vouch for me."

"Give me their name and address and I'll send a wire out immediately. Meanwhile, you can check into the hotel."

"Damnation, you do believe her!"

"Until I find out differently, Jess, I have no choice but to accept her story."

"Marshal Hawks," Ariel said, embarrassed, "I have very little cash."

Because she had been strictly forbidden to travel to Texas alone, Ariel had taken only the money she had on hand, which was sufficient for her trip but left little extra. And only a small amount of that was pinned to her bodice; the rest had been stolen. Ariel knew from the lawyer's correspondence that her father had left a sizable sum of money in her name in the bank in Waco. All those letters and more were among the articles stolen from the stage.

"If you'd be so kind as to extend me a loan I'll repay you as soon as I reach Waco. My father left me a prosperous ranch as well as money in the bank. Perhaps you'd also wire Mr. Jason Burns, my father's lawyer, and tell him I've been delayed in Fort Worth."

"I'll see to the wires. About the loan—"

"I'll loan Ariel the money," Jess interjected, forestalling Caleb's answer. He knew from experience how little a town marshal was paid and didn't want Caleb to throw away money he could ill afford to spare. On the other hand, Jess had earned a considerable amount collecting rewards the past two years, which was just sitting around in the bank drawing dust.

Caleb flushed, but looked grateful. Before Ariel could voice protest, Caleb said, "Why don't you settle Miss Leland at the hotel while I send the telegrams.''

Jess nodded. "I'll meet you back here later. If there's a reward for a pair of desperadoes named Blackie Rowe and Luke Wilkes I aim to collect it. I buried them somewhere between here and Texarkana. But first I have to report a raid on the Butterfield way station. Injuns made off with the stock.''

"Anyone hurt?''

"Nope. Those rascals were only interested in horses.''

"If I'm not mistaken there's a five-hundred-dollar reward offered for each of those two characters, dead or alive. You got proof?''

"In my saddlebag. I also have a witness.'' He motioned toward Ariel. "The pair tried to kill me so they could get to Ariel.''

"That right, Miss Leland?'' Caleb asked.

"Yes,'' Ariel said, lending credence to Jess' claim. "Jess Wilder is handy with a gun, I'll give him that much.''

A few minutes later Ariel and Jess walked toward the hotel while Caleb strode over to the telegraph office to dispatch the telegrams. To Ariel's chagrin Jess held her tightly by the elbow.

"I don't want your money,'' Ariel spat, shrugging free of his grasp and stopping abruptly as she whirled to face him. "You still don't believe I'm Ariel Leland, do you?''

"Nope.'' His short, curt answer said it all. "Move your butt, I've got business to attend to.''

"I told you, I don't want your money.''

"Where will you sleep? How will you eat?''

"I have some money. Even the street is preferable to accepting anything from you.''

Jess' silver eyes glinted dangerously. "I could take you to Miss Jolene's. It's not as fancy as some bawdy houses but I reckon it wouldn't matter to someone who's not choosy about who they bed.

The girls there earn a decent wage. Then again,''
Jess taunted, wondering why he let her get under
his skin like she did, ''the street's not too bad a
place if you're hankering to get fixed up with a
cowboy. Plenty of them around.''

A dull red crept up Ariel's neck, flushing her
cheeks and disappearing into the roots of her hair.
She was so angry that her feeble efforts at coherent speech failed miserably.

''Well, what will it be?'' Jess prodded. ''Miss
Jolene's, the street, or the best hotel in town?''

''I asked Marshal Hawks for a loan, not you.''

''Caleb can't afford to lend the money.''

''And you can?''

Jess grinned with devastating effect. No matter
how far the arrogant rogue pushed her Ariel
couldn't help but be affected by his raw masculine appeal. A shiver trembled down her spine;
suddenly she was afraid of the way he made her
feel, of the strange way his touch made her body
react. How could one experience hatred and attraction at the same time?

''I'm not as poor as you might think,'' Jess informed her. ''Bounty hunting has provided me
with a damn good living.''

''I'll bet,'' Ariel remarked dryly. She wanted
desperately to refuse Jess' money but was too
practical to allow her anger to distort her good
sense. ''You'll have your money the moment I
reach Waco.''

They turned again in the direction of the hotel.
But once again were stopped in their tracks, this
time by a young woman with bouncing blonde
curls, blue eyes, and voluptuous curves enticingly
displayed in a pink and white voile dress. She
came rushing out of the mercantile, throwing herself into Jess' arms with a squeal of delight.

''You're back! I've missed you, darling, really
missed you.'' Then to Ariel's dismay the attractive young woman planted an exuberant kiss on

Jess' lips. What really disgusted Ariel was the fact that Jess appeared to enjoy the woman's vulgar display, responding by kissing her back. Then he set her aside, laughing.

"Behave yourself, Ellie Lu, what will people think?"

"Oh, pooh, I don't give a fig what they think," Ellie Lu said, pouting. Her lower lip was full, red, and sensual. Ariel hated her on sight. "Are you here to stay?"

"I wish I could tell you my search was over, honey, but I can't," Jess said.

Ariel stiffened. Honey. He called her honey.

"Give it up, Jess, let the law take care of it. You're wasting your life chasing Judd's killer."

"Sorry, Ellie Lu, I can't do that. I've sworn a solemn oath to bring Bart Dillon and Tilly Cowles to justice and I will."

Suddenly Ellie seemed to notice Ariel who stood slightly behind Jess, watching through hooded eyes. "Who is she?" Ellie Lu asked. Her big blue eyes settled on Ariel with a hostility Ariel found disconcerting.

"This is—Ariel Leland," Jess said, stumbling over the name. "The stage she was riding overturned." He omitted any mention of their meeting and details of the time they spent together. "I'm taking her to the hotel. Ariel, this is Ellie Lu Dodge. Her daddy owns the mercantile."

When Ariel offered a polite greeting, Ellie Lu deliberately ignored her gesture by turning up her pert nose. "Come for supper tonight, Jess, my parents will be as happy to see you as I am. We can go for a walk afterward and maybe I can persuade you to stick around this time."

Her eyes promised delights she dare not speak of.

"I accept, Ellie Lu." Jess smiled. "But I really have to go now."

"If you insist," Ellie Lu replied. Her shrill voice

grated on Ariel's nerves. ''Until tonight.'' She raised herself on tiptoes and kissed Jess again, glancing at Ariel to see if she was watching. She was. Then she turned and walked away, her hips swaying provocatively.

Chapter 5

Never had a bath felt so delicious, Ariel thought as she stretched languidly in the tub of water she'd ordered the moment Jess left her. The room he secured for her was large and comfortable though not nearly so grand as those she'd occupied in Eastern cities. She wondered how long it would take to get an answer to the telegrams sent by Marshal Hawks. She couldn't wait to leave Fort Worth behind. According to her calculations she had just enough money pinned inside the bodice of her dress to purchase a ticket to Waco with perhaps a little extra to buy a change of clothes.

Suddenly Ariel's ruminations were interrupted by a knock on the door. Thinking it was the maid with fresh towels, Ariel bade her enter.

"Please set the towels on the chair, I can manage on my own," she called over her shoulder.

Jess strode into the room, Ariel's meager bundle of belongings slung under his arm. He had already been to the Butterfield office and on his way to the barber shop remembered Ariel's things in his saddlebag. He knew she'd want them. He could have sent them over by messenger but for some obscure reason the thought of sparring with Ariel again sent a shot of adrenaline surging through his veins. What he saw when he stepped through the door caused the breath to slam out of him.

One leg raised out of the water, Ariel slid the washcloth along her slim calf, leaving a trail of soap in its wake. Her arms were bare and alluringly curved, innocent yet seductive. Her smooth ivory breasts bobbed above the water, their pert pink nipples making him forget that the tantalizing witch was wanted for any reason but to provide pleasure for a man. And he'd sure as hell like to be that man.

"I'm pretty good at scrubbing backs," Jess drawled lazily. His voice was low and husky, his eyes dark with desire.

"You!" Ariel sputtered, sinking beneath the water until only her neck and head were visible. Or so she assumed. "Get out of here."

Nothing short of death could have stopped Jess from moving forward until he stood beside the tub. Wild excitement shuddered through him as he gazed down at Ariel. Every curve, each cleverly fashioned inch of her was clearly visible beneath the water's surface. He stared in mute fascination at the dark triangle crowning the apex of her thighs. Rampant desire swelled his loins.

"You heard me, get out of here. Now!"

"I'd be happy to wash your back," Jess repeated, flashing a mischievous grin. He dipped a hand into the water, deliberately brushing her thigh.

Ariel drew in a shuddering sigh. The sweeping emotions this man's mere touch evoked in her both thrilled and frightened her. He might not be considered handsome in a classical sense but he was ruggedly appealing and literally reeked of male sexuality. Ariel had enjoyed her share of beaux in St. Louis but none could compare with big, vital Jess Wilder. Especially not Denton Dobbs, the man her mother and stepfather hoped she'd marry.

"I'm perfectly capable of washing my own back," she hissed, trying to shield her nakedness with a tiny scrap of washcloth she held in her hand.

She heard Jess chuckle, a low rumble deep in his throat, and then the cloth was plucked away. "Hand me the soap."

"Are you hard of hearing? I said I can wash my own back. Please leave before the maid returns with the towels."

He fished for the soap himself, found it, and lathered the cloth with slow relish. "Sit up."

"You're the most infuriating, exasperating, ornery, contemptible man I've ever had the *dis*pleasure of meeting!"

"And you're the most stubborn, contrary, shrewdest little wildcat I've ever come across. You're also damn enticing and pure woman, from your pink toes to those pert little nipples you're trying so damn hard to hide."

Ariel gasped in outrage. "You have the manners of a toad and are certainly no gentleman."

"Never said I was." He positioned himself at her back. "Are you gonna sit up?"

"Do you promise to leave if I do? I could scream for help."

"But you won't." His tone of mocking sarcasm made her want to slap him in the face.

Defeated, Ariel sat up, hugging her arms in front of her. Was there no end to this man's audacity? Were all Texans so—so—damn hardheaded? She flinched when she felt the cloth slide over her back. All her nerve endings seemed to come alive at his touch. Even through the cloth her flesh was sensitive to his gentle massage.

"Now, was that so difficult?" Jess whispered in her ear.

He knew he was deliberately baiting her but couldn't seem to help himself. Her anger and frustration served only to enhance her beauty and he delighted in taunting her, in seeing her green eyes turn dark and defiant. He knew he was placing himself in potentially dangerous territory, that he was deliberately disregarding every instinct that warned him to turn tail and run as far as he could from this bewitching little termagant.

But this was one time he ignored his inner voices and followed—what? What prompted him to act so outrageously toward Ariel Leland—or Tilly Cowles—or whatever her name was? The answer was simple, he told himself. He was driven by lust. He wanted her, lusted after her; he couldn't remember when a woman had affected him in ways he neither liked nor needed right now. His life was complicated enough without taking up with a woman who was either a devious liar or an innocent virgin caught in unfortunate circumstances. Fearing he might be tempted to learn the truth in the most basic way known to man, Jess rose suddenly and left the room.

"Thank goodness, it's about time you left!" Ariel swiveled her head to peer over her shoulder, shocked to find herself dismayed that Jess had left. "Insufferable swine," she muttered sourly. It had become increasingly evident that God had put Jess Wilder on earth merely to torment her.

When a knock sounded on the door a few minutes later Ariel wasn't about to make the same mistake twice. "Who is it?"

"The maid, miss, I have your towels. Sorry it took so long."

Ariel bade the girl enter then sent her on her way after she set the towels on a chair beside the tub. Afterward Ariel ordered supper sent to her room and went straight to bed. Traveling with Jess Wilder had exhausted her both mentally and physically. Let Ellie Lu Dodge put up with him tonight, she thought, wondering at the conflicting emotions that statement evoked in her. Her last thought before she fell asleep was strange indeed for a virgin untutored in the ways of love. Every instinct told her that Jess Wilder would be a wonderfully passionate lover, capable of giving a woman exquisite pleasure. Unfortunately she wasn't that woman—nor was she ever likely to be.

Soon that irritating scoundrel would be out of her life forever. Soon she'd be running her own ranch, proving to her mother and stepfather that a woman was as competent as a man when it came to ranching and managing her own property. Clinging to that satisfying thought, Ariel drifted into a slumber fraught with dreams of a big silver-eyed Texan who had sold his soul to the devil.

The next morning Ariel counted her money and left the hotel for the Butterfield Stage Line office. She was disappointed to learn the Butterfield stage made only one run a week to Waco and she'd just missed it by one day. When she found she had enough money with which to purchase the ticket she thanked the agent and left. Fortunately she wouldn't have to ask Jess for another loan.

It was nearly noon when Ariel approached the marshal's office. She hoped that by now he had an answer to the telegrams sent the day before. She paused outside the door, her hand on the knob as the sound of voices drifted to her through the open window. One belonged to Marshal Hawks, the other to Jess Wilder. The bounty hunter's voice was raised in anger.

"Dammit, Caleb, those telegrams prove nothing except that a woman named Ariel Leland left St. Louis on June 16th, her probable destination Waco, Texas. For all we know the real Ariel is dead and buried amid the sagebrush. Tilly Cowles is clever—very clever."

"Tarnation, Jess, I've never known you to be so dang mule-headed or all-fired obstinate. I believe Ariel is who she claims to be. Even that lawyer fellow said Ariel Leland was expected in Waco. What further proof do you need?''

''Does anything in either of those telegrams positively identify Ariel Leland?'' Jess asked.

''No, but— What in tarnation are you gettin' at?''

''Look, Caleb, why don't you wire Ariel's mother for positive identification? A birthmark, maybe, or anything at all that will help us solve this mystery.''

''If this woman *is* Tilly Cowles, how do you 'spose she knew all about Ariel and was able to supply us with the names of her mother, stepfather, and lawyer in Waco?'' Caleb asked.

Jess paused. He had no answer. Nothing seemed to make sense anymore. Was he so obsessed with the need to catch Judd's killers that he no longer had the ability to tell right from wrong, good from bad?

''I don't know, Caleb, I purely don't know,'' Jess admitted, shaking his head in bewilderment. ''But if there is even a remote possibility that Ariel Leland could be Tilly Cowles, I'll not let her out of my sight until I learn the truth. I've devoted too many years of my life to finding Judd's killers to stop now, or make a mistake that will set me back months.''

''Dammit, Jess, what do you want me to do?'' Caleb asked, exasperated. ''I can't hold the woman without good reason.''

''Just a few days, Caleb, while you wire for something more conclusive.''

''I'm sorry, Jess, I just can't do it,'' Caleb replied. ''I'm goin' 'round to the hotel on my way home this evenin' and tell Miss Leland I'm sending her back to St. Louis on the next stage east. Her mother and stepfather requested that I return her to them. Seems they're not too happy about her comin' to Texas without their permission.''

"You're the marshal," Jess said bitterly. "But that little lady isn't going anywhere without me on her tail. If for any reason she leaves the stage between here and St. Louis I'll know she's not who she claims to be."

"Suit yourself, Jess, but this time you're barkin' up the wrong tree."

Ariel didn't wait around to hear more. She was free to leave and that's all that mattered. But she certainly wasn't going back to St. Louis. And she didn't want the likes of Jess Wilder anywhere near her. When she left Fort Worth it had to be without the knowledge of either Jess or the marshal. And she knew exactly how to do it. Not one to waste time, Ariel turned toward the mercantile.

The clerk looked at Ariel strangely when she purchased a set of boy's clothing and a wide-brimmed Stetson. It took all of her money save for a dollar or two to purchase supplies and a gun and ammunition. She wasn't exactly familiar with weapons but considered it a necessary expenditure for what she had in mind. The clerk was helpful enough to show her how to load, aim, and fire the Smith and Wesson revolver. He also gave her directions to Waco, explaining that the road was well-defined and easily accessible to travelers.

As for transportation, Ariel had that all figured out. She'd merely "borrow" the horse stabled at the livery, the one she'd ridden to Fort Worth and had once belonged to Blackie Rowe. Horse, saddle, saddlebags, and everything she needed was hers for the taking. She figured Jess Wilder owed it to her for all the grief he'd caused her these past few days. After paying for her purchases, Ariel picked up her bundle and left the store. To her chagrin she bumped into Ellie Lu Dodge.

"Why, Miss Leland, how nice to see you again. Will you be staying long in town?"

"Hello, Miss Dodge," Ariel returned pleasantly, though inwardly she was gritting her teeth in frustration. "I plan to leave Fort Worth very soon."

Not soon enough, Ellie Lu thought spitefully. Seeing Ariel with Jess just hadn't set right with her. Perhaps she was being overly suspicious, but she'd certainly breathe easier when the dark-haired beauty was out of Jess' life. Ellie Lu never did hear how it happened that Jess was escorting Ariel to the hotel yesterday. "Tell me, how well do you know Jess Wilder?"

Ellie Lu just *had* to ask that question. Though Jess hadn't mentioned Ariel when he came to visit last night his mind certainly had been occupied with something besides her. She hadn't seen Jess in months, yet when they were alone he hardly acted like a man starved for female companionship. Finally, he had apologized for his preoccupation and left, the peck he bestowed on her lips bearing little resemblance to the ardent kisses she knew him capable of.

"I don't know Jess Wilder at all," Ariel replied, anxious to escape as quickly as possible. "We only spent a few days together, and none of them pleasant."

Ellie Lu gasped. "You—what! You spent *days* with Jess? Alone?" She had been told blessed little about Ariel, except that she was the sole survivor of a stage wreck. She'd assumed that Jess was merely doing Marshal Hawks a favor by taking her to a hotel, never questioning how Ariel had reached Fort Worth, or with whom. A nagging suspicion took root in her brain and refused to be dislodged.

"I—yes, I thought you knew. Weren't you with Jess last night? Surely he must have told you about me."

"We had more important things to—talk about," Ellie Lu hinted. The look in her eyes sug-

gested long hours of stolen pleasure that she
didn't dare reveal.

"I'll bet," Ariel said wryly. "I assure you, Miss
Dodge, I am no threat to you where Jess Wilder
is concerned. We can scarcely stand one another.
Besides, I'm leaving soon—very soon."

"I didn't mean to imply anything improper,"
Ellie Lu sniffed, "but Jess and I have an understanding. I'm a jealous woman, Miss Leland."

"Ariel."

"You're a beautiful woman, Ariel, and I had to
be sure there was nothing between you and Jess."

"You have my word, Jess is all yours. Now I
really must go."

Ellie Lu made no move to stop Ariel when she
pushed past her, clutching her bundle of purchases to her chest. She went directly to the hotel
where she told the maid she was going to rest and
didn't want to be disturbed until morning. Once
inside her room Ariel donned the boy's clothes,
jammed her long hair under the Stetson, and
shoved the gun inside her belt. Then she packed
everything else in a pillowcase. Making certain the
hall was deserted, she took her bundle and
slipped down the back staircase that led to the
alley behind the row of businesses along the main
street. At the end of the long alley she came to
the livery.

Ariel located with little difficulty the horse she
had ridden into town. He was a fine animal. Not
nearly so fine as Soldier but a respectable mount
nevertheless. After the stable boy had saddled
him for her she packed the saddlebags, mounted,
and prepared to leave.

"What about the boardin' fees?" the stable boy
asked. "Are ya fixin' to bring him back or are ya
leavin' town?"

"Jess Wilder will pay when he returns for Soldier." Ariel felt no guilt over leaving Jess with
livery charges after the high-handed way he'd

treated her. "I'm going to—to visit friends in north Texas," she lied. She kept her voice deliberately pitched low and her head down. No sense leaving a trail for Jess to follow, she thought shrewdly. Let him think what he wanted when he found her gone.

Since the stable boy was acquainted with Jess and knew he wouldn't try to light out of town without paying, he agreed to the arrangement. Jess had brought in both horses to be boarded, thus accepting full responsibility for payment. Though he didn't recognize the lad he assumed he was a friend of Jess'.

Fortunately Ariel didn't have to pass the marshal's office on her way out of town. Not that she feared being recognized dressed as she was. Still, she breathed a sigh of relief when she easily located the trail leading south to Waco, and was more than happy to shake the dust of Fort Worth from her feet. If she was lucky she might never have to see Jess Wilder's sardonic face again. The man disturbed her in ways she didn't understand and liked even less. He was the main reason for her hasty leave-taking from Fort Worth. She gathered from his conversation with Marshal Hawks that he intended to trail her wherever she went, and the last thing she wanted was Jess Wilder's obnoxious company. If the marshal believed her why couldn't Jess Wilder?

Ariel refused to accept the possibility that Jess would eventually find her. When he discovered her gone would he think the worst, that she was Tilly Cowles and had gone off somewhere to meet Bart Dillon? she wondered glumly. She answered her own question: of course he would.

Not allowing herself to be intimidated or hindered in any way by Jess Wilder, Ariel rode till it was too dark to travel. Then she found a sheltering grove of trees and made camp.

* * *

Marshal Hawks left instructions for the night with his deputy then headed home for supper. Things were quiet tonight, as opposed to Saturday night when cowboys from nearby ranches came to town to drink and carouse. On his way home he made a detour to the hotel to inform Ariel about the telegrams he had received in answer to those he'd sent the day before. He also needed to tell her that he had already made arrangements to send her back to St. Louis according to instructions from her mother and stepfather.

Caleb couldn't get over Jess' stubbornness regarding the pert brunette and wondered what had happened during those long days and nights when they had been alone. As closemouthed as Jess was, Caleb reckoned he'd never find out. Putting those two together was like mixing oil and water. Jess was convinced that Ariel Leland was Tilly Cowles despite the fact that any fool could see Ariel was no common desperado. Nor was she a whore like Tilly was reputed to be. Jess Wilder was right about a lot of things, but this certainly wasn't one of them.

Caleb paused before Ariel's room, intending to knock on the door, but the maid who happened by forestalled him.

"Miss Leland is resting, Marshal. She left instructions not to be disturbed tonight."

Caleb hesitated, undecided whether to insist on seeing Ariel tonight or to wait until morning to give her the good news. If she didn't wish to be bothered she certainly had a right to privacy, Caleb thought.

"If you see Miss Leland tell her to come to my office first thing in the mornin'," Caleb instructed the maid as he turned to leave. Addie had promised him an apple pie tonight and he didn't want to be late for supper.

* * *

Jess was restless tonight. He thought he'd visit Ellie Lu then changed his mind. For some reason she didn't seem nearly as appealing as she used to. When had she grown so possessive, so cling-ing—so annoying? Deciding he needed a playful romp in bed, he moseyed over to Miss Jolene's bawdy house, selected a lively blonde with danc-ing blue eyes, then changed his mind and left abruptly. It annoyed him to think that a certain green-eyed, black-haired young woman intruded upon the most private part of his life, but it was only too true. It being still too early for bed, Jess decided to call on Caleb and Addie.

Addie Hawks was a cheerful, matronly woman in her forties with a comfortable figure and a spry step. She had birthed four babes and the only one to live was a daughter now married and residing in the East. Addie was tickled to see Jess and in-sisted he try her apple pie.

The two men exchanged idle chatter while Addie was out of the room.

"Thought you'd be courtin' Ellie Lu Dodge to-night," Caleb teased.

"I'm not ready to settle down yet, Caleb."

"Hear tell Miss Jolene's got some mighty fine girls, have you tried them yet?"

"Caleb Hawks, you ought to be ashamed of yourself!" Addie scolded. She had just returned to the room with Jess' pie and heard Caleb's words.

"Aw, Addie, you know how it is with young men."

Jess accepted the pie, struggling to keep a straight face.

"Jess ought to be thinking about marriage and a family, not sporting with soiled doves."

Jess nearly choked to keep from laughing out loud.

"That's what I was just tellin' Jess, Addie. This

vendetta of his to get Judd's killers is gonna make an old man of him before his time.''

"I know Ellie Lu Dodge is sweet on you, Jess. She won't wait forever,'' Addie warned good-naturedly.

"I don't expect her to, Addie,'' Jess returned thoughtfully. "In fact, I'm glad you brought it up. It wouldn't be fair to Ellie Lu to ask her to wait for me. I made a promise to Judd as he lay dying and I aim to fulfill it. Nothing or no one is important enough to me to make me break my solemn promise. Not even Ellie Lu.''

They chatted a few minutes longer and then Addie excused herself, astute enough to realize the men wanted a few minutes alone. Once she was gone Jess broached the subject that had brought him here.

"What did Ariel say when you told her she was free to leave? Was she upset to learn you were sending her back to St. Louis? Wherever she goes I'll be right behind her, at least until I'm damn certain she is Ariel Leland.''

"Didn't see her,'' Caleb replied. "She told the maid she didn't want to be disturbed till mornin' so I didn't bother her. Tomorrow is soon enough to tell her she's a free woman.''

Caleb's words brought a startled look to Jess' face. Some sixth sense warned him that something wasn't right. He thought he knew Ariel well enough to know she'd be on pins and needles waiting for those telegrams to arrive. Now he suspected she was up to no good. If the little wildcat was trying to pull the wool over his eyes he'd skin the lovely little hide from her delectable body!

"Something tells me the lady has some devious purpose in mind.'' Jess scowled, unhappy with this new development.

"Why would you think that?'' Caleb objected.

"Don't know, just a feeling I have. Maybe

you're right. Maybe I'm just getting too sensitive about this whole damn situation. Guess I'll vamoose. I wanna go around to the livery and see if Soldier is all right before I turn in."

The stable boy, young Hank Tanner, was just closing up when Jess arrived at the livery.

"Yer horse is jest fine, Mr. Wilder," Hank said eagerly. "Took care of him myself. Gave him extra oats, too, jest like ya said."

"Much obliged, Hank, but I'll check anyway. Soldier and I go a long way back. We've been through a lot together."

Soldier nickered in welcome as Jess neared his stall. Jess stroked his nose and spoke to him in soothing tones for a few minutes before turning to leave. Almost as an afterthought he paused before a nearby stall and raised the lantern high over his head. It was empty.

"Hank!" he bellowed.

Hank came running. "Somethin' wrong, Mr. Wilder?"

"Damn right! Where's the horse I brought in with Soldier? Did you move him to another stall?"

"Don't you know? Your friend took him out this afternoon. Said you'd pay the tab."

"Damnation! I shoulda known the little wildcat had something up her sleeve."

"Did—did I do somethin' wrong, Mr. Wilder? Wasn't the lad yer friend?"

"Lad? Did you say lad?"

"Yessir."

Jess muttered a foul oath, noted Hank's distress, and said, "It's not your fault, Hank. I reckon I shouldn't have let my guard down. Did the 'lad' say where 'he' was goin'?"

"I recollect he did. Said he was goin' ta north Texas ta visit friends."

"Friends!" Jess snorted in derision. She'd almost had him convinced that she really was Ariel Leland. But this latest stunt served to reinforce his original belief that she was Tilly Cowles. More than likely she was on her way to join up with Bart Dillon. In fact, every sign pointed that way. But Jess wasn't about to let her get away with it. No sirree. Come morning he'd be riding north and hopefully catch up with the wildcat before nightfall. Didn't she realize how dangerous it was for a woman traveling alone in untamed country? Marauding Kiowa and Comanche roamed the area and desperadoes on the run were a common sight.

Now where in the hell did that thought come from? Jess wondered curiously. Why should he care what happened to Tilly Cowles? If she really was Tilly Cowles. And Jess had to admit the doubt existed in his mind. That's why he was set on following her. There were too many unanswered questions, too many things he didn't understand. But he'd find out soon enough. Once he found the little wildcat he'd wring the truth from her.

Chapter 6

A riel was back in the saddle at first light after a breakfast of biscuits and black coffee. She had slept with the loaded gun within reach but luckily did not have to use it. She might not be able to shoot straight but at least the store clerk had shown her how to load and aim the weapon.

Ariel set a course due south, following the ruts made by the stage. She was careful not to tire her mount, resting him often. It amazed Ariel, who was basically a city girl, how well she was able to survive on her own in this vast wild state. But she was her father's daughter, wasn't she? Just because her mother hated Texas and had left shortly after she bore her husband a daughter didn't mean Ariel would hate it too. Ariel felt oddly at home on a horse, riding through the rough rolling terrain of central Texas as if she'd been born to it.

Perhaps it was due to her need to prove to everyone, herself included, that she was perfectly capable of managing on her own. Her father must have thought so too or he wouldn't have left her his ranch. He must have known her adventurous spirit would demand she try her hand at ranching despite her mother's vigorous objection and her stepfather's stern disapproval.

Ariel deliberately steered clear of the towns; she wanted no hassles, no trouble in any form. She'd already had enough of that with Jess Wilder. Ariel shook her head. Why did she have to go and think of that obnoxious bounty hunter now when he was miles away? she asked herself. Most of the time she didn't even like him. He had gone out of his way to be hateful to her. He thought her a woman capable of committing vile acts. If Miss Ellie Lu Dodge knew what he was *really* like she wouldn't want him.

If only his handsome, rugged face didn't keep popping up before her eyes to taunt and torment her. He was too arrogant, too confident—too overwhelmingly male! Ariel was too aware of every intimidating inch of him. Hopefully she'd never have to set eyes on Jess Wilder again.

Jess left Fort Worth early on the morning after Ariel's departure. He didn't bother with purchasing supplies, intending to stop at a small town along the way to obtain what he needed. He hoped to pick up Ariel's trail outside of town but for the life of him he didn't know what he was going to do with her once he found her. He only knew he couldn't let the little wildcat out of his sight until he was damn certain she wasn't Tilly Cowles. But if she was heading north instead of south to Waco he'd bet his ass she was going to join Bart Dillon.

Jess rode north for an hour, failing to pick out Ariel's tracks on the dusty trail. It began as a niggling suspicion, but as the hours ticked by it became increasingly evident that he had been had. If Ariel—he'd rather think of her as Ariel instead of Tilly—really intended to go north would she tell anyone? Jess knew Ariel was clever, too clever to leave clues—unless they were deliberately meant to mislead. Was that her game? Did she lie so he wouldn't follow her? Reining Soldier in the opposite direction, Jess rode hell-bent for leather back to Fort Worth. He'd get to the bottom of this yet.

Marshal Hawks was of little help. He didn't know what to think when he learned Ariel had left town so abruptly. But since he had no reason to hold her there was little he could do about it. He told Jess as much when he came bursting into the office later that day.

"Let her go, Jess," Caleb advised. "Continue your search for Bart Dillon if you must, but leave Ariel Leland out of it."

"Sorry, Caleb, I can't do that. I might miss my one chance at Dillon if I let Ariel go so easily."

Jess left the marshal's office soon afterward. Ellie Lu saw him from across the street and hailed him. He waited somewhat impatiently for Ellie Lu to join him.

"Jess, where were you last night? I waited and waited but you didn't come. I was afraid you'd left town without telling me."

Jess flushed guiltily. That's exactly what he had done, without giving Ellie Lu a second thought. "Sorry, Ellie Lu," he apologized. "I had business last night with Marshal Hawks."

"Always business." Ellie Lu pouted. "I declare I'm getting mighty tired of you walking in and out of my life. If I didn't know that Ariel Leland planned on leaving town I'd think you thought more of her than you do me."

Jess' attention sharpened. "What do you know about Ariel?"

"I know you two spent several days alone, something you conveniently forgot to tell me."

"How do you know that?"

"Ariel told me."

"You saw Ariel? When?"

"I bumped into her outside the mercantile yesterday. We—chatted. She said she was leaving town very soon."

"Did she mention where she was going?"

"No. Why? Is it important?" Ellie Lu's eyes hardened with suspicion.

"I can't explain now, Ellie Lu, but I have to find out where Ariel went and catch up with her."

"Jess Wilder!" Ellie Lu scolded, her hands on her hips. "If you go chasing off after that woman we're through. I've put up with your wandering for two years. If I was smart I'd marry Richard Long. At least he's a homebody who wouldn't find one excuse after another to leave me."

"Maybe you should, Ellie Lu," Jess said slowly. "I'm not free to devote my life to a woman until Judd's killer is either dead or behind bars. I'm sorry if I led you on. You deserve better."

Ellie Lu's mouth flew open in dismay. "Jess, you don't mean that!"

"Sorry," he muttered again. "I have to go, Ellie Lu. You'll be better off without me whether you marry Long or not. He's a good man. You could do worse." He tipped his hat, spun on his heel, and strode away, leaving Ellie Lu standing with her mouth hanging open in stunned disbelief.

Jess' step was surprisingly light as he entered the mercantile. At one time he'd thought Ellie Lu was the woman he wanted, the type of woman he needed to give stability to his life. His future with Ellie Lu was more or less assured until he'd met Ariel. To his everlasting regret Ariel was fast becoming an obsession with him, whether he liked it or wanted it. Everything about her was perfect, from her sweetly rounded curves to her temptingly lush lips. His life hadn't been the same since he met her. She injected an excitement in his life he hadn't felt in years.

Jess quickly purchased the supplies he needed and then, almost as an afterthought, questioned the clerk about Ariel's presence in the store the day before.

"Yes indeed, Mr. Wilder, the lady was in the store yesterday afternoon. Funny thing," he mused curiously. "She bought a set of boy's duds and a gun. Didn't even know how to shoot," he added.

It fit with what the stable boy had told him about a "lad" taking the spare horse. "Did she say anything? About her plans, I mean?"

The clerk thought for a few moments then said, "She asked directions to Waco. Don't recollect her sayin' anythin' else."

"Much obliged," Jess said, tossing down the coin to pay for his supplies.

"What's this all about, Mr. Wilder?" the clerk called after Jess' departing back.

"Nothing that concerns you. But you've been a big help."

Ten minutes later Jess had his saddlebags packed and rode south out of town. Waco, he thought in silent contemplation. Was Dillon in Waco? Or was the little wildcat actually going to claim the ranch left to Ariel Leland? He'd find out the truth soon enough, he told himself smugly. There wasn't a woman alive smart enough or wily enough to fool Jess Wilder. Tilly or Ariel—one way or another he'd get to the bottom of it.

By the end of the second day Ariel had stopped looking behind her, certain now that Jess had either washed his hands of her and said good riddance or was riding north on a wild goose chase. Either way she was finally shed of the tenacious bounty hunter. That obnoxious man refused to give up, not even when the truth stared him in the face. Things were finally going her way, she thought gleefully. If only the weather would cooperate and it wasn't so darn hot. Using her sleeve she wiped away the sweat dripping down her brow. Texas was suffering a mid-July hot spell. By mid-morning the temperatures would soar, and by afternoon Ariel was wilting beneath the brutal sun. Heat lightning lit up the night sky

but brought empty promises of rain. Not even the
breezes offered relief, searing her, drying her skin
until it felt like parchment stretched across her
bones.

That evening Ariel was pleasantly surprised to
find a stream with water still flowing within its
narrow banks. It wasn't deep but it contained
enough water with which to sponge the choking
dust from her body. She longed for an honest-to-
goodness bath in a real tub, but all that would
have to wait until she reached the ranch. It
couldn't be too soon to suit her. She couldn't wait
for this nightmare to be over and done with so
she could settle down to ranch life, learning everything she needed to know to make her the best
damn rancher in Texas.

Ariel built a small campfire, pleased with her
ability to do so with such ease. She puzzled over
her mother's hatred for this vast untamed state,
for truth to tell she herself seemed to thrive in this
stark hostile environment. Out here on the prairie
she could be herself, do as she pleased, be free of
any man's domination. She was forever grateful
to her father for trusting her to administer her
legacy without outside interference. Few women
her age were offered the opportunity to be independent.

If her mother and stepfather had their way she
would have remained in St. Louis and married
boring Denton Dobbs, who thought excitement
consisted of taking a drive in the country on a
Sunday afternoon. Thank God she had enough
gumption to pack up and leave. She had more of
her father in her than anyone knew. Her father
had written countless letters to her during the
years she had lived in St. Louis. Each one was
filled with descriptions of the ranch and the day-
to-day problems encountered in running a profitable enterprise. Buck Leland had visited her
several times while she was growing up, regaling

her with stories of Texas until Ariel felt a part of
the place. If she had remained in St. Louis her
future would have been mapped out for her.
Thank goodness she had taken matters into her
own hands before it was too late to escape the
rigid standards set by a society where women
were subjected to men's whims.

After a supper of canned beans, hard biscuits,
and canned peaches, Ariel settled down by the
fire, dreamily staring off into space. She couldn't
believe how easy it had been to escape Jess Wilder. Fortunately her luck had held and she'd encountered no threatening situations since she left
Fort Worth, or even met another traveler. Texas
wasn't as wild and dangerous as most people had
led her to believe. She was feeling quite smug
when she decided to turn in. And then she found
just how ill-equipped she was to survive on her
own when three riders suddenly appeared as if
from nowhere. They stood poised at the outer
fringes of the campsite and it truly frightened Ariel to think she hadn't heard them approach.

"Evenin', sonny," one of the men said as he
nudged his horse to where Ariel stood rooted to
the ground.

Ariel gasped in wordless terror as the man dismounted. Light from the dying campfire fell
across his face and she knew him instantly. It was
the man from the stagecoach, the one Jess called
Bart Dillon. The same man who had killed Jess'
brother!

"What's wrong, cat got yer tongue?"

Ariel's hand hovered near the gun shoved in
her belt. "N-no, you startled me, that's all." She
lowered her head and pitched her voice as low as
it would go. She felt she was safe only as long as
they thought she was a boy.

The other two men dismounted and ranged
themselves behind Dillon. Ariel nearly collapsed
on the spot when Dillon eyed her with mild cu-

riosity. Instinctively she pulled her Stetson lower over her eyes and tucked down her head.

"A mite young to be out here on yer own, ain't ya? Does yer mama know yer out traipsin' over the countryside in the dead of night?"

His mocking words brought a chuckle from his companions.

"Ain't got no maw," Ariel mumbled, using the rough language of an uneducated bumpkin. "She died and I'm gonna join up with my paw in Waco."

The answer seemed to satisfy Dillon. "How 'bout some of that coffee. We smelled it a mile away." He ambled over to the campfire and poured coffee from the tin pot into the cup Ariel had used earlier. He drank deeply then handed the cup to one of his companions, who followed suit.

"Ya make a damn fine cup of coffee, sonny," Dillon complimented.

"Much obliged, mister."

"The name's Dillon, Bart Dillon. This here's Pecos Pete and the other fella is Gandy."

"H-howdy." Ariel gulped nervously, afraid Dillon would recognize her as the woman on the stagecoach. She wondered what had happened to Tilly Cowles for she was nowhere in sight. "I'm— Art. Art Lee," she improvised when Dillon seemed to be waiting for her to supply him with a name.

Suddenly Dillon gave Ariel a puzzled look. "Ain't ya never heard of us?"

"N-no, should I have? I lived on a small spread in north Texas, didn't get into town much."

"Never mind, I reckon it's best ya don't know nothin'. Much obliged fer the coffee, sonny. Maybe we can return the favor one day. Look us up when yer a mite older and we'll give ya a job if ya ain't too particular what ya do."

"We'd sure as hell have to be hard up to hire a hayseed like this kid to ride with us." Pecos Pete snorted derisively.

"Yeah," echoed Gandy. "Don't need no wet-behind-the-ears kid ridin' with us."

"Aw, leave the kid alone," Dillon said. "I kinda like him. Takes guts fer a scrap like him to travel alone. C'mon, boys, let's make tracks. We got a heap of ridin' before we reach the border. You can bet yer ass that no-account bounty hunter is on our tail by now."

"I can't believe yer lettin' a damn bounty hunter chase ya outta the country," Pecos Pete said challengingly.

"Don't get all riled up, Pecos, we'll be back soon as things cool off up here. Pickin's ain't too good in Mexico and I don't plan on learnin' the language."

Ariel held her breath while the three men mounted and rode off. "So long, sonny," Dillon called over his shoulder. "Don't forget, look me up if ya ever need help."

Even after they were gone Ariel couldn't stop shaking. It seemed incredible that her gender had gone undetected and she had escaped unscathed. If Dillon had showed up in the daylight she might not have gotten away with her deception so easily. Thank God she had had the foresight to purchase clothes baggy enough to hide all traces of her femininity.

By now any thought of sleep was out of the question. Despite the heat Ariel shivered as she hunkered down beside the fire and fed it small sticks and brush she had gathered earlier. With deadly purpose she checked and rechecked her gun, making certain she had released the safety just like the store clerk had shown her.

Ariel had no idea how long she sat there, clutching the gun until her fingers were numb. It was a still night, stars twinkled above her and heat lightning danced across the sky. She could have been sitting for hours—or was it only minutes since Dillon and his companions rode off into the night? She sat peering into the darkness until her palms grew sweaty and her hands shook. Her mouth was dry and her tongue felt swollen. Her breath was a loud rasp that sounded like thunder in the stillness of the night. Her ears were attuned to the slightest noise; the rustle of leaves in the breeze, the call of the night owl, the snapping of a twig . . .

Twig! Ariel froze, her trigger finger automatically tightening. The snapping of a twig spelled company. Had Dillon and his pals realized she was a woman and returned for her? They weren't going to surprise her again, she silently vowed, aiming into the darkness. Suddenly a form materialized from out of the shadows, taking the shape of a man. A rather large man—wearing a Stetson. Dillon! It had to be. No one else knew she was here. The gun in her hands wavered, exhaustion and fear combining to send Ariel into a panic-induced frenzy. The man stepped closer and Ariel jerked, her reflexive action sending off six bullets in quick succession.

"Jesus H. Christ! You damn near shot my ba—ears off, Ariel!"

"Jess? Damn you, Jess Wilder! How dare you sneak up on me like that!"

Jess moved into the small circle of light provided by the campfire.

"What in holy hell are you doing sitting there in the dark with a gun in your hand?"

"What in holy hell are you doing here at all?" Ariel retorted.

"Christ, you're shaking like a leaf! What happened?" Jess hunkered down beside her, carefully removed the gun from her hands, and set it out of reach.

"I—I thought they came back."

"Came back? Who? What happened tonight, Ariel?"

"Dillon."

Jess looked thunderstruck. "Dillon was here? Of all the rotten luck!" It rankled to think he was so close to Dillon yet had managed somehow to miss him. "Was he alone?"

"No. He rode with two men. Pecos Pete and a man named Gandy."

"Gandy Reese. There are wanted posters out on both men." He searched Ariel's features. "Why did Dillon leave you behind?"

Rage and frustration combined to send Ariel's temper soaring. "You mule-headed bastard! When will you get it through your thick skull that I'm not Tilly Cowles? Why do you think I was sitting here with a gun in my hand, afraid that Dillon had realized I'm not a boy and come back? If I was Tilly Cowles would I deliberately try to hide my identity from Dillon? Use the sense God gave you, Jess Wilder!"

Never had Jess seen Ariel so furious. She looked so comical sitting there in baggy trousers, a jacket miles too big for her, and a battered Stetson jammed down over her shiny black hair that he wanted to laugh. He was so enthralled by Ariel and the way her anger made her green eyes ignite and her tiny body bristle inside her too-large clothing that she caught him completely by surprise when she launched herself at him in a fit of uncontrollable anger.

Unprepared and unsuspecting, Jess was shoved to the ground by the violence of Ariel's attack. She fell on top of him and Jess howled in pain when her nails raked across his face.

"You little wildcat! What in tarnation are you doing? Trying to maim me?"

"If that's what it takes to knock some sense into you," Ariel panted, pummeling his chest with her fists.

Recovering from his astonishment, Jess grasped Ariel's wrists, dragging them above her head as he rolled her beneath him. His body was hot and hard and eager as he pressed her into the unyielding sunbaked ground. Ariel squirmed, panic seizing her as she felt Jess' body respond to her in a way that both thrilled and frightened her. His blatantly sexual response went far beyond her meager knowledge of what happened between a man and woman and left her hungry to learn more.

Suddenly Jess leaned forward to capture her mouth. His manhood reacted instinctively and swiftly, swelling against the confinement of his tight trousers to boldly prod her abdomen. A strange trembling sensation erupted in the pit of her stomach and Ariel renewed her efforts to escape Jess' relentless ardor. Her efforts proved futile.

At first there was no hint of tenderness in his kiss. Indeed, the emotion that drove him was a surge of anger as his lips moved over hers, searching with an almost desperate urgency. Fighting for control, Ariel was determined that this exasperating man neither master nor subdue her into meek compliance. The hard earth beneath them became their battleground as they rolled over and over, each fighting for mastery, neither willing to budge an inch in their struggle for domination.

Ariel felt the difference the moment Jess' kiss grew soft. It suddenly became filled with such passion and tenderness she could feel the anger drain from his body, could literally taste a sweeter, more urgent need fill the void left by his anger. He was like an invading army, demanding total surrender, a surrender Ariel swore she would not give. If and when she let a man take her it would be because she wanted it, not because a man demanded it.

Chapter 7

Did she want Jess Wilder? Ariel asked herself. Did she want him in the same way a woman wants a man? Did she want him enough to surrender to him? Surrender? No! Emphatically no! There would be no surrender. If she allowed this closeness to go any farther—and she wasn't certain at this point whether she would—it would be an equal sharing. There was something volatile and searing between her and Jess Wilder, something she could neither deny nor ignore. This explosion between them was inevitable; it had been ordained from the moment they met. In the beginning Ariel had known only the ice of Jess' anger but now she knew the searing hellfire of his passion.

Suddenly Jess shattered her thoughts with the reckless plunder of his tongue. The erotic assault was like nothing Ariel had ever experienced before, or likely to experience again with any other man. It was a journey into foreign territory, a voyage into the unknown, and Ariel suddenly thirsted for the special knowledge that only this big tough bounty hunter could give her. But she wanted it on her terms.

They rolled again, this time Ariel ending up on top. Without warning Jess released her arms. When their mouths parted so they might catch their breaths, Jess growled, "Fight me if you must, wildcat, but don't try to tell me you don't want this.''

"I don't know what I want, Jess Wilder, except the right to make my own decision.''

"Let me help you make the right decision, sweetheart,'' Jess gasped, in an agony of need so pressing his body throbbed from it.

Then he was kissing her again, his mouth hot and demanding, his tongue probing her soul. He tried to shift her beneath him but Ariel stubbornly resisted, pounding his chest, his shoulders, gripping his slim hips with her legs, refusing to be mastered in the way he intended.

Jess growled deep in his throat, his hands going to her shirt, stripping the buttons from their holes, searching for and finding smooth silken flesh beneath the thin chemise shielding her breasts. Ariel felt his hands on her breasts, caressing the naked flesh, his palms rough with callouses yet painfully exciting. His lips left hers in ragged passion to press against her throat. She was aware of her shirt being stripped down her arms, of her chemise being pulled over her head and tossed aside. And of his lips encircling her breast, his tongue rasping against her nipple, bringing an anguished cry from her lips.

Jess pulled back slightly and stared at the tantalizing flesh bared to his hot gaze. In the moonlight her breasts appeared as rose-tinted ivory, high and firm, the nipples full and hard. He drew one erect tip into his mouth, sucking, teasing; all the while his hands tore frantically at her britches, working them past her hips. Since she still straddled his hips he was finding the task nearly beyond him, hindered by Ariel's stubborn resistance. In an abrupt move that took her by surprise, Jess reversed their positions, trapping her beneath him.

"Damn you, Jess Wilder, I'm not going to make this easy for you!''

"I didn't reckon you would." She didn't have to see his face to know he was grinning. "I'm gonna make love to you, wildcat. Do you still wanna fight me?" He finally got a grip on her britches and slid them down her legs.

Ariel found time for only a brief reply as his lips seized hers again. "I don't know."

His kiss was not a gentleman's kiss—nothing about Jess Wilder was gentle. He was bold, insolent, uncivilized, rude, and mule-headed, yet he had protected and comforted her on more than one occasion with amazing understanding and—yes, even tenderness. Did she really want Jess Wilder to make love to her? If she was perfectly honest with herself the answer would have to be a resounding yes. Should she melt in his arms and let him have his way? she wondered with a hint of resentment. Hell no! Jess had called her a wildcat and she would show him he couldn't make a docile pet of her.

Jess' kiss seemed to go on forever as his hands roamed freely, as if memorizing the smooth texture of her skin and tempting contours of her body. Suddenly Ariel decided Jess Wilder had had things his way long enough. Taking advantage of his distraction she shifted positions, placing herself on top once again. Straddling his hips, she tore at his clothes, wanting him as naked as she was. She saw no reason why Jess should remain fully clothed while her nude body was at his disposal, to do with as he pleased. Eager to oblige, Jess shed his shirt and vest.

"Damnation, I can't remember when I've wanted a woman as fiercely as I want you," he said raggedly. "May my soul rot in hell for what I'm gonna do, I can't stop now. Raise your hips, sweetheart, so I can slide off my pants."

If she intended to stop this before it went any further, now was the time to do so, Ariel realized. But she was astute enough to know that she wanted this exasperating man. His kisses made her burn for more; his bold caresses sent her blood singing through her veins and made her body yearn for fulfillment. Because it was her wish to do so, Ariel raised her hips and helped Jess remove his pants and boots. She nearly lost her nerve when his manhood sprang free, rising like a pillar of pale ivory.

Ariel gasped in shock. She had no idea the male body could be so intimidating—so beautiful. It didn't seem possible that they could fit together. She knew there would be some discomfort for it appeared as if Jess was much too large for her, and she began to have second thoughts. Did she want this? Really want it? Then Jess was kissing her again, her initial protest smothered by the pressure of his lips. In order to make her wishes known, Ariel pounded on his chest. His arms held her firmly in place, denying her unspoken request, attempting to slide her beneath him.

Dragging her mouth away from his seductive kisses, Ariel gasped, "Jess, no, I—I've changed my mind."

"I haven't," Jess growled in reply. "Don't stop me now, sweetheart, I've come too far. I promise you won't be sorry if you let me do this my way."

"No!" Ariel answered stubbornly. "If we're going to do this at all it's going to be my way. You've had things your way long enough."

Locking her legs around his slim hips, Ariel refused to be dislodged, unwilling to give Jess unfair advantage over her yet resigned to the fact that she wanted him to make love to her. She wasn't certain this clash of wills was what making love was all about, but whatever it was she wanted to share equally in the adventure. When Jess again tried to tuck Ariel beneath him she fastened her mouth to his, raised her hips, and slid smoothly down over his erection.

Jess' silver eyes widened with astonishment as

he felt hot flesh tighten around him. Ariel jerked upright, startled by the sudden jolt of pain as she stretched to accommodate Jess' huge erection. It was much worse than she had imagined and if Jess hadn't been holding her firmly in place she would have thrown herself off of him.

A gasp of dismay left Jess' throat when the tip of his shaft reached the barrier of Ariel's virginity. Oh, God, no! How could Tilly Cowles be a virgin?

"Jesus H. Christ! Who in hell are you?" His voice was raw with need as he struggled desperately to rein in his galloping passion.

Ariel shuddered, wanting Jess to complete the act now that it was nearly done. She was disappointed when he made as if to pull away. She had gone too far to stop now. If her virginity was a problem she'd put an end to it here and now. Gritting her teeth, she tangled her fingers in the thatch of hair covering his chest and pushed herself down as hard as she could. A muffled scream forced itself past her lips, joining Jess' shout of pure pleasure.

It was done.

Jess nearly exploded in instant climax but forced himself to breathe deeply and concentrate on anything but how wonderful it felt to be buried to the hilt inside Ariel's sweet body. Never had he felt anything so tight, so hot—so damn *good*. He wanted to pound into her until she cried for mercy, until he shattered and spilled his seed.

But he didn't.

For reasons unknown to him he wanted Ariel to feel the same things he did, to experience fulfillment for the first time with him. He waited until he felt her relax and grow accustomed to the size and feel of him before moving smooth and deep inside her. She was so small and so new to this he realized he was causing her pain and suffered a momentary twinge of regret. But whatever reservations he might have had disappeared when Ariel made a highly erotic move with her hips.

By then it was far beyond too late. With a will of their own his hands sought her breasts, toying with the nipples. Raising his head he drew an erect tip into his mouth, laving it with the rough moistness of his tongue, nipping gently then kissing the hurt away.

As the initial pain receded, Ariel thrilled to the need Jess was creating in her. Her body vibrated with strange sensations, more pleasure now than pain, and she quickly learned the rhythm, discovering for herself which motions offered her the most enjoyment. Jess' mouth continued to nurse her breasts as his hands slid to her waist and then her buttocks, moving her up and down the length of his rigid staff. Suddenly she was beneath him as he began a new assault of slow rise and fall against her tingling flesh.

Ariel soared. She burned. She yearned for something that dangled just out of reach.

"Jess! What's happening?"

"You're doing fine, sweetheart." His words were a strangled groan. "Let me take you there. You'll know when it's time."

Time for what? Ariel wondered, panting and moaning as she felt herself on the verge of a great discovery. She was more than a little startled by the savagery of Jess' passion as he neared his own reward but soon her own body's dictates made her oblivious to all but the terrible need driving her. It began as a tiny spark deep in her loins, intensifying, magnifying, until it claimed and devoured her body and soul. Jess let loose a satisfied groan as he felt Ariel tremble and heard her cry out.

The end came to him explosively, fiercely. He arched hard and held, then collapsed, his head coming to rest against her breast. She had drained him of lust and anger at the same time. Only one thought occupied his mind now. It seemed highly unlikely that Tilly Cowles would be a virgin. He searched Ariel's face with a mixture of awe and disbelief. It was nearly dawn now and he could see her clearly. Her eyes were still glazed with passion, her lips swollen from his kisses.

"You're too damn passionate to be a virgin," he said slowly. "And yet—I know for a fact I was the first. You gotta lot of explaining to do, lady." He levered himself upward and away from her, feeling strangely bereft when he left the warmth of her body.

Ariel felt it too and reached immediately for her clothes. She must have been crazy to let this happen. But if it did nothing else, it helped convince Jess she was really Ariel Leland.

"What's to explain?" she asked with bitter emphasis. "If your brains were dynamite you wouldn't have enough to blow your nose. I've been telling you for days and days that I'm not Tilly Cowles. If you weren't so mule-headed you would have realized it immediately. Tilly Cowles and Bart Dillon are still out there someplace as free as birds."

That didn't set well with Jess. He'd thought he had it all figured out, but nothing was what it seemed. Ariel wasn't Tilly, Tilly wasn't Ariel, and if that was true he had just taken the virginity of a lady he had no business seducing.

"Ariel, I don't know what to say," Jess said, gesturing helplessly.

"Saying you're sorry might be a good place to start."

"I'm sorry about the mix-up but not about making love to you. You gave me one hell of a ride, sweetheart. Now why don't you start from the beginning and tell me what you're doing in Texas and why you're traveling alone."

"Aren't you going to get dressed first?" She couldn't think straight with Jess sitting there buck-naked and apparently unconcerned with his nudity.

A lazy smile curved the corner of Jess' lips. "Does it bother you?"

"I—yes. I'm unaccustomed to seeing men sitting around unclothed."

Ariel turned away as Jess reached for his pants and slid into them. To be brutally frank the sight of his nude body produced feelings she wasn't prepared to deal with.

"You don't have to worry, Ariel, I won't touch you again. Not unless you want me to," Jess added. "But you gotta admit we both enjoyed it."

"That's besides the point," Ariel contended somewhat sheepishly. She'd had no idea she'd react to Jess' loving with such overwhelming passion. "You are right about one thing, though. This has been brewing between us for a long time. Now that it's out of our systems we can each go our own way and forget this whole unfortunate episode. You've got desperadoes to catch and I've got a ranch to run."

"I'm dressed now, you can turn around. Tell me about your ranch."

"My father died six months ago and left me his ranch south of Waco on the Brazos River. My mother hated the idea of my living in Texas and wired Father's lawyer to sell the property against my wishes."

"Why weren't your father and mother living together?"

"Mama despised Texas and refused to live there with Father. They separated when I was a child and later divorced. Father came to St. Louis once a year to visit me. I loved him dearly. Then six months ago he was gored by a bull and died of infection. When I learned he left me the ranch I was determined to justify his faith in me and become the best darn rancher in Texas."

"Quite an undertaking for a mite like you. I'm willing to bet you're not even twenty-one yet."

"I—just turned twenty. But that doesn't mean I'm not capable of running a ranch," Ariel added in a slightly belligerent tone.

Jess sent her a measuring glance. "I reckon you can do just about anything you set your mind to. You handled me right fine."

Ariel flushed. Just how did he mean that?

"So you left St. Louis without your mother's permission."

"Both Mama and Tom, my stepfather, were adamantly opposed to my coming to Texas. They said Texas was no place for a proper young lady. I must admit," Ariel observed wryly, "that if what I've encountered so far is any indication, they were partly right. They just failed to realize how determined I was to carry out Father's wishes and succeed at ranching."

"Admirable, but not too smart," Jess remarked. "Traveling alone is definitely a bad idea. Especially for a woman who doesn't know beans about life, or ranching, or taking care of herself."

Ariel shot him a fulminating look. "I'm no child! I can take care of myself. And I can learn about ranching. Father's letters were full of advice and information about ranch life. I'll feel right at home on the ranch."

"Didn't you say your mother put the ranch up for sale?"

"It's not hers to sell."

"You're underage," Jess reminded her.

"No matter, the ranch is mine. I'd still have to know when it was sold. That's why it's imperative I reach Waco before Mr. Burns sells the ranch on Mother's orders."

Jess regarded Ariel before seeming to come to a decision. "I'll take you back to Fort Worth. You can catch a stage from there to go home."

"Go back home? Are you mad? I've come this far, I'll not go back like a naughty child. Besides, Texas is my home now."

"You're mother and stepfather will be worried. The telegram Caleb sent must of scared the sh— daylights outta them. They want you home."

"I'm not going home, Jess," Ariel said with firm conviction. Her mind was made up; nothing would change it. "I'm going to Waco. Father wanted me to have his ranch and I'll show the world I'm capable of managing my own affairs.

"I'll wire Mama as soon as I get to Waco. Don't worry, Jess, I don't hold you responsible for anything that happened between us. When we part we need never see one another again or be reminded of—of—anything," she added lamely.

Jess' face grew thoughtful. Her words caused a response in him that made him decidedly uncomfortable. Not see Ariel again? Is that what he wanted? It wouldn't be easy to forget Ariel after making love to her. He wasn't even certain he wanted to.

Then he thought of the solemn vow he had made over his dying brother's body. Until Bart Dillon and Tilly Cowles were behind bars he had no room in his life for a woman like Ariel Leland. For two years he'd made do with occasional whores, thinking one day he'd marry Ellie Lu Dodge. Strange. Now he couldn't even remember what Ellie Lu looked like or recall one reason why he'd wanted to marry her. He suddenly became aware of Ariel's probing gaze and turned away.

"Go to sleep, Ariel, there's still time to snatch a couple hours of shut-eye."

"What are you going to do?"

"I've got a heap of thinking to do."

"Are—will you leave before I wake up?"

"Nope."

Satisfied, Ariel stretched out on her bedroll, suddenly exhausted. A man she thought she hated, and maybe still did, had just made a woman of her. And in all likelihood she would never see him again once they parted. Why did she care?

Chapter 8

The delicious aroma of boiling coffee slowly roused Ariel from a deep slumber. She heard Jess walking around the campsite and opened her eyes. She saw him immediately, bending over the fire stirring something in a skillet. Black stubble shadowed his chin and he looked as if he hadn't slept all night—which of course he hadn't. He seemed to sense her eyes on him and turned, a slow smile lifting the corners of his lips.

"Coffee's ready."

"You're still here."

"I told you I wouldn't leave."

Ariel sent him a skeptical look. "You haven't given me much reason to trust you."

"If you're talking 'bout last night . . ."

"I'm referring to everything that's happened between us since we first met. You refused to believe a simple truth, embarrassed and humiliated me and that's not all. I—I'm not even sure I like you."

"You have an odd way of showing your dislike," Jess replied with wry amusement.

Ariel had the grace to blush. "If you were a gentleman you wouldn't remind me of—of my lapse."

"Lapse? Sweetheart, when we made love it was what we both wanted. You're a goldarn wildcat in bed. If I was a gentleman I'd apologize instead of wishing I had the time to make love to you again."

"It *won't* happen again," Ariel insisted, stung by his words. "We'll likely never see one another again." It rankled to think that she had wanted Jess as badly as he wanted her, and had actually rolled on the ground with him like a bitch in heat.

Mama would be horrified. And she had a suspicion even Father wouldn't have approved were he alive. Her behavior with Jess Wilder was shocking. Her only excuse was no excuse at all. The man was impossibly arrogant, magnificently male, totally without morals, and so packed with raw sex appeal he put Denton Dobbs to shame. Obviously Jess Wilder was a man any decent woman should steer clear of.

"I reckon you're right," Jess concurred, unable to look Ariel in the eye. Not that he was ashamed of what he had done, but he feared Ariel would detect the flicker of emotion he was unable to suppress. "Every second I waste puts Bart Dillon closer to the Mexican border."

"Are you still so determined to find Dillon?"

"I swore an oath over my brother's body. I'll get him all right. It might not be tomorrow, or next month, or maybe not even next year, but I'll get him."

"Don't let me hold you back, Jess, I can get to Waco on my own."

"I reckon you can but Waco isn't out of my way none. I'll see that you get there safe and sound and be on my way. Dillon can't be too far ahead of me."

Ariel didn't trust herself to answer. In one way she was anxious for Jess' company but in another the notion of being with him a few more days filled her with dread. She couldn't afford an involvement with a man dedicated to violence and death. Jess Wilder was a user, a man accustomed to getting his own way, a womanizer and mule-stubborn.

Jess had called what they did last night "making love." But it seemed to her it was more like an explosive conflict of wills. The harder she fought him the more determined he became, until their tempers turned to violence—the kind of violence that led to . . . The most humiliating experience of her life—and the most stimulating. She hated Jess Wilder for the way he made her feel, for trying to master her, for making her want him until she ached from it.

"I don't need your company, Jess Wilder!" Ariel claimed obstinately. "Just go do what it is you have to do. I wish you luck."

"Quit jawing at me, wildcat, I'm trying my best to do what's right but you're making it damn difficult."

"You have no conception of right or wrong," Ariel returned smartly. "You've been nothing but an aggravation to me from the beginning. If you weren't so darn fool stubborn I'd be in Waco right now."

Her stinging barbs bounced off his tough hide, leaving no scars. "If you weren't so determined to have your own way you'd have stayed in St. Louis where you belong."

Ariel opened her mouth to fling back a scathing retort, wrinkled her nose, then asked, "What's burning?"

"Damnation! The biscuits. You do have a way of distracting a man."

"And you have a way of riling a woman."

After choking down burnt biscuits and beans they left the campsite and continued on to Waco. Jess said no more about his intentions but seemed in no particular hurry to leave her and go his own way. It occurred to Ariel that she'd have to suffer his obnoxious company the entire distance to Waco.

They stopped for a brief nooning then forged on, camping that night in the shadow of a flat ridge. Jess shot a pair of rabbits and they feasted heartily on the succulent meat. This time Jess took care not to burn the biscuits. They spoke little. Neither willing to submit to the urges driving them, both aware that opening dialogue between them would only lead to angry words and false accusations—and a far deeper emotion whose surface had only been scratched. Exhausted from lack of sleep the previous night, Ariel bedded down immediately after supper.

"Good night," she called to Jess, who remained sitting beside the fire staring broodingly into the dying flames. He merely grunted in reply. Ariel shrugged, turned on her side, and promptly fell asleep. Nothing short of an earthquake could have roused her.

Had Ariel noticed the enigmatic way Jess stared at her after she turned her back on him she would have been dismayed. His silver eyes turned smoky with desire as he recalled to mind their violent lovemaking the night before. Words failed to describe the way she made him feel when she took him into the tight warmth of her body. She was so hot, so tight, so damn incredible, and if he didn't stop thinking about it he'd lose his mind. If he had bedded Tilly Cowles he would have felt no emotion or guilt, but making love to Ariel Leland presented more problems than he needed right now.

They had come together in furious combat and mutual need and Jess wasn't certain who had emerged the winner. He had taken Ariel's virginity but in truth it had been Ariel who had brought the act to its final conclusion. From the moment she shoved herself onto his manhood he remembered little except that she had embraced passion

as fully as she embraced life, with fervor and
abandon. Once her body had accommodated him
fully she turned wanton, biting, scratching, taking him on the most incredible ride of his life. He
wanted her again.

Now.

More than once.

All night.

Need drove him as he lurched to his feet and
prepared to go to her. One step—two steps.
Abruptly he halted, recalling with painful clarity
the promise he had made to his brother. Heaving
a ragged sigh of regret and longing, Jess turned
away and sought his own lonely bed. There was
nothing in life more important than finding Judd's
killers—was there?

The next day was a repeat of the first two. Ariel
fought the heat, the dust—and her attraction to
Jess.

Jess fought the heat, the dust—and his obsession with Ariel.

Both fought a losing battle.

That night they camped beneath a rocky over-
hang butted up against a ridge. Rain, a rarity this
time of year, had threatened most of the day. For
that reason Jess chose a sheltered spot when it
came time to make camp. There was nothing he
hated worse than getting rained on while he slept.
Ariel being somewhat of a tenderfoot he reckoned
she would hate sleeping wet as much as he did.

"We should reach Waco late tomorrow afternoon," Jess informed her as they ate meagerly
from their dwindling rations.

"Thank God," Ariel said with heartfelt relief.
Silently she wondered why she also felt a twinge
of regret.

All she'd thought about for days was reaching
the ranch and bidding good-bye to Jess Wilder.
Being with Jess like this was sheer torture. She'd
tried her best to forget the night they had made

love. She wanted to block it from her mind forever. She wasn't proud of her behavior with that obstinate rogue, but she didn't regret it. It was inevitable. But obviously it meant nothing to Jess. His heart and mind were filled with too much hate to let a mere woman pierce his tough hide. Jess was single-minded when it came to his brother's killer.

Only one emotion drove Jess Wilder. Revenge. With singular purpose he pursued those responsible for Judd Wilder's untimely death. Ariel wondered what it would be like to be loved with such fierce devotion. Especially by a man like Jess Wilder. Unfortunately she'd never know, and probably be better off for it. Loving a man like Jess could only lead to heartache and disappointment. It would utterly consume her until there was nothing left of herself.

"Are you so anxious to be rid of me?" Jess asked, misinterpreting her remark.

"To be perfectly honest, Jess, we seem to rub one another the wrong way. Every time we open our mouths we're either at each other's throats or trading insults."

"Or making love," Jess reminded her, his eyes twinkling. "I can think of at least one time we were in total agreement."

Ariel flushed and lowered her eyes. "Even while making love we fought a battle," she whispered softly.

"The most incredible battle I've ever had the pleasure of fighting. Ariel . . ." He reached out to her, then let his hand drop helplessly to his side when she deliberately turned away.

Ariel could easily have fallen into Jess' arms, could have yielded sweetly to the lure of his masculine appeal. But if she did she'd be forever lost—forever damned to an empty life, yearning for something that wasn't hers. And so she did exactly the opposite of what her heart demanded of her. She turned away.

God help her!

Though she might desire Jess Wilder with every fiber of her being Ariel knew he wasn't the man for her. His life was too consumed with hatred and vengeance to trust her heart to him. The kind of man she needed was one who would devote more time to her than he would to useless vendettas.

"Good night, Jess. If we're lucky this may very well be the last night we'll be forced to spend together."

Jess watched in mute appeal as Ariel rolled up in her blanket and turned her back on him. It was the most difficult thing she had ever done. How could she dislike a man so thoroughly yet want him with the same intensity?

Jess had been wise in selecting their campsite that night. Shortly after midnight the heavens opened up. Rain poured down in buckets, a real gully-washer. It pounded the ledge sheltering them, which fortunately kept them relatively dry. Lightning set off spectacular fireworks across the sky and angry claps of thunder reverberated over the plains. Too tired to let it bother her, Ariel merely grunted and rolled over, clapping her hands over her ears when thunder jolted her awake.

Morning arrived on the wings of soggy gray skies. Intermittent rain still fell but not in torrents like the night before. Not a glimmer of sunshine greeted Ariel when she awakened. Nor the smell of boiling coffee. Nor the sound of Jess moving around their campsite. It was highly unusual that Jess wasn't already up and seeing to their horses or breakfast. She supposed the dismal weather had persuaded him to lay abed longer than was his usual custom, and glanced over at his bedroll. Jess lay on his back, still as death. Not a muscle twitched, not even an eyelid. Stranger still, Jess' eyes were wide open. He appeared to be staring at the ground beside him.

Intrigued as well as curious, Ariel rose up on her haunches, tossing the blanket aside. Fear and apprehension seized her when Jess made no move to greet or acknowledge her. His eyes did not waver from whatever he was staring at so intently, every muscle alert and tautly drawn.

"Jess?"

Ariel rose unsteadily to her feet, intending to investigate, when Jess's urgent whispering halted her in her tracks.

"Don't move."

"What! Jess, what is it?"

Then she saw it. Coiled at Jess' side, its head reared in deadly appraisal. A rattlesnake. She heard it now. The numerous rattles on its tail sounded like a harbinger of death, dry and raspy and menacing. Ariel's breath caught painfully in her throat. Panic seized her when she noted that Jess could neither move nor speak for fear of riling the rattler and causing his own death. If the rattler bit him he was likely to perish before she could get him to town.

"Tell me what to do."

Her voice shook and her hands trembled. Never had she been so frightened for another human being. He was an arrogant, black-hearted devil but he didn't deserve to die a painful death out here on the prairie.

Jess remained silent. Ariel saw beads of sweat dewing his brow and knew he was focusing every ounce of strength he possessed into remaining motionless. She had no idea how long he had remained like that but realized it took an enormous amount of control to remain perfectly still. She had to help him. But how?

"Ariel." His voice was a mere whisper. A hollow sound rising from his throat. "Shoot the damn thing."

"Shoot it?" Ariel repeated in a stunned voice. "I'm not a good shot. Is there no other way?"

"Christ! Just do it. I don't know how much longer I can hold out."

Gulping back a spurt of raw terror, Ariel fumbled for her gun. She had placed it next to her bedroll when she went to sleep. It was loaded. All she had to do was aim and shoot. No small task when the target was incredibly tiny and her hand shaking so badly. What if she missed? What if she hit Jess? What if she killed him!

Looking down the barrel of the Smith and Wesson, Ariel heartily wished she had taken the time to learn how to shoot straight. She felt certain she could hit a large target but the head of a snake was nearly impossible. She closed her eyes, her finger on the target, praying for all she was worth.

"Open your eyes, for Chrissake."

Jess' terse words seemed to annoy the rattler for it stretched its neck, its forked tongue darting out in silent menace. A spurt of adrenaline churned through Ariel as she realized it was now or never, that Jess' life depended on her and she couldn't let him down. Taking careful aim, she squeezed the trigger before she lost her nerve.

Then she closed her eyes.

"You can open your eyes now." Jess' voice was the most beautiful sound she'd ever heard.

The gun slipped from her fingers, falling to the ground with a soft thud. Ariel never even noticed.

Slowly and with great trepidation, she forced herself to open her eyes, first one, then the other, fearful of what she'd find. Parts of the rattler lay splattered on the ground beside Jess. It was dead. She had actually hit the damn thing! It was beyond belief but wonderfully satisfying to know she had saved Jess' life. What happened next could only be described as a natural reaction to the tension and high drama these last few minutes had wrought.

Seeing Jess alive and knowing she had saved him sent Ariel soaring. "You're alive! I did it! Jess, oh, Jess, I was so afraid I'd shoot you."

He didn't have time to rise to his feet before Ariel had thrown herself at him, laughing and crying, planting kisses wherever she could reach.

With a will of their own his arms tightened around her, pulling her on top of him. His lips found her mouth, his tongue boldly parting her lips to venture into sweet forbidden territory. Ariel was too excited to protest when his hands slid beneath her shirt and fondled her breasts. Suddenly what had begun as an innocent expression of gratitude and elation ended as a heated exchange of passion and need. The culmination of desperate wanting, and something else both Ariel and Jess refused to name. Ariel gasped for air as his searing kiss robbed her of breath, of reason, of her very soul.

"I've wanted you—Christ, I've wanted you," Jess whispered hoarsely as he claimed her mouth again and again.

Ariel locked her arms around his neck and was lost. She no longer thought of right or wrong or of the danger this man presented to her plans for the future. All she knew was that she wanted Jess to make love to her. Returning his kisses with feverish abandon, Ariel tugged at his clothes, eager to feel naked flesh against naked flesh. She couldn't wait, she wanted him now—immediately!

"Damnation, sweetheart, give me time to get outta my clothes. This time we're gonna do it slow and easy like we should have done the first time if I hadn't been so hot for you."

Ariel appeared not to have heard him as she finally succeeded in tearing open his shirt.

"Ariel, slow down, sweetheart, we got lots of time for this. Why are you in such an all-fired hurry? I want you as hot for me as I am for you."

He finally got through to her.

"Jess, I don't think—"

"Relax, sweetheart, don't think. Let me take you there, let me show you how good it can be. Let me—let me—"

With amazing dexterity Jess rid her of her clothes then shucked his own. He pulled her close and she felt his arousal prod boldly against her stomach. Then his fingers found the velvet of her inner thigh, stroking upward. Ariel felt a warm wetness flood her loins and sighed. He was probing inward now, penetrating her, his gentle massage setting off waves of gut-grinding pulsations deep inside her. Just when Ariel thought she'd savored the ultimate in enjoyment, Jess' mouth found her breast. He tugged and suckled the erect tip while his hand continued touching her between the legs in the most intimate of ways. Jolts of pure fire shot along her nerve endings. She kissed him, over and over, wildly, arching and quivering as his hands did marvelous things to her.

She cried out his name.

Suddenly it wasn't enough to be the recipient of his ardor; Ariel wanted to give as well as receive. Her hands slid over his sweat-slicked muscles, taut with barely controlled passion. She explored his nipples, following the thick matting of dark hair on his broad chest downward over his hard flat stomach.

Jess exhaled sharply.

Ariel continued her erotic journey, discovering the two taut mounds of his buttocks. She appeared as delighted with Jess as he was with her. Then her hand curled around the smooth hardness of his manhood. Hot. Thick. Throbbing with a life of its own. It felt like tempered steel sheathed in the softest velvet.

Jess jerked in violent reaction.

She stroked him gently, holding him firmly in both hands, amazed at his size and strength.

Jess wanted to explode—and explode—and explode—Ariel was driving him crazy— But he didn't. He merely gritted his teeth and persevered, until he could stand it no longer. A ferocious growl ripped past his lips as he rolled Ariel beneath him.

"Now it's your turn, sweetheart," he said with slow relish. "Two can play this game."

He cupped his hand against the downy hair at the juncture of her thighs, tenderly parting her with his fingers until he could rub inside her, until she grew slick and strained against him. Then he moved down and lowered his head and found her with his mouth.

Ariel jerked violently, stunned. What was he doing? It wasn't—decent. "Jess, stop!"

"Stop?" he repeated, raising his head to stare at her. He chuckled softly. "Not on your life, sweetheart." His voice was low, rich, made harsh with passion. "I wouldn't, even supposing I could." Then he continued his tender torment, his mouth hot, his tongue probing her with ruthless urgency— deep—deeper . . . He was famished; she was his sustenance.

Grasping her hips, he held her with firm insistence as she writhed and arched and begged him to cease. Then it was too late as her breath came in quick desperate pants; she was achingly aware of the sensation, rising in splendor and bursting with glorious ecstasy.

"Jess!"

Then he was over her, in her, filling her with himself, hard, hot, thrusting, again and again. She felt his urgency, was inflamed anew by it; felt the shuddering ferocity of passion, responding instinctively.

"Oh, God, don't let me go, Jess!"

"Hang on, sweetheart."

Sudden release beat through Ariel's veins and vibrated through her body. She cried out, her words incoherent, her mind blank. Nothing made sense but what Jess was doing to her. Abruptly his hands tightened on her buttocks and he was pulsating inside her. He grew rigid, then still, as she felt hot liquid spill inside her. The world spun crazily, tilted, then settled down to an erratic orbit.

"Jesus H. Christ, Ariel, I think I've died and gone to heaven!"

Chapter 9

"I'm ready to leave whenever you are, Ariel."

Jess stood beside his horse watching Ariel stuff her long ebony tresses beneath the battered Stetson she had jammed down over her head. She looked adorable. "We can make Waco before dark if we hurry," he went on.

"I'm ready, Jess."

Ariel had a difficult time looking Jess in the eye this morning after the way she had behaved the day before. She had turned wild and wanton in his arms, literally begging him to make love to her in a moment of weakness when she thought she might have killed him. It had been wonderful! More thrilling than anything she had known before. And it would never happen again. When they parted at Waco their lives would necessarily take different courses. More than likely Jess would marry Ellie Lu one day and she—she would probably never marry. Finding someone to fill Jess' shoes seemed an impossible task.

After boosting Ariel aboard her horse, Jess mounted Soldier. Ariel looked back only once at their campsite, her expression soft and wistful. Then, with a determined shake of her head, she turned away. She had much to lose and nothing to gain from dwelling on what she and Jess shared mere hours ago. If he could forget everything that had happened between them so could she.

Jess was far from forgetting the moment of stolen love they had shared. He recalled everything. How good Ariel felt in his arms, how wonderfully she made love and how incredibly passionate she was. She was everything he could ever want in a woman—if he was free to settle down.

At noon they stopped and finished the last of their supplies, drinking from the canteen when no stream was available. They spoke little; no words seemed appropriate to convey what each was feeling. Jess was driven by a solemn vow and lust for revenge, while the need to prove herself capable of handling her own affairs rode Ariel. Neither was willing to relent or retreat, neither willing to admit to an attraction for one another more powerful than pursuing their separate dreams.

They stopped once more before reaching town so that Ariel might change into a dress and look more presentable. Deliberately Jess turned his back while she washed with water from the canteen then donned the one dress she had brought along with her. When he turned around Ariel was properly adorned in a stripped linen frock, minus corset and numerous petticoats, but nevertheless tasteful and attractive. If he thought she was adorable before, dressed in boy's duds, she looked beautiful now. With a pang of regret Jess was willing to bet she'd be married within six months. There wasn't a man alive who could resist the charms of Ariel Leland, and he was the first to admit it.

Dusk was a breath away when they rode into Waco. It looked very much like any other Texas town to Ariel. The normal number of businesses and saloons lined both sides of the street, the same dusty road led down the main thoroughfare, the usual number of cowboys milled about aimlessly.

"I'll get us a room at the hotel. It's probably too late to call on the lawyer," Jess said. They were the first words he had spoken in hours.

Ariel looked startled. "Make it two rooms, Jess."

He regarded her keenly for several tense seconds then nodded.

"Have you been to Waco before?" Ariel asked curiously.

"Yup. Been to darn near every city in Texas. The Brazos River is an important cattle crossing and the town is nearly always bursting at the seams with cowboys. There's a couple of good hotels."

"Whatever you think," Ariel replied without real interest. Now that she was here she could think of nothing but settling matters with the lawyer and moving out to the ranch.

The hotel Jess selected was rather new. She let him take care of all the particulars and followed him somewhat distractedly when he showed her to her room.

"I'll see to the horses and meet you in the dining room in an hour," Jess said, handing her the key.

"You're going to stay?"

"Just overnight. I'll light outta here as soon as I buy supplies."

"I want to pay you back the money you loaned me."

"It's not necessary. It's the least I can do to repay you for the misery I've caused you."

Words failed Ariel; she merely nodded. Jess frowned, puzzled at her strange preoccupation, then turned and strode down the hall to his own room.

* * *

The dining room was full when Ariel was ushered to her table. Jess hadn't arrived yet and a terrible thought entered her mind. Had Jess already left town? Had the words they spoke a short time ago been their farewell? It was inconceivable that Jess would leave without a proper good-bye. She was so enmeshed in her thoughts that she failed to notice how the eye of every male in the room was turned on her, their interest clearly piqued.

"Every man in the room is envying me right now," Jess said as he seated himself across from her.

"Jess! I thought— It doesn't matter. Let's order, I'm famished."

"So am I," he replied, his meaning definitely different from hers.

The service was so efficient that the meal was concluded before Ariel was ready for it to end. Having drawn the evening out as long as she dared, Ariel rose to her feet. "Shall we leave?"

Jess walked her to her room, pausing before the door as she fumbled for the key. He took it from her hands and slipped it in the lock.

"Is there anything you need? I'll be happy to lend you some money to tide you over."

"I don't need your money, Jess, there's money waiting for me in the bank."

"Do you want me to call on the lawyer with you?"

"No, thank you, I'm capable of handling my own affairs."

"You handled *me* just fine."

Ariel flushed a becoming pink, unable to look him in the eye.

"I'll be leaving in the morning, soon as I can purchase supplies."

"I—wish you luck, Jess." Why did it sound so final? Why did it have to be like this?

Jess merely stared at her. After a long, poignant

pause, he stunned her by saying. "I want to make love to you again before I leave."

While making love with Jess had been the most incredible experience of her life, to do so now would be a mistake. Somehow it seemed right out in the wilderness where they could very well be the only two people to inhabit the earth. But once back in civilization, such as it was, it seemed wrong. Jess was still a rough, tough bounty hunter, dangerous and intimidating, with one purpose in life. Letting him love her again would not change him or keep him from chasing desperadoes. Nor would it convince her to give up her claim on the ranch and follow him from one end of Texas to the other. They had nothing in common except this overwhelming passion for one another. In the end there was but one answer available to Ariel.

"What you ask is impossible, Jess. Making love again can't possibly do either of us any good." Had he said he loved her it might have altered the entire course of their lives. But Ariel thought it highly unlikely that love existed anywhere in Jess Wilder's remarkable body.

"Is that your final answer?"

"Everything about this parting is final."

"I'll be finished with all this one day."

Was he trying to tell her something? Ariel wondered curiously. If he was asking her to wait for him he'd have to be more explicit than that.

"I know."

Silence.

Even if Jess had offered a commitment Ariel wasn't certain she could have made one in return.

It was on the tip of Jess' tongue to ask Ariel to wait for him but second thoughts made him change his mind. As beautiful as Ariel was he wouldn't be surprised to see her married in six months. He'd seen the way the men in the dining room had ogled her, and he couldn't blame them.

But in all fairness he couldn't ask Ariel to wait for a man who could be dead tomorrow. Bounty hunting was a dangerous profession. Until he gave up the life he had no right to ask any woman for a commitment. Especially a woman like Ariel who had everything to lose and nothing to gain by attaching herself to a man like him. A swift, clean parting was best for all involved.

"A kiss then. Surely that's not too much to ask."

What harm could a kiss do, she thought and lifted her face to his.

If she'd expected a gentle kiss she was disappointed, for Jess' kiss was anything but gentle. It was more like a savage attack upon her senses. It was hard and demanding and so utterly devouring that Ariel's knees buckled beneath her. Breathing became a distant memory as his tongue parted her lips and his mouth stole the air from her lungs. He deepened the kiss, his hands grasping her hips and bringing their bodies together until there was nothing between them but the clothes they wore. Then he found her breasts, his long fingers toying with their tips through the barrier of her bodice.

He broke off the kiss as suddenly as it had begun. Stunned, Ariel stared at him in astonishment as he tenderly touched her cheek then spun on his heel. "Remember me, wildcat—I know I'll never forget you." Then he was gone. Ariel's hand flew to her cheek, the imprint of his caress a burning memory that would likely remain with her until her dying day.

Ariel was up bright and early the next morning after a sleepless night. Every instinct urged her to go to Jess, to let him make love to her one last time. But her practical nature warned her it would be the wrong thing to do. In the end her practical nature became the victor. Were life's decisions always so difficult?

Ariel's first order of business was to look up Jason Burns, her father's lawyer. The hotel clerk gave her directions to his office and she set out shortly after eight o'clock that morning. Mr. Burns' office was on the second floor above the hardware store. With great anticipation Ariel climbed the stairs, composing in her mind what she intended to tell him. She hoped he hadn't found a buyer for the ranch yet and that he wouldn't be too disappointed when she told him she had no intention of selling it.

Ariel saw neither hide nor hair of Jess this morning, nor did she expect to. More than likely he was already gone, so why torture herself thinking of the obstinate devil? Easier said than done, she snorted in self-derision.

She had reached the top of the stairs now and focused her attention on the matter at hand. Jess Wilder might not be available to her but her ranch more than compensated for her loss, didn't it?

The lawyer's office was locked and Ariel assumed she had arrived too early. Until she noticed the sign tacked to the door. Lawyer Burns was out of town and wouldn't be back in Waco until the end of the week. Damn! Of all the rotten luck. What to do now? Go out to the ranch, she told herself. It was hers and she had a right to live on her own property. It seemed the right thing to do.

A short time later Ariel checked out of the hotel, not surprised to learn that Jess had taken care of the bill. Nor was she surprised that he had checked out of his own room earlier that morning. She found her horse at the livery—she still hadn't named the poor animal—and learned that the boarding fees had already been taken care of. Jess again. He certainly was doing his best to make up for any anguish he might have caused her, she thought as she mounted and rode slowly out of town.

Ariel had no need to ask directions to the Leland Ranch; she knew them by heart. Her father's letters had been full of tidbits of information concerning the ranch, its location, and its day-to-day operations. She felt she could move right in and take up where her father left off without missing a beat. When she thought back on it she realized his letters had served a purpose. They had instilled in her a sense of what Texas was all about, with a love of the land and pride in all that her father had accomplished. She knew now that Buck Leland had been preparing his only child for a time when all he'd worked and sweated for rested entirely in her hands. The ranch was her future, her security, her independence. She saw it all clearly now and thanked God her father had seen it too.

Ariel followed the Brazos River south, recalling her father's directions as if she had his letters before her. Though she had left Texas when she was a small child she occasionally remembered bits and pieces of the happy life she had enjoyed at the ranch with her father and mother. Life was simple then, until her mother decided she could no longer stand the isolation of ranch life and left. Having no choice in the matter, Ariel was whisked away to the more lively atmosphere of St. Louis. But she had never forgotten her father or the happiness she'd enjoyed in Texas.

The long dusty road angling off from the river wasn't much but Ariel knew immediately it was the road leading to the ranch house. She had been on her own land now for the last few miles. She gazed around her with something akin to awe. Every tree, each blade of sere brown grass, every watering hole belonged to her. Off in the distance she could see sleek cows foraging for tender shoots of grass, tended by men on horseback she assumed to be hands employed by her father.

That surprised Ariel. She'd assumed the cowboys had left after her father's death. How were they being paid? It suddenly occurred to her that her father's will would have taken care of all those details and left it up to the lawyer to pay the hands out of the estate. Evidently everything was running smoothly and she'd encounter little difficulty taking over the reins of authority of such a well-organized operation.

Ariel paused before passing under the gate and signpost that arched above the road leading into the yard. LELAND RANCH. The words tasted sweet on her tongue and she savored them fully before continuing. After a few minutes, excitement at being *home* again drove her forward through the entrance and into the yard. Then her eyes were everywhere at once, feasting on the sight, taking mental note of everything she saw.

The stables looked new. Had her father ordered them built sometime before his death? She was surprised he hadn't mentioned it in his letters. The fence around the yard looked in good repair and she could see places where it had been mended recently. The corral held several rangy workhorses and a few others whose bloodlines were much purer. Ariel was pleased with what she saw and intended to compliment lawyer Burns the moment she saw him. Saving the best for last, Ariel turned to inspect the ranch house.

Made entirely of logs, the house was two stories tall, with a front porch running the full width of the house. It was a comfortable house, made for living with none of the fancy fripperies of Eastern homes but comfortable and pleasing in its simplicity. Ariel couldn't understand why her mother had not liked it.

All the hands must have been occupied elsewhere for no one appeared to greet Ariel when she dismounted and flipped the reins over the porch rail. With mild curiosity she noted another saddled horse close to the corral and wondered if it belonged to Rosalie, her father's housekeeper. If Rosalie was still here, that is. For all she knew the Mexican woman her father wrote about was long gone by now.

Ariel's legs shook as she approached the front door. She had gone through so much to get here it was like the end to a bad dream. Except for Jess Wilder. *He* was no dream. Bigger than life, the man had exploded into her world like a volcano and withdrew from it just as quickly, leaving behind the white-hot memory of his passion.

The front door opened at her touch. She thought it strange to find it unlatched but again assumed the housekeeper was still in residence. The moment she entered Ariel felt as if she had truly come home. The front door led into a small foyer and then opened directly into the parlor. Large and comfortable, the rustic furniture and wall hangings reflected her father's taste and preference and suited Ariel perfectly. The chairs and couch were built to accommodate a large man who valued his comfort and were placed around a huge stone fireplace that took up one entire wall. Everything looked clean and fresh, as if she had been expected.

With fond remembrance she walked around the room, picking up items she thought she recalled from her younger days, inspecting others that may have meant something to her father. On one of the tables was a photograph of her when she was a child, and Ariel lamented that she hadn't given him a later one to take its place. The child in the photograph was small with dark hair and smiled back at her with the same features she saw every time she looked in the mirror.

"Who are you? What are you doing here?"

Startled, Ariel whirled. She had been so immersed in childhood recollections she hadn't heard anyone enter the room. She relaxed somewhat when she saw that it was a beautiful, blonde young woman who had addressed her. Surely not the Mexican housekeeper! "More to the point, who are you?" Ariel said.

"I'm Trudy Walters. My brother owns this house. I've come to select items I might want from the furnishings before the house is rented."

"Rent the house?" Ariel repeated, stunned.

"We have no need for the house and Kirk says we may as well rent it and get some good out of it. Our house is ever so much more grand. Buck Leland didn't go much for extravagance."

"You knew Buck Leland?"

"Of course—he was our neighbor. Our spread is just down the road." Suddenly Trudy seemed to realize she was running off at the mouth and asked, "Are you here to rent the house? Did you hear in town that it was for rent?"

"Are you certain your brother bought the ranch?" Ariel questioned sharply.

"Of course. The deal is as good as done," Trudy boasted. "The papers have already been sent to St. Louis for Miss Leland's signature. Evidently the woman has no head for ranching and put the ranch up for sale. Of course Kirk jumped at the chance to buy it. It's a good piece of land and the price was right."

Ariel stared at Trudy, suddenly at a loss for words. What she saw was a tall, slim woman about her age with eyes the color of bluebells and hair more silver than blonde. She wore it in braids coiled around her head like a coronet. She looked cool and regal and beautiful. In comparison Ariel felt small and grubby wearing clothes she had dragged around in her saddlebag for weeks.

Finally Ariel decided to put an end to all this. She didn't like the haughty Trudy Walters and definitely didn't like the proprietary air she as-

sumed when speaking of *her* house. "I'm Ariel
Leland. This is *my* house and *my* land. I fear your
brother is in for a big disappointment as I'm keeping the ranch."

"What! Why—that's impossible! Jason said the
deal was all but done. It only needed your signature. Why are you doing this? We were told
you had no interest in the land."

"That was my mother and stepfather speaking.
I've never wanted to sell the ranch. I've come to
clarify my wishes once and for all." Thank God
she arrived in time to keep her mother from taking matters in her own hands and signing the papers without her consent. That certainly would
have muddied the waters.

"You can't do this!" Trudy declared. "Wait till
Kirk hears about this. And Jason."

"Jason. I assume you're referring to lawyer Jason Burns."

"Yes. He's worked hard to see this through.
He'll not be pleased with this development."

"I'll explain everything to Mr. Burns."

"*Gracias a dios*, you've come! And just in time."

"This is none of your concern, Rosalie," Trudy
warned, addressing the Mexican woman who had
just entered the room. She was small and dark
with generous curves and beautiful black eyes that
slanted upward at their outer corners. She was
very pretty, about forty years old with silver
threads streaking her coal-black hair. Rosalie,
Father's housekeeper. He spoke often and quite
fondly about Rosalie in his letters but somehow
Ariel had imagined her much older and not quite
so striking.

"You know who I am?" Ariel asked as Rosalie
stared at her with genuine welcome.

"Of course." Rosalie spoke with a slight accent
but her words were easily understood. "You are
Señorita Leland, Buck's daughter. I have prayed
to the Virgin that you would change your mind

about selling the land your father loved so dearly. He wanted you to live here."

Ariel took note of the way Rosalie referred to her father. She had called him Buck, not Mr. Leland.

"How did you know me so quickly?" she asked.

Rosalie's dark gaze drifted to the photograph sitting on the table. "You have not changed so much. Besides, Buck spoke of you so often I felt I already knew you. Welcome, Señorita Leland, welcome to Texas and Leland Ranch."

"That will do, Rosalie, get on with your packing," Trudy ordered sternly. She was dismayed by the turn of events but was determined to keep the upper hand. Until Jason Burns said otherwise, little Miss Ariel Leland was interfering where she didn't belong.

Rosalie looked to Ariel for confirmation.

"Are you leaving, Rosalie?" Ariel asked innocently.

"Sí, señorita, I have been discharged."

"Discharged? By whom?"

"By Señorita Walters."

"Are you responsible for keeping the place in order since Father's death? It looks wonderful."

"Sí," Rosalie said shyly. "It was the least I could do. This has been my home for—many years."

"Where will you go?"

Rosalie looked accusingly at Trudy. "The Walterses have offered me a position."

"Do you want to leave?"

"See here, Miss Leland, this is none of your business."

"This has everything to do with me," Ariel contended. "Rosalie has been with my father a good many years. I'm sure he would have wanted her to be taken care of." She redirected the question to Rosalie. "Do you want to leave, Rosalie?"

"Oh, no. Leaving is not my choice, Señorita Leland."

"Then you may stay. I will have need of a housekeeper. I plan to devote my time to running the ranch and will have little time to see to the house or cooking."

"Kirk isn't going to like this," Trudy muttered. "He is accustomed to being obeyed."

"Your brother has no authority over my house or property," Ariel replied with as much grace as she could muster. She was anxious to be rid of Trudy Walters and settle down in her own house. "I'll be happy to speak with him after I've had time to rest up from my long journey. We're neighbors, after all, and I'm sure he'll understand once I've explained everything to him."

Trudy recognized a dismissal when she heard one. She wasn't accustomed to being spoken to this way by a woman who looked more like a hoyden than a proper young lady from St. Louis. She'd go, all right, but Ariel Leland hadn't heard the last from her. She was certain Kirk wouldn't let her get away with this. He wanted the ranch, wanted it badly, and would do whatever it took to convince Ariel Leland to go back to St. Louis where she belonged.

Chapter 10

"I am glad you have come, Señorita Leland," Rosalie said once Trudy was on her
way. "I do not like the Walterses. Your father
would not have liked it if they had taken over his
land. Kirk Walters tried to buy it many times but
your father would not sell."

"Why would Kirk Walters want this land?" Ariel asked curiously.

"I am not sure but I suspect it is because of the
water."

"Water?"

"*Sí.* You know. The river. Señor Walters' property does not have access to the Brazos River."

Ariel chewed on that thought for a while and
decided it was as good a reason as any. But right
now she didn't give a hoot about the Walterses.
Of more importance was getting acquainted with
her own home.

"Where is your luggage, Señorita Leland?"
Rosalie asked. "I will put your clothes away while
you bathe and freshen up."

"I have no luggage, Rosalie. It's a long story
but suffice it to say this hasn't been an easy trip.
I should have been here days ago but was un-
avoidably detained by the law."

Rosalie's eyes grew wide with wonder. "The
law, señorita?"

"I'll tell you all about it later, Rosalie. Right

130

now that bath sounds wonderful. And something light to eat. I had no time for breakfast this morning." And no money, she thought but didn't say aloud. "And please call me Ariel. I know my father thought a lot of you and I want us to be friends."

"*Sí*, Ariel, that is my wish too. But we will have to do something about clothes for you."

"I have no ready cash and Mr. Burns won't be back in his office for days yet to release Father's bank account to me."

"No matter, storekeepers will be happy to extend credit to the daughter of Buck Leland. He was much respected in Waco. We will ride into town and replenish your wardrobe tomorrow. There are also staples that must be purchased to stock the larder. I have been allowed to buy nothing since Buck's—death." She choked on the last words, her voice sad and remote.

Just what did Rosalie and Father mean to one another? Ariel wondered, intrigued by the possibilities. Her answers would have to wait for a more appropriate time.

The bath felt wonderful and Ariel soaked until the water grew cool. Then she washed her hair and lay back, her head resting on the rim of the tub. She had been delighted by so many things since she reached the ranch, but nothing delighted her more than the room Rosalie assured her was hers. It was a room Father had prepared for her long before anyone knew she was coming to Texas. Done in her favorite colors of blue and peach, it had obviously been decorated with her in mind. Soft peach walls, thick blue carpet, and sheer white curtains. The four-poster bed was big and soft and covered with a quilt whose colors were predominantly blue. Evidently Father had anticipated a visit from her and done the room for her use. It made Ariel realize just how much he had loved her and how glad she was that she had decided to come to Texas against all opposition. She knew she could count on Rosalie for help, and nervously looked forward to telling the hands when they returned from the range that she was their new boss. Ariel knew there might be some resentment on their part but hoped most would elect to remain. Rosalie had told her the foreman was a man named Lew Pike, and she intended to speak with him first to see where he stood in regard to her bid to keep the ranch.

Rosalie was a marvelous cook and Ariel ate ravenously. Except for the meal with Jess in the hotel last night her diet had been singularly boring these past weeks. She could tell immediately she wouldn't be bored by Rosalie's cooking, and to show her appreciation ate everything on her plate.

"What time will the hands return?" Ariel asked as she pushed her plate away.

"Some will stay with the cows but most will return at dusk," Rosalie replied. "There are ten hired hands, all of them cowboys who have been with Buck for several years."

"Do you think they will resent me?"

"I think they will like you better than they would Señor Walters," Rosalie ventured sagely. "He is one mean hombre and most cowboys don't care to work for him."

"What is Kirk Walters like?" Ariel asked curiously. She hoped he was nothing like his haughty sister.

"He is very handsome," Rosalie said slowly. "He is blond, like his sister. He has the same blue eyes and is big and tall."

"He doesn't sound so bad," Ariel decided aloud. "Did Father like him?"

"They got along well enough," Rosalie allowed grudgingly. "It was me who didn't trust him but Buck laughed at my concern. Señor Walters has never done anything to justify my feelings, but . . .''

''. . . You still don't like him,'' Ariel said, completing the sentence.

''No, Ariel, I do not like him. But that is something you must judge for yourself. I think you will not have too long to wait.''

Rosalie was correct. Kirk Walters presented himself at the door shortly after supper.

He certainly is big, Ariel thought as Rosalie showed Kirk Walters into the parlor where she waited. But not as big as Jess. Damn, where did that thought come from? She'd done her darnedest not to think of Jess Wilder. Kirk Walters wasn't as handsome as Jess, either, though he certainly held his own with the best of them. His hair was so blond it was nearly white and his eyes so pale they appeared nearly colorless. Jess' eyes were silver. She'd never forget them.

''Miss Leland,'' Kirk Walters greeted her warmly, extending a hand. ''You can't imagine how surprised I was when Trudy told me you were here at the ranch. The bill of sale for the ranch has already been forwarded to St. Louis for your signature.''

''How do you do, Mr. Walters. Surely your sister mentioned that I don't wish to sell the ranch, didn't she?''

''She did say something to that effect,'' Kirk bluffed, ''but I thought she had misunderstood. All the details were settled weeks ago.''

''Not to my satisfaction,'' Ariel replied promptly.

Her answer left him somewhat flustered. ''Would you kindly explain, Miss Leland?''

''It's simple, really,'' Ariel informed him. ''Selling the ranch was never my idea. It was what my mother and stepfather thought best for me. I didn't agree and came to Texas to claim what is mine by law.''

"I see," he said slowly, regarding Ariel with keen appreciation. He always did like small women and Ariel was certainly pleasing to the eye, with her dramatic dark coloring and exquisitely fashioned body.

Kirk Walters could be a charming man when he chose and he suddenly decided that this was one time charm would work better on a woman than either anger or force. Besides, being charming to Ariel would be a pleasure—a real pleasure. She was probably an empty-headed bit of fluff who didn't know what she was getting into when she came to Texas. He'd be willing to bet she'd be begging him to take the ranch off her hands within the month.

"I'm sorry if I've inconvenienced you, Mr. Walters," Ariel said by way of an apology.

"You must call me Kirk and I'll call you Ariel," he instructed, offering Ariel a beguiling smile. "I can't say I'm not disappointed with your decision but I'll abide by it. Having you for a neighbor will more than compensate for my loss. I look forward to a lasting friendship, Ariel."

Why, what a nice man, Ariel thought with a pang of guilt. Nothing like what she had been led to believe. How could Rosalie be so wrong? And Trudy's remarks had led her to believe that Kirk Walters was a man who didn't accept defeat lightly. What a pleasant surprise to find a charming, educated man as her neighbor.

"Thank you for being so understanding, Kirk," Ariel said sincerely. "I'm most happy to have you for a friend. Except for Rosalie I have no one in Texas I can count on."

You have Jess, she reminded herself. But you can't count on him, her mind responded.

"You have only to call on me for help," Kirk returned, smugly satisfied with Ariel's response to his friendly overtures. "Our homes are but five miles apart; I assure you we will see one another often.''

''I'll count on it,'' Ariel said.

He left a few minutes later, after extending an invitation for Ariel to visit at any time, for any reason.

''You aren't taken in by that man's fine manners, are you?'' Rosalie asked after Kirk rode off.

''You were eavesdropping,'' Ariel accused. Far from being angry with the housekeeper, she was touched that Rosalie cared and worried about what happened to her. But Rosalie was mistaken in her opinion of Kirk Walters.

''*Sí*,'' Rosalie admitted without a speck of remorse. ''I was nearby should you have need of me.''

''Thank you, Rosalie, but I'm quite capable of handling Kirk Walters myself. He was a perfect gentleman and very considerate of my decision not to sell the ranch. I think you misjudge him.''

''Time will tell,'' Rosalie sniffed, refusing to alter her opinion. ''The hands are in the bunkhouse now. Did you want to speak with them?''

''I'm really tired tonight, Rosalie, perhaps I'll speak to the foreman and let him tell the hands. What do you think?''

''*Sí*, I will call him. You will like him, I think. He is a good man. Your father depended on him.''

Ariel's interview with Lew Pike went well. If the stringy cowboy was surprised to see the daughter of Buck Leland in Texas, he was polite enough not to mention it. He merely listened attentively to Ariel, his stoic, weather-worn face revealing nothing. To Ariel, Lew Pike was the epitome of the Western cowboy. Tall, gaunt, and wiry, his legs slightly bowed from constant riding, he was polite, respectful, and quiet as he waited for her to finish. What surprised Ariel about Lew Pike was his age. He was young, really young. Yet he must have been competent or else his father wouldn't have hired him.

Ariel was later to learn that most cowboys were young, most still in their twenties. They valued their horses, their hats, and their boots above all else and lived by a code of honor with regard to good women. Most were shy, particularly where women were concerned, but they worked harder than any other breed of men she knew.

When Ariel finished speaking, Pike merely nodded his head and said, "I'll tell the hands." He turned to leave.

"Pike, wait," Ariel called, unaccustomed to cowboys' natural reticence. "Will they work for me? You never said how they will like working for a woman."

"They'll like it right fine, Miss Leland," Pike replied softly. "We all liked yer paw and respect his wishes. You can depend on us, ma'am." It was the most words he had strung together in some time.

"Thank you, Pike, that's all I need to know. We'll talk later, when I have a better idea of the workings of the ranch. Until then I'll depend on you and the hands to do what is needed."

He turned to leave then thought of something else he wanted to say. "What about Mr. Walters?"

"Kirk Walters is out of the picture where the ranch is concerned. I'm not selling, not for any reason. You'll all be paid as usual so you need not worry about money."

Her answer seemed to satisfy Pike. Without another word he left the small office where Buck Leland usually conducted business. But truth to tell Pike was worried. He knew Kirk Walters, knew he wouldn't accept the loss of the ranch so easily, and thought Ariel had bitten off more than she could chew. Of one thing he was certain, though. Every dang cowboy on the Leland spread was behind Buck Leland's daughter no matter what she decided to do.

Kirk Walters was quiet and thoughtful after he returned home from seeing Ariel. He had done a lot of thinking on the return trip back to his own ranch, and reached a decision that suited his purposes quite nicely. He broached the subject to Trudy as they sat over coffee in the parlor that night.

"What do you think of Ariel Leland?" Kirk asked bluntly.

Trudy made a wry face. "I don't care for her at all. She seems a wild sort. How many young women do you know would travel all the way to Texas alone? I'll bet she could tell some wild tales."

"You'd better get used to the woman, Trudy, she's going to be my wife. I'll not have the women in my household disrupting my life with petty arguments."

"What! Marry Ariel Leland? You must be joking. You just met her. What if she has a fiancé tucked away someplace? How do you know she'll even have you?"

"Don't be shrewish, Trudy, I've made up my mind," Kirk said with firm conviction. "You know how important you are to me but if the only way I can get Leland Ranch is by marrying the owner, then I'll marry her. I don't care how many fiancés she has tucked away, once I've decided on something there's no turning back. The only thing that will change my mind is for Ariel to sell me the ranch and go back to St. Louis, and that seems unlikely. Somehow that little lady didn't strike me as a quitter. She's quite determined, in fact. But I'm just as determined as she is."

"Is the Leland property so important to you?" Trudy asked petulantly.

"Damn right it is. I'll do anything to get it. I

hated it every time I had to ask permission to drive my cattle across Leland land to get to the river. Every summer when my water holes dry up it's either ask for permission to drive the stock to the Brazos River or let them die. I was elated when I learned the Leland heir didn't want anything to do with ranching. Then the little bitch turns up out of the blue and ruins everything."

"Is there no other way to get what you want? Marriage is so—final. I don't want you to marry."

"Perhaps marriage is final, and then again . . ." His words trailed off, bringing a brilliant smile to Trudy's face. She understood her crafty brother perfectly.

"For your sake I'll try to tolerate Ariel . . ." She pouted. ". . . for a short time anyway. I don't intend to live with you forever."

"If you're referring to marriage you'd best forget it for the time being. I'm not ready to let you go yet."

"One day the right man will come along," Trudy said wistfully.

"I'm not certain he will, sis," Kirk scoffed derisively. "I've spoiled you for another man. You're too damn particular."

Peeved, Trudy sniffed and turned away. "If you're planning on marrying Ariel Leland I'd say you're not particular enough."

Ariel met most of the hands the next day. Back East cowboys had a heroic image as hard-riding, fast-shooting hombres. But as she came to know the group of young men working for her she realized they were overworked laborers who fried their brains under a prairie sun, rode endless miles in rain, wind, and snow to mend fences or look for lost calves.

Leland Ranch boasted ten cowboys and within two weeks Ariel knew each one of them by name. Some she liked better than others but all were unfailingly polite. When she voiced her desire to learn the ropes they offered no objection, patiently explaining each and every function Ariel asked about. A week went by so fast Ariel was shocked when Rosalie suggested they go into town. By now lawyer Burns was back from wherever he went and she could no longer delay replenishing her wardrobe.

They took the wagon into town. Rosalie drove and Willis, one of the cowboys, went along to help load the supplies. It was a beautiful day, not too hot yet, and Ariel's mind wandered aimlessly as she sat beside Rosalie. She'd tried not to think of Jess these past few days. And in truth had been too busy to give him more than a passing thought. Except at night. Tired as she was after a day learning and doing things she had never done before in her life, Jess appeared in her bed. Not the flesh-and-blood Jess but the memory of what it had been like in his arms. Some nights he even made love to her, her vivid imagination recreating each wondrous caress, every gasp and sigh. He came so often to her late at night that Ariel wondered if she'd always have to depend on dreams to find the kind of joy Jess brought her.

"What's his name?"

"What!" Ariel flushed guiltily. Could Rosalie read her mind?

"The way you're sighing could only mean one thing. You never did mention a special man you might have left behind in St. Louis."

"There is no special man in St. Louis."

"There is a special man somewhere," Rosalie said with keen perception. "You seem so preoccupied at times I've often wondered who you were thinking of."

"There could have been a man," Ariel confided, "if he didn't have more important things on his mind than me. And if he wasn't the most arrogant, exasperating, mule-headed man I've ever met."

Rosalie smiled a secret smile. "I do not think this man is in St. Louis."

"You're right," Ariel confirmed, refusing to divulge another word about Jess Wilder.

"Only a Texan could be all the things you described. You have not been in Texas very long, señorita," Rosalie mused, curious as to the identity of the man who had struck Ariel's fancy.

"Long enough."

"Perhaps things will work out for you and this special man."

"I've already forgotten him, Rosalie," Ariel lied. "The ranch is my future. I don't need a man to make my life complete."

"Sí, Ariel," Rosalie replied agreeably. Somehow she doubted that Ariel had seen the last of her "special" man. She was willing to bet he hadn't forgotten her. What man in his right mind could forget Buck's striking daughter?

Ariel left Rosalie and Willis at the mercantile and went directly to Jason Burns' office. This time she was in luck; the lawyer was in his office. In fact, Ariel was Burns' second visitor that morning. Kirk Walters had already been there and left. When Ariel stated her name Burns welcomed her to Texas and invited her to sit down.

"I know you must have many questions to ask me after that telegram from Marshal Hawks in Fort Worth," Ariel began somewhat hesitantly. "But you must have had some inkling why I was in Texas."

"I had to leave town rather abruptly after that telegram arrived," Jason Burns admitted, "and haven't had much time to consider your motives. At the time I was too rushed to ride out to the Walters spread and tell Kirk that you were on your way to Waco. Would you care to explain what happened in Fort Worth that compelled the marshal to question your identity?"

At least fifty years old and looking every bit his age, Jason Burns was a short, stocky man with a balding head and quick intelligent blue eyes. He'd practiced law in Waco for a good many years and knew just about every soul who lived in the area. He was as trustworthy as most lawyers but not above working out deals that benefited his own pocket. He had never done anything that could be called dishonest but on more occasions than one had bent the law to suit his purposes and those of his clients.

"It's a long story," Ariel sighed, "but you have a right to know." Then she proceeded to relate all the events that led up to the telegrams being sent to both her mother and Jason Burns.

Burns was both dismayed and horrified by Ariel's tale. He admired her for her ability to overcome the misadventure with such amazing resilience. Kirk Walters was right, he observed thoughtfully. Ariel Leland was the kind of woman who would not be dissuaded from something once she set her mind to it. Obviously she was determined to keep her land.

"An amazing story, my dear, I'm glad you came out of the ordeal unscathed. I'm happy to have been of service. Although I had never met you I knew from the telegram you sent from St. Louis that you were coming to Waco. I just wasn't sure why. That's why I didn't mention it to Kirk. I had already sent the papers to you to sign but when I learned you were on your way here I prepared new ones."

"Surely you must realize by now that I'm not selling the ranch."

"All that's needed to complete the transaction is your signature on the bill of sale. The offer from Kirk Walters is an excellent one; you'll be a very rich young lady if you accept."

"I'm not going to sell, Mr. Burns."

Burns regarded her keenly. "Have you thought it over very carefully, my dear Miss Leland? Ranching is a man's job. Can you handle a dozen cowboys and transact all the business necessary to show a profit?"

"I think so," Ariel said firmly. "I'm sorry if I've caused you any inconvenience. You'll be compensated for your trouble."

"It's not me I'm thinking of, Miss Leland. Kirk Walters is the one who will have to be pacified. He was counting on that land."

"I've already spoken to Mr. Walters and he was quite generous about understanding my decision. I've come a long way, encountered many delays, and suffered untold anguish in order to carry out my father's wishes in regard to the ranch."

"I had a visitor this morning," Burns said slowly. "Kirk Walters wanted me to impress upon you the difficulty a young woman would encounter managing a ranch the size of your father's. For your own good I must concur. But if it is your wish to plunge into the business of ranching I'll do all in my power to help. At least with the business end of things."

Burns knew Walters wouldn't approve of his abetting Ariel in this matter but he felt the young woman deserved a chance. Besides, he'd known Buck Leland well and the man wouldn't have left his ranch to his daughter if he didn't think she could handle it. In fact, he wasn't even going to tell Ariel about the telegram he received just this morning from her mother, urging him to sell the ranch and send Ariel back home. The girl certainly was old enough to know her own mind. He intended to wire Willa Brady and tell her if she wanted her daughter she'd have to come after her herself.

The smile Ariel bestowed on Jason Burns more than compensated for the loss of any revenue he'd have received from the sale of the ranch. "I'm truly grateful for any help you give me, Mr. Burns. Despite his great disappointment Kirk Walters also offered his support. It's certainly good to know I have friends. My first request is that you release the funds in the bank to me. Rosalie is buying supplies that must be paid for and I need a new wardrobe."

"Certainly, my dear, I'll come with you personally to the bank and see to the transfer. Your father was a good manager and the ranch quite profitable. You'll be surprised at the amount he left you. Handle it wisely and in time you'll be a very wealthy young woman."

"Thank you, Mr. Burns. Father chose his lawyer well." She offered him her hand.

Jason Burns took Ariel's tiny hand in his, thinking he'd never met so beguiling a creature. Yet he couldn't suppress a shiver of fear for her welfare. She was a woman, alone and vulnerable and unaware of how far Kirk Walters was willing to go to get the ranch. That was something even he didn't know. Kirk had made no threats but left little doubt in Burns' mind that one way or another Leland Ranch would be his.

Chapter 11

⌒◯◯⌒

The following days were long and exhausting for Ariel. She pushed herself relentlessly in order to learn all there was to know about the ranch in as short a time as possible. Comfortably dressed now in denim pants or a split leather skirt to accommodate her long hours spent in the saddle, she could usually be found somewhere on her countless acres watching the hands perform their duties. Strangely, they didn't seem to mind her questions or resent her interference. She learned how to brand a calf, rope, and where to search for strays. Of course there were some things she preferred to leave to the men, such as castrating the young bulls.

In addition to these duties she spent most evenings going over the account books provided by lawyer Burns. Going to Buck Leland's small office every night after supper became a ritual. Sometimes she stayed so late Rosalie had to literally shoo her from the room to her bed. During that first month she learned so much that sometimes her head spun with all the knowledge she had stored there.

Kirk Walters was a frequent visitor, much to Rosalie's consternation. He generously offered Ariel the wisdom of his advice and knowledge of ranching, which in most instances proved sound. Before long Ariel considered the handsome rancher one of her most valued friends. One day Kirk arrived with a letter from her mother. He had been in town to conduct business and pick up mail and had collected her mail at the same time.

Ariel excused herself while she read her letter. After a few minutes she frowned, placed it back in its envelope, and shoved it in her pocket. Kirk burned with curiosity.

"Bad news?"

"Not really." Ariel shrugged, still frowning. "Even though Mother knows I'm determined to make the ranch work she wants me to return to St. Louis. She threatened to send someone after me. But it won't work. I'll be twenty-one soon. If I can hold out that long she'll have no say over what I do."

"Are you still so determined to remain in Texas?" Kirk asked, annoyed by Ariel's persistence.

"Yes. I love it here. Father knew I would; that's why he left the ranch to me."

"You say that now because everything seems to be going your way. No emergencies have arisen, nothing's gone amiss to challenge your authority."

"Nothing will," Ariel asserted. "Each day I learn more, become more experienced. Soon I'll be able to handle everything pertaining to the ranch."

"You're a remarkable woman, Ariel Leland," he said. Oddly, he meant every word. Not that it would stop him from deliberately wresting the ranch from her hands, even if it took marriage to accomplish it.

Ariel still couldn't bring herself to like Trudy Walters. She thought the girl vain and self-serving. She could have used a friend her own age but unfortunately Trudy wasn't someone whose friendship she wished to cultivate. On those rare occasions Trudy accompanied her brother to Leland Ranch, Ariel was coolly polite but wary. She thought Trudy could learn a lot from her brother when it came to charm.

One day in August Kirk arrived alone and invited Ariel on a picnic. At first Ariel refused, carefully enumerating all the things that needed doing that day—and the next—and the next. But Kirk was so adamant, piquing her interest by describing the perfect spot he had in mind, that in the end she agreed to accompany him. Lord knew she could use a day off. They planned the picnic for the following day. Kirk was to pick her up at ten o'clock the next morning and provide the food. His plans sounded so intriguing that Ariel looked forward with relish to the outing. Kirk was delightful company, seemed genuinely fond of her, and wouldn't take no for an answer.

Not a cloud darkened the morning sky as Ariel dressed for the picnic with Kirk. She couldn't remember when she had last been on a picnic, and she was looking forward to a few relaxing hours in pleasant company. It had been ages since she'd been in the company of an eligible man, not since— No, she wouldn't think of Jess now—not now. Besides, she wouldn't exactly call Jess Wilder an eligible man. He was an exasperating man, a mule-headed man—a magnificent man! She hated him—she wanted him—she couldn't have him.

Rosalie joined Ariel as she waited for Kirk on the porch. "Are you sure you wish to do this, señorita?" she asked, clucking her tongue in consternation.

"I'm only going on a picnic, Rosalie," Ariel replied, annoyed by the housekeeper's constant badgering about Kirk.

"I do not like it. You are not safe with that man."

"For heaven's sake, Rosalie, what could happen? Kirk is my friend. I've learned to trust him this past month and I think you should too.''

''I have talked with his servants and know what he is capable of. Even his hands fear him.''

''Well, I don't fear him. And neither should you. Father always said talk was cheap.''

Rosalie grew quiet after that remark, and then Kirk arrived promptly at ten, driving a buckboard.

It took nearly an hour to reach their destination on the Brazos River. It was a beautiful spot, and somewhat secluded beneath the cottonwood trees where Kirk laid out their blanket.

''You're on your own property,'' Kirk said as Ariel walked to the river's edge to stare out at its broad expanse. It pleased him to think he was so knowledgeable about Leland land. He had to be if it was going to be his one day. ''There's a fording place just downstream a ways but no one should bother us here.''

''It's a lovely spot; thank you for showing it to me. There are places on the property I haven't had the occasion to visit yet. I'm so busy all the time . . .''

''Ariel, come and sit down, you look exhausted. You work too hard. You need a man, someone to help you with the ranch.''

Ariel bristled indignantly. ''I'm doing just fine.''

''Of course you are, and I'm proud of you, but ranching is difficult work for a woman.''

He led her over to the blanket. Ariel sank to the ground, tucking her legs beneath her. Kirk followed, placing his arm around her shoulders. She stiffened, then chided herself for being so foolish; Kirk was only being friendly. Kirk felt Ariel relax and smiled inwardly. Soon she would be eating out of his hand, he thought with smug satisfaction.

''Have you ever thought of marrying?''

"Doesn't every woman?" Ariel replied non-committally. "Perhaps I will marry one day—who knows?"

"I've known you but a short time, Ariel, but I've come to care a great deal for you."

"You have?" Ariel said guardedly.

"Haven't you guessed by now? I hoped you felt the same way about me."

Ariel gulped. She wasn't exactly sure where this conversation was leading but it was decidedly uncomfortable talking about marriage with Kirk. "I—admire you, Kirk. You've proven yourself an indispensable friend."

"Just a friend? I had hoped for more, much more. Is there someone in St. Louis you care about?"

Ariel thought about Denton Dobbs and wrinkled her nose. "I've left no beaux behind in St. Louis."

Kirk smiled, delighted that he'd have no competition for Ariel's affections. She was young, vulnerable, lonely, and ripe for what he had in mind.

"I've thought about this at great length, Ariel, and I want you to be my wife. You're everything I've ever wanted in a woman—warm, lovely, giving, and as determined in your ways as I am. Combined, our spreads will be one of the largest in Texas. We've so much going for us. Please say yes."

Ariel was stunned—absolutely stunned. She liked Kirk but marriage was a serious matter. Still, it would stop her mother from interfering with her life and trying to make her return to St. Louis. What was she thinking! Ariel scolded herself. Marriage after such a short acquaintance was impossible. Besides, she didn't love Kirk.

"I'm flattered, Kirk, but marriage is out of the question. At least for now. I hardly know you.

Give us time to get acquainted before you ask me again."

"Why should we wait? I know what I want and if you'll give yourself half a chance you'll find the idea has much to offer." When Ariel looked troubled, he added, "Will you think about it?"

"I—yes, of course, and I truly am flattered. It's just that you've taken me by surprise. I don't know if I feel for you in—*that* way."

"How do you know? I've never even kissed you."

Ariel chewed her lower lip thoughtfully. Kirk was partly right. How could she know how she felt about the man if she'd never thought about him in a romantic sense? He was a friend, nothing more. Was she missing an opportunity to learn if another man affected her the way Jess Wilder did? It would be interesting to know if she responded to another man's touch in the same way she did to Jess' kisses and caresses. Jess made her burn with wanting. His touch created a need in her that couldn't be duplicated by another. Or could it? There was only one way to find out.

"Kiss me, Kirk," Ariel whispered, raising her mouth invitingly.

Kirk grinned slyly. He had been right all along. Winning Ariel over had been easier than he thought. Much easier than using force or coercion. With a confidence born of male conceit, he pulled Ariel into his arms. Slowly his mouth covered hers, savoring her lips.

Ariel felt nothing.

When Ariel didn't object, Kirk nearly crowed with elation, exploring inward with the tip of his tongue.

Still nothing.

Then his tongue grew bold, forcing itself past the barrier of her teeth to deepen the kiss. Ariel responded by returning the kiss, waiting for the explosion of feeling to jolt her to awareness. When none came she pulled slightly away and stared at him with a mixture of consternation and bewilderment. But by now Kirk was consumed by a discovery of his own. Ariel wasn't the shy little thing he had first supposed her to be. He found her to be a woman capable of passion, and he intended to explore it to the fullest. Perhaps this marriage wouldn't be as dull as he'd thought. Spurred by Ariel's willingness and fired by a lust that surprised him, Kirk threw caution to the wind. Seizing Ariel, he pulled her back into his arms.

His mouth on hers grew hard and demanding, his hands seeking intimacies she had no intention of allowing. When he grasped her breast Ariel knew Kirk had more on his mind than mere kissing. Yet the fault wasn't entirely his for she had deliberately encouraged him, waiting for the same delicious sensations she experienced when Jess kissed her. When none came she was too involved with delving into her discovery to really concern herself with what Kirk would think when she voiced no objection to his intimacies. This time she pulled away with firm insistence, though his hand still rested on her breast.

"No, Kirk—I'm sorry if I led you on. I'm not experienced at this sort of thing."

"You're a passionate woman, Ariel, why deny how I make you feel? I told you I'd marry you so why do you hesitate? No one will know the difference if we anticipate the wedding by a few weeks."

"I never agreed to marriage, Kirk, just a few kisses. This can go no further."

"Don't be shy, sweet, I won't hurt you. I promise you'll enjoy what I do to you."

"You have the wrong idea about me, Kirk, I—"

By now Kirk was beyond words. He was a man of action and he wanted to prove his mastery over

Ariel in the most basic way known to man. He
seized her lips, pressing her down onto the hard
surface of the blanket. His hands were all over
her, her breasts, her hips, her buttocks, everywhere. He was so obsessed with having Ariel and
Ariel so obsessed with defending herself that neither heard the splash as a man on horseback
crossed the river and came ashore mere feet away
from where they struggled on the blanket.

The soft nicker of his horse greeting the new-
comer was what finally alerted Kirk. He released
Ariel instantly, whirled, and reached for his
weapon. Ariel lay there stunned, wondering how
things had advanced so quickly. One kiss had
driven Kirk to the point where he wanted more.
Was there some flaw in her character that made
men think of her as someone easy to bed? she
wondered bleakly. When she finally became
aware that they weren't alone, Kirk had already
rolled away from her.

"Howdy."

"What do you want?" Kirk asked belligerently.
"What are you doing here?"

"Crossing the river. Is there a law against it?"

"No, I just wondered why you chose this spot.
This is Leland property."

"Do tell. Are you Mr. Leland?"

"No," Kirk admitted reluctantly. "But this is
Miss Leland and she'll tell you you're trespassing."

"That a fact? Am I trespassing, miss?"

Ariel blinked, closed her eyes, then blinked
again. He was still there. Big—God, was he big—
ruggedly handsome and magnificently male. He
sat his horse with an easy grace that suggested
long hours in the saddle. His Stetson was pulled
down over his eyes to shade them from the sun
but Ariel would know him anywhere. Suddenly
it occurred to her that he had seen her and Kirk
rolling around on the ground like animals. She

flushed, the color rising slowly from her neck to the top of her head. Jess must have known exactly what she was thinking for he asked, "I hope I didn't interrupt anything."

"Jess? I can't believe my eyes! What are you doing here?"

"Crossing the river."

Ariel sat up, brushing her split skirt primly. He always was exasperating. "You know what I mean."

"You two know one another?" Kirk asked, numb with disbelief. Where in the world would Ariel meet a dangerous hombre like this one? he wondered curiously.

"We've met," Jess said, tipping his hat in Ariel's direction.

Ariel could tell from Jess' carefully controlled movement and tight smile that he was mad—mad enough to spit nails. His smile and careless ease didn't fool her one damn bit. He had seen enough to draw the wrong conclusion.

"Kirk, this is Jess Wilder. Jess, meet my neighbor, Kirk Walters. Kirk has been a big help to me with the ranch."

"I'll bet," Jess said with sly innuendo.

Neither man offered the other the courtesy of a handshake, both aware from the beginning that friendship would never exist between them.

"You haven't answered my question," Ariel said. "What are you doing here? I thought you had business in Mexico."

"Changed my mind," Jess said cryptically. He slanted her a meaningful glance. "It wasn't out of my way none to swing by to visit an old friend."

Kirk glanced from Ariel to Jess, aware of some deep undercurrent but unable to fathom what dark secret existed between them.

"How—thoughtful of you to remember me."

"You're damn hard to forget," Jess muttered beneath his breath.

"What?"

"Never mind. Is ranch life all that you expected?"

Ariel's eyes shone with happiness. "More than I ever imagined. I love it; I love Texas. I arrived just in time. Kirk was all set to buy the property until I arrived and altered his plans. I must say he took the news with amazing good grace."

"Right nice of you, Walters. Ariel can be quite convincing when she wants to be."

Suddenly Jess glanced around, took in the picnic basket and the spread blanket and asked, "Having a picnic?"

"We were until you interrupted," Kirk said pointedly. "We haven't gotten around to eating yet."

Kirk hoped his hint would send Jess on his way. He didn't like his showing up at so crucial a moment. Another few minutes and Ariel would have been his. Once he bedded her she would have agreed to their marriage without second thoughts. A whole morning wasted, he thought glumly, all due to some nosy cowboy Ariel happened to know. Kirk wanted Jess gone, and gone fast. He didn't want a man that handsome hanging around Ariel for any length of time. And the two of them seemed better acquainted than he would like to think. His instincts were usually right on target and Kirk's instincts told him that Jess Wilder posed a threat in his own relationship with Ariel.

"Haven't eaten myself," Jess drawled lazily. "Last decent meal I had was in San Antone." He looked with interest at the picnic basket.

"Will you join us?" Ariel asked, ignoring Kirk's groan. "I'm sure Kirk brought more than either of us could eat."

Grinning from ear to ear, Jess dismounted.

"See here, Wilder, this is a private party," Kirk objected. "You're not wanted. You've already paid your respects to Miss Leland. Now be on your way."

Ariel bristled angrily. Kirk had no business talking to Jess that way. He didn't own her; no one did. This was her land and if she invited Jess to share their food he shouldn't be so mean about it. Truth to tell, she was delighted that Jess had showed up when he did, even if he did see her in Kirk's arms and arrived at the wrong conclusion. Jess had no claim on her—he had left her in Waco without a second thought.

"Kirk, I invited Jess and—"

"Miss Leland, thank God I found ya!"

A rider skidded to a halt beside them, out of breath, his face flushed from hard riding. It was Bud, one of the hands.

"Rosalie said ya might be headed in this direction."

"What is it, Bud? Has something happened at the ranch?"

"Yes, ma'am. Pike was breakin' a bronco and got throwed. Busted him up pretty good. Rosalie said to bring ya home quick."

"I'm on my way," Ariel called to him as she hurried toward the buckboard. Kirk picked up the blanket and basket and threw them into the back then hopped into the driver's seat.

"I can get you there faster," Jess said, scooping Ariel up before she reached the buckboard and tossing her aboard Soldier. Then he vaulted up behind her. She made no protest when Jess set Soldier into motion with a click of his tongue.

"Ariel!" Kirk's words were lost to the wind as Jess and Ariel left him in their dust. His face turned ugly, and he let out a string of curses.

Kirk didn't like this latest development, not one damn bit. Jess Wilder was an unwanted nuisance and an interference he hadn't counted on. Hopefully Wilder would be gone before he did too much damage to the relationship Kirk was developing with Ariel. If not, Kirk intended to make damn certain the man knew how things stood between him and Ariel.

Less than an hour later Ariel and Jess arrived at the ranch. It had been a wild ride, one not conducive to conversation; they had spoken little during that time. Yet it was exhilarating to find herself in Jess' arms again, pressed against the unyielding hardness of his body. Memories assailed her mercilessly. Memories she had tried to suppress but never succeeded. God, she hated him—and wanted him—and wished he had never returned to remind her of the passion they once shared. Until she learned exactly why he showed up in her life again she wasn't about to let her guard down with him. He had a sneaky way of getting under her skin and making himself indispensable to her.

Rosalie waited for them on the porch. She seemed startled when Ariel showed up with Jess but her concern at the moment was for the injured man. She gave Jess no more than a brief glance before turning her attention back to Ariel.

"How is Pike, Rosalie?" Ariel asked, worried.

"In pain, señorita. I have done all I could."

"Has someone gone for the doctor?"

"Sí, Dewey rode into town but I don't expect him back for another hour."

"Perhaps I can help," Jess offered.

Rosalie regarded Jess keenly, taking note of the breadth and width of his broad frame, gaping in amazement at the outrageous size of his muscles. She liked what she saw, very much, and looked to Ariel for an explanation. The explanation was absurdly brief.

"This is Jess Wilder. Jess, Rosalie is my housekeeper and friend."

"Howdy, Rosalie." Jess smiled, tipping his hat.

"Ai yi yi," Rosalie chuckled softly, "you are one *macho* hombre, señor. I wish I was ten years younger."

Jess' grin widened while Ariel groaned in frustration. Just what she needed, a smitten housekeeper. "Take us to Pike, Rosalie. I don't know what Jess can do to help but it's worth a try."

"*Sí*, señorita, he is in my room."

Just then Kirk rolled into the yard and leaped from the buckboard. Now Rosalie's eyes did grow wide, and she nearly burst with curiosity. He joined Ariel and Jess as they walked into the house. The injured foreman lay writhing and moaning on the bed in Rosalie's small room just off the kitchen. Jess went to him immediately and knelt by his side.

"You'll be right as rain soon, cowboy," he said soothingly, amazed at how a man this young had attained the position of foreman. "The doctor is on his way."

As he talked his hands skimmed Pike's arms and legs, locating the problem immediately. He rose to his feet and walked back to where Ariel and Kirk were standing.

"Broken left leg and right arm," he said. "Don't know how much damage was done when they moved him."

"Is there nothing we can do?" Ariel asked worriedly. Her tender heart went out to the poor young man.

"Reckon we'll have to wait until the doctor arrives. Do you have any laudanum? It will ease the pain some."

"*Sí*, I have some," Rosalie answered. "I keep it for times when something like this happens."

"Give him some," Ariel said softly.

Nearly an hour later, Pike was resting more comfortably but was obviously still in pain. Then Dewey returned, alone.

"Where's the doctor?" Ariel cried out in alarm. "Couldn't you find him?"

"I found him, ma'am, but he couldn't come. Miz Lacy is givin' birth and likely to die from it. He said to tell ya he'd be here as soon as he could."

Ariel groaned aloud and Kirk eased his frustration by uttering a foul oath. Jess merely gritted his teeth and announced, "I can set the limbs. Done it more than once."

"Jess, are you sure?"

"You're crazy if you let that rough cowboy touch Pike," Kirk advised.

"What do you need?" Ariel asked, ignoring Kirk. She trusted Jess. If he said he could set broken bones, then he could.

Jess quickly stated his needs, sending Rosalie in search of the items. When she returned he sent everyone except Rosalie out of the room and then he went to work. Pike screamed once when his leg was snapped back into place and again when the process was repeated with his arm. Then he fainted.

"Fortunately both breaks were simple," Jess said when he rejoined Ariel and Kirk in the parlor a long time later. He looked tired and was sweating profusely from the exertion.

"I don't know how to thank you, Jess," Ariel said. Was there no end to this man's capabilities? "Looks like I'll be without a foreman for a long time."

Just then Bud entered the room, having come to inquire about Pike. "How is he, Miss Leland?"

"Hopefully he'll mend, but that leaves the ranch without a foreman. Will you take the job, Bud?"

Bud looked properly horrified. "Me? Oh, no, ma'am, I ain't no foreman. I'm jest a cowboy who follows orders."

"What about one of the other hands? Dewey or Casey or Mose?"

"They won't want the job no more than me. Ain't none of them wantin' to be foreman."

Kirk straightened in his chair, proud of the fact that he could offer Ariel something Jess Wilder couldn't. "Don't fret, Ariel, I'll send one of my best men over to take over as foreman. You won't even have to pay him. He'll remain under my employ but work for you until Pike is on his feet again."

"You'd do that for me?" Ariel asked gratefully.

"Of course. What are friends for? I told you before I care for you a great deal and am concerned about your being alone out here."

"How touching," Jess said with a hint of scorn. "There's no need to put yourself out, Walters. As it happens I'm not doing anything at the moment and would be glad to help Ariel out."

"You?" Ariel said, astounded. "You'd be my foreman?"

"What do you know about ranching?" Kirk asked derisively.

"I've put in my time," Jess replied cryptically.

"Are you going to accept his offer, Ariel?" Kirk asked, offended. "I thought you trusted my judgment."

"I do, Kirk, but I don't think Jess would take on something he couldn't handle. If he—needs a job I'll be happy to hire him on as foreman."

Kirk seethed.

Jess grinned.

Rosalie smothered a chuckle.

Bud looked relieved.

Ariel sighed, unwilling at this time to explore the complications of having Jess living on the ranch.

Chapter 12

Kirk made a belated departure, reluctant to leave Ariel alone with Jess Wilder but unable to find a valid reason to remain. Bud and Rosalie also left. Only Ariel and Jess remained in the parlor. Ariel appeared to be at a loss for words while Jess merely stared at Ariel as if starved, unaware that he was staring. His eyes couldn't get enough of her. Evidently Texas agreed with her for she looked wonderful. Her exposed flesh was tinged a becoming tan and her body was lean and supple. He recalled with vivid clarity how well that body fit his arms, how he had brought her to ecstasy and made a woman of her. He shuddered from the erotic memories his thoughts evoked.

A slow flush crawled up Ariel's cheeks. She knew without being told what Jess was thinking and it flustered her. The damn rogue, she thought, exasperated. He was doing it deliberately, trying to embarrass her by making her feel uncomfortable. She'd put an end to that quick enough.

"What are you doing here, Jess? I assumed you'd be in Mexico. Did you find Dillon?"

With great difficulty Jess forced himself to concentrate on Ariel's words, not on the way she looked. "Dillon is holed up across the border, probably riding with desperadoes who make their headquarters in the hills. I tracked him across the

Rio Grande before I lost his trail. Going into those hills alone would be foolish. I'm not ready to die yet.''

"You gave up?" Ariel asked, dumbfounded. Jess didn't seem the type to give up so easily.

"Give up? Hell no! Dillon will be back. Pickings are slim in Mexico. I'll give him a few weeks before Texas lures him back. One day we'll hear he's robbed a bank or stagecoach and I'll be waiting.''

"What are you doing here at the ranch?"

"Curiosity, I reckon. Besides, it wasn't out of my way," he explained lamely. "Thought I'd see how you were getting on.''

"And you volunteered for the foreman's job because you had nothing better to do," Ariel prompted, not completely satisfied with his explanation.

"You might say that.''

"Jess Wilder! You're the most exasperating man I know.''

"And you're the most exciting female I've ever met. Damnation, Ariel, why are we standing here jawing at one another like polite strangers when all I want to do is kiss you?''

"Because for once in my life I'm being smart where you're concerned. I don't need you complicating my life when you'll take off again at the drop of a hat. This is strictly a business arrangement. I should have listened to Kirk and accepted his offer of one of his men.''

"Kirk.'' Jess spat the name derisively. "If he has his way you'll be wedded and bedded before you catch your breath.''

"Would that be so bad?" Ariel asked defensively. "At least his offer is a legitimate one. Most girls desire marriage.''

The barb had the desired effect. "You don't love Walters.''

"You couldn't possibly know that," Ariel fumed. How dare Jess dictate to her? Popping in and out of her life whenever it suited him gave him absolutely no hold over her.

"I can damn well prove it to you."

His speed amazed her. She was in his arms in the space of a heartbeat, pressed against the hard wall of his chest, his mouth hungry on hers. Then he was kissing her, his tongue a hot shaft thrusting past her lips, tasting, branding her in his own special way.

"I've missed you. I've missed *this*," Jess groaned against her lips.

Ariel couldn't speak, she could only feel. She felt his heat, his quick passion, his arousal. She was stunned, confused, bemused—and suddenly filled with rage. Did the big, arrogant Texan think he could bounce into her life and claim her whenever he felt the need? She wasn't stupid enough to fall into his arms or take up with him where they'd left off weeks ago. She'd soon show him he couldn't have things his way all the time. If Jess Wilder wanted to bed a woman he could damn well visit a bawdy house in Waco. Freeing herself from his embrace was the most difficult task she had ever set for herself but she accomplished it with amazing dexterity.

"The job of foreman doesn't include getting familiar with the boss," she upbraided him. "I suggest you settle in at the bunkhouse and acquaint yourself with the hands."

Jess flashed an arrogant grin. "Sure thing, boss lady, but I think I've proved my point. No woman in love with someone else would respond to my kiss like you just did." Then he turned and sauntered from the room with that loose-hipped gait that made Ariel grit her teeth in pure frustration.

"Damn exasperating man," she muttered beneath her breath.

"Is he the one, señorita?"

Rosalie walked into the parlor just as Jess walked out the front door.

"What are you talking about, Rosalie?"

"You do not fool Rosalie, Ariel. Señor Wilder is the 'special man' you spoke of. Those hot looks he gives you would melt my bones if they were directed at me."

"You're imagining things," Ariel scoffed. She lowered her lashes, shuttering her thoughts from the perceptive housekeeper.

"I do not imagine things, señorita. It will do you no good to lie."

"You're right as usual, Rosalie, you're much too canny to fool. But you're dead wrong about Jess Wilder. He's a man with a cause; I mean nothing to him. He enjoys women and unfortunately I'm handy while he waits for—never mind. Suffice it to say Jess Wilder will disappear from my life as abruptly as he appeared. Nothing I do or say will keep him here."

"I think you misjudge Señor Wilder," Rosalie observed softly. "Intuition tells me he has strong feelings for you. And from what I saw you return those feelings."

Was nothing private around here? Ariel fumed, turning away from Rosalie's keen scrutiny. Rosalie had the amazing ability to look deep into her soul and see things Ariel wasn't ready to admit to herself.

"You were eavesdropping again," Ariel accused sourly. "But you may as well know the truth. There are times I actually hate Jess Wilder. He's the most obstinate man I know. He's never wrong and won't take no for an answer. If you really must know, Rosalie, Jess is the man who refused to believe I'm Ariel Leland, stubbornly insisting until the very end that I was Tilly Cowles, a—a common criminal wanted for various crimes."

Rosalie's dark eyes grew wide. Ariel had already told her the story but had conveniently left out Jess' name. "Ai yi yi, so he is the hombre that caused you such grief. You were alone with him many days, were you not?''

Her simple question opened the door to a score of others Ariel had no intention of answering.

''Perhaps you should see to Pike,'' Ariel said tightly. She didn't want to be reminded of the way Jess made her feel, all hot and cold and shaky inside.

Suppressing a secret smile, Rosalie left Ariel to her own brooding thoughts.

The doctor arrived from town a short time later. ''Not much for me to do here,'' he pronounced as he examined the splints on Pike's arm and leg. ''Whoever did this did a mighty fine job.'' He made a few adjustments, left a vial of laudanum along with instructions, and left, promising to return in a day or two. ''He'll be laid up six weeks or so but you can move him out to the bunkhouse in a few days. I imagine he'll be more comfortable with the hands than here in the house.''

Six weeks, Ariel thought morosely as she showed the doctor out. Six weeks of seeing Jess every day. How in the world was she to survive?

Kirk Walters slammed the door and stormed into his house like a raging bull. Nothing was going his way. He'd nearly had Ariel eating out of his hand until that damn cowboy, Jess Wilder, showed up.

''What in the world is going on down there?'' Trudy called from the top of the stairs. ''Is your picnic over so soon?''

''What there was of it,'' Kirk spat. Trudy came the rest of the way downstairs but the furious expression in Kirk's eyes made her halt abruptly. ''An accident at the ranch brought it to an early end.'' His eyes grew thoughtful as he scrutinized his sister with frank appraisal.

He saw a beautiful blonde with seductive blue eyes and a figure most men would drool over.

Though her looks were cool and regal she was anything but cold-blooded. Kirk knew firsthand that she was a passionate little bitch who would bed every cowboy on the place if he allowed it. Until now he'd selfishly refrained from finding her a husband, but suddenly he saw a way to make use of Trudy's experience and felt no guilt over what he was about to suggest. He'd supported her and satisfied her every whim all these years and the least she could do was help him out when he needed it. Besides, he reckoned Trudy would find his request more of a pleasure than duty.

"What—what are you looking at?" Trudy asked, puzzled by Kirk's interest.

"You. You're a beautiful, passionate woman—it's been a mistake to keep you to myself when you could be such a help to me. I'll bet you could wind a man around your little finger very easily."

"What are you hinting at, Kirk?" Her skin warmed all over at the intensity of his gaze. Kirk had a devious mind but she'd learned early on that their minds often ran in the same direction.

"I've found a man for you."

"You what! If I wanted a man I'd find one myself."

"Not like this one. I'm more adept at judging women but even I have to admit this man is someone you would appreciate. He's a big, tall Texan with the kind of rugged good looks you seem to prefer. He strikes me as being tough, too, and dangerous. But I think you can handle him."

"Who is this man?" Trudy asked, her interest definitely piqued. "Where did you meet him?"

"His name is Jess Wilder and he just appeared out of nowhere. I had Ariel all set to marry me. She was literally eating out of my hand when he showed up. I was stunned to learn they knew one another. And quite well, judging from their conversation."

"Where would Ariel meet a man like that?" Trudy asked. The man sounded like a dream, too good for the likes of Ariel Leland.

"Damned if I know. About that time a rider showed up from the ranch with the news that the foreman had been injured. Ariel hightailed it home and I wasn't able to speak with her alone after that. I stuck around as long as I could but she only had eyes for the cowboy. I don't like it, not one damn bit."

"What are you going to do about it?"

"You're going to attract Wilder's attention and keep him away from Ariel long enough for me to make her my wife."

"Me! What makes you think I'd be interested?"

"Ha!" scoffed Kirk. "I know you. You'll definitely be interested in Jess Wilder. Besides, whatever you do will be for your benefit as well as mine."

"Are you asking me to bed the man?"

"If that's what it takes. Don't pretend outrage, you're always hot for a good bedding. I ought to know, I've been taking care of your—needs since you were sixteen. If you do as I ask and Leland land becomes mine, this ranch will be your dowry."

"I want that in writing, Kirk," Trudy said shrewdly.

"You'll have it," Kirk promised, "if you agree to divert Wilder long enough for me to convince Ariel to marry me."

"What if I like him well enough to want him for a husband?"

"He's all yours as long as you didn't bring him around too often to visit."

"Done," agreed Trudy with a smug smile. She'd never known a man she couldn't seduce. She'd just never found one she wanted to wed. Kirk might be her brother but he was all the man she needed. She sincerely hoped Jess Wilder could topple Kirk from his pedestal. She certainly wished it was so.

Pike improved enough to be moved to the bunkhouse. In fact, he requested the move after languishing in Rosalie's room for several days. The doctor hadn't been far off the mark when he said the cowboy would prefer to be among his own kind. Rosalie and Ariel still saw to his needs but now he had the company and support of the other hands.

Ariel saw Jess only when absolutely necessary. He was usually so busy they spoke only in regard to his duties, which he was performing with amazing skill. Kirk dropped by once or twice asking after Pike and to remind Ariel that he hadn't received an answer to his proposal. He also mentioned that he had to leave town for a few days, and surprised Ariel by asking if Trudy might stay with her in his absence, saying that he hated to leave her alone on the ranch while he was gone. Of course Ariel agreed, though she knew Trudy's visit wouldn't be a happy one. Trudy didn't like her any better than she liked Trudy.

A few days later Kirk returned with his sister and enough luggage in the back of the buckboard to ensure Trudy a lengthy stay. Ariel welcomed the blonde with as much enthusiasm as she could muster. Entertaining a guest was far down on her list of priorities.

"It's so nice of you to invite me," Trudy said as Kirk swung her down from the buckboard. "I couldn't bear being alone while Kirk was gone."

"My pleasure," Ariel replied politely. "Rosalie will show you to your room and you can settle in. One of the hands will bring your luggage up later."

"Enjoy your stay, sis," Kirk called. "I'll try not to be gone too long."

"Don't worry about me, I'll be just fine," Trudy returned, flashing him a confident grin.

"This really is kind of you," Kirk said once Trudy had entered the house. "Trudy can be somewhat of a pest. I'm afraid our parents spoiled her terribly. Are you sure you don't mind?"

"I said it was all right," Ariel said shortly. Thinking that she sounded anything but happy, her tone softened. "Don't worry, Kirk, we'll be fine."

"Will you think about my proposal while I'm gone?"

"I—perhaps." It was all she could think of to say. It certainly wouldn't be right to give him hope where none existed.

"I'll want an answer when I return," Kirk insisted. "Is it too much to ask for a kiss? I'll miss you dreadfully."

Ariel flushed. She didn't want to kiss Kirk, especially not here where anyone could see them. She opened her mouth to protest but her words came out as a squeak when Kirk refused to be denied. His lips were hot and hard on hers, pressing her head against his arm as he ravaged her mouth. He hadn't meant to force his kiss on her but he had seen Jess approach the house and couldn't resist the opportunity to show the cowboy that Ariel belonged to him. After a sufficient time he released her, gloating when he saw Jess glaring at them with an expression that could only be described as murderous.

Reeling from his kiss, Ariel watched Kirk leave. Not that his kiss evoked any sort of response—just the opposite. It was the degree of his conceit that stunned her. He seemed to think she should fall into his arms and act grateful that he wanted to make her his wife. She stood there staring after him, pressing her fingertips to her lips.

"Have you bedded him yet?"

Ariel whirled. "What! What are you doing

sneaking up on me like that, Jess Wilder? Can't a girl have a private moment with a—friend?''

"I asked you a question, Ariel. Did you bed him yet?'' His face was red with anger. "He kissed you like he owned you. The day I interrupted your picnic he had his hands all over you.''

"It's none of your business, Jess Wilder! You have no claim on me. I'll bed whomever I want.''

"Like hell!'' Jess snarled, seizing her wrist and pulling her close.

"Am I interrupting?''

Jess released Ariel instantly. If his dark scowl was any indication, Trudy couldn't have picked a worse—or better—time to intrude.

"Kirk told me you had a new foreman.'' She regarded Jess with keen appreciation, thinking that Kirk hadn't adequately described Jess Wilder at all. He was big and tall, yes, but he was so virile, handsome, and loaded with potent male sensuality, just looking at him nearly bowled her over. A jolt of raw lust ran through her body. "Are you going to introduce us, Ariel?''

Ariel hadn't missed Trudy's avid scrutiny of Jess, nor the way her blue eyes settled so possessively on him. She almost groaned in frustration. Did the big Texan affect all women that way? First Rosalie and now Trudy. Well, at least *she* had the sense to resist him.

"Sorry,'' Ariel mumbled, "I didn't mean to be rude. This is Jess Wilder, my foreman until Pike recovers. Jess, this is Trudy Walters, Kirk's sister.''

"Howdy, ma'am,'' Jess drawled, aware of the effect he had on Trudy. "Are all women in this part of Texas as pretty as you?''

His words produced the desired effect. If he meant to make Ariel jealous he was succeeding only too well. She gritted her teeth in frustration and watched Jess charm Trudy, whose inflated ego was already beyond endurance.

"I'm afraid you're a better judge of that than I am," Trudy said coyly. She batted her long lashes, forcing Ariel to suppress another groan. "Please call me Trudy. 'Ma'am' sounds so—so formal. And I'll call you Jess. Are you from around these parts, Jess?"

"Nope. I was born near Fort Worth but I've been around some."

"I'll bet," Trudy said breathlessly.

"Don't you have work to do, Jess?" Ariel intervened. Trudy looked as if she could devour Jess and Jess was basking in her adulation like a pleased puppy. Too bad Trudy didn't know what the real Jess Wilder was like, she thought uncharitably.

Jess flashed Ariel an impudent grin. "I got plenty of work to do, boss lady. None of it as pleasant as standing here talking with two beautiful women. But I reckon it's gotta get done so I'll see you ladies later."

"You can count on it, Jess Wilder," Trudy called to his departing back.

The sound that came from Ariel's throat was anything but ladylike.

During the following days Trudy was underfoot every waking hour. When she wasn't intruding in every aspect of Ariel's business she was following Jess around like an extra appendage. One day Ariel came upon her running her hands over his bulging biceps, oohing and aahing like a lovesick calf. Or so it seemed to Ariel. Another time the blonde was perched on the corral fence with her dress hiked up high enough to give Jess, who was working with one of the horses, a good view of her trim calves and a tantalizing glimpse of more tender flesh higher up. Obviously the woman was trying to entice Jess and it irked Ariel to think that her feminine wiles were working so

well. She had thought him immune to such female tricks. Or was it just her he was immune to?

Trudy had been a houseguest for nearly two
weeks and Ariel began to wonder just how far she
was willing to go to snare Jess. She didn't have
long to wonder. She was in the yard when she
saw the blonde disappear into the stables with the
big Texan.

Trudy was elated when she saw the opportunity to get Jess alone. So far she'd had little luck
luring him into a compromising position. Kirk
would be back soon and he expected to find Jess
completely out of the picture where Ariel was
concerned. And Kirk hated to be disappointed.
Trudy had been talking with Jess while he worked
near the corral and when he excused himself she
merely tagged along when she saw he was headed
toward the stables. She knew none of the hands
were around this time of day and smiled in anticipation at what was likely to happen once she got
him alone. He was a man, wasn't he? A virile
man at that. She knew he'd be the kind of lover
she'd always dreamed about.

"Did you want something, Trudy?" Jess asked
when she boldly followed him inside the dim stables redolent with the earthy smell of horse and
hay and manure.

"I like being with you, Jess. You don't mind,
do you?"

Appreciative as Jess was of a stunning female
like Trudy Walters, he wasn't taken in by her. He
knew she was up to something but didn't know
what. She could be just a flirt, or a woman who
craved men, or—really enthralled by him.

" 'Course I don't mind, Trudy, but the boss
lady won't like it if I neglect my work to talk to
you."

"Oh, hang the boss lady! Forget Ariel for a few
minutes and think of me."

Forget Ariel? Jess thought, silently scoffing at

the idea. Trudy's blonde prettiness couldn't compare with Ariel's violet-eyed, smoldering beauty. "I don't know what you want of me, Trudy."

Trudy thought his honesty refreshing and sought to enlighten him. "I want *you*, Jess Wilder. I've never met a man like you."

"There must be plenty of men you could have," Jess said slowly. "Why do you want a poor cowboy like me?"

"You don't have to remain a poor cowboy all your life, Jess. I have enough money for both of us. Have you ever thought of being a rancher? One day soon the Walters ranch will be mine. I'll need a husband to run it."

"You want me for a husband?" Jess asked, astounded.

"Among other things," Trudy purred. Winding her arms around his neck she pulled his head down until she could reach his lips. "I can make you happy, Jess, real happy."

Her kiss was bold and insinuating. Her instant passion so startled Jess it was a challenge to keep his own under strict control. He wasn't entirely successful as Trudy did things with her tongue that sorely tried his endurance. He wrapped his arms around her waist in order to set her aside and her refusal to be dislodged surprised him. He didn't want to hurt her but neither did he want to bed the flirtatious beauty.

When both Jess and Trudy remained in the stables longer than Ariel considered a reasonable length of time, her curiosity got the best of her.

"Why don't you go and see what the little witch is up to?"

"Rosalie! You do have a way of sneaking up on people. How long have you been standing there?"

"Long enough. Are you going to let Trudy steal your man?" Rosalie goaded.

"Jess Wilder isn't my man."

"Of course not. Are you going to let Trudy have him without a fight?"

Ariel looked toward the stables, then back at Rosalie.

"You must decide, señorita." After that piece of sage advice Rosalie tactfully returned to the house.

Ariel hesitated but a moment before walking resolutely toward the stable. In her heart she knew what she would find but a practical part of her told her Jess was too smart to fall under Trudy's spell. The stable was dim, and after being in the strong sunlight she had to wait until her eyes adjusted once she entered. It took only a few seconds but what she saw would last her a lifetime.

Jess and Trudy were in a clinch that left little doubt as to their intention. Her hands were around his neck, his clutched her waist as they strained toward one another. Their kiss went on and on, not even a breath stirred between them. Ariel could feel their passion, taste the heated exchange between them, and a sob caught in her throat. When she saw them drop to the ground she turned and fled.

Damn! Jess thought as Trudy grew limp in his arms and dropped to the ground. He didn't want her to hurt herself so he hung on and followed, intending only to cushion her fall. He certainly didn't want the cool blonde in the same way he wanted Ariel. Then from the corner of his eye he caught a movement, someone fleeing out the door. Instinctively he knew it was Ariel and a curse slipped past his lips. He hit the ground and rolled away from Trudy.

Determined to have Jess, Trudy grabbed for him—and found nothing but air. Slowly she roused herself from her stupor, staring at Jess dazedly.

"What's wrong? I thought you wanted me as much as I want you."

"You're a damn enticing woman, Trudy, but I can't take advantage of you," Jess said gallantly.

"Don't you understand?" Trudy said, her voice rising. "I want you! Not just for a few minutes but for a lifetime. You won't be taking advantage of me if we marry soon."

"I'm not the marrying kind, Trudy. Find someone worthy of your love."

"What about Ariel?"

"What about her?" Jess asked defensively.

"I know you're attracted to her. Is that why you won't respond to me? Don't you know she's going to marry my brother?"

"Has Ariel told you that?"

"Well, no," she admitted reluctantly, "but once Kirk makes up his mind he'll let nothing or no one stand in his way."

Jess rose to his feet and extended his hand to Trudy. "You're a fetching woman, Trudy, but I'm not in the market for a wife. Best you go now. I've got a heap of work to do."

"I won't give up so easily, Jess. Every man has a breaking point and I'll find yours. I can offer you everything you've ever dreamed of. You can be your own boss and have me in the bargain. I'd be a loving wife, Jess, a *very* loving wife. Think about it."

Jess watched Trudy flounce out of the stable, her skirts swishing enticingly about her slender ankles. But he wasn't thinking of Trudy, he was thinking about Ariel. How much had she seen? he wondered dismally. Trudy had been like a bitch in heat and nothing he'd said seemed to discourage her. It was time to have a private talk with Ariel, he decided. He'd been here over two weeks and in all that time she'd avoided him like the plague. If she truly was indifferent to him, having him around wouldn't bother her in the least. The Lord knew he wasn't indifferent to her. Every time he saw her only renewed his passion in ways that made his heart beat faster and his loins burn. Tonight, he thought with staunch determination. One way or another he and Ariel would have a long-overdue talk tonight.

Actually, talking was the last thing on Jess Wilder's mind.

Ariel lingered on the porch long past her usual time for retiring. It was a hot night, too hot to sleep, too hot for September. Rosalie had already gone to bed and so had Trudy. Ariel could hardly look at Trudy tonight over supper. She kept seeing the little witch in Jess' arms, thinking of what went on in the stable after she'd left. God, she hated him!

Finally the mosquitos drove her inside. After lighting a lamp she climbed the stairs and entered her room. It wasn't much cooler but at least there was a screen on the window to keep out those pesky insects. She set the lamp on her nightstand and began undressing. Once she had all her clothes carefully folded, she reached for the nightgown Rosalie always left at the foot of her bed. It wasn't there.

"Are you looking for this, sweetheart?" a familiar voice asked.

Chapter 13

J ess stood in the corner shrouded in shadows. He had entered earlier while Ariel still lingered outside. He hadn't had a moment alone with her in weeks and was determined this time to talk without interruptions, without either Trudy or Rosalie intruding on their privacy. His patience was rewarded when Ariel finally entered her room and began undressing for bed. He hadn't meant it to go so far but the sight of her peeling off the layers of her clothing completely enthralled him. Not until every inch of her skin was gilded by the pale glow of lamplight did he finally make his presence known. And then reluctantly. He could look at her like this forever and never grow tired of the sight.

Ariel gasped and whirled, stunned to see Jess standing nearby, holding out her nightgown. "Jess Wilder! How dare you sneak into my room?" She snatched the nightgown from his hand and held it before her like a shield. "What are you doing here?"

"I want to talk to you."

"We'll talk tomorrow. Get out of here."

"Damnation, Ariel, there's never a time when we can talk privately without someone intruding. I'm here now, so why can't you just listen to what I have to say?"

"A lady's bedroom is no place to hold a conversation," Ariel persisted.

Jess' eyes roamed hungrily over her scantily clad curves, barely covered by the nightgown held protectively against her bosom. "I can't think of a better place." His voice was low and so filled with longing that Ariel's knees turned weak.

"You can forget what you're thinking," she said stiffly. "If you need a woman I'm sure Trudy will be glad to accommodate you. What kind of man are you? After that roll in the hay this afternoon you should be sated."

"Are you jealous?" Jess said softly.

"Jealous? Of you and Trudy? I don't care what you and that little witch do as long as you don't neglect your work."

Slowly Jess advanced, one step at a time. Ariel retreated, until the back of her knees came into contact with the bed. "All right, dammit, talk," she relented, "but let me put on my nightgown first."

"Go ahead."

Ariel did a slow turn. "Turn your back."

Rather than anger her further, Jess complied.

"Say what it is you came to say and get out of here before someone hears you."

Jess took that as a signal that Ariel was now decently clad in her long flowing nightgown. He turned, and sucked in his breath sharply. The lamp was behind Ariel and every luscious curve was clearly outlined beneath the fine linen garment. Jess had to force his eyes upward from the dark shadow between her legs, and it wasn't easy.

"Well, I'm waiting. What's so important that it couldn't wait until tomorrow?"

Jess seemed to be having trouble breathing. When he spoke his words came out as strangled gasps. "First of all let me set you straight about Trudy."

"I don't want to hear it," Ariel returned shortly.

"You'll listen anyway. I know what you saw in the stable this afternoon but it was misleading."

"Of course," Ariel said sarcastically. "You were merely groping one another for no other reason than to scratch each other's back. Do you think me stupid? Not that it really matters what you and Trudy do," she added sourly.

"I don't want Trudy," Jess stated. "I told her so this afternoon."

"You could have fooled me."

"Obviously you didn't stay around long enough to see the outcome of that little scene she initiated."

"I saw all I wanted to see."

"Ariel, I swear I didn't touch Trudy. How can I, when I want you so damn bad you've spoiled me for any other woman? Let me show you how much I want you."

If he touched her she'd go up in smoke. "Is that all you came here to say, Jess?"

Jess spewed out an oath beneath his breath. "No, dammit, that's not all. I want to know if you plan on marrying Kirk Walters. Has he done anything else but kiss you? Just thinking about him touching you makes me mad enough to kill the bastard."

"I don't know why it should concern you," Ariel said, then relented. "But for your information I have no intention of becoming Kirk's wife."

"That's not what Trudy says."

"Trudy has no right to speak for me. She certainly isn't someone I would confide in."

"What about the other?" Jess asked tightly. "How far have you gone with him?" He had no idea his hands were clenched at his sides until he felt his nails dig into his palms.

"I can't imagine why my private life should concern you, but if it will make you go away then

I'll tell you. Except for a kiss or two Kirk hasn't laid a hand on me. Now are you satisfied?''

Jess released his breath in a long ragged sigh. ''Yep, but I'm not ready to go yet. There's still something else I wanna say.''

''Then say it,'' Ariel demanded, wishing he'd leave while she still had the willpower to send him away.

''I care about you, Ariel, I care what happens to you. I just wanna make damn certain you aren't taken in by Kirk Walters. When I leave here I wanna know that you won't let him pressure you into marrying him. I don't trust the phony bastard. I think both he and Trudy are up to something, I just don't know what.''

Ariel never got past his words about leaving. ''Will—will you leave soon?''

''Not until Pike is back on his feet. Besides, the marshal in Waco hasn't heard anything concerning Dillon so I have no reason to leave yet.''

''Dillon!'' Ariel spat disgustedly. ''Your life seems to revolve around that man.''

''Not entirely,'' Jess admitted somewhat reluctantly. ''Lately a violet-eyed wildcat has me wishing I never heard of a man named Dillon. I find my priorities have changed since you dropped into my life, and I'm not sure I like it.''

''Have I really changed your life?'' Ariel asked. She was bewildered by Jess' admission and uncertain what it meant in regard to a relationship between them.

''Jesus H. Christ! You're with me every damn hour of every damn day. If that isn't changing my life I don't know what is. I've never wanted a woman like I want you. Just being near you makes me forget my promise to Judd and that's not good. But I can't help it. I've got feelings for you I've never had before.''

''Do—do you love me, Jess?'' There, she'd said it. Though Jess' words were the closest she'd ever

heard to an admission of love, Ariel wanted to
hear him say it.

"Love? I—don't rightly know. I've never experienced love before so how can I say? I do know
no other woman affects me like you do, or feels
so good in my arms, or gets me hard by just looking at her, or—or—Jesus H. Christ! Maybe I do
love you!"

Ariel smiled dreamily. It wasn't exactly a romantic declaration but it would do. "I could easily love you, Jess, if you gave us half a chance."

It was an outright lie, for Ariel knew without a
doubt she already loved Jess. When she wasn't
hating him. The fine line between love and hate
was sometimes difficult to distinguish and often
the two emotions merged into one. It had taken
a long time to realize she could love and hate at
the same time until one emotion devoured the
other, leaving the stronger one behind.

"You know I can't stay, sweetheart. A solemn
promise is a solemn promise. My life is not my
own until Dillon is behind bars or dead. Revenge
is a powerful emotion."

"More powerful than love?"

"I—don't know. This thing between us is too
new yet to judge how it will affect my thinking."

Ariel sighed and turned her back on him. "I
can't see how anything has changed between us,
Jess. Getting closer to you can only lead to heartache."

"Hurting you is the last thing I want to do,"
Jess said softly.

She felt his hands on her shoulders and stiffened, his mere touch a brand searing her skin.
He tried to turn her to face him but she resisted.

"Ariel, look at me."

She turned then, raising her sooty black lashes
to stare at him. Her eyes revealed emotions better
left unsaid. Jess had no difficulty deciphering
them. His answer to her unspoken fears was to

kiss her deeply, hungrily, conveying to her his silent promise to love her always no matter what fate had in store for them.

He kissed her eyes, her cheeks, his lips following the ridge of her cheekbone to her ear then downward to where the pulse in her throat beat erratically.

"You're the most exciting female I've ever laid eyes on," he groaned, pushing the neck of her gown aside to caress her bare shoulder. Then lower to bare her breast. "I'll always want you, just like I want you now."

His mouth covered her nipple and Ariel gasped. With a deft movement Jess bared her other breast, then the nightgown slid to the floor. Bending his knees, he scooped her up and carried her to the bed. "I'm gonna make love to you, sweetheart. All night long."

Ariel wanted to say no but couldn't. She had dreamed of this moment for so long, she wanted it as much as he did. So much time had elapsed since the last time they had made love she needed to feel him deep inside her, needed him to satisfy the longing that had been building inside her. There was no past, no present, no future, only Jess and this sublime moment that defied reality. If he must leave, then she'd at least have this much to remember him by.

"My God, you're beautiful," Jess said reverently as he cupped the fullness of her breasts, lightly stroking the pearly pink tips with his thumbs. Licks of fire brushed her skin. She gasped and arched her back, pressing against his hands. He rewarded the movement with deepening strokes, gently kneading her flesh until Ariel was breathless, panting, and flushed with a deeper need.

"Tell me what you feel," Jess whispered hoarsely.

"It's like no other feeling," Ariel said breathlessly. "Your hands on me—I can't begin to describe it. I'm on fire! I feel hungry—and I ache! I—I want you inside me."

Ariel whimpered when Jess suddenly removed his hands and moved away. But she grew quiet when he began to undress, the sight of his body nude and ready for her more than compensating for any discomfort he was causing her by halting their lovemaking. "You look like a god," Ariel said in a strangled voice. "I could look at you forever."

"If you keep looking at me like that I'll explode before I get a chance to show you how much I want you." Jess chuckled softly.

Then he was beside her. His hard, calloused hands cupped her buttocks as his mouth found her breasts again, this time sucking strong and hard until she cried out. When he raised his head he said, "I want to taste you, sweetheart, every part of you." He slid down her body, bringing her up to his mouth.

"Jess, I don't think—"

"Don't think, just feel."

His words were muffled, his head buried between her legs. A shriek left Ariel's lips as his tongue parted the tender flesh and delved inside to tease and caress with bold strokes that left her gasping for breath. She clutched his head, hers rolling from side to side as ecstasy built inside her.

"Jess, stop, please, I can't take any more!"

"Let it come, sweetheart, I won't leave you."

Her climax burst upon her with the sudden fury of a summer storm and she began a mad spiral into rapture's realm. It was glorious! Like a wild whirlpool she spun faster and faster. Her breath came in gulps and spurts until she reached the ultimate peak of rapture. She squeezed her eyes tightly shut and when she opened them again Jess was hovering above her, pushing deep inside her.

"I can still feel you quiver inside," he rasped, his face contorted with intense pleasure. "You're so warm, so smooth, I wanna stay here forever."

His bold words and powerful strokes within her sent hot slivers of pleasure shooting through her.

"Let me take you there again," he whispered against her lips.

"God, Jess, I don't think I can."

The words had no sooner left her lips than Jess began a torrid assault upon her senses that proved her wrong. He was kissing her, his tongue plunging into her mouth in tempo with his thrusting down below. His hands, oh, God, those hands were stroking her breasts, traveling the warm, naked length of her, awakening her senses and renewing a need in her to match his own.

Faster, harder, he plunged into her with reckless abandon. His eyes narrowed, his jaw clenched against the almost unbearable pleasure driving him to completion. "Hurry, Ariel!"

Her own face strained, Ariel reached for that shimmering peak and found it. Together they raced to touch the top, hovered there briefly, then tumbled down—down—down . . . Unable to bear it, Ariel shut her eyes and hung on for dear life.

"Wake up, wildcat, I don't want you to sleep the night away. As soon as I've rested I want to love you again."

Ariel opened her eyes unaware that she had fallen asleep. "You're insatiable," she groaned. "What will it take to satisfy you?"

"A lifetime, I reckon. Do you realize how long it's been since we've loved like this?"

Since Jess seemed not to expect an answer she gave none. But she did know. She had counted every damn minute since the last time Jess had made love to her. "It doesn't have to be like that."

Jess made an exasperated sound deep in his

throat. "If things were different . . . If I was free . . ."

"You are free, Jess. Let the law take care of Dillon."

"If I thought that were possible I'd give it up in a minute. But it just won't happen, sweetheart. There are too many desperadoes like Dillon in Texas and too few lawmen to bring them to justice. I would have remained marshal if I wanted to sit on my behind and wait for him to fall into my lap. I'm not so selfish as to ask you to wait for me, Ariel, but if you're still here when I return . . ."

What he didn't say held more meaning for Ariel than what he said. "I thought you're not the marrying kind."

"I'm not. Not now, anyway. But I want a wife and kids just like the next man. You'd be a good mother to my kids."

It was as close to a proposal as she was going to get.

"Jess Wilder, you are one exasperating man! But more man than any I've ever known. Rosalie is right, you know."

"About what?"

"You're one *macho* hombre. You have a way of turning me into that wildcat you're always calling me. Have you rested yet?"

For an answer he guided her hand to his groin. "Judge for yourself."

A soft sigh slid past Ariel's lips as her fingers curled around the hard strength of his erection. With exquisite slowness she moved her hand up and down his magnificent length; she felt him jerk in response and realized he was capable of being aroused in the same manner he practiced on her. She was about to put her theory to the test when Jess suddenly grasped her waist and lifted her onto his loins where he slid into her with effortless ease. Then his skillful hands set fire to her flesh, flames that burned out of control even while she was drowning in a sea of ecstasy.

They loved again and yet again before exhaustion sent Ariel into a dark, dreamless slumber. The next thing she knew Rosalie was shaking her awake.

"Señorita, it's time to get up!"

"Go away!" She was tired, so tired.

"You wanted to go with the hands on roundup. Are you sick? Perhaps I should summon the doctor."

Rosalie's last sentence did the trick. "No, I'm not sick," Ariel insisted, "just tired. I'm up now."

With languid grace she sat up and stretched. The sheet fell away, baring the upper portion of her nude body to Rosalie. When Ariel realized Rosalie was staring at her curiously she flushed and explained, "It was hot last night."

"*Sí*, very hot," Rosalie said cryptically.

Ariel had no idea she how looked—her hair tousled, her lips slightly swollen, and her eyes still glazed with passion. Rosalie recognized the look. Her eyes settled on the mussed bed and she quickly added two and two and came up with the right answer. Besides, the room reeked of sex. She was not too old to remember how it had been with her and Buck. But wisely she decided not to pursue the matter. If Ariel wanted to confide in her she would. She only hoped Ariel knew what she was doing for she had grown very fond of the girl.

"Breakfast is ready," Rosalie said, looking anywhere but at Ariel's flushed body. "Come down when you're dressed." Then she left, closing the door softly behind her.

Ariel yawned, then stretched again. There wasn't a place she didn't ache. But it was a pleasant ache, one that made her realize she had been thoroughly and utterly loved. She washed quickly, dressed, and hurried downstairs where a substantial breakfast awaited her. Normally Ariel downed a hasty cup of coffee and a biscuit but this morning she sat down and devoured the entire plate of food Rosalie set before her.

"You have a good appetite this morning, señorita." Rosalie chuckled knowingly.

"I don't know how long I'll be out this morning," Ariel said sheepishly. "I may not return till dusk. I don't think I'll get hungry but if I do I'll eat with the hands." After finishing a second cup of coffee she hurried off before Rosalie had time for more of her infernal questions.

The hands were ready to ride when she arrived at the corral. Someone had already saddled her horse. Jess was standing by the fence waiting for her.

"Didn't you sleep well, boss lady?" he teased mercilessly. "You look tired."

"Damn you, Jess Wilder!" she hissed from between clenched teeth. Aloud, she said, "Well enough. Are we ready to ride?"

"Whenever you are." She nodded her head and he handed her up into the saddle, his hands lingering on her waist longer than was necessary. Their eyes met and so much heat passed between them Ariel had to look away. She slapped the reins against her mount and took off before every one of the hands could hear the pounding of her heart.

After a day spent in the saddle rounding up strays, Ariel returned at dusk more tired than she had ever been in her life. But it was a good kind of tired. They had accomplished much today. They had rounded up over a hundred strays and the next few days would be devoted to branding.

Two days later Kirk Walters returned from his "trip." He came for his sister just as they were sitting down to supper. Ariel invited him to share the meal and he graciously accepted.

"I'm sorry to have imposed on you so long," he said as he helped himself to a generous portion of roast beef. "You must be tired of Trudy by now. My business took longer than anticipated."

You don't know how tired I am of Trudy, Ariel thought but didn't say aloud. "I'm afraid I had little time to devote to Trudy. Ranch life keeps me busy."

"You work too hard," Kirk said smoothly. "You need a man to see to your affairs. I'd like to be that man. Have you thought any more about my proposal?"

"I doubt if Ariel thought about you at all while you were gone," Trudy remarked. Her snide remark drew a frown from Kirk.

"I hope Trudy is wrong but I can see that now is not the time to discuss this," he said. "I'll be around in a day or two; perhaps by then you will have come to a decision."

Ariel was happy to bid both Kirk and Trudy good-bye after supper was concluded. Fortunately Kirk stayed only long enough for Trudy to pack up her clothes. "I'll be around in the buckboard to pick up Trudy's luggage later," he said as Ariel walked outside with them. "I've missed you. Being away from you made me realize how much I really care for you." Ariel anticipated his kiss and turned her head, his lips falling harmlessly on her cheek. Scowling darkly, he hurried off after Trudy who waited for him by the horses.

They were well out of hearing when Kirk asked, "Did you accomplish anything in my absence? Is that cowboy still panting after Ariel or did you manage to distract him?"

"Jess Wilder is like no other man I've ever known," Trudy complained. "No matter what I did, it didn't seem to have any effect on him. I went so far as to offer myself to him but he turned gallant and refused. Yet I saw nothing to indicate

that he and Ariel are anything but boss and foreman."

"You little bitch, can't you do anything right!"
It was said in such a savage tone, Trudy flinched.
"I thought for sure you'd have Wilder eating out
of your hand by now."

Her face grew hot under his bitter outburst. "I
tried, Kirk, truly I did. I wanted the man! Really
wanted him. I would never have suspected him
of being hard to get but he resisted my every effort to seduce him. God, he's magnificent. Why
don't you seduce Ariel? I'll wait around to snare
Jess when he realizes that you've bedded Ariel."

Kirk mulled over everything Trudy said. "Are
you sure you noticed nothing going on between
them? It's hard to believe. The air seems to vi-
brate around them whenever they are together.
Why else would a man like that stick around if he
and Ariel weren't involved in one way or another?"

Trudy shrugged. "I only know what I saw. I
was with the man as much as his work allowed.
He had no time for Ariel."

"What about the nights?"

Trudy's eyes grew wide. "I never thought of
that."

"Well, I did and I don't trust the man, not one
damn bit. I want Jess Wilder out of Ariel's life. I
want Ariel and I want Leland Ranch. If I can't get
rid of Wilder one way I'll do it another."

Ariel glanced out the kitchen window and saw
a cowboy she didn't recognize talking to Jess. She
thought no more about it until they both walked
up to the house. Assuming they wanted to see
her she went outside to meet them.

"This is Slim Wicks, boss lady, he's looking for
a job," Jess said.

"Do we need another hand?" Ariel asked,
looking over the tall lanky cowboy. Though there

was little to differentiate him from any of the other cowboys working the ranch Ariel had a strange feeling about him.

"We could use him right now with branding and all. Winter's coming on and there's lots to do before snow flies."

"Where are you from, Wicks?" Ariel asked, still wary.

"San Antone, ma'am," Wicks said politely, doffing his hat as he spoke.

"Why did you leave?" Jess interjected.

Wicks slanted him a strange look. "The climate got a mite too hot to suit me. I'm workin' my way up to Fort Worth."

Since the code Texans lived by forbade personal questions, Jess relented. "Reckon that's a good enough reason. Used it once or twice myself."

Ariel wasn't satisfied. "Are you wanted by the law?"

"No, ma'am, never been in trouble with the law. You can check with the marshal's office in Waco if you don't believe me."

"I suggest we hire the man, boss lady. It's only temporary and that's fine with him. He doesn't want to hang around long in these parts anyway."

"All right, Jess, you're the foreman. Show him what to do."

She watched them walk away, wishing she knew why she felt so uneasy.

That night Jess came to her room again. It had been over a week since they had made love last and their hunger for one another was as ravenous as it was then. His kisses and caresses drove her wild, until she begged him to take her, to make her whole with his loving. Jess needed no encouragement as he slid into her full and deep and drove her to the brink of insanity.

"Love me, sweetheart, love me with fury."

Chapter 14

Kirk Walters came for his sister's baggage and again posed the question of marriage to Ariel.

"You've been a wonderful friend to me, Kirk, but I don't love you. I don't want to hurt your feelings but marriage is out of the question for us."

Kirk's eyes narrowed suspiciously. "Is there another man in your life?"

There was Jess. How could another man mean anything to her with Jess in her life? But she prudently refrained from speaking her mind. No matter how much they cared for one another she knew Jess would be leaving one day. Perhaps he would return—she prayed he would—and perhaps he wouldn't. Telling Kirk about Jess now would only complicate matters.

The deliberate lie did not come easy to her. "There is no other man in my life at this time."

"Is that your final answer? Will you at least consider my proposal?"

"I'm sorry, Kirk, I *have* considered it and my answer remains the same."

"I'm sorry, too, Ariel," Kirk said. His voice had a sharp edge that puzzled Ariel. "Our marriage would take some of the responsibilities of ranching off your shoulders, but you don't see it that way. Don't say I didn't try to warn you when you face a crisis and there are difficult decisions to make.''

''I truly appreciate your concern, Kirk, and I want us to remain friends. I just don't think marriage will work for us.''

''Well, then, I'd best be going. I'll come around in a few days to see how things are going with you. How is your new foreman working out?''

''Jess is a godsend,'' Ariel said, drawing a frown from Kirk. ''He's proven quite capable in every aspect of ranching. The men seem to like and respect him.''

''I'm glad things are going well,'' Kirk said dryly. ''Let me know if I can be of further help.''

Ariel stood in the yard for a few minutes, watching Kirk drive away. He was such a nice man and she hated to disappoint him, but she loved Jess too much to even think about marriage to another.

''What in the hell did he want?''

Speak of the devil. Jess had approached on silent feet, evidently watching while Ariel and Kirk conversed.

''He came after Trudy's things,'' Ariel informed him.

''His conversation was rather intense; did he bring up marriage again?''

''Yes,'' she admitted, ''but I told him I didn't love him.''

''The bastard won't give up.''

''Why do you dislike him, Jess? Kirk has been a good friend to me. If I needed him he'd be here in a minute.''

''I reckon he would,'' Jess said with a hint of derision. ''I don't trust the bastard. He wants something. He's much too friendly for a man deprived of a piece of land he's wanted for a long time.''

''How do you know that?''

''I've been talking to Rosalie. She says Walters

offered many times to buy this land from Buck. Water is a valuable asset and his land has limited access to water.''

''Rosalie talks too much and you're too suspicious,'' Ariel scoffed. ''I've already told Kirk I won't marry him so I see nothing more to discuss.''

''I reckon you're right, wildcat, but just the same I'll keep my eye on him when he comes around again. I got no right to be so damn jealous but I can't help it.''

''You have every right,'' Ariel said, her eyes shining. ''You gained that right when you made me yours.''

Jess flushed, her words reminding him that no matter how much he might want Ariel there were things that stood in the way of making her his forever. ''Ariel, you know I can't . . .''

''No, Jess, don't say it,'' Ariel interrupted, placing a finger on his lips. ''I know what you're going to say and I'd rather not hear it. You must realize I'll do all in my power to keep you from leaving when the time comes.''

Stricken with guilt and remorse, Jess hung his head. ''I wish to God Dillon would never return to Texas.''

His anguished plea held a ring of sincerity Ariel couldn't deny, but it didn't change a thing.

A few days later Ariel got her first taste of some of the problems and dangers associated with ranching. She was out in the north range with the hands when the herd they had been gathering together to drive to market stampeded for no apparent reason. Ariel and Dewey were the only two standing on the ground when it happened; the others were still mounted, engaged in other duties. Their two horses were loosely tethered to a bush nearby. One minute they were contentedly munching grass and the next they were rearing, pulling free, and galloping off, their reins dragging on the ground. Both Ariel and Dewey made a mad dash for the trailing reins but were too late. A moment later they saw what had spooked the horses.

Coming at them full speed, their hooves thundering, sending clods of dirt flying, were two hundred head of cattle that had been rounded up to drive to Waco in order to be sold. Ariel froze when she saw them coming and realized that she and Dewey had no place to go to escape. They couldn't outrun them on foot, there were no sturdy trees in the area and no large rocks to hide behind.

"Run, boss, run!" Dewey hollered over the din of pounding hooves.

When Ariel made no effort to move Dewey grabbed her hand and pulled her along. But it soon became evident that they wouldn't be able to outdistance the spooked herd. In desperation Ariel looked around to see if Jess or any of the cowboys had seen her and Dewey. They had, but were still too far away to be of help. Some had ridden ahead to head off the herd while others rode off to the side to keep them from scattering. She had nearly resigned herself to being trampled to death along with Dewey when from the corner of her eye she saw two riders racing toward them hell-bent for leather. She wasn't sure they would make it in time but prayed harder than she ever had in her life. Loyal to the end, Dewey positioned himself in front of her in order to take the brunt of the attack.

Jess heard the stampede before he saw it. He was some distance away rescuing a stray that had gotten itself caught in a briar patch. When he looked up he saw the herd thundering across the open range toward a narrow ravine. If they hit the ravine at that speed they would all be killed. Leaping on Soldier's back, he spurred him mercilessly, hoping to stop the herd before the damage could be done. Then he saw Ariel, standing directly in the path of the rampaging cattle. Dewey was with her, shielding her with his body as if expecting his meager efforts to save her.

Jess' heart was pounding; never had he been so frightened for another human being. He had seen stampedes before, knew exactly what those sharp hooves could do to human flesh. With unaccustomed cruelty he lashed the reins across Soldier's lathered withers, urging him into even greater speed. With gallant effort the stallion responded, stretching his legs to literally fly over the ground.

Little by little Jess gained on the herd until he was nearly even with them. From the corner of his eye he saw that one of the hands was close on his heels, obviously someone closer than he had been to the herd when they stampeded. Now Jess was ahead of the herd and nearly to the place where Ariel and Dewey stood rooted to the ground awaiting the vicious onslaught. Then he reached her, only seconds before the herd would have trampled her to death.

"Hang on!" Jess yelled in her ear as he leaned low over Soldier and swooped her off her feet.

Then he was lifting her into the saddle before him as cows thundered past, thudding against the sturdy mount from all sides. But Soldier held steadfast, experienced enough to hold his own against the rampaging herd. Ariel felt the cows brush against her legs, knowing she'd be full of bruises tomorrow but happy to be alive. If not for Jess she'd be lying beneath hundreds of hooves, pounded into pulp. Then the herd was gone, thundering off in the distance. But miraculously the hands had managed to slow them and before Ariel knew it, it was all over.

"Are you all right?" Jess asked shakily. He had

come so close to losing her he couldn't bear to think about it.

"Yes, thanks to you." Suddenly she remembered Dewey. "What happened to Dewey?"

They both turned around at the same time. Three men were bending over someone lying on the ground.

"Oh, God," Ariel sobbed, "he's hurt, or maybe even dead."

Jess turned Soldier to where the hands were gathered. He slid to the ground; Ariel followed. She heaved a sigh of gratitude when she saw that Dewey's eyes were open, though he was obviously in a great deal of pain. Jess made a quick examination, then announced, "He's lucky, only a few broken ribs. The doc will tape him up and he'll be good as new in no time."

"Thank God," Ariel said fervently.

"I tried to reach him in time," Bud interjected, "but at least I managed to keep the herd from tramplin' him to death."

"You saved my life." Dewey grimaced. Just speaking was painful. "If it weren't for you dancin' yer horse 'round me I for sure woulda been dead."

"Bud, you and Wicks help him back to the bunkhouse and get the doc out here. The rest of you men keep a close eye on the herd, we don't want anything else spooking them today."

Dewey groaned as Bud and Wicks lifted him onto Bud's horse. Then Bud mounted behind him in order to hold him in the saddle. They rode off at a slow pace, Wicks trailing behind them.

"What do you think spooked the herd, Jess?" one of the hands asked.

"Damned if I know," Jess replied, more than a little puzzled himself. "One minute they were as calm as could be and the next they were racing toward the ravine. I'll come back and nose around some as soon as I take the boss lady home. Looks mighty suspicious to me. We'll be days rounding up all the strays."

"Find my horse and I can get home on my own," Ariel said shakily. Despite her words to the contrary, she was still upset from the experience and seriously doubted her ability to function on her own.

"No way, sweetheart," he said for her ears alone. "I mean to see you get home safely—and have you stay there," he added pointedly.

"Do you really think someone deliberately stampeded the herd?" Ariel asked after they rode off.

"It's possible." His answer told her nothing.

"Dammit, Jess, this is my business too. Tell me if you suspect someone."

"I can't say yet, Ariel. I have no reason to suspect anyone of deliberately stampeding the herd. It's just a feeling I have. Believe me, you'll be the first to know if I discover that someone is out to sabotage you."

"I hope you're wrong."

"I do too. I thought I'd die when I saw how close you came to being trampled out there. What if Soldier hadn't been fast enough to save you?" He shuddered, the thought too horrible to contemplate. "I don't want anything like that to happen again. I want you to stick close to the house for the next few days. At least until I get to the bottom of this."

Ariel bristled. "I can't promise you that! This is my ranch; I need to know what's going on at all times."

"That kind of thinking will get you killed," Jess said sourly. "Just this once listen to me, wildcat."

"I—I'll think about it."

She did, for all of one day. When Jess told her he could find no evidence of foul play with regard to the stampede, she started helping the hands again with whatever duties she was able to perform. What she didn't realize was that whenever she left the house either Jess or one of the hands made a point of being close at hand should she need them.

During this time Pike's broken bones began to heal and he was able to hobble around with the help of a crutch. Ariel refused to think about what Jess would do once Pike was able to resume his duties. She knew he was only biding his time until definite word of Dillon reached him. Meanwhile she welcomed him to her bed whenever his heavy workload eased up a bit and he was able to visit her at night. In her heart she knew Jess loved her, and though a commitment might not be possible at this time his actions proved that he wanted no other woman but her.

Nearly a week passed after the stampede before Jess found the opportunity to visit Ariel late one night. She was already asleep when he quietly entered her room, though she had left the lamp burning low in case he showed up. Since that first time Jess had found his way to her room she nearly always left the back door unlatched to provide him with easy entry. Tonight was no different.

Reluctant to disturb her, Jess stood beside Ariel, staring down at her with a look of such love and longing on his face that Ariel would have been stunned to learn the true depth of his emotion. She was so beautiful, he thought wistfully, with her black hair spread around her like a silken cloud. She looked so peaceful that he nearly turned and left. But something prevented him. Something so powerful, so compelling, he felt that if he left the room it would utterly destroy him. He quickly stripped and slid into bed beside her.

Ariel didn't awaken right away. She merely sighed and settled herself more comfortably into

the curve of his body. He kissed the nape of her
neck, her shoulder, his hands moving along her
spine to her buttocks where they lingered to caress and fondle the taut mounds. Her breasts
drew his hands next. Even in sleep her nipples
grew erect as his fingers pulled and stroked at the
tender buds. Ariel stirred, murmured something
unintelligible, and panted softly as Jess continued
his slow arousal. She awoke just as Jess pressed
into her from behind. Being awakened like this
felt so delicious she purred and arched her back
like a satisfied cat.

"I'm glad you finally woke up," he teased. "I'd
hate for you to miss this."

"I'd like to wake up like this every morning of
my life," Ariel returned dreamily.

"Am I hurting you?"

"I love it. Any way you want to love me is fine
with me, just don't stop loving me."

"As if I could," Jess scoffed. "Lift your leg,
sweetheart."

She complied instantly and felt herself stretch
as he filled her with more of himself. With slow,
measured strokes he began to move, sliding full
and deep then withdrawing, leaving her hovering
on the edge until he filled her again. He kissed
her nape, her shoulder, her back, wherever he
could reach while his hands stroked and kneaded
her breasts; all the while he thrust into her from
behind.

Ariel felt herself floating, spinning out of control, yearning for release but wishing for it never
to end. But like all good things, it did end.

"That's it, sweetheart, don't hold back. God, I
love to hear you when you find that special place.
Did you know I can feel you quiver inside?"

His words drove her that final inch and she
exploded in a million pieces. When she came
down to earth Jess was still hard and throbbing
inside her. Puzzled, she turned to peer over her

shoulder at him. He grinned back at her. With a
deft movement, Jess slid her beneath him, still
embedded deep inside her. His control was
amazing, Ariel thought as he renewed his efforts
to bring her to another climax before seeking his
own. It was the last coherent thought she had
for a long time. When Jess finally sought his own
release it was with the knowledge that no one
could satisfy Ariel like he could. Ariel never
doubted it.

They had fallen asleep in each other's arms
when the first sign of disaster reared its ugly head.
It was late, very late. And black as pitch outside.
Jess had no idea what awakened him but something did. He stirred uneasily, trying to force
himself back to sleep for another hour or two before it was time to leave Ariel. A prickly sensation
crawling over his flesh was the first inkling he
had that something was wrong, terribly wrong.
Suddenly the room was filled with light. Not the
light of day or lamplight, but something eerie and
mysterious. The light flickered ominously against
the windowpane and suddenly Jess realized what
it was. Fire!

He moved so fast that Ariel sat up, bewildered.
"What is it, Jess?"

"Fire, sweetheart."

He struggled into his pants and shirt and carried his boots out the door with him. He was
putting them on when he met Rosalie coming up
the stairs to awaken Ariel. She carried a lamp in
her hands and stopped abruptly when she saw
Jess.

"The stable is on fire, señor."

She said no more but stood silently aside while
he raced past her, more than a little concerned
by the censuring glance she aimed at him as he
fled by. He hadn't meant for it to happen this
way. Ariel meant too much to him to have her
reputation damaged by his carelessness. Rosalie

was the last person in the world he wanted angry at him. But he had too much on his mind right now to consider the repercussions of Rosalie's discovery.

The fire had gotten a good start, for the stable was already engulfed in flames. Jess could hear the animals inside screeching and fighting to escape. By now one or two of the men were staggering out of the bunkhouse and Jess yelled out orders to awaken the others and start a bucket brigade. Meanwhile Ariel had dressed and was now at his side. She had rushed out of her room even before Rosalie reached the top of the stairs and so had no idea that the housekeeper had seen Jess leave her room.

"What can I do?"

"Stay out of the way," Jess shot back. "I don't wanna have to worry about you." He took off his shirt and wet it in the horse trough.

"What are you going to do?"

"I'm going in after Soldier and any of the other animals I can save."

"You can't go in there now—the roof will cave in at any minute."

He sent her a withering glance. "I'm going in." Wrapping his wet shirt over his head and shoulders he dashed inside the blazing stable. Ariel screamed for him to stop but her words were lost to the roaring inferno.

By now the hands had all emerged from the bunkhouse, even recovering invalids Pike and Dewey, and had formed a bucket brigade, but it all seemed so useless. Ariel's eyes never wavered from the spot where Jess had entered the stable and her lips moved in silent prayer. Suddenly he emerged, coughing and sputtering, leading two of the more valuable horses by the reins. Neither of them was Soldier. Then, before Ariel realized what he meant to do, he turned

around and disappeared into the flames and
smoke once again.

"No-o-o!"

She started after him but found Bud's arms
wrapped tightly around her. "You can't go in
there, boss." Rosalie came up beside her and Bud
released her into Rosalie's keeping. "Don't let go
of her," he warned.

"Let me go, I have to go to Jess!"

"No, señorita, it's too dangerous. Señor Jess
can take care of himself."

"You don't understand," Ariel sobbed, by now
too distraught to realize what she was saying. "I
love him."

"I know, I know," Rosalie clucked soothingly.
"Do you think he would want you to risk your
life for him?"

"I don't care what he wants, I'm going in anyway. He's been in there too long, I know something dreadful has happened."

With a spurt of strength she didn't know she
possessed, Ariel pulled from Rosalie's grasp and
dashed toward the stable. She had just entered
the smoke-filled inferno when she saw Jess coming toward her leading Soldier and another wildly
protesting stallion. Flames licked all around him,
his boots smoked and his hair was singed. He
staggered slightly and he was gasping for breath.
Ariel started forward to help him when he saw
her. His eyes grew wide with horror and he motioned her back. Ariel ignored him. The smoke
grew worse now, more dense as the fire spread
with amazing speed. Ariel began coughing now
herself; her eyes watered and her flesh felt as if it
was peeling from her bones.

Suddenly she heard a terrible noise. A beam
from the ceiling crashed to the ground, burst into
flames, and blocked her path. "Jess!" She could
no longer see him.

Just then Soldier and the other horse Jess was

leading burst past her and out the door to safety. Ariel didn't follow them. With grim determination she continued forward, each step more difficult than the last, each breath an agony. Then she saw him, lying on the ground, his foot pinned beneath the fallen beam. He was struggling to free himself.

"Dammit, Ariel, get outta here," he gasped when he saw her bending over him. "Do you want us both to die?"

"I don't want either of us to die, Jess," she choked out, wiping tears from her eyes. "Can you get your foot out of the boot?"

"What in the hell do you think I'm trying to do?"

"Let me help." She grasped his ankle and pulled. It didn't budge an inch.

The beam was burning a path toward Jess' leg, flames spewed out all around them, and it was obvious that neither of them were going to be able to escape alive if something wasn't done within minutes.

"Ariel, it's no use. Leave me, sweetheart, save yourself. You've got too much to live for."

"I'm not going," Ariel said stubbornly. "Let's try again."

Suddenly the hem of her skirt caught fire and Jess beat it out with his hands. "What in the hell will it take to get you to leave? Jesus H. Christ, wildcat, I love you. Did you hear? *I love you!* I don't want to see you die."

"Miss Leland! Jess! Where are you?"

"It's Bud! Did you hear that, Jess? Over here, Bud. Hurry, Jess is in trouble!"

"What's the use," Jess muttered beneath his breath. "It'll take more than one man to lift this beam."

As if in answer to a prayer, Bud and three other men all emerged through the thick fog of smoke and flames. They had retrieved blankets from the bunkhouse, wet them down, and entered the burning stable at the risk of their lives. Bud sized up the situation immediately and set to work.

"Get Ariel out of here before you do anything," Jess ordered curtly.

Before she could voice a protest a wet blanket was thrown over her head. Then she was lifted off her feet and carried bodily out of the flaming stable. The moment her feet touched the ground she tore off the blanket and trained her eyes on the stable as she waited for Jess and the others to emerge. Long agonizing minutes dragged by before she saw them. They nearly didn't make it. Behind them the entire stable crumbled inward and collapsed. Jess and the three men were mere steps ahead of it. All of them were gasping for breath, all had singed eyebrows and hair and one had burns on both hands. That they had survived was a miracle.

Rosalie examined the extent of the men's injuries and bustled into action. She had already anticipated injuries and had assembled soothing salves and lotions with which to treat the burns.

Of all the men Jess looked the worse. Not only were his hair and eyebrows singed but the hair on his hands and arms was also seared. His clothing and boots smoldered and there was a large burn on his shoulder as well as on both his hands where he'd tried to pry the beam off his foot. His breath was labored and his eyes were raw and watering.

Ariel wasn't nearly in as bad a shape but she too had suffered from smoke and flames. Her eyebrows had escaped the flames but the ends of her long hair were singed. The hem of her skirt had burnt clear up to her knees and the soles of her boots had burnt completely through. In addition, her right palm bore a severe burn she hadn't even been aware of. Rosalie clucked sympathetically as she treated the burns to the best of her ability.

As for the stable, it would have to be rebuilt from the ground up. Nothing remained but burning embers. Only four horses including Soldier had been saved. All the animals in the stable had been valuable stock and would be expensive to replace. Everything had been happening too fast lately. First Pike, then the stampede and Dewey's injury, now this. What next? Ariel asked herself glumly. Is this what Kirk meant when he said ranching was a dangerous business? She deeply regretted the injuries and loss of animals but she wasn't going to let a spell of bad luck change her mind about ranching.

All the men had returned to the bunkhouse now except for Jess, who still sat on the ground nursing a bruised ankle. Fortunately it hadn't been broken when the beam fell across it. He looked up at Ariel, his expression stormy.

"You sure as hell are one stubborn female. Why didn't you listen to me when I told you to leave? You could have been killed."

"Don't harp at me, Jess, you know I wouldn't leave you to die. Did you really mean it?"

"Mean what?"

"You said you loved me."

For a moment he looked stunned. "I said that?" Gravely she nodded her head. "Well, I'll be damned. They say dying men never lie." His mouth turned up in a grin that ended in a grimace when his tender skin stretched too far.

"I love you too, you obstinate fool."

"Ariel, forget that for a moment, there's something else we need to talk about."

"Nothing is more important than that."

"This is. I think someone is deliberately trying to run you off the ranch. They're deliberately causing mischief so you'll sell out and leave. Or else they're trying to kill you outright."

Ariel sputtered in disbelief. "Who would want to do that? And for what reason?"

"Don't know, but I sure as hell aim to find out."

Chapter 15

It took several days to round up strays after the stampede, during which Jess had little time to devote to finding the culprit responsible for setting fire to the stable. There was no doubt in his mind that it had been deliberate, for there had been no storm that night or lightning to ignite the blaze. Furthermore, Wicks had sworn no lantern had been left lit in the building. It was a mystery but one Jess intended to solve.

The day after the fire Kirk Walters appeared, expressing his concern and his relief that no one had been hurt. He stood before the rubble of the burnt structure shaking his head sadly. He said, "All those valuable animals. But it could have been worse. Human lives could have been lost. I heard your foreman went in after his horse and very nearly didn't make it out."

"Jess could have been killed," Ariel acknowledged, "if some of the hands hadn't risked their lives to save him."

"How fortunate for him," Kirk said dryly. "Now do you understand what I meant when I said ranching is dangerous business for a woman? Are you ready to give it up yet and let someone else shoulder the burden?"

"No!" Ariel said. The stubborn tilt to her chin warned Kirk that his words were only making Ariel more determined than ever to succeed. He decided to let the matter drop.

"I'd be happy to lend you men to help rebuild the stable," he offered magnanimously. "I imagine most of your hands are busy preparing for winter."

"The boss lady decided not to rebuild till spring." While Kirk and Ariel conversed, Jess had ridden in from the range, saw them talking, and was determined not to leave Ariel alone with the man.

Kirk's expression grew stony when Jess rode up and interrupted their private conversation. "Is that true, Ariel?" he asked, deliberately disdaining Jess' authority.

"We had talked about rebuilding and then decided to wait until spring."

"By 'we' I take it you mean Wilder and yourself."

"I trust Jess' judgment," Ariel said with a hint of censure.

"How is Pike doing? Is he ready to resume his duties yet?"

"Pike is up and around and doing right well," Jess interjected. "Anything else you want to know, Walters?"

"Jess, Kirk is concerned over what happens here," Ariel said quickly. The last thing she wanted was for Jess and Kirk to be at each other's throats.

Jess snorted derisively. He wouldn't put it past Walters to be behind all the misfortunes Ariel had had to deal with recently. But he had no proof, nothing to link Walters with any of the "accidents" that had happened lately. Walters didn't strike him as a man who would give up easily once he set his mind on something.

"Your foreman doesn't like me, Ariel. But I can assure you both that I have Ariel's best interests at heart. I'm willing to help in any way I can."

"I'll bet you'll even buy her land if she decides to sell," Jess remarked dryly.

Kirk shifted uncomfortably. "Perhaps I'd better leave, Ariel. Will you have supper with me and Trudy on Sunday? I haven't repaid you for keeping Trudy in my absence."

Ariel wanted to refuse but didn't have the heart. "Of course. What time?"

Kirk smiled at Jess smugly. "I'll come for you around noon. You can spend the afternoon. I'd like to show you my spread."

There were no words to describe the noise Jess made in his throat.

Kirt left shortly afterward. The moment he left Jess flew into a rage.

"Are you loco? I don't want you going anywhere with that man. I told you I don't trust him."

Ariel bristled indignantly. "Kirk is my friend. Besides, you have no right to tell me who I can or can't see."

"Dammit, wildcat, can't you see through that man? He wants you. He wants your land. He'll do anything to get what he wants."

"You're just being jealous and spiteful," Ariel accused. Secretly she was pleased that Jess was so jealous of Kirk; it made her feel more secure in his affections. But she wasn't doing it deliberately to annoy Jess. She truly liked Kirk and he was such a nice helpful man that she hated to hurt him by refusing. She had already refused his proposal; the least she could do was have supper with him and Trudy. Jess would just have to get over his petty grievances and learn to get along with Kirk.

Jess decided to set a trap for the culprit responsible for all the mischief and senseless injuries that had beset the ranch during the past few weeks. He told Ariel of his plan and took only Bud,

Dewey, and Pike into his confidence, men who Rosalie told him had been in Buck Leland's employ for many years and were trustworthy. Nothing had happened for a week after the fire but Jess was taking no chances. His greatest fear was that something would happen to Ariel, so he set a nightly guard around the house, alternating between the three men and himself. It meant he wouldn't be able to be with Ariel for a while but her life was more important than his selfish pleasure.

A week passed without mishap and Jess hoped it meant the end of their problems, but he kept the night guards posted nevertheless.

On Sunday Kirk arrived promptly in the buckboard to pick up Ariel. Despite Jess' stormy looks and Rosalie's grumbling, she waved merrily and drove off with Kirk without a fear in the world. Jess didn't like it one damn bit.

It was cold; the wind held a definite hint of winter and Ariel pulled her collar up around her neck. Jess had looked so miserable she wished now she had refused Kirk's invitation. Besides, she didn't exactly relish spending the day with Trudy.

The drive to the Walters ranch took a half hour, spent in friendly conversation with Kirk. When they arrived Ariel was surprised and more than a little uncomfortable to learn that Trudy was not there.

"Trudy is spending the day with friends," Kirk said smoothly. "Besides, I know you two don't care for one another. The visit will be more pleasant for you without her here making snide remarks."

Ariel said nothing, wishing she had listened to Jess and Rosalie. Not that Kirk had done or said anything to give her cause for alarm. But she couldn't suppress the frisson of apprehension that worked its way up her spine. When she saw

Kirk's housekeeper setting the table she felt somewhat easier, but not entirely. Hoping to disarm her, Kirk invited Ariel for a tour of his ranch. Ariel eagerly accepted. They spent an enjoyable two hours riding around the sprawling ranch before returning, ravenous and chilled to the bone.

Ariel studied the parlor. It was larger than hers, and the furnishings more ornate and numerous. There was nothing rustic about Kirk Walters or his home. Though the house was lovely Ariel preferred her own snug home.

"Do you like it?" Kirk asked, watching her closely.

"It's very nice," Ariel remarked casually.

"It could be yours. All you have to do is say yes."

Ariel flushed. "I'm not ready for marriage."

"Supper is ready, señor."

The housekeeper stood timidly in the doorway.

"Thank you, Rita. Shall we go into the dining room?" Kirk invited Ariel. She rose and allowed him to take her arm and then seat her at the table.

The food was delicious, the conversation lively, and Ariel began to relax. She felt foolish for thinking that Trudy's absence meant Kirk had some devious plan in mind. She began to enjoy herself.

Jess was restless. He decided to ride into town while Ariel was with Kirk and inquire of the marshal if he'd received any word of Dillon. Pike was nearly completely recovered now and Jess didn't feel right usurping the young man's position as foreman. Leaving Ariel was the last thing he wanted to do, but when the time came he would do what he must. He loved Ariel and hoped she understood why he had to do what he had to do. He wouldn't leave, though, until he had put a stop to the accidents plaguing her. Dillon would keep until he made certain nothing bad happened to the woman he loved.

Jess' first stop in town was the marshal's office, where he learned that Dillon hadn't been seen in Texas in weeks. So much for that, now what? he thought, wandering aimlessly down the street. He was upset over Ariel's refusal to take his warning about Walters to heart; he was worried about her. Yet he knew that if he'd trailed her to Walters' ranch Ariel would have been livid. Damn obstinate woman, he thought, heading toward the saloon. What he needed were a couple of good belts of whiskey to ease his mind. Suddenly he halted in his tracks, his brain refusing to believe what he saw. Trudy Walters was tripping down the street toward him in the company of another woman. Trudy saw him and hurried her steps.

"Why, Jess Wilder, how nice to see you," she gushed, batting her long lashes. "I'm annoyed that you haven't been out to the ranch once to visit me. Is Ariel such a slave driver that you can't get away?"

"What in tarnation are you doing here, Trudy?" Jess growled. His voice was so fierce that Trudy stepped back in alarm.

"Whatever is wrong, Jess?" she asked innocently.

"You know damn well what I'm talking about. You're supposed to be home right now having supper with Ariel."

"Whoever gave you that idea?"

"Your brother," Jess ground out tightly. "He has Ariel alone at your ranch right now."

Trudy stated, "They're both old enough to know what they're doing."

"Kirk knows what he's doing but Ariel has no idea what she's getting into."

"Forget Ariel, Jess. I'd like you to meet my friend, Mary Ann Ames. Perhaps you'll join us for a stroll around town."

Jess acknowledged the introduction with a curt nod. "Sorry, Trudy, there's something urgent I

gotta do." Then he was gone, leaving Trudy and
her friend standing with their mouths agape.

Ariel enjoyed the meal and Kirk's company but
decided it was time to go home. Since Kirk had
spoken to the housekeeper in Spanish after their
meal was served she'd seen neither hide nor hair
of the woman and that same uneasy feeling she'd
had earlier made her anxious to leave. Kirk had
other ideas.

"It's still early, Ariel," he replied when Ariel
suggested he take her home. "I hoped to spend
some time convincing you to marry me."

"As pleasant as it has been, Kirk, I really should
be going. Rosalie will be worried."

"Just Rosalie?" Kirk hinted with sly innuendo.
"Are you sure you aren't worrying about what
Jess Wilder will think if you're alone in my com-
pany too long?"

"You don't know what you're talking about,"
Ariel said, growing angry.

"Don't I? I'm neither blind nor stupid. I see the
way he looks at you. You're lovers, aren't you?"

Ariel rose to her feet. "Take me home, Kirk. I
don't like your insinuations or your tone of
voice."

Kirk grabbed her arm and pulled her back down
beside him on the sofa. "And I don't like the way
you've been treating me. How could you prefer
that rough cowboy to me? Maybe you like your
men tough. Maybe you like to be slapped around
and roughed up. Is that it, Ariel? Are you a hot
little bitch who wants her loving administered
with a heavy hand? Had you agreed to marry me
I would have been good to you," he lied. "You
could have had anything you wanted. Yet you
continually thwart my every effort to win you. If
you want rough, I'll show you what rough is.
When I'm done you'll be begging me to marry
you."

Ariel was stunned, and more than a little frightened. She'd never seen Kirk like this. Never realized he harbored such vile thoughts inside him. She should have listened to Jess, she realized, growing frantic when Kirk's hold tightened on her arm.

"Kirk, you're hurting me."

"And you like it, don't you?"

"If you don't let me go I'll scream!"

Kirk laughed. "No one will come. I sent Rita home hours ago. I'm going to bed you, you little bitch, right here on the floor. I can be as much an animal as Jess Wilder."

"How can you turn on me like this? What happened to you? I thought you were my friend!" Nothing she said seemed to get through to him. Did he think she'd like him any better if he raped her?

"I never wanted to be your friend. All I wanted was your ranch. I would have married you to get it but you were stubborn. After a while I wanted you merely because I couldn't have you. Tonight I'll satisfy one craving. Tomorrow when we get married I'll satisfy the other."

"I'll never marry you! Not tomorrow or ever," Ariel cried, struggling now in earnest. "Raping me won't change my mind."

"I think it will. I'm a good lover. Once you find that out for yourself you'll forget that penniless cowboy. Together we can have the biggest spread in Texas. Now be a good girl and hold still."

He began tearing at her clothes like a man possessed, cursing when her nails dug a furrow down his cheek. He slapped her hard and grabbed a handful of her hair, pulling her down so he could reach her lips. His kiss was hurtful. Nothing about the man reminded her of the gentle friend she'd once considered him to be. His tongue stabbed repeatedly against her lips, finally forcing them apart so he could ravage the inside of her mouth. He moaned, so aroused by his use of force that

he scooped her up and fell with her to the floor.
The breath was driven from Ariel's lungs as Kirk
fell heavily atop her. Through the layers of their
clothing she could feel his manhood swell and
strain against her.

Sobbing in frustration, Ariel felt her dress slide
up around her waist and Kirk's hands touch her
flesh. She shuddered; his touch made her skin
crawl. Only Jess had the right to touch her like
that. Only Jess . . . Jess . . . Oh, God, where was
Jess when she needed him? Why hadn't she
heeded his warning? Was the price of her stubbornness to be rape?

"I want to hear you scream, Ariel," Kirk
gasped, lost in the throes of lust. "Scream with
joy, scream because I satisfy you so well."

"You're crazy," Ariel sobbed, in an effort to
diffuse his savage attack.

"Damn right. I was crazy to think you wanted
gentleness when this is what you wanted all
along."

"Jess will kill you!"

"I think not. Once you're my wife there's nothing he can do about it."

"Ariel will never be your wife!"

Suddenly the oppressive weight was lifted from
her and Ariel sobbed in relief, her chest heaving
from the futile effort of her struggles. Ariel had
identified her rescuer immediately. Jess' commanding voice was as familiar to her as her own.
The bond between them was so strong he seemed
to know exactly when she needed him and appeared when all seemed to be lost.

Kirk flew over Ariel's head. Though only
slightly shorter and weighing nearly as much as
Jess, Jess had flung him aside as if he were a
featherweight. Jess was so enraged he wanted to
kill the man on the spot. And would have if he
hadn't seen the condition Ariel was in and paused
to cover her legs and help her to her feet.

"Did the bastard hurt you, sweetheart?"

Ariel wagged her head from side to side in furious denial, too shaken to speak.

"It's my fault for letting you come here by yourself. I knew Walters was up to no good but you seemed so confident the man was your friend that I ignored my inner warnings."

He glanced to where Kirk lay still sprawled on the floor, his pants down around his knees. Jess snorted in disgust at the sight of Kirk's flaccid manhood now lying limp between his legs, shriveled to a harmless piece of flesh.

"Get up, Walters, I never kill a man without giving him a chance to defend himself."

Kirk struggled to his feet, pulling up his pants on the way. He was scared, really scared. Never had he seen a man as fierce as Jess Wilder. There was something about him that was dangerous and deadly, something that made him want to turn and flee. Sweat beaded his forehead yet his lips were so dry his tongue flicked out to moisten them.

"I don't have a gun, Wilder. Look," he pleaded, "we're both men, you know how things can get out of hand. I'll make it worth your while if you forget this. No harm was done."

"You filthy scum!" Jess growled. "You can't buy me. What did you hope to gain by forcing Ariel? Not her love. I'm gonna kill you whether you arm yourself or not so I suggest you find a gun pronto."

When Kirk failed to move, Ariel found her tongue. "Jess, no, he's not worth the bullet. Take me home. Please. I don't want bloodshed."

Jess was all for killing Kirk; it wouldn't bother him in the least to blow him away for what he tried to do to Ariel. But Ariel sounded so utterly distraught that he relented. If Kirk's unprovoked attack proved anything it showed Ariel exactly the kind of man he was.

"If you ever show your face on Leland land again I won't be so lenient," Jess promised.

"And if Jess doesn't shoot you I will," Ariel added for good measure.

Jess took Ariel before him on Soldier, his hands gentle as they came around her. "Are you sure he didn't—hurt you, sweetheart?"

"He didn't rape me, Jess, you arrived in time. I don't know what brought you here but I'm grateful."

"You can thank Trudy." Jess grinned, fully aware of how that statement would shock Ariel.

"Trudy! What has she to do with all this? I would assume she was in on her brother's little game."

"I don't know how much Trudy knew of Walters' plans for you, but when I saw her in town I knew you were alone with him. I hightailed it out there as soon as I could. I'm not usually a praying man but I recited every prayer I could think of on my way. If I hadn't arrived in time I would have never forgiven myself."

"It was all my fault, Jess, for not listening to your warning about Kirk. Even Rosalie tried to tell me what he was like but I refused to heed either of you. I was completely taken in my him. I'm sorry for doubting your judgment."

Jess stayed with Ariel that night, making such tender love to her it brought tears to her eyes. When he finished she couldn't even recall a man named Kirk Walters or the vile act he'd tried to force on her. All she remembered was Jess loving her, filling her with himself, driving away everything but the love they shared and the wonderful way he had of demonstrating that love.

Jess was so convinced that Kirk Walters had been responsible for the stable fire and various accidents at Leland Ranch that he called off the nightly guard. He felt certain they had seen and heard the last from Kirk Walters. The man was a coward, and once his devious tricks were brought out in the open he wasn't likely to continue them. What Jess failed to realize was that Kirk Walters was more determined than most men.

November arrived, bringing the first heavy frost of the season. The hands had cut wood in their spare time and stacked it up in the woodshed. Three of the hands had already moved to town where they would spend the winter. Among those who remained were Pike, Bud, Dewey, and Wicks. Pike was now able to ride and Jess relinquished his job as foreman. Pike seemed relieved; he'd assumed Jess meant to keep the job. Ariel was thrilled when Jess made no effort to leave once Pike resumed his duties as foreman. It was her belief he remained because he didn't want to leave her.

Her assumption was only partly correct. It was true the thought of leaving Ariel was painful for Jess, but what kept him from going was his fear that the accidents would resume once he left. The hands that remained had been told to shoot on sight should Walters step foot anywhere on Leland property, but Jess worried that the precaution wasn't enough without him around to enforce it.

When Jess went to town in the middle of November he learned that Bart Dillon had robbed a bank in San Antone. Judd's killer was back in Texas and Jess' heart was torn. No matter how much he loved Ariel the fact remained that he had sworn to hunt down and punish Judd's killer. He couldn't do that sitting on his duff all comfy and cozy at Leland Ranch. Why couldn't life be simple? he silently implored. If not for Dillon he'd be happy spending the rest of his life with Ariel on Leland Ranch. He'd liked being marshal but ranching had its rewards too.

"Damn," he cursed beneath his breath. He had

gone to bed that night at the normal time but sleep wouldn't come. He needed to talk to Ariel. He wanted to tell her he loved her, wanted her to understand why he had to leave—and it couldn't wait. Rising quietly so as not to awaken the other men, Jess slipped into his pants, grabbed his boots, and tiptoed out the door. A blast of cold air hit him in the face and he shivered. He hadn't thought to bring a coat.

It was pitch-black outside; not even a sliver of moon lit the overcast sky. But Jess had traveled this route so many times in the past weeks he needed no light to guide his way. As he neared the rear of the house a noise brought him instantly alert. He reached for his gun and realized he had left it behind, finding no need for it in Ariel's bedroom. He moved around to the back door, knowing he would find it unlatched and cursing himself for being so stupid as to allow it. It had never occurred to him that someone might try to harm Ariel in her own house. He found the door standing ajar and raw panic danced down his spine.

He nearly stumbled over Rosalie's prone form, and stopped to feel for a pulse. He was relieved to find it beating strong and steady. Then he stepped over her body and continued toward the stairs. On his way he detoured to the parlor to retrieve the loaded rifle propped against the fireplace that Ariel always kept handy in case of emergency. A stair creaked beneath his foot and Jess froze. When no response was forthcoming he moved stealthily upward. On the landing he saw a light coming through the partially opened door to Ariel's room and realized she must have been expecting him. That would account for her not crying out in alarm when someone entered her room. Peering around the door, Jess saw the man now. He was standing in partial shadow. He held a knife in his hand, too clever to use a gun and rouse the hands.

Ariel must have been exhausted for she lay on her back, sleeping soundly. In another minute her life would have been taken from her without her ever knowing danger existed. The man raised his arm, the knife poised downward, and Jess didn't think twice before pulling the trigger. His aim was true: the man was dead before he hit the floor. Jess grunted in satisfaction, certain it was Kirk Walters.

The shot sounded like thunder magnified a hundred times. Ariel awoke in panic to find herself splattered with blood. At first she thought it was her own until she saw Jess standing across the room, a smoking rifle held loosely in his hand.

"Jess! What happened? I don't understand." Ariel was confused and disoriented.

"The bastard tried to kill you," Jess told her.

"Who? Who tried to kill me? My God, his blood is all over me!"

"I don't know, sweetheart, let's have a look." He knelt and turned the man over. "Jesus H. Christ, it's Wicks!"

"Wicks? Why would he want to kill me?"

"That's something we'll never find out. He's dead."

Then confusion reigned. The men in the bunkhouse had heard the shot and soon filled the room, asking questions, stunned by what had happened. Jess offered a terse explanation that told them little except that the evidence added up to Wicks being the man responsible for all the accidents on Leland Ranch.

"Put the bastard in the woodshed," Jess said tightly. "We'll take his body into town tomorrow and turn him over to the marshal."

They all filed out, leaving Jess and Ariel alone. Jess went to the washstand, wet a cloth, and came back to wipe the blood from Ariel's face and arms.

Just then Rosalie came staggering in. One of the hands had found her where she had fallen and revived her. She had been clubbed on the head when she heard a noise and went to investigate.

"Thank God you are all right, señorita," Rosalie said shakily. "I would never forgive myself if you were harmed."

"What about you, Rosalie, are you hurt?" Jess asked.

"Just my head, señor, and that will heal."

"What happened?"

"I heard something. At first I thought it was you, but something about him didn't look right. I tried to light a lamp but he came up behind me and hit me. I knew no more until Dewey found me."

"The man is dead, Rosalie, he'll be causing no further trouble," Ariel said soothingly. "Go to bed, I'm fine now."

"Sí, señorita," Rosalie said, sliding a sidelong glance at Jess as she left.

"I'm afraid she doesn't approve of me spending nights in your bedroom," Jess said unhappily. "But this is one time I'm sure she's glad I came to you. I don't like sneaking around any more than she likes me doing it."

"I know of a way we could gain her approval," Ariel said. Her wits had finally returned after the shock of being awakened to find herself splattered with her would-be killer's blood. "You've saved my life so many times I belong to you body and soul. Make me yours forever, Jess."

Jess groaned. "I want to, wildcat, more than anything in the world—except—"

"Except for finding Judd's killer and bringing him to justice," Ariel finished when he faltered. "I don't think Dillon intends to leave Mexico," she said hopefully. "Maybe he's already dead. Men like him live short lives. Maybe you're chasing a ghost."

"He's back in Texas, sweetheart. I learned today that Dillon robbed a bank in San Antone."

"Oh, God." Her face contorted in agony. "You're leaving."

"I have to. It doesn't mean I don't love you any less. This is something I've sworn to do. I'll come back. Nothing will keep me from returning to you once I've finished with Dillon."

"You're never going to be finished with Dillon!" Ariel shouted angrily. "I thought I meant something to you. Is this stupid vendetta more important to you than I am?"

Never had Ariel been so thoroughly infuriated. Everything that had happened to her these past few weeks, combined with Jess' devastating announcement, drove her to say things she might later regret. But at the moment everything she said sounded reasonable to her. She had given freely of herself, holding nothing back, allowing Jess to use her for his own pleasure. That she gained as much pleasure as he did from their loving made little difference. Each time he came to her room she faced Rosalie's stern disapproval and yet she hadn't cared. But if he left her now she'd never forgive him.

"You mean everything to me, sweetheart; this has nothing to do with you. The danger to you is gone now that Wicks is dead, and I don't think Walters is brave enough to bother you again. I'm gonna get Dillon this time, I can feel it in my bones."

Ariel's face grew hard; her chin rose defiantly and her violet eyes turned dark and brooding. She knew if she didn't make a stand now Jess would be forever walking in and out of her life, breaking her heart each time he left until nothing remained but an empty shell.

"If you leave me now, Jess, I don't ever want to see you again."

"You don't mean that, sweetheart."

''You do what you have to do and I'll do what I have to do to retain my pride. Walk out on me now, Jess, and you can forget me.''

Jess grew still, his face a study of agony and distress. Torn between duty and love, he took a course that his own pride demanded.

''Good-bye, wildcat, I'll light outta here at dawn. I gotta do this for my own peace of mind. I'd make a lousy husband if I didn't.''

He didn't seem to expect a reply. Ariel didn't disappoint him.

Chapter 16

⟡ ⟡

The first few days after Jess left Ariel functioned in a daze. She felt empty, devoid of all feeling and emotion. Jess had been the catalyst that gave her life meaning. Of course she still had the ranch, nothing or no one could change that, but somehow nothing looked as bright or promising as it did when Jess was around to light up her days and nights. Since Jess' departure she'd reverted back to her old ways of loving and hating him at the same time. He had left of his own free will, nothing could alter that fact, but why did she have to be so darn obstinate about it and tell him she never wanted to see him again?

She truly understood how he felt about his brother's killer, but that still didn't make his opting to leave her any easier to swallow. He loved her yet there was something else he desired more. Revenge. He had spoken of peace of mind and pride, but Ariel had pride too. And peace of mind to her was having Jess by her side as her husband. Didn't he realize how much she needed him—loved him? Didn't he realize she didn't mean all those angry words she flung at him before he left?

"Señorita, brooding will not bring him back."

Rosalie stood quietly in the doorway of the parlor where Ariel sat staring moodily into the flames dancing in the hearth.

"I don't want him back," Ariel declared heatedly. "Jess left of his own accord after I begged him not to go. I know you didn't approve of him, Rosalie, but I loved him. And I thought he loved me."

"I think Señor Jess will make you a fine husband," Rosalie allowed. "What troubled me was his failure to do so. It hurt me to think he was taking advantage of you but I could find no other reason for his reluctance to make you his wife."

"Jess has other priorities," Ariel said with bitter emphasis. "He is driven by a thirst for revenge."

"Revenge is a strong emotion, Ariel. Perhaps you should explain. It would clear up many questions in my mind."

"There are many things I didn't tell you about Jess," Ariel said. "Our first meeting was rather explosive and the days that followed anything but serene. I told you he thought I was Tilly Cowles, a woman wanted by the law. What I didn't tell you was that Jess was a bounty hunter. He's spent two years searching for a man named Dillon, Tilly's partner, who had gunned down his brother in cold blood. Jess swore to bring the man to justice."

"Two years is a very long time. A man could easily become obsessed with his prey in that time," Rosalie said astutely.

"That's just what happened." Ariel sighed despondently. "Jess is a man obsessed with finding his brother's killer. Judd was the only family Jess had. I knew from the very beginning not to become involved with a man too obstinate to know when to give up, but love knows no boundaries or limits. At first I hated Jess Wilder. Then my hate turned in another direction. Jess felt the same way; we were so attracted to one another we couldn't bear being apart or keep our feelings under control."

"If Señor Jess was so obsessed with Dillon, why did he come back to the ranch?" Rosalie asked curiously.

"Dillon escaped over the border and Jess decided to bide his time until the desperado returned."

"So, this Dillon has come back to Texas and Señor Jess has left to fulfill his vow made to his brother's memory," Rosalie surmised.

"Exactly," Ariel said glumly.

"But he will come back, Ariel, I am sure of it. Has he not said he will return?"

"Yes," Ariel admitted slowly, "but I told him I never wanted to see him again. I was hurt and saddened to think he could leave me so easily after—after all we had been to one another. At the time I said it I meant it with all my heart. But now that my temper has cooled I realize that I spoke out of anger and disappointment. I want Jess back, Rosalie."

"He will come, señorita, he will come," Rosalie assured her with a confidence Ariel wished she could duplicate. "But you must not allow yourself to grow despondent. Before Buck died I promised I would look after his daughter if she came to Texas and I do not take my vow lightly."

Once again Ariel noted that note of tenderness whenever Rosalie spoke of her father. This time she decided to satisfy her curiosity.

"You must have been very fond of my father," she hinted, her violet eyes intent upon Rosalie's face.

Rosalie's expression grew dreamy. "I was with him ten years. I loved him," she said simply.

"I suspected as much," Ariel said softly. "Ten years is a long time; why didn't you marry? Didn't Father feel the same about you?"

"Buck was an honorable man," Rosalie replied. "He loved me as much as I loved him, but we could not marry." She paused, as if finding it difficult to express herself. "I was already married."

"What! You have a husband? I—I don't understand."

"Few people would understand, that's why we kept our relationship a secret. Buck would do nothing to dishonor me."

"Where is your husband now?"

"I do not know. At fifteen I was young and foolish and let his wild ways and handsome face entrance me. I ran off with him against my parents' wishes and eventually we married. It wasn't until weeks later that I learned he was a desperado on the run from the law. He robbed banks, trains, stagecoaches, and even killed," Rosalie said in a distant voice.

"When I complained he beat me. When he threatened to share me with his outlaw friends I became tame and meek and never complained aloud again."

Tears sprang to Ariel's eyes, feeling compassion for the fifteen-year-old abused by her husband. "Why didn't you leave him?"

"Where could I go? Not back to my parents who had already disowned me. After ten years of terror and living from day to day, never knowing if the law would catch up to us, my husband tired of me. He abandoned me in Waco. I never saw him again."

"What did you do then?"

"I worked, Ariel, at any job that earned me money with which to eat and keep a roof over my head. I am not proud of some of the jobs I performed," she said, "but I survived. Then I met Buck. The most wonderful man that ever lived. Your mother had divorced him and he was lonely. I won't tell you how or where we met, only that he offered me the job as housekeeper. I eagerly accepted. We fell deeply in love."

"Why didn't you divorce your husband so you could marry my father?"

"I was married by a priest; Catholics do not divorce."

"So you and Father became lovers."

"I am not ashamed of it," Rosalie said defiantly.

"Nor am I," Ariel returned, hugging the woman. "All that matters is that you gave Father the happiness he lacked with Mother. It is not my place to condemn when Jess and I—" She faltered, unwilling to give a name to their relationship. She knew Rosalie understood. "I am glad you told me about you and Father, Rosalie. I am relieved to know he had someone all those years he was deprived of his family. I hope he took care of you in his will. If not, I—"

"Buck was generous," Rosalie interrupted. "He left me enough to live on for the rest of my life. I remain here because it is the only home I've known for many years and I wanted the opportunity to meet his daughter."

"I'm glad you stayed," Ariel said sincerely.

After that talk a new closeness developed between Ariel and Rosalie, but it in no way lessened Ariel's loneliness and longing for Jess. He had been gone a week when lawyer Burns arrived unannounced one day.

"Mr. Burns, how nice to see you," Ariel greeted him warmly. "I was coming to town in a day or two to pay you a visit. I need some financial advice. I hope to buy more blooded horses to replace those lost in the fire and I need to know if I can afford to purchase them as well as rebuild the stable."

"You should have sufficient funds for both, my dear." Burns smiled. "All those accidents you've suffered have been regrettable but since the man behind them is dead I'm certain nothing else unforeseen will occur. Too bad he died before you learned why he acted as he did.''

The whole town knew of the unfortunate accidents at Leland Ranch. It was difficult to keep anything of that magnitude quiet. When the hands went into town on Saturday nights they spoke among themselves about the happenings at the various ranches at which they worked. Soon it became common knowledge.

''All that is behind us now,'' Ariel said, with more confidence than she felt. ''Obviously the man was deranged.''

''Yes, well, there is another matter I'd like to discuss with you. It concerns Kirk Walters.''

Ariel's lips tightened. Kirk Walters was the last man she wished to talk about. She said as much to Burns.

''I don't know what happened between you two, my dear, but the man is truly repentant. He asked me to come here and speak on his behalf. He's sorry and asks your forgiveness. He'd like to be friends again.''

''That's impossible,'' Ariel replied coldly. ''I want nothing to do with Kirk Walters or his friendship.''

After Jess left, Kirk had tried to see Ariel, but the hands, following orders, had turned him away the moment he stepped on Leland land. Kirk was livid and had sought the lawyer's help in placating Ariel.

''Kirk has been a good friend to you. Don't let a little misunderstanding come between you.''

''Little misunderstanding!'' Ariel raged. ''Is that what he called it? The man tried to rape me!''

''I—no, I don't believe it,'' Burns sputtered, unwilling to believe Kirk Walters would attempt such a vile deed. ''Perhaps you're being too hasty and should think over what you just accused Walters of doing.''

''I know what I'm talking about, Mr. Burns,''

came Ariel's adamant reply. Did Kirk have everyone duped? she wondered. Did none of his acquaintances know what he was really like? "Please tell Mr. Walters for me that I refuse to see him or allow him on my land. Now, is there something else you wanted to discuss?"

Jason Burns left shortly afterward. He didn't know whether or not to believe Ariel, but he had known Kirk Walters a long time. True, the man could be hard and ruthless at times, but he'd never known him to abuse a woman.

Winter was a mild one that year. There was a cold snap in late November that produced snow and then a warm spell in early December. Everything at Leland Ranch was thriving except for the owner. Ariel couldn't seem to pull herself out of the terrible despondency she fell into when Jess left. Her appetite declined and much-needed flesh melted from her already slim proportions. Despite Rosalie's scolding and the tempting array of food placed before her, Ariel found little enthusiasm for eating. In fact, the very smell of the food Rosalie tried to force down her seemed to sicken her.

When the weather held she took to riding every day, hoping to lose her longing for Jess somewhere on her vast acres. But even the ranch and all she'd accomplished thus far failed to cheer her. Rosalie was beside herself with worry and truly feared for Ariel's well-being. Then one day something occurred that revived Ariel's flagging spirits. Not only did it jolt her out of her unaccustomed despondency, it made her mad—mad enough to fight for what was hers.

Lawyer Jason Burns paid Ariel another visit. He wasn't alone.

Lawyer Burns pulled up to Ariel's front door in a closed carriage. That alone was cause for thought as he usually came on horseback. Ariel

was standing at the front door to greet him. She
watched curiously as he turned to help someone
behind him alight. She saw the telltale swish of
skirts and knew it was a woman. Besides Rosalie
and Trudy, Ariel knew few women in Texas. She
was isolated out here and far too busy with the
ranch to cultivate female companionship.

The woman's face was hidden by a huge bonnet and it wasn't until she was standing before
Ariel and raised her head that Ariel recognized
her. The color drained from Ariel's face and she
gasped in shock and disbelief. In some ways she
could have been looking at her sister. The woman
was small, just as she was, with dark hair and
violet eyes. But there the similarity ended. She
was slightly older than Ariel and her face showed
fine lines around her mouth and eyes that suggested a life far different from the one Ariel had
lived these twenty years.

The face was a familiar one in more ways than
one.

Ariel knew the woman.

Her name was Tilly Cowles.

"What is she doing here?" Ariel choked out,
anger and dismay nearly robbing her of her voice.

"May we come in?" Burns asked, regarding
Ariel's reaction keenly. Without waiting for an
answer he pushed inside. Tilly Cowles followed,
sweeping past Ariel with a look of utter disdain.

"So this is the woman who's been impersonating me," Tilly said haughtily. "I don't know
how you could have all been taken in by the impostor; she looks nothing like me."

"We haven't established yet that she is an impostor, Miss—Leland," Burns contradicted. "For
expediency's sake I will refer to you as Miss Leland and the—other lady as Ariel." He turned to
Ariel. "You seem to recognize this woman."

Numb with disbelief, Ariel said, "Of course I
do—she is Tilly Cowles. What I can't figure out is

why you've brought her here. She's wanted by the law."

"She claims to be Ariel Leland."

"*I am* Ariel Leland," Tilly said with firm conviction. If Ariel didn't know better, she'd have sworn that the woman really was Ariel Leland, so convincing was she.

"I don't understand any of this," Ariel said, reeling from shock. "Would someone care to explain?"

"Please, both of you sit down," Burns suggested. He himself chose to remain standing. "This may take some time."

"What will take some time?" Ariel asked.

"Finding out which of you is Ariel Leland."

"*I am* Ariel Leland," Ariel insisted indignantly. She pointed to Tilly. "That woman is the impostor. What in the world possessed you to believe such a preposterous lie? Has Tilly Cowles somehow duped you into believing she is me?"

"I don't know if duped is the right word," Burns said, completely baffled by this quirk of fate. "Miss Leland—" He nodded toward Tilly. "—has come to me with the proper identification papers, letters, and personal property of a woman named Ariel Leland, while you came here empty-handed. I foolishly took your word that you actually were Ariel Leland without requiring adequate proof."

"I told you, all my personal property and money was stolen," Ariel persisted, praying she was having a bad dream and would wake up at any moment.

"She lies," Tilly hissed.

"That's what we're here to determine," Burns said.

"How do you explain the fact that I knew everything about the ranch and Buck Leland?" Ariel asked smugly.

"That's easy," Tilly interjected. "You listened

to everything I said when I spoke with the lawman on the stage. I told him about the ranch and
my father and I even mentioned lawyer Burns'
name in conversation. It was a long, uncomfortable trip and talking was one way to ease the
boredom. Only in this instance I talked too much.
I had no idea you'd escape and turn everything I
said to your own advantage.''

''Can't you see she's lying?'' Ariel appealed to
Burns. ''Her story has too many holes in it. For
instance, where has she been all this time? I've
been at the ranch for over four months.''

''She has already explained it to my satisfaction
but I'll let her tell you herself,'' Burns said.

Ariel slanted Tilly a challenging glance. ''I'll be
anxious to hear what Tilly has to say.''

Tilly remained unperturbed. ''I'll be glad to tell
my story again. Why not, it's true. We all know
the stagecoach overturned so I'll omit that part.
Tilly Cowles was rendered unconscious in the accident and so was I. When I came to I heard Bart
Dillon talking to the desperadoes chasing the
stage. Evidently it was all planned. They were
friends of Dillon's and meant to set him free.''

''Who killed the sheriff?'' Ariel asked.

''One of the desperadoes, I don't know who.''
Tilly shrugged, sending Ariel a withering glance.
''May I go on with my story?''

Ariel flushed but said nothing more.

''Please do,'' Burns urged.

''When the desperadoes saw I was still alive
they discussed what they should do with me. Dillon suggested holding me for ransom. He had
heard my conversation with the sheriff and knew
I wasn't without means or property. They decided to take me along with them.''

''Why did they leave Tilly behind?'' Ariel
asked, finding the fabrication fascinating as well
as clever. And utterly false.

''From what I gathered, Dillon was tired of

you," Tilly said. "You were becoming too possessive and beginning to get in his way. He left you behind simply because he no longer cared what happened to you."

"I am not Tilly Cowles!" Ariel shouted, sick of this stupid charade. She turned to Burns. "Can't you see she is making this all up?"

Burns looked at Ariel in consternation. "Right now I find this entire situation incredible."

"Go on with your story," Ariel hissed.

"Yes, well, as I said, the desperadoes took me with them, thinking to hold me for ransom. But they're a stupid bunch; I managed to escape three days later while they slept. It was dark and I didn't have a horse but I hid in a hollow tree until they gave up the search the next day. Then I walked, having no idea where I was. I fell into a ravine and that's when I broke my leg. I don't know how long I lay there before I was able to crawl out. I should have died but I was fortunate. I collapsed by a water hole and was found by a cowboy riding a remote range looking for strays.

"I was ill and delirious from pain and exposure and it was a long time before I knew who I was or how I had gotten to the ranch where I was treated for my injuries. The rancher and his wife were very kind to me. I was ill a long time but eventually recovered, and here I am."

"With all your valuables and identification intact," Ariel said dryly.

"Of course. I had taken the precaution of pinning everything to the inside of my corset," Tilly said smugly. "If you don't believe me you have only to contact the rancher who gave me shelter. His name is Al Leach, and he owns the Circle L Ranch. It's north of Fort Worth."

Tilly sounded so sincere Ariel couldn't believe this was happening. Much of her story could be checked out and if it held where would that put her? She wondered dismally. The only people who could positively identify her were far away in St. Louis. She'd thought this nasty business with identification was all behind her months ago, but she was wrong—wrong—wrong!

"You understand, of course, that I must verify your story before I make a decision," Burns told Tilly.

"You'd be better informed if you wired my mother," Ariel contended. "She and my stepfather are the only ones who can positively identify Ariel Leland."

"I shall wire them immediately for help in this matter."

"Would you like refreshments, señorita?"

Rosalie stood in the doorway, uncertain whether or not to interrupt. The conversation seemed so intense that Rosalie's curiosity was piqued.

"Ah, Rosalie," Burns said, "please come in." Burns was well-acquainted with the housekeeper, and because of Buck's bequeathal concerning Rosalie he was aware of the special relationship between her and her employer. "Had you ever seen Ariel Leland before she showed up at the ranch?"

"No, señor, but Buck talked constantly of his daughter."

"Too bad." Burns sighed, disappointed.

"Is there a problem, señor?"

"A very grave problem, Rosalie. We seem to have two Ariel Lelands."

"No, señor." Rosalie smiled, gesturing toward Ariel. "There is only one Ariel Leland."

"She has fooled everyone," Tilly remarked with a sneer. "I am Ariel Leland. The other woman is an impostor. Her name is Tilly Cowles and she is wanted by the law."

Rosalie bristled indignantly. "I know which of you is Ariel Leland and it is not you." Her words brought a smile of gratitude to Ariel's lips.

"How can you be so sure, Rosalie?" Burns asked curiously.

Immediately Rosalie went to the table where the photograph of Ariel when she was a child rested. She picked it up and shoved it under Burns' nose. "This is Ariel Leland. She has the same look as the woman whom I have known and grown to love these past months."

Burns studied the photograph closely, but it told him little. It could have been either woman—or neither. He shook his head, more confused than ever. "I'm sorry, Rosalie, I have to side with the woman who has all the proper identification and letters written by Buck Leland."

Ariel couldn't believe her ears. Surely Burns didn't believe a woman whose life consisted of committing crimes and running from the law. "You need more proof than that, Mr. Burns." No one was going to take her land from her, certainly not Tilly Cowles. "If you think I'll walk off and hand everything over to this—this dishonest bitch you're dead wrong."

Burns looked properly shocked. "Of course not. Before I do anything or go to the law with this story I will check out Miss Leland's story carefully. I will also contact Ariel's mother and stepfather for some positive method of identification. Meanwhile, I'll order the bank account frozen so no one can take from it while I'm making the decision."

Tilly looked disconcerted but made no objection. "This can't be settled too soon for me."

"Nor me," Ariel said tightly. "Meanwhile, I don't want this woman in my house. Put her up in town but don't expect me to keep her while you're awaiting word. She'll steal me blind."

"Perhaps it *would* be best if Miss Leland stays in town," Burns said thoughtfully. "It will take an investigator two or three weeks to find Al Leach and return with the information. Perhaps by then Ariel's mother will shed some light on the subject of her daughter's identification. Shall we go, Miss Leland?''

"There is nothing more I have to say to this woman,'' Tilly declared as she rose to her feet.

Burns turned to Ariel, sending her an apologetic look. "You must consider my dilemma and not think too badly of me for wanting to be absolutely certain I haven't turned Buck's ranch over to the wrong woman. I will make my final judgment when all the facts have been verified.''

"Save your apologies for the day you come and tell me you are sorry for even thinking I'm not Ariel Leland,'' Ariel said, far from appeased.

"If it comes to that I will be the first to say I was wrong.''

Ariel stood in the doorway fuming as Burns and Tilly drove away. This whole thing was so preposterous she wanted to laugh and cry at the same time. What did Tilly hope to accomplish by impersonating her? Ariel wondered. The money in the bank account was lost to both of them for the time being and surely one day soon the truth would come out. Then suddenly the answer burst upon Ariel. If Tilly had read Ariel's letters and correspondence she knew there was a buyer for the ranch. Conceivably Tilly could sell the ranch and take off with the money before anyone was the wiser.

"Come inside, señorita,'' Rosalie urged as she led Ariel into the house and closed the door behind her. "Things will work out, you'll see. The woman is a liar, anyone can see that.''

"Anyone but Jason Burns,'' Ariel said bitterly. "What if she convinces Mr. Burns that she really is me? What will happen?''

"That won't happen, Ariel, believe me.''

"I pray you're right, Rosalie.''

The next day Ariel confronted the hands remaining on the ranch and explained to them what had happened. She preferred to tell them herself rather than have them hear false gossip in town. As she suspected, they were shocked and angered. Nothing or no one would ever convince them that she wasn't Ariel Leland. Ariel appreciated their loyalty but it did nothing to alleviate her fear.

"Just say the word, boss, and we'll run that impostor outta town," Pike offered. "If Jess was here he'd put a stop to this nonsense."

That only made Ariel feel worse. Jess had doubted her from the beginning. He might even side with Tilly now that she had showed up with all the proper identification. Still, having her hired hands behind her and Rosalie at her side went a long way in bolstering her confidence. If only she didn't feel so damn rotten most of the time. Ariel had no idea what was wrong with her and even considered going to the doctor next time she went to town. That would have to wait now until this mess with Tilly Cowles was all cleared up.

Ariel heard nothing about the matter for over a week. When Rosalie went into town for supplies she refused to accompany her, excusing herself by saying she had too much to do to. Rosalie wasn't fooled for a minute. She was worried about Ariel, really worried. She barely picked at her food and sometimes at night Rosalie could hear her crying. Rosalie knew Ariel's tears weren't due entirely to Tilly Cowles. Oh, no, it had more to do with Jess Wilder. If that obstinate hombre would come back, half Ariel's problems would be solved.

About the same time Rosalie was driving the buckboard into town Tilly Cowles was riding in the opposite direction on a rented horse. She rode steadily for an hour then stopped when she reached a huge boulder that had been previously decided on as a place for a clandestine meeting. The man she was to meet was already there.

" 'Bout time you showed up," he grumbled. "Did everythin' go as planned?"

"Without a hitch," Tilly crowed gleefully. "I've got that lawyer eating out of my hand. Even the people in town think I'm Ariel Leland. Everyone except the Mexican housekeeper and she's nobody to worry about. I've even found a man who wants to buy Leland Ranch. His name is Kirk Walters. You were right, Bart, this is a cinch."

"Knew it would be." Bart Dillon grinned. "When I saw them papers you stole from Ariel Leland and saw how closely you two resembled one another it all fit together."

"I always said you were smart, Bart."

"Have you cleaned out the bank account yet?" Bart asked eagerly.

Tilly scowled. "That's the one hitch I hadn't counted on. The lawyer is a sly one. He ordered the account closed until he makes up his mind which one of us is Tilly Cowles. He's going to check my story about the rancher and send a telegram to Ariel's mother."

That bit of news didn't sit well with Dillon. "The rancher will tell the same story you did," he said, "but I ain't so sure about the mother. It could get sticky."

"We'll be out of here with the money before anyone from St. Louis arrives," Tilly stated. "This Walters fellow wants the ranch so bad he's willing to strike a deal if I sign the ranch over to him. He's got something against Ariel and it serves his purposes to think she's a fraud."

"You got more talent than I gave you credit for, Tilly." Dillon guffawed. "I'll be in touch. I've been growin' a beard so's I'll be harder to spot in town. In a few days I'll drop by yer hotel room to see if yer makin' any headway with this Walters fella."

Excited by their accomplishment and giddy with

Chapter 17

A riel walked out of the doctor's office stunned. When another week had passed without improvement in her strange illness she could put off the visit no longer. Especially since she needed her wits about her now more than ever. She could no longer dismiss the nauseous feeling she experienced more than half the day. She wasn't prepared for what the doctor told her, didn't know if she would ever be. Ariel had no idea how she would handle this new development except to take each day as it came.

Since she was in town Ariel stopped at the post office for the mail and received her second shock of the day. A letter awaited her from her mother. It was written nearly a month ago. In it Willa Brady expressed her disappointment with Ariel for leaving St. Louis without permission. She had waited for Ariel to return of her own free will and when she did not she had dispatched someone to come and get her. Ariel checked the date on the letter again and using simple arithmetic realized that whoever her mother had sent would be showing up at any time. She read on.

Since Ariel was not yet twenty-one Willa expected to be obeyed. She did offer a slight concession. She would allow Ariel to keep the ranch as long as someone else ran it in her stead. *Until a girl is married her place is with her family*, Willa went on to say. *Please don't be obstinate about this. Come home as soon as your escort arrives.*

"Damn," Ariel cursed beneath her breath. Didn't she have enough to worry about without Mother sending a nursemaid to see her home like a naughty child? When Ariel reread the letter, she noticed that Willa had not mentioned who she was sending to Texas. As much as Willa hated Texas Ariel knew it wouldn't be her mother. The only logical choice was Tom, her stepfather. Since he was her legal guardian he could make things rather difficult for her if she refused to accompany him back to St. Louis. But at least he would serve a purpose, Ariel decided. Tom Brady would put this whole ugly business to rest by identifying the real Ariel Leland.

Stuffing the letter in her pocket, Ariel hurried off to pay a call on lawyer Burns. This new development was sure to change his mind about who was Tilly Cowles and who was Ariel Leland. On the way she received her third shock of the day. She saw Tilly Cowles strolling down the street on the arm of a man. The man was Kirk Walters. Their heads were together and they were obviously engaged in earnest conversation.

All kinds of wild thoughts rushed through Ariel's brain. She hadn't counted on those two getting together but it was remiss of her not to expect it. Tilly was in Waco for one reason. Money. There had to be money in it for her somewhere and the only way she could realize a profit of any kind was to convince everyone she was Ariel Leland and sell the ranch for a tidy sum. Kirk was the obvious buyer. He wanted the land bad enough to believe anything Tilly told him. As luck would have it they saw her and waited for her to approach. Ariel considered crossing the street but changed her mind. Only a coward or someone with something to hide would deliberately avoid a confrontation, and Ariel was neither.

"Hello, Tilly," Ariel said when she stood face-to-face with Tilly and Kirk. With willful purpose she refused to acknowledge Kirk.

Kirk scowled but Tilly merely smiled. "You may as well give up the charade," she advised. "Everyone knows you're the impostor. Kirk believes me, don't you, Kirk?" She turned to Kirk, waiting for him to lend his support. She wasn't disappointed.

"I knew from the beginning you weren't who you pretended to be," he said, addressing Ariel. "The real Ariel Leland would have sold the ranch to me without a moment's hesitation. Only Tilly Cowles would have held out."

"Why would Tilly Cowles do that?" Ariel asked curiously.

"To drive up the price, of course. And to make sure she had cleaned out Buck Leland's bank account before disappearing."

"You think you have it all figured out, don't you?" Ariel said to Tilly Cowles, struggling to keep her temper from exploding. "We will learn the truth sooner than you expect. A letter just arrived from St. Louis. Someone from my family is on their way to Texas. It won't be long before you're behind bars where you belong. He left several weeks ago and should arrive any day."

Kirk looked confused.

Tilly visibly paled.

Ariel felt confident for the first time in weeks—despite the fact that it meant she'd be forced to return to St. Louis.

"You don't believe her, do you?" Tilly asked, looking at Kirk with such helpless appeal that Ariel wanted to gag. "The sooner someone arrives to identify me the better I'll like it."

Tilly's mind worked furiously. If Ariel was telling the truth, she had to work fast and get out of Waco pronto. Fortunately she was expecting Bart Dillon at her hotel room that night and together

they would plan how to fleece Walters out of his
money. Walters was so gullible he was already
eating out of her hand. It wouldn't take much to
part him from his money and provide him with a
worthless bill of sale for the land.

"Of course I don't believe her, Ariel," Kirk
said. "No one in their right mind would, when
you have all the proof you need to prove your
identity. She came here with nothing, no luggage, no identification, only her word that she
was Ariel Leland."

"Thank you, Kirk," Tilly trilled. "You'll find
I'm not unappreciative of your support." Her
broad hint brought a smile to Kirk's face.

"You two are despicable!" Ariel spat, turning
on her heel and stomping off. She'd had just
about all she could take of Tilly Cowles. Thank
God this nightmare was nearly over. She continued on to the lawyer's office so that she might
fling her letter beneath Jason Burns' nose and demand that he put Tilly behind bars where she belonged.

"Your letter doesn't prove a thing, Ariel,"
Burns said once he'd read Ariel's letter, "except
that Willa Brady wants her daughter back home
badly enough to send someone after her. When
your guardian gets here he can put this matter to
rest once and for all."

"I guess I'll just have to content myself to wait
a few more days," Ariel observed sourly.

"It might interest you to know that the other
young lady's story checked out. My investigator
returned and Al Leach corroborated her explanation of why she was so late in getting here. Personally," he said, lowering his voice, "I'd much
prefer you to be the real Ariel Leland."

"A lot of good that does me now," Ariel muttered with a hint of contempt.

When she returned to the ranch she went directly to her room, in no mood to be questioned

by Rosalie. Before her visit to the doctor she had
only one problem; now she had two. Both of them
serious, only one of them reversible.

Sporting a newly grown beard and mustache,
Bart Dillon entered the hotel and asked at the desk
for the room number of Ariel Leland. Pausing before her door, he rapped once. It opened immediately.

"Come in," Tilly said, glancing down the hall
to make sure no one was looking.

"I made sure no one saw me," Dillon said,
slipping inside.

"You couldn't have come at a better time.
Things are happening fast around here."

"What kind of things?" Dillon asked sharply.
"Is that lawyer fella gettin' suspicious?"

"No, nothing like that. Ariel received a letter
saying someone from St. Louis is on their way to
Waco. That means trouble for us."

A string of curses left Dillon's lips. "Shit, just
when things are goin' our way. The money from
the San Antone bank is nearly gone, and I was
countin' on this to tide us over fer a spell. Havin'
to divide with Pecos and Gandy makes things a
mite tight."

"Send those two on their way, we don't need
them."

"Naw, they come in handy in a pinch. Things
will be easier once we sell the ranch. How ya
comin' with that Walters fella?"

"I've got him nearly convinced. It won't take
much to get him to buy the ranch in return for a
bill of sale. He told me the Leland woman's folks
want her back home bad but she don't want to
leave Texas. It got me to thinking. What if Ariel
disappears before her guardian gets here? Everyone will think she left because she was afraid of
being identified as Tilly Cowles. Even the lawyer
will have to agree that I am Ariel Leland. I can

sell the ranch to Walters and light out of there without anyone the wiser.''

''Won't they get suspicious if you disappear too?''

''They'll think Ariel took off because she didn't want to go back to St. Louis. And of course they'll think I am Ariel.''

A wide grin split Dillon's features. ''This is easier than robbin' banks or holdin' up stagecoaches.''

''I'll leave it to you to work out the details of Ariel's disappearance. It has to be within a day or two. We're cutting it close as it is.''

''Leave it to me, Tilly, no one will ever see or hear from Ariel Leland after I get my hands on her.''

''You're to keep your hands *off* of her, you hear, Bart? Kill her but don't do anything else. You know what I mean. You're my man, I don't want you bedding no other woman.''

''Aw, Tilly, I wouldn't do no such thing.''

''See that you don't. Where should we meet after I leave here with the money?''

Dillon pondered the question for several minutes. ''I'll wait at our hideout south of San Antone. I ain't used it fer some time so no one will think to look there. Not that anyone will connect me with you since we ain't been seen together fer quite a spell.''

''I'll be there,'' Tilly promised. Dillon made to leave but Tilly stopped him with a hand on his arm. Her eyes were dark and inviting. ''Do you have to leave so soon?''

Dillon grinned with wicked delight. ''Naw, I got plenty of time.'' He eyed the bed. ''Looks mighty invitin'.''

Slowly Tilly unbuttoned her blouse.

Jess sat with his back to the wall. Old habits die hard. He had learned early on how foolish it was to leave your back unprotected. With his hat pulled low over his eyes and a blue-black stubble dusting his chin he looked as dangerous as any of the desperadoes in the cantina. He took a healthy swig of the bad whiskey they served in the cantina and grimaced. He had been sitting there a long time, too damn long. His sharp silver eyes roved restlessly over each new customer as he entered, then fell away in disappointment when he saw it wasn't the one he sought.

Jess reached San Antonio only to learn Bart Dillon had virtually dropped off the face of the earth after he robbed the bank. Either he was laying low at one of his many hideouts or he had fled across the border again. Jess chose to believe the latter. He nosed around San Antonio for a couple of weeks, frequented some of the seedier saloons seeking information, and when none was forthcoming, headed for Mexico. And here he sat, nursing a drink and thinking about Ariel.

He wondered if she was all right and if she truly meant what she had said at their turbulent parting. He didn't blame her for hating him; he didn't deserve her love. She had no idea how difficult it was to leave her, to choose a course that would uphold his honor but did little to ease his conscience or inspire Ariel's love. Loving Ariel was the one constant in his life. Things came and went but his love for her would never change. Jesus H. Christ! Jess thought fervently, didn't Ariel realize he would come back to her if he was physically able?

"Would you like company, señor?"

Jess had been so engrossed in his misery he hadn't noticed the stunning woman who sidled up to him. He had seen her in the cantina before. She was a fiery dancer who performed nightly for the customers.

"I wouldn't be good company," Jess muttered dimissively.

The woman looked puzzled. Few men would refuse such an invitation from Lolita Morengo. She was much sought after by Mexicans and gringo alike. "Perhaps another time," she suggested coyly. She liked Jess' looks. He was cleaner, bigger, and more powerful than most men who frequented the cantina.

"Sure, another time," Jess said absently. The dancer started to walk away when suddenly Jess came to life. Perhaps she could help him. "Wait! I've changed my mind. Sit down, señorita, let me buy you a drink."

"My name is Lolita."

"Sit down, Lolita."

Lolita glided into the chair beside Jess, her short skirt riding up to her thigh. "You are a handsome hombre, señor. American?"

"Texan." Jess smiled pleasantly. "I imagine many Texans come here."

"A few," Lolita said warily. "But why do we speak of them? There are much more pleasant things to talk about."

Short on patience, Jess gritted his teeth in frustration. Patience, he told himself. He snapped his fingers and a short time later the bartender arrived and set a glass in front of Lolita. She picked it up and sipped daintily.

"What brings you to Mexico, señor?"

"The name is Jess. I'm looking for a man, Lolita. Perhaps you've seen him."

"How can I know if I don't know what he looks like?"

Jess pulled the well-worn poster from his vest pocket. "This is the man I seek, Lolita."

Lolita perused the poster with interest. "I cannot read the words."

"The man is Bart Dillon. He's wanted by the law."

"Are you a lawman?"

"No, I'm a bounty hunter. Have you seen this man recently?"

"Perhaps," Lolita said cagily.

Jess reached in his pocket and pulled out several folded bills. He put them in Lolita's hand. "Now have you seen him?"

He was surprised when Lolita handed the money back to him. "It is not your money I want, señor." Her dark eyes were filled with wild promise.

Jess went still. He hadn't had a woman since Ariel—hadn't wanted one. But he had come this far and wasn't about to back down now. He had run into a dead end. If Lolita had information he could use he'd go to any lengths to obtain it. "Where is your room, Lolita?"

Lolita smiled beguilingly and rose to her feet. "Follow me, señor." Jess nodded and followed her outside. She walked around to the rear of the cantina and opened a door that led into a small room. "I rent this from the owner for only a few pesos. It isn't much but I do not intend to remain here long."

Jess looked around curiously, saying little but paying close attention to details in case he needed to make a hasty exit. He saw at a glance that there was only one exit, the one they had just used. The room was clean but sparsely furnished, a bed taking up most of the space. There was a small table and two chairs but nothing on which to prepare food.

"I eat at the cantina," Lolita said as if anticipating his question. "Would you like a drink, Jess?"

"Nope," Jess said tersely.

Lolita took his curt answer to mean that he was anxious to get on with it without wasting time on preliminaries. She was in perfect accord as she slowly began to undress. Jess made no move to do the same, merely watching her from beneath lowered lids. When she finished she moved with sinuous grace into his arms. She lifted her mouth, her lips moist and expectant.

She had a dancer's body—lithe, supple, and delightfully fashioned with small firm breasts, minuscule waist, and long lean thighs and legs. Since she expected it, Jess kissed her. She felt soft and warm and smelled deliciously of aroused female. She kissed with the avid expertise of a practiced whore and the enthusiasm of an animal in heat. She was beautiful, sexy, beguiling—Jess didn't want her. When her hands began unfastening his clothing, he set her aside. As experienced as she was Jess realized she would be able to tell immediately that he wasn't aroused by her. Most men would think him loco but he couldn't help it if only one woman appealed to him.

"What's wrong, Jess?" Lolita pouted.

"Nothing. Let's talk first."

"Talk? You want to talk now? Don't you like Lolita?"

"I like you just fine but I want to know about that desperado before we both forget." His wicked leer suggested that they'd soon be too busy to think about such trivial matters.

"You mean Dillon," Lolita said. Her nimble fingers moved impatiently over the broad expanse of his chest and shoulders.

"That's right. Have you seen him recently?"

"*Sí*, I have seen him."

Jess grew excited. "When?"

Lolita's smooth brow wrinkled in thought. "He was here at the cantina with two of his friends three or four months ago, I can't remember exactly."

Keen disappointment jolted through Jess. "That long? You haven't seen him since?"

"No," Lolita said sourly, growing tired of the subject. "Forget Dillon. After we make love I will tell you all I know about the man."

"What else do you know?" Jess asked, his attention sharpening.

"Later, señor, much later," Lolita said, drawing him toward the bed.

Jess didn't resist, but his mind divorced itself from what his body must do as Lolita continued to undress him. He kissed her and concentrated on another raven-haired beauty, one with violet eyes and a feisty spirit and who was too damn stubborn for her own good. Jesus, he loved Ariel. Loved her too much to make love to Lolita. No wonder his manhood refused to cooperate. Fortunately Lolita was too excited to notice as she writhed and panted beneath him.

Taking advantage of her state of arousal, Jess asked, "What else do you know about Dillon, sweetheart?"

"Who?" Lolita asked, gasping as Jess teased her nipple with his tongue.

"You know, Bart Dillon, the man I'm looking for."

Deliberately he tormented her with his hands and mouth until she was sobbing for release. Then he sat back, watching her through narrowed silver slits.

'Don't stop! *Dios*, don't stop!"

"Tell me what you know," Jess prompted.

"I heard Dillon talking. He has a hideout in the hills south of San Antonio. He goes there when he needs to escape from the law."

"Is he there now?"

"I don't know. Jess, please!"

"I'm sorry, Lolita, sometimes I'm a real bastard. Especially when it concerns Bart Dillon. I've got nothing against you, it's just that I don't wanna make love to you."

"What kind of man are you?" Lolita cried, her eyes moist with tears.

"I've asked myself that same question many

times,'' Jess muttered. Hadn't Ariel asked him the same thing?

Suddenly he felt sorry for what he had done to Lolita; she hadn't deserved it. Neither had Ariel deserved to be abandoned by him. If he couldn't right one wrong he'd right the other. He rolled over toward Lolita and kissed her lightly on her lips.

"I won't leave you like this." Then he used his hands to bring her the relief she sought.

Less than an hour later Jess had fetched Soldier, bought supplies, and headed north across the border. Lolita was a distant memory while Ariel was a constant ache in his heart. He had brought Lolita to climax with cold precision but had gained no satisfaction from it. Would Ariel understand? he wondered dismally. Would he ever get the chance to find out? a little voice inside him asked.

That night Jess camped beside the Rio Grande River, rolled up in his blanket, and tried to sleep. Finally he dozed fitfully and began to dream. The dream was so real that cold sweat ran down his armpits despite the chill and his body shook with an unnamed fear. He saw Ariel, racing across her land, her midnight hair streaming behind her like an ebony banner. Then he saw her face and she was frightened. He had never seen her so frightened, not even when she was threatened by Kirk Walters. Though Jess' eyes never left her as she rode across the prairie, she suddenly disappeared into thin air. He searched the spot where he had last seen her, frantic with worry. But she was gone. Nothing of Ariel remained. He rode back to the ranch to alert the hands, but they seemed unconcerned. When he questioned Rosalie she merely smiled, pointed to a small dark-haired woman standing in the doorway, and said, "You worry for nothing, señor, Ariel is waiting for you."

The woman beckoning to him was not Ariel.

She resembled Ariel somewhat but it wasn't the woman he loved.

Jess woke up screaming. He was shaking. He was cold. He was hot. And he knew in his heart something was dreadfully wrong. Ariel needed him, needed him desperately. And Bart Dillon could be found at his hideout near San Antonio. Pulled in both directions, it no longer became a contest between love and duty.

"Duty, hell!" Jess swore aloud as he shook his fist at the star-studded sky. "The devil take you, Bart Dillon, for I no longer want you!"

Never had Jess' mind been so at peace as it was at that moment. For the first time in over two years he was thinking clearly. What a fool he had been to leave Ariel when she was his life, his future. The past was dead. He had done some terrible things in his life and regretted most of them, but not as much as he regretted leaving Ariel. If by some miracle she forgave him he'd give her no further cause to doubt him.

What about Bart Dillon? his mind asked, still inspired by the lust for vengeance. The answer came easily. He had only to ask his heart to speak for him. One day the law would catch up with Bart Dillon, for Jess no longer had the will or inclination to pursue the man. Jess knew Judd would forgive him if he were alive because his brother had not been a vengeful man.

Jess was in the saddle at dawn, spurred on by the sinking feeling that Ariel needed him. He wished he could sprout wings to fly to his love but had to satisfy himself with Soldier's valiant efforts.

"I'm driving the buckboard into town, Ariel, do you wish to come with me?" Rosalie asked.

It was a Saturday and Rosalie had decided to drive to Waco to purchase supplies for the holidays. The hands who had remained on the ranch for the winter had already departed for their weekly Saturday-night carousing.

Recalling her last trip to town and her confrontation with Tilly and Kirk, Ariel declined. She just didn't feel up to a bumpy ride to town today. "I think I'll stay home and go over the books, Rosalie. There is nothing I need in town anyway. Bundle up, it's brisk outside."

Rosalie frowned in consternation. She hated leaving Ariel alone but the errand could not be put off. "Sí, señorita, but will you be all right by yourself?"

Ariel smiled wanly. "You shouldn't worry about me so much. I'm fine."

"You don't look fine. I would feel better if you let the doctor look at you."

"Shouldn't you be going?" Ariel asked pointedly.

"Sí," Rosalie grumbled sourly. "But one day you will have to tell me what is bothering you." Then she turned and stomped out.

Ariel watched in silent contemplation as Rosalie drove away in the buckboard. She wondered if the housekeeper suspected anything and knew that before long she must be told. Having a baby without being married would cause a scandal. Most people would shun her but Ariel knew Rosalie would be sympathetic and supportive. If her mother and stepfather knew, Ariel thought glumly, they would be horrified and never live down the shame. That's why they must never know. Somehow she had to remain in Texas no matter how much coercion they used to force her back to St. Louis.

The sound of approaching riders interrupted Ariel's musings but she paid it little heed, thinking one of the hands had forgotten something and returned. It wasn't until the front door burst open and three men spilled into the room that Ariel realized how wrong she had been. A spurt of black terror pumped through her veins as she stared at the three rough men whose menacing looks and advancing steps presented a threat to her very life.

"What do you want? Who are you?"

Bart Dillon removed his Stetson and grinned.

"You!" Ariel gasped, stunned. "I know you. You're Tilly Cowles'—partner."

"You got a good memory, lady," Dillon said. "These two pretty boys with me are my friends Pecos Pete and Gandy."

Both Pecos and Gandy broke into raucous laughter. "Aw, Dillon, yer always joshin'," Pecos said. "You know dang well we ain't all that good-lookin'." Pecos might have been good-looking once but time and the wild life he led had taken its toll. As for Gandy, he could never be described as being anything but ugly.

As Ariel stared at the three men it was as if a curtain had been lifted and she saw everything perfectly clearly for the first time. Bart Dillon and Tilly Cowles were in cahoots. They had planned this mixed-up mess together in order to fleece her out of her inheritance. Once they had opened the bag they stole from her and read all the important letters and papers it contained, they'd decided to help themselves to her father's money and property.

"What do you want?" she asked shakily. Did they intend to kill her so that no one would dispute Tilly's false claim?

"Get yer wrap, yer comin' with us," Dillon ordered tersely.

"I'll do no such thing!" Ariel returned.

"And pack a bag with some of yer clothes. That way everyone'll think you lit outta here so's yer kin couldn't identify you as bein' Tilly Cowles."

"I—don't understand. When my stepfather arrives everyone will know Tilly isn't Ariel Leland. What good is all this going to do you?"

"Tilly ain't gonna be around when yer kin gets here." Dillon grinned wickedly. "We got it all figured out, see. When you leave they'll think it was because you were afraid of bein' unmasked. When Tilly leaves they'll think she didn't want to go back to St. Louis. Only by then Tilly will have already sold the ranch to Kirk Walters. It's all so simple when you know what yer doin'."

"I'm not going with you," Ariel said defiantly.

Dillon fixed her with a baleful look, nodded at Pecos, and said, "See that she does as she's told."

Pecos grasped her arm and pulled her behind him up the stairs. "Where's yer room?" he asked, shaking her roughly.

"Jest see that her bag is packed and get back down here pronto," Dillon called up to them. "That means no foolin' around, Pecos."

Pecos grumbled beneath his breath but offered no objection.

"You won't get away with this," Ariel said tightly as she shoved clothes in the carpetbag Pecos had found beneath the bed.

"Wanna bet?" Pecos smiled nastily.

"What—what are you going to do to me?"

"That's up to Dillon. He's the one what figured this all out. Tilly's a cold-blooded little bitch, she says to kill ya, but i reckon Dillon will make up his own mind. Hurry," he prodded, gouging her cruelly with the barrel of his gun. "Just pack enough so's yer friends will think ya took off in a hurry."

Fifteen minutes later Ariel was back downstairs. Dillon was there alone. "C'mon, Gandy's got her horse saddled and is waitin'. No tellin' when that housekeeper Tilly told us about will return."

Ariel was hustled out of the house and into the

cold crisp air, wondering if she'd ever see her ranch again. Was this to be the end of her short life? If she died her babe would die with her. No! her mind protested in vigorous denial. She wouldn't let her unborn child—Jess' child—perish. Jess had a right to know he had fathered a child and she damn well intended to live to tell him. Providing he ever showed up. As long as she kept her wits about her there was a chance for survival.

They laughed at Ariel's feeble struggles as they tossed her unceremoniously atop her mount, trying her hands to the saddle horn. Dillon slapped her horse's rump and they all rode off at a furious pace. Ariel held on for dear life, determined not to lose Jess' child. Even if her babe's father didn't want him, she did.

Jess, I need you! she cried in silent supplication.

Chapter 18

Petrified with fear, Rosalie glanced out the window one more time to see if Ariel had returned yet. She had arrived home at dusk and was surprised to find Ariel gone. It wasn't like Ariel to take off without telling her where she went or to remain away so long. She immediately checked the corral and discovered that Ariel's horse was missing. Assuming she had gone riding, Rosalie was somewhat mollified. But as the minutes ticked by and the skies darkened, Rosalie was assailed by a terrible fear.

Why did Ariel go riding on such a cold day? Why would she remain gone so long? Ariel could have had an accident and since the hired hands were in town there was no one around to search for her, Rosalie thought, all kinds of things going through her mind. She prepared supper, hoping to take her mind off her fears. It didn't work. She kept picturing Ariel lying somewhere on her vast property, injured and helpless. Rosalie thought about taking the buckboard and searching, but where would she look? In which direction should she go? Many men and horses were needed to carry out a search of Leland land. In the end Rosalie built up the fire in the parlor and waited— and waited—and waited—

With dawn came the unspoken certainty that something dreadful had happened to Ariel, and

Rosalie knew she had to do more than sit and wait and worry. She hitched up the buckboard.

Jason Burns was still abed when Rosalie arrived at his house. It took several minutes of frantic banging on the door before the disheveled lawyer answered the summons.

"Don't you know today is Sunday, woman?" he growled as he peered at Rosalie through sleep-drugged eyes. "What could possibly be important enough to take me from my bed this early in the morning?"

"It is Ariel, señor, she is missing," Rosalie blurted out, undaunted by the lawyer's anger.

"Missing? What are you babbling about, Rosalie?"

"When I returned from town yesterday Ariel was gone. Her horse was missing and I assumed she had gone riding. But she did not come back."

"She was out all night?" Burns asked, his attention sharpening.

"Sí, señor, and Ariel would not do such a thing. I fear something has happened to her."

"Have you sent the hands out to search for her?"

"No, señor, they have not returned from town yet. You must do something. Perhaps she was thrown from her horse, or—or worse." She was referring to desperadoes whose misdeeds were well-documented in these parts.

"Come inside, Rosalie, while I dress. Then we'll round up the hands and begin an immediate search," Burns said with crisp authority. "You could very well be right. Ariel may be lying injured somewhere on the property."

As good as his word, Burns did exactly as he said, even riding out with the hands to search the area. Not a trace of Ariel was found. At dusk the search was called off and Burns had decided to inform the marshal of suspected foul play when

Tilly Cowles arrived at the ranch with Kirk Walters.

"I heard in town that my imposter is missing," Tilly said smugly. She didn't seem at all surprised, which didn't set well with Rosalie.

"Obviously Ariel went riding and was abducted by desperadoes," Burns informed them.

"Have you checked her closet and drawers?" Tilly suggested slyly.

"What for?" Rosalie asked, immediately defensive. She knew what Tilly was suggesting but thought the notion preposterous.

"Just do as I say and if my theory is correct I'll explain."

"I think Ariel," Kirk said, nodding vigorously toward Tilly, "is on to something."

"I reckon it can't hurt," Burns replied, ready to grasp at any straw.

Together they trooped upstairs. Reluctantly Rosalie threw open the door to Ariel's room and stood aside as they filed inside.

"Is anything missing, Rosalie?" Kirk asked eagerly.

Grumbling beneath her breath, Rosalie went to the closet, gasping in shock when she opened it and realized several of Ariel's favorite outfits were missing, including the split skirts she favored. Turning away she began flinging open drawers, noting immediately that underwear and blouses that had been neatly folded and put away just yesterday were also missing. Still she refused to believe the obvious, until she checked under the bed and discovered the carpetbag had been removed from where it had been stored.

"Well?" Burns asked, aware by the look on Rosalie's face that something was wrong. "Is anything missing?"

Rosalie said nothing, the miserable look on her face more than conveying her dismay.

"I knew it!" Tilly crowed delightedly. Bart

hadn't failed her. By now Ariel Leland was miles away from here. Maybe even dead.

"Why would she leave like this?" Rosalie asked, utterly confused. She didn't believe Ariel would leave without a word to anyone, not when the ranch meant so much to her.

"It's simple," Tilly explained, enjoying her moment of triumph. "I am the real Ariel Leland and that other woman feared exposure when her kin arrived from St. Louis. Jail held little appeal so she quietly disappeared."

"No! The *puta* lies!" Rosalie cried, her black eyes blazing defiantly. "Something happened to Ariel, I tell you, something terrible. You must not give up the search."

"Admit it, Rosalie," Kirk advised, "the woman had us all fooled. She did a damn fine job of acting. By now she's miles away with her accomplice."

Jason Burns had to agree with the woman he now assumed to be Ariel Leland though in his heart wished it wasn't so. As much as he wanted it otherwise the woman standing before him was the real Ariel Leland and the one who had taken off so abruptly was Tilly Cowles. "I know you've grown mighty fond of the woman, Rosalie, but I'm ready to admit that the real Ariel Leland is right here in this room. We no longer need her kin to point out the impostor."

"You will never convince me of that, señor," Rosalie replied staunchly.

"As long as that is all settled," Tilly said, turning to Burns, "I'll expect my bank account opened so that I might draw out necessary funds. Then I want the papers prepared for the sale of Leland Ranch to Kirk Walters. I don't mind telling you that I don't expect to be here when my—stepfather arrives from St. Louis."

"You want to sell the ranch?" Burns asked suspiciously.

"Of course. That was always my intention. They only reason I came to Texas was to escape my mother and stepfather's authority. They wanted me to marry someone unacceptable to me."

She had gleaned this information from the letters written by Buck Leland to his daughter. When Ariel complained about her mother's choice of husband, her father had advised standing firm against them.

"All I want is what's due me from my father so I might live my life as I see fit."

"I can have the money tomorrow," Kirk said eagerly. "I know Burns already has the necessary legal papers in his possession so there should be no problem sealing the deal."

At first Burns expressed concern at executing so hasty a transaction. But after he considered it more carefully it made good sense. A young woman like Ariel had no business trying to run a ranch on her own. He had advised the impostor many times to sell out and return to St. Louis. So why should he balk when the real Ariel Leland wanted to do exactly what he had been advising for months? Even though she wasn't returning to St. Louis she'd be ridding herself of a burden she was ill-prepared to handle.

"If that's your wish, Miss Leland, then I'll have the papers ready for your signature tomorrow afternoon."

Everything was happening so fast that Rosalie was horrified. *Her* Ariel wouldn't lie. *Her* Ariel wouldn't leave like a thief in the night without a word to anyone. *Her* Ariel was Buck's daughter, not the *puta* standing before her with a smug smile on her face. How could these stupid men allow such a travesty to occur? There was only one man she knew of who could solve this mystery and Jess Wilder wasn't here. Rosalie was beside herself with worry and frustration. She needed help, needed it fast.

"You may remain here until I rent the house," Kirk said to Rosalie magnanimously. He was so elated by the turn of events he could afford to be generous. "I have no desire to live here myself as the house is inferior to mine. Trudy would be displeased if I moved her here bag and baggage."

"*Sí*, I will remain," Rosalie agreed grudgingly. She wanted to be here when Ariel returned—*if* she returned.

The next day Tilly Cowles affixed Ariel's name to the bill of sale and deed to Leland Ranch. The day after that she took the stage to San Antonio. Her bags were packed with more money than she had seen in her life. Once in San Antonio she intended to buy a horse and ride out to the hideout where she was to meet Bart Dillon and the others. The money would more than make up for the difficult life she'd been forced to lead all these years. If not for Bart Dillon she would have been dead at thirteen, the age at which her stepfather had raped her and forced his child on her. After she lost the child her mother threw her out of the house, refusing to believe her husband had been responsible.

Bart Dillon found the forlorn waif working in a bawdy house in Fort Worth and had taken her under his wing. He led her from a life of prostitution into a life of crime. When the law pursued them too vigorously in one place, they found more fertile ground elsewhere. Tilly's life consisted of running from place to place, robbing, shooting when it became necessary, and being Dillon's lover. In his own fashion, Tilly knew Bart loved her, as much as he could love anyone, and believed he was reasonably true to her. He hadn't abandoned her after all these years and that meant a lot to Tilly. It meant enough to keep her loyal and faithful to Bart Dillon.

* * *

Jess rode hell-bent for leather, propelled by inner warnings and premonitions of danger. He stopped only when he couldn't safely stay in the saddle, catching a few hours' sleep and downing a hasty meal before vaulting in the saddle again to continue his journey. Even the light snow dusting the ground failed to slow him down. He passed the San Antonio stage but gave it little heed. It could have been carrying Bart Dillon and Tilly Cowles for all Jess cared; he was no longer concerned with them. Nothing mattered but Ariel, his love for her and their future—if she forgave him for being such an obstinate fool.

The ranch looked strangely deserted when Jess rode into the yard. He frowned, wondering where the hands were. There was little to do on the range at this time of year and he would have expected them to be engaged in jobs around the house and outbuildings. He put Soldier in the corral and stopped off at the bunkhouse first. It was empty. All the bunks were neatly made but it was cold and deserted. Jess was puzzled when he noted that no fire had been built in the stove, nor had been for days. Bounding out of the bunkhouse, he sprinted the short distance to the house and flung open the unlatched door.

Rosalie sat in a chair, staring blankly into space. She barely roused herself when Jess stormed into the house despite his noisy entrance. He stopped in his tracks, staring at Rosalie in bewilderment before realizing the woman was in shock. Being very careful not to startle her, Jess knelt down beside her and touched her shoulder.

"Rosalie, it's Jess Wilder. What happened here? Where is Ariel?"

Rosalie was slow to react and even slower to acknowledge Jess. He was stunned by the look of utter hopelessness in her dark gaze. It was a look he'd seen many times in the eyes of trapped an-

imals and men who would rather shoot it out to
the death than end up behind bars. But somehow
Jess got through to her and she began to wail and
shake her head from side to side.

"She is gone, señor, Buck's Ariel is gone."

"Gone? I don't understand. Gone where?"

"I do not know, señor. Why did you leave? Ariel loved you. If you had remained nothing would
have happened to her."

"Rosalie, I can't make sense out of what you're
saying. Please try to compose yourself and tell me
exactly what happened."

Rosalie drew in a ragged breath, making a valiant effort to speak clearly and rationally. Ariel
had been gone for days now and all she could
think of was that the girl she had come to love as
her own was dead. "Ariel has disappeared, Señor Jess. One minute she is here, and poof, she
is gone."

"How could that be?"

"I went to town, Ariel did not want to go.
When I returned she was gone. She had taken her
horse and some of her clothes."

"Why would Ariel leave?" Jess asked, skeptical.

"I forget, señor, you do not know the trouble
we have had. Shortly after you left another
woman appeared in town claiming to be Ariel Leland. But I knew she was lying. She had identification and letters to back up her claim."

Jess sat back on his heels, stunned. Another
woman? Tilly Cowles? Or the real Ariel Leland?
Had he been duped along with everyone else by
a woman posing as Ariel Leland? Had he really
fallen in love with Tilly Cowles? Jess shuddered,
that thought bringing more agony than he was
prepared to deal with.

"Ariel tried to tell those fools the truth but because of the papers and identification they did not
believe her," Rosalie continued raggedly. "One

of her kin is on his way from St. Louis to identify her but she disappeared before he arrived. Both Señor Burns and Señor Walters think she left to keep from going to jail.''

''What of the other woman?'' Jess asked, more confused than ever.

''With Ariel out of the way the other woman sold the ranch and left town. Señor Walters is the new owner. I fear Ariel is dead.'' Her sentence ended on a wail.

''What about the hands? Did they see nothing?''

''It was Saturday, they had already left for town. Señor Jess,'' Rosalie pleaded, grasping his hands in desperation, ''you do not think like the others, do you? *My* Ariel would not lie. Ariel is Buck's true daughter. The other woman is a *puta* who had tricked everyone.''

Jess went still. Rosalie's question threw him off balance. He needed time to think but there was no time. Did he believe the woman he knew as Ariel Leland was an impostor? Did he love Tilly Cowles? His heart gave him the answer and his mind accepted it. He could not love Tilly Cowles. His entire body rebelled at the thought. For a brief time he did think Ariel was Tilly Cowles, but it didn't take long for him to be disabused of that notion. Truth to tell, he had known from the beginning that the beguiling creature he rescued from the overturned stage wasn't Tilly Cowles but was too dang stubborn to admit it. He wanted Bart Dillon and Tilly Cowles so bad he couldn't see the truth when it was staring him in the face. But he saw it now, knew it with every fiber of his being, felt it in the depths of his soul.

''No, Rosalie, I don't think Ariel lied,'' Jess finally said. ''I *know* which woman is Ariel Leland, just as you know.''

''What can we do, señor? She has lost the ranch, maybe she has lost her life.''

"Rosalie, I'm gonna ask you an important question and I want you to think very hard before answering. Did you see a strange man around the ranch before Ariel disappeared? One who looks like this man?" He reached in his pocket for the poster he'd been carrying around for over two years, carefully unfolded it, and held it up for Rosalie's perusal.

Rosalie studied it intently, then shook her head sadly. "No, señor, I have never seen that man. But I recognize the name. Ariel told me all about Bart Dillon and how he killed your brother. Do you think he is responsible for Ariel's disappearance?"

"I don't know but I aim to find out," Jess said tightly. "If the woman posing as Ariel is Tilly Cowles, and I reckon she is, then Bart Dillon is working with her. I lost track of the bastard in San Antone. Went clear to Mexico thinking he was there but learned he was still in Texas. He's been here all the time, in Waco with Tilly Cowles."

"Do—do you think they have hurt Ariel?" Rosalie asked fearfully.

It was a question Jess didn't want to answer. If he was in Dillon's place he would have killed Ariel and gotten rid of her forever. The man had no scruples and though he'd never to Jess' knowledge killed a woman, there was always a first time. If he still traveled with Pecos Pete and Gandy the danger was even greater for both men were ruthless killers. For Rosalie's sake and his own peace of mind Jess told a deliberate lie.

"Don't fret, Rosalie, they won't kill Ariel. Once Tilly joins them with the loot they'll probably let Ariel go. It doesn't make sense to kill her. They'll hightail it to Mexico and live like kings on Walters' money."

Though Rosalie wasn't entirely convinced, Jess' confident manner helped put some of her worst fears to rest. His next words brought a tentative smile to her tear-ravaged face.

"I will find Ariel, Rosalie. I swear on my brother's dead body that I will find her and bring her home where she belongs. What about Ariel's kin? When will he arrive?"

"He will come soon, señor. What will I tell him?"

"Let Burns take care of it, but whatever you do try to keep him here until I return. Once he identifies Ariel this problem will be laid to rest forever."

"What if he insists on taking Ariel back to St. Louis?"

"Let's worry about that when the time comes. I gotta find her first."

"Sí, señor, I will do as you say, and pray to God you succeed."

"One more thing, Rosalie. Where are Bud and Dewey and Pike? I want to question them."

"They no longer work here, señor. They do not like Señor Walters. None of them believe Ariel is not Buck's daughter."

Jess paced the marshal's office in angry frustration. He had wasted precious time trying to convince the stubborn man to form a posse to search for Ariel Leland. Jess had ridden directly from the ranch to Waco. His first stop had been the lawyer's office where his revelation was met with open skepticism. In the first place Burns regarded the rough cowboy as being unqualified to make a judgment in regard to Ariel Leland. He hadn't been around to see the evidence. Besides, Burns hated to think he could have been wrong and allowed an impostor to sell Buck Leland's ranch. The marshal said much the same thing when Jess arrived with his demands for a posse.

"You might have been a U.S. marshal at one time, Jess, but you have no right now to come in here and tell me what to do," Marshal Henry Bills said. "Burns told me about this whole nasty business and I'm sorry Tilly Cowles got away before I could put her behind bars. But I have no reason to believe Tilly Cowles fleeced Walters out of his money and Ariel Leland was abducted. Until you can prove to me that we were all duped I see no reason to send a posse out on a wild goose chase."

That was his final word on the subject.

Since it was nearly dark by that time and Soldier needed rest, Jess arranged for a room in town. At dawn he was back in the saddle, his destination San Antonio. It was a long shot, but it was the only clue Jess had as to where Dillon might take Ariel. Tilly had to meet up with him somewhere and that seemed the most likely place. It wasn't far from there to the border and he fully expected Dillon and his gang to head for Mexico with Walters' money.

Ariel was colder than she had ever been in her entire life. Wind stung her cheeks and she was certain that her hands, tied to the saddle horn, were frost-bitten. They rode throughout most the night, putting as much distance as they could between them and Waco. Dillon knew that once Ariel's disappearance was discovered there would likely be a search and he wanted to be as far away as possible before daylight. He trusted Tilly to convince the men to abandon the search and accept her as the real Ariel Leland. Once she did that, nothing stood in the way of selling the ranch and hightailing it out of town with the money.

Reeling from exhaustion, Ariel sobbed with relief when they stopped at daylight. Gandy prepared a makeshift meal. Ariel was offered a plate but she shook her head. All she wanted was to lie down and sleep. She lay against a rock, dozing, while nearby the three men spoke of what they intended to do with the money Tilly was bringing. They made no effort to lower their voices for none of them expected Ariel to live to tell the tale. At the moment Ariel couldn't have cared less as she slid into slumber. It seemed only minutes later that she was prodded awake with the toe of Dillon's boot.

"Time to go," he growled.

"Where are we going?" Ariel asked, somewhat refreshed after her nap.

Pecos guffawed, obviously amused. "We're goin' ta Mexico but I don't reckon you'll be joinin' us."

Gandy snickered and glanced at Dillon. "Ya gonna do it now, Dillon?"

Dillon looked at Ariel and scowled. He'd done many vile things in his life but he'd never killed a woman. "Later," he said gruffly. "We gotta keep movin'." He didn't want Pecos and Gandy to think he had a soft streak in him. Maybe later he'd muster the courage to do what had to be done.

They rode most of the day, stopping only to rest the horses and eat food Ariel found barely palatable. She forced herself to choke down whatever they gave her, realizing she must not become weak for she had no one to depend upon but herself.

To Ariel's vast relief they camped that night for a real rest, assuming by now they had no cause for worry. Ariel sat at the opposite side of the campfire from the three men, devouring her plate of beans and washing it down with bitter coffee. It reminded her of the night she had shared her coffee with the same three men who at the time thought she was a young boy. A far away look came over her features as she recalled that night and their conversation. She was so engrossed in her recollections that she paid little heed to the talk around the campfire until she realized they were discussing her and her fate.

"I wanna poke her before ya kill her," Gandy said, licking his meaty lips.

"Wouldn't mind it myself," Pecos concurred.

Privately Dillon felt the same but Tilly was a jealous sort and likely to raise all kinds of hell if she found out. He and Tilly had been together a long time and made a good team; he didn't cotton to having her leave him at this point. Truth to tell, he might even call what he felt for Tilly love.

Dillon was silent so long Ariel feared he was considering giving her to Pecos and Gandy, and maybe even raping her himself. Raw panic surged through her and she blurted out the only thing she could think of at the time.

"I'm expecting a child. It you harm me in any way you'll kill an innocent child. Do you want that on your conscience?"

"Yer growin' a baby?" Dillon asked, stunned.

"Aw, Dillon, ya ain't gonna believe her, are ya?" This from Gandy who was already anticipating a night of pleasure. "She ain't even married."

"Since when does a woman have to be married to have a child?" Ariel challenged.

"Who's the father?" Pecos asked shrewdly.

"My—my foreman," Ariel admitted. "We were going to get married. I wouldn't lie to you about something like that."

"Well now," Dillon said, scratching his chin in consternation, "if this don't beat all. If the woman is tellin' the truth I ain't gonna be responsible for killin' no baby."

"She's lyin'," Gandy insisted.

"Could be," Dillon agreed. "But I ain't convinced one way or another. Do either of you wanna do it?"

"Not me," Pecos replied. "I had me a wife once. The sorriest thin' I ever did was abandon her. We coulda had a kid fer all I know. Rosalie was young, and sweet, too. Gotta admit I wasn't the best of husbands. Sometimes I think about her and wonder if she survived."

Ariel was stunned. Rosalie? Could Pecos Pete be Rosalie's husband? Rosalie would be gratified to know that the man suffered remorse over his vile treatment of her. But letting Pecos know where Rosalie could be found was the furthest thing from Ariel's mind. Her friend was better off without the desperado. One day his life would end as violently as he lived it.

"Aw, shit, are ya both goin' soft on me?" Gandy spat disgustedly. "I reckon it's up ta me ta get the job done. *After* I poke her." He ogled Ariel lewdly and left his spot by the campfire.

As he made his way slowly toward her fear raced down Ariel's spine. She couldn't die, not now, not when she had Jess' child to live for. Her mind worked furiously. Then suddenly she recalled what it was she was thinking about before this conversation had taken place. It was a slim hope but she clung to it with a desperation that lent her courage.

"Mr. Dillon, you can't let Mr. Gandy kill me," she said on a note of rising panic. "Do you recall a young boy named Art Lee?"

Dillon went still. The name sounded familiar. "Are ya talkin' 'bout a kid travelin' by hisself from Fort Worth to Waco?" he asked. Clearly his curiosity was piqued.

"Yes," Ariel said eagerly. "Do you remember what you said to him?"

"What in the hell does this have ta do with a kid?" Gandy asked irritably.

"Let her talk, Gandy," Dillon ordered tersely.

Gratified, Ariel continued. She might be grasping at straws but her life was at stake. "I was that boy, Art Lee. I was traveling alone to my ranch disguised as a boy. I offered you coffee. You drank

with me and said maybe someday you could return the favor. Well, I'm calling in that favor now.
I want my life, Mr. Dillon, and the life of my unborn child.''

Dillon observed Ariel as if she had just lost her
mind. "You? A boy? You're joshin'."

"No, it's true," Ariel cried in renewed panic.
She had to make Dillon believe her! "I told you I
was going to join my father in Waco. You said
you liked my spunk."

The expression on Dillon's face changed from
outright disbelief to grudging acceptance. "I
reckon I recall sayin' that. Why were you travelin'
alone?"

"There was a bounty hunter on my trail." She
had to make this sound good. "He thought I was
Tilly Cowles." Dillon chuckled. "The marshal in
Fort Worth hadn't enough evidence to hold me
so I was free to go, but that bounty hunter was
determined. So I deliberately set a false trail and
took off alone for Waco before he knew what I
was about."

"That same bounty hunter has been after me
for months," Dillon boasted, "but I always manage to keep one step ahead of him. Did ya recognize me when I came upon yer camp that
night?"

Slowly Ariel nodded.

"I'll be damned. Ya got spunk, all right, more
than I gave ya credit for. Any other woman
woulda been hysterical."

"You promised to return my favor," Ariel persisted. "Are you going to keep that promise?"

Dillon grew thoughtful. Ariel had proved herself a woman who could survive on her wits and
he had no desire to snuff out her life. Especially
if she carried a child. She had just presented him
with a plausible excuse for not killing her and he
intended to use it.

"Bart Dillon ain't a welsher. If I told ya I'd return yer favor than ya can damn well count on it. I won't kill ya, lady."

"Dillon, are ya loco? What are we gonna do with her? We can't bring her ta Mexico with us and we can't jest turn her loose. Not until we're outta Texas, anyway." Gandy made a viable point and Pecos was quick to add his support.

"I'll think of somethin'," Dillon grumbled distractedly. Tilly wouldn't be pleased, not one damn bit.

"I know of a man in San Antone who buys women fer whorehouses in Mexico," Pecos volunteered. "We wouldn't be killin' her but she wouldn't be free to spill her guts 'bout us."

Dillon's frown turned into a sly smile. "Sounds good ta me. It ain't our fault if her belly starts ta swell once they get her down in Mexico. Leastways we ain't killin' a woman growin' a baby." His mind was so corrupted he saw this as the lesser of two evils.

"No!" Ariel cried. "You might as well kill me, it would be the same thing."

"Hush up, lady, or I'll give ya ta Gandy," Dillon warned. "The only reason I ain't lettin' him have ya now is because of my respect fer motherhood."

He saw no contradiction in his words.

Chapter 19

Dillon and the others were careful to skirt San Antonio as they traveled to the hideout. It hadn't been too long ago that they'd robbed a bank in town and now they didn't dare show their faces, at least not three of them all at once. They traveled south into the rugged country below the Alamo, forcing Ariel to endure long days in the saddle and food not fit for human consumption. Often at night she caught Gandy staring at her strangely, but so far he had made no move to harm her. Pecos told him she would bring a good price and evidently Gandy relished money more than he did her. But it didn't stop him from looking—and wishing.

Ariel knew she was being taken to some sort of hideout near San Antonio where they would wait for Tilly to arrive with the money she'd obtained by fraudulently selling her ranch. She supposed the desperadoes would continue on to Mexico— after they got rid of her. It occurred to Ariel that the closer they got to the hideout the more remote her chances were for escape.

That night they reached the hideout. The small, crudely constructed log cabin nestled against a brown hill that protected it from unwanted visitors. It was off the beaten path and unless one knew exactly where to find it it was unlikely to be discovered. Ariel was pulled roughly from the saddle and shoved inside. It was as dark and dank and cold as the inside of a tomb. A lamp was found and lit and Ariel's spirits sank even further, if that was possible. She couldn't imagine sleeping in such a squalid place. Nevertheless, Dillon lit a fire in the stove with wood left there from his last visit. It did dispel some of the gloom and chill but offered Ariel little comfort.

Two cots sat against one wall, covered by shabby blankets. The two windows were so dingy one could barely see out of them and a layer of dust covered everything. A table with one leg shorter than the other was flanked by four chairs and several tin plates and cups were piled atop its scarred surface. Several pieces of cookware, utensils, and assorted tins of food were scattered about the shelves built into one wall.

"It ain't much but it's better than jail," Dillon said, chuckling when he noted the arrested look on Ariel's face. He had no idea she was studying her surroundings with rapt attention, weighing her chances of escaping.

"Can ya cook?" Dillon asked hopefully. "I'm sick of Gandy's cookin'."

Ariel flushed. Cooking definitely wasn't one of her talents, but if it meant the difference between being tied to one place and a measure of freedom she definitely preferred cooking. "I'm not the best cook in the world, but I can do better than Gandy."

"I'll fetch some water from the creek nearby while you rustle us up some grub. Gandy, bring in more firewood. And Pecos, stick around inside in case the lady decides to leave us."

In Ariel's opinion the meal she prepared was palatable, barely, but the men seemed to enjoy it, smacking their lips in appreciation. They sat around the table and talked while she ate from the leftovers and cleaned up.

"How soon do ya expect Tilly?" Pecos asked, picking his teeth with a straw from the broom.

"Two, three days," Dillon speculated. "We gotta get rid of the girl first or Tilly will have fits. Do ya know where ta get in touch with the man ya told me about? The one who buys women fer whorehouses in Mexico?"

"I don't know him personally," Pecos admitted somewhat sheepishly, "but I know how to contact him. An old acquaintance of mine owns a bawdy house in town and she's the one told me about him. All I gotta do is tell Clara Mae and she'll take it from there."

"Do ya reckon he'll come out here? It's too risky ta take the girl ta town."

"I can arrange ta meet him at the edge of town and bring him out here, otherwise he'd never find the way," Pecos suggested. "Ya want I should leave now?"

"Wait till mornin'," Dillon advised. "We could all use a good night's rest. There's a ridge five miles north of here, looks like a camel with two humps. Tell Clara Mae ta have the man meet ya there. Be sure and tell her how fetchin' the girl is so she can convince him it's worth the trip out here."

Later Dillon tied Ariel's wrists and ankles together and tossed a blanket over her. Then he stretched out on one bunk while Gandy and Pecos drew straws for the other. Ariel curled up on the floor, trying to find a comfortable position. She considered it some kind of miracle that she hadn't already been molested and offered a prayer of thanks, though she could tell Gandy was close to defying the other men where she was concerned. She spent an uncomfortable night attempting to stay awake, too afraid to sleep. The next morning Pecos left for San Antonio.

* * *

Clara Mae was sleeping soundly when Pecos appeared at her door. She was furious until she learned who had disturbed her sleep.

"Pecos Pete, if you ain't a sight for sore eyes," she greeted him as she opened the door. "Ain't you taking a chance coming to town after that bank robbery you and your friends pulled a while back?"

"I wouldn't be here now if I didn't need yer help, Clara Mae." Pecos eyed her with slow relish, liking what he saw.

"Well, sit down and spit it out," Clara Mae invited archly.

A buxom woman well past the first bloom of youth, Clara Mae looked charmingly disheveled in her nightgown and wrapper. Her hair was dyed a garish red and her complexion was slightly mottled from sleep but she was still a handsome woman, considering how long she'd been around in her profession. Pecos wet his lips and nearly forgot his reason for being here.

He shook his head and reluctantly pulled his thoughts up from below his belt to concentrate on the matter at hand. "You recollect that friend ya told me 'bout, Clara Mae? The one who buys women for whorehouses in Mexico?"

"Reckon I do. Why?"

"We got a woman we wanna sell. She's a real beauty, with coal-black hair hangin' down ta her waist and eyes a kinda violet color with long thick lashes."

"Why waste her in Mexico?" Clara Mae asked, clearly interested. "You could sell her to me. My customers would go crazy for a woman like you just described."

"Naw, we want her outta Texas. Can ya help us?"

"It's a pity to waste her on Mexicans but if that's what you want . . . But before I agree to anything you got to tell me what this is all about."

"We pulled a little job up around Waco and the

woman kinda got in our way. There's nothin'
more ya need ta know. Either ya help us or ya
won't."

"What's in it for me?" Clara Mae asked
shrewdly.

Pecos and Dillon had already talked about that
detail, expecting Clara Mae to ask for something
for her trouble. With the money Tilly was bringing they were prepared to buy the madam's compliance. "One hundred dollars just fer tellin' yer
friend about the woman."

"I want it now," Clara Mae said, her eyes
gleaming greedily.

Pecos nodded, forking over the money they had
pooled to get enough to pay off Clara Mae.

"My friend ain't in town but he'll be back in a
day or two. Bring the girl here and he'll take a
look at her."

"Naw, too risky. He can come out ta the hideout."

"How in the hell is he supposed to get there?"

"I'll meet him and take him there." He proceeded to tell Clara Mae exactly where he would
meet the man.

"All right, I'll do what I can," Clara Mae promised. "Be there in two days. His name is Mick
Garner."

When Pecos made no move to leave, Clara Mae
asked, "Is there something else?"

"Yeah, it's been a long time since I had a
woman and I just gave you a hell of a lot of
money. It oughta include somethin' extra fer me."

Clara Mae was well-acquainted with Pecos Pete.
He was hung like a bull and lusty as a cowboy
just off a cattle drive. Despite the early hour she
wouldn't mind a romp in bed with him. She
smiled coyly and began removing her robe.

Pecos grinned foolishly, relishing the idea of
telling Gandy he'd gotten laid in town.

* * *

Jess arrived in San Antonio mere hours after Tilly Cowles. Able to travel at a faster pace than the stage, he had pushed Soldier to the limit of his endurance. He was counting heavily on finding Ariel at Dillon's hideout and prayed he'd be able to locate the place. Jess knew it would be cleverly hidden but somehow he would find it. For Ariel's sake he had to! As it turned out, the answer to his dilemma fell into his hand like a ripe plum. He was tying Soldier to the hitching post outside the saloon when Tilly Cowles walked right by him as big as life. She carried two large carpetbags and was walking in the direction of the livery. It appeared as if she had just recently arrived in town.

As a matter of fact, Tilly had arrived in San Antonio the previous afternoon and decided to rent a room for the night instead of riding directly out to the hideout. She needed to buy some decent clothes and a good horse and it was too late to do all that and arrive at the hideout before dark. By the time Jess spotted her the next day she had made her purchases and had only to buy a horse before leaving town.

With cautious steps Jess followed Tilly, realizing that even if she did notice him she wouldn't know who he was. Neither she nor Dillon had ever seen Jess Wilder. And to the best of his knowledge neither had Pecos or Gandy. Hanging around outside the livery, Jess heard Tilly bargaining for a horse. When a bargain was struck, Jess went to get Soldier and returned to the livery in time to see Tilly riding off. Adept at trailing a man without being seen, Jess followed, certain Tilly would lead him directly to the hideout.

Jess was elated. He knew he had been right in assuming Dillon would wait for Tilly at his hideout and thanked God fate had led him to Lolita. Even though he'd had to employ devious methods, Lolita had provided him with the valuable information pertaining to the hideout. But one burning question remained. A question that struck terror in Jess' heart. Was Ariel still alive or had Dillon already done away with her?

Jess followed Tilly for more than two hours. Once he thought he'd lost her, only to pick up her trail again a short time later. She crossed a narrow creek, rode over a slight rise, and reined in, staring at the cabin before deciding that all was well so she could enter. Dillon heard her approach and came out to greet her. Jess watched from a safe distance, straining his eyes for any sign that might indicate Ariel was being held in the cabin.

"Ya got here sooner than I reckoned," Dillon said, grinning. "Ya got the money?"

Tilly patted the carpetbags tied onto the saddle. "Right here, Bart. Every penny except for my fare to San Antonio, decent clothes, and this horse. Kirk Walters was anxious to get the papers signed so everything was taken care of a day or two after you left with the Leland woman. Did you take care of her like I said?"

"Well," he blustered, "there was a hitch but we got it all taken care of. She'll be off our hands in a day or two."

"You still have her?" Tilly asked, scowling darkly.

"Come inside, Tilly, I'll explain."

Tilly dismounted and Dillon sprang forward to help her with the bags carrying the money. Then they disappeared into the house.

Jess could hear none of the conversation that had just ensued, nor did he see any sign of Ariel. His heart beat so rapidly it sounded like thunder in his ears. Could they have already gotten rid of her? he wondered. Stark black fear curled in his gut and he knew he had to get closer to the cabin in order to find out if Ariel was in there. Tethering Soldier to a bush well out of sight of the cabin,

Jess approached the hideout with the stealth of a jungle cat. A master at stalking and capturing desperadoes, his steps were soundless, his breathing slow and even.

"This better be good, Bart," Tilly warned as she slanted an annoyed glance in Ariel's direction. "I thought I told you to get rid of the woman."

"Aw, Tilly, ya know I ain't never killed a woman," Dillon said in a placating tone.

"Just what do you expect to do with her, take her to Mexico with us? What about Pecos and Gandy?"

Ariel sat on one of the bunks, listening carefully but saying little. From what she knew of Tilly the woman wouldn't be any more inclined to release her than the three men had been. In fact, if their conversation was any indication, Tilly wanted her dead.

"I ain't gonna kill no woman carryin' a baby," Pecos said sourly. "Ya want her dead, ya do it yerself."

"Baby!" Tilly gasped, stunned. "And you three fools believe her?"

"Not me," Gandy announced, "but these two decided to get rid of her another way."

It was at this point that Jess reached the cabin, crouching beside the window as the occupants continued their conversation. He heard Dillon say, "Pecos has this friend in town who knows a man who buys women for whorehouses in Mexico. Why should we kill the woman when we can earn a little extra profit we weren't countin' on?"

Dillon knew Tilly well and appealing to her practical side was the best way he knew to turn her anger around. Besides, he seriously doubted Tilly would kill a pregnant woman.

"Sell her, huh?" Tilly repeated thoughtfully. Her mouth curled in a slow smile. "Got to hand it to you, Bart, you think of all the angles."

Bart's inflated ego soared.

"Hey, I'm the one what thought of the idea," Pecos grumbled. "Dillon don't deserve all the credit."

Jess' blood ran cold. Peering through the filthy window he could barely make out Ariel's small form crouched on the bunk across the room. He couldn't see her face at all and so had no idea if she had been hurt or abused by the three desperadoes. He had no notion how he was going to do it but he would not allow Ariel to be sold to a whoremaster. The people inside the cabin were talking again and he listened intently to their words.

"Just how are you going to work out this deal?" Tilly asked.

"Pecos is gonna meet the man, his name is Mick Garner, and bring him out here."

"Meet him where? You three don't dare show your faces in town."

"I'm gonna meet him south of the Alamo at that ridge with two humps," Pecos replied. "We're to meet at noon tomorrow. In two days we'll be on our way ta Mexico ta live like kings."

Jess' mind worked furiously. As bad as he wanted to storm through the door with guns blazing, he realized it was the worst thing he could possibly do. The odds were four to one against him. But that wasn't what bothered him; he'd faced greater odds before. It was his concern over Ariel that gave him second thoughts. In the ensuing melee she could be hurt or even killed by the exchange of bullets.

He could ride into town and enlist the marshal's help, but in Jess' opinion that idea was even more dangerous. More men meant more flying bullets and a greater chance of Ariel's being shot. If he was going to rescue Ariel he had to do it alone. As much as he hated leaving Ariel with these desperadoes, Jess knew she would be safe until Mick Garner arrived to carry her off with him. Jess prayed that having Tilly in the cabin would prevent any of the men from abusing Ariel physically. Lord knew what she'd been through already. But he couldn't think about that, not now, not when he needed a clear mind to plan Ariel's rescue.

"Fix us some grub, woman!" Dillon bellowed at Ariel as he opened the carpetbags Tilly brought. He dumped the contents onto the table and the men whooped and yelled and began counting their ill-gotten loot.

With the others occupied, Jess was able to concentrate on Ariel. She stood closer to the window now, listlessly shifting through tins of food. Jess nearly cried aloud in relief; she looked tired and wan but otherwise unharmed. He wanted to reach out to her, to pull her into his arms and comfort and protect her. He wanted—he wanted—Jesus, all he wanted was to love Ariel every day for the rest of his life. Soon, sweetheart, he silently vowed, trying to convey the message through the power of mental concentration.

Jess remained crouched beside the window until both Gandy and Pecos went outside to fetch water and wood for the fire. Then he melted silently into the bushes and made his way back to Soldier. There was much to be done before tomorrow noon.

Ariel felt a tingling sensation creep along her spine, the same sensation she experienced when she was in Jess' presence. Glancing toward the window, she expected to see his face pressed against the dirty pane. She saw nothing. But the feeling persisted. Did she wish for him so desperately that she conjured him up out of nowhere? she wondered bleakly. During the past two days Ariel had found no means of escape, formulated no plan to get out of this horrible situation. With three men guarding her she'd had no opportunity to slip past their surveillance. Since Tilly arrived escape seemed even more remote. Her only hope now was to somehow escape from the man who was taking her to Mexico.

His silver eyes narrowed into watchful slits, Jess scouted the area, his relief evident when he saw he had arrived in plenty of time. The position of the sun in the sky told him it wasn't yet noon. Cleanly shaved, his hair trimmed, and looking dapper in a new suit of clothes, Jess waited for Mick Garner to arrive for his rendezvous with Pecos Pete. He counted on Garner arriving early, or else he'd be forced to change his plan. He had no idea what the white slaver looked like but was comforted by the fact that none of the desperadoes had ever seen Garner. Nor did any of them know Jess Wilder. If luck was with him he would get Ariel away without a shot being fired or her life endangered. Later he'd come back with the law and make short work of Judd's killers.

Soldier heard the rider approach seconds before Jess and nickered softly in warning. Jess had no idea if he'd see Pecos or Garner, and grinned in satisfaction when Garner came into view. The man saw him and reined in.

Garner looked Jess over carefully. "Are you Pecos Pete?"

Jess nodded.

"You're not what I expected. Clara Mae spoke highly of you but I thought you'd be a rougher type."

"Don't let my looks fool you," Jess replied.

"Where's the girl?"

"At the cabin."

"She better be all you say to bring me clear out here."

Jess wanted to smash him in the face. "She is, and much more."

"Let's get going. I want time to sample her be-fore I take her back to San Antone."

Jess could take no more. "You slimy bastard!" he snarled. "Where you're going you won't be taking innocent women across the border for il-legal purposes."

Jess' intention was to disarm the man, tie him up, and place him temporarily out of commission until he came back with the marshal. But Garner had other ideas. A man who lived by his wits and fast draw, Garner realized too late the man stand-ing before him was not Pecos Pete. He reached for his gun. Jess was faster. Though Jess hadn't wanted to kill the man it was either shoot or be shot. He fired mere seconds before Garner. His aim was true; Garner never felt the bullet that killed him.

Cursing beneath his breath, Jess dragged Gar-ner out of sight. There was no time to bury him now for Pecos was expected at any moment. Then he searched Garner's pockets, removing identifi-cation and money, surprised to find the man car-ried such a large amount of cash. Jess hoped Pecos hadn't heard the shot but quickly made up a story in case he had. Then, slapping Garner's horse on the rump, he sent him racing toward town. When Pecos arrived he was sitting calmly on a rock, par-ing his nails with his knife.

Pecos Pete reined in sharply when he saw Jess. "You Mick Garner?"

"That's right," Jess returned. "You Pecos Pete?"

Pecos nodded. "Thought I heard a shot a few minutes ago. Know anythin' 'bout it?"

"Hunters," Jess said with a careless shrug. "Wouldn't worry too much about it."

"Mount up. I'll take ya ta the cabin."

Jess complied eagerly. The sooner he got Ariel away from that place the happier he'd be. His one fear was that she'd give him away when she saw him. Yet there had been no way possible for him to warn her ahead of time. He'd have to trust in God and luck that he could pull this off without anyone the wiser.

"They're here." Dillon had stationed himself at the window, waiting for Pecos and Garner to arrive.

Ariel heard the crunch of hooves on the ground and then footsteps as the man walked to the cabin. Inwardly she cringed, wondering what kind of man would buy women for whorehouses. He had to be cruel and devious and lower than a snake to be engaged in such a vile business. The kind who would ignore her plea for mercy, Ariel decided. She mentally prepared herself for the worst kind of villain imaginable.

What she wasn't prepared for was Jess Wilder. Big as life and twice as handsome. He filled the doorway with his bulk, dressed as she had never seen him before. He looked alert and dangerous and was so welcome a sight that Ariel nearly screamed at the sight of him. Jess found her immediately, his silver eyes flashing a warning Ariel heeded instantly. She couldn't have said a word even if she wanted to. Her tongue was frozen to the roof of her mouth and her legs wobbled beneath her like jelly. So many questions flashed through her brain that her entire thinking process broke down.

What was Jess doing here? How did he know where to find her? Was Mick Garner someone he knew well? Did he expect to take her away from here without Dillon becoming suspicious? Ariel searched for answers and found none. All she could do was pray Jess knew what he was doing, pray for a safe deliverance, pray they wouldn't both die.

Jess found Ariel with his eyes, noting her pallor, the violet smudges beneath her eyes and the look of utter hopelessness on her face. Their gazes locked, his shooting an instant warning, hers reflecting her shock. Time seemed suspended as Jess conveyed his silent message and Ariel received it with a jerky nod of her head.

" 'Bout time," Dillon grumbled. "Ya get lost?"

"Got here as quick as we could," Pecos said. "This here is Mick Garner." To Jess, he said, "These are my friends Bart Dillon, Gandy, and Tilly Cowles."

"Howdy," Jess replied, forcing himself to remain calm. "Is that the woman?" He motioned toward Ariel.

"Yep," Dillon said. "Right purty, ain't she?"

"A little too skinny for my taste. Haven't you been feedin' her?"

"Fed her good," Gandy interjected. "Can't help it if she don't have much appetite."

"How much?" Jess asked, going right to the point.

Dillon started to speak but Tilly forestalled him. When it came to bargaining she considered herself far superior to any of the three men present.

"Seven hundred and fifty dollars," Tilly said, her small tongue flicking out to moisten her lips.

"What!" Jess said, pretending outrage. He didn't want to seem too eager—acting as he thought Mick Garner might. "Seven hundred and fifty dollars for one scrawny woman?"

"And worth every penny," Tilly declared. "She's a virgin and you can demand top dollar for her the first time." By the time Garner learned the truth Tilly expected to be long gone and beyond his reach.

"A virgin?" Jess said, pretending interest. "Five hundred, that's all I'm prepared to pay."

"Six fifty," Tilly haggled.

"Six hundred," Jess returned, prepared to pay three times that amount.

"Done," Dillon said, afraid they'd lose out altogether if Tilly was allowed to continue. "In case yer interested her name is Ariel Leland."

Jess stared at Ariel a moment, nodded, then counted out the money, placing it in Dillon's hand. Abruptly Dillon turned and went to where Ariel stood watching the proceedings in a kind of daze. He grasped her arm and pulled her close enough to whisper in her ear, "If ya tell him you're growin' a baby and he brings ya back we'll kill ya. If yer smart ya won't tell no one."

"She's my property now, get your hands off her," Jess growled, his temper exploding.

"Just tellin' her good-bye." Dillon shrugged, backing away. Mick Garner was a man he didn't care to tangle with.

Gandy watched the proceedings with a puzzled look on his face, staring at Jess as if he was trying to remember something, something important. "Haven't we met before?" he finally asked.

Jess fixed him with a baleful glare. "Not that I know of."

"Funny, I seem to remember—oh, well, I reckon it's not important."

Turning away, Jess beckoned to Ariel. "C'mon, woman, I haven't got all day." Then to Dillon, "What about her clothes?"

Dillon pointed to a carpetbag dumped next to the door. "She ain't got much but ya can have what there is."

Jess nodded and picked up the bag, expecting Ariel to follow without being told. He tried to act As Garner would, without being too solicitous or caring. Ariel was slow to react, finding it difficult to believe she was actually getting out of here alive, without Jess' deception being discovered or anyone getting hurt. For a moment she feared Gandy would ruin everything, but fortunately his memory failed him at the right moment. When she finally realized she was free to go with Jess she willed her frozen limbs to move.

They were nearly out the door when Dillon called out to them, "Wait!"

Terror slammed through Ariel, and she could tell by the way Jess' shoulders tensed that he was prepared for the worst.

"Ya'll find her horse out back."

"Much obliged," Jess called over his shoulder.

His steps were unhurried as he went around to the rear of the cabin, but the moment they were out of sight he grasped Ariel about the waist and threw her onto the horse's back, handed her the carpetbag and reins, and slapped the animal's rump. He was quick to follow, vaulting aboard Soldier and spurring him into motion.

Ariel hung on for dear life, holding her breath until she was certain no one was following.

Chapter 20

After fifteen minutes Jess slowed the furious pace he had set, certain now that no one inside the cabin suspected a thing.

"Are you all right, sweetheart?" They were riding side by side at a more leisurely clip, allowing Ariel time to catch her breath.

"I'm fine, Jess, but how—"

"Explanations will have to wait until I have you safe in San Antone. I don't think we're being followed but I'm not taking any chances. Even if they do get suspicious they won't dare follow us to town where they might be recognized."

Ariel nodded, her mind still reeling from the shock of seeing Jess. What had happened to Mick Garner? How did Jess know she'd been abducted? How did he know where to find her? Why did none of the desperadoes seem to recognize Jess? Not until Ariel saw San Antonio rising in the distance did she finally believe she was safe. She was with Jess, he had extracted her from a situation she probably couldn't have gotten out of herself, and, more importantly, he loved her enough to come after her.

Jess called a halt on the outskirts of town, no longer driven by the urgency that brought him this far. He dismounted and reached out for Ariel. She slid into his arms with little effort as he set her on her feet. But he didn't release her; he kept her tightly enfolded in his embrace. He didn't ever want to let her go.

"Are you sure you're all right, sweetheart? They—didn't hurt you, did they?"

"They didn't harm me in any way, Jess," Ariel assured him.

"When I get you back home I'm never gonna let you out of my sight, woman."

"Is that a proposal, Jess?"

"Damn right. As soon as I take care of some unfinished business we'll be married in Waco. But first I'll get you settled in the hotel room I rented in San Antone last night."

"Thank you for being here when I needed you. There are so many questions I want to ask I don't know where to begin."

"Save them, sweetheart, there will be plenty of time later for questions. All I want to do right now is hold you and kiss you and thank God for bringing me to you in time."

She lifted her mouth and his lips covered hers. His kiss spoke eloquently of his love, his need for her, and his commitment to their future together. It also told her how frightened he had been for her, told her of his anger and helplessness when he'd learned she had been abducted by Dillon. Clinging together, their bodies greeted one another in rapturous reunion as Jess' hands boldly roamed the hills and valleys he knew so well. Ariel felt him swell and throb through the barrier of their clothes.

Jess was the first to break off the kiss. "Jesus H. Christ! Forgive me, sweetheart, for being a selfish bastard. I reckon I've been too long without you. After all you've been through you deserve better than being pawed out here on the prairie. I'll settle you in at the hotel where you can take a hot bath and get some decent food in you. You look so thin they couldn't have been feeding you."

Ariel recalled the reason for her lack of appetite the past few weeks and smiled. She hoped Jess would be as pleased as she was to learn their love had made a baby. They'd go back to the ranch and— Her mind skidded to a halt. Did she have a ranch? Would the law side with Kirk and say that he had bought Leland Ranch in good faith? Was this to be the end of everything? Had she gone through all this travail for nothing? She remained quietly thoughtful during the remainder of the ride to San Antonio. Jess assumed she was exhausted after her long ordeal and left her to her reverie.

"You've no cause to worry that it will look bad for us to be staying together in the same room," Jess said as they reined in outside the hotel. "I registered as Mr. and Mrs. Jess Wilder. It won't be long till we're married anyway."

The room was comfortable and clean and Ariel eyed the bed gratefully. After curling up on the ground and floor these past several days, sleeping in a bed would be sheer bliss. Especially if Jess was beside her. She wondered when they would return to Waco. It couldn't be any too soon for her. By now her stepfather would be at the ranch and hopefully setting everyone straight on her identity. Ariel knew he probably expected to take her back to St. Louis, but once she married he'd have no jurisdiction over her.

To Ariel's consternation Jess prepared to leave almost immediately. "Where are you going?" she asked as he changed into his normal attire of denim pants, checkered shirt, and vest. When she first saw him shedding his clothes she thought . . . But when he began dressing again she grew alarmed.

"I told you I had unfinished business, sweetheart." Leaving Ariel right now was the hardest thing he'd ever done, but this time he'd be gone only a short while.

"You're going after Dillon!" Ariel said, comprehension dawning. "You aren't even going to stay long enough to answer all my questions, are you?"

"I'm not gonna leave you tonight, wildcat. Not even Dillon can drag me from this bed tonight. I'm gonna go see the marshal. He needs to be told about Dillon and where he can be found. It takes time to round up a posse."

"You're coming back?" Ariel asked, still skeptical.

"Wild horses couldn't drag me away from you tonight." He said nothing of tomorrow but Ariel drew her own conclusions. "I'll order you a bath and food. Sleep for a while if you want; I'll be back as soon as I can."

The delicious odor of the food Jess ordered miraculously restored Ariel's appetite. She ate everything on the plate and asked for another helping of dessert. When the dishes were cleared away she spread her hands across her stomach, surprised that a child could be growing inside her when there was still no visible sign of it. She looked as flat as she had ever been. Now that she no longer felt nauseous most of the day and her appetite had returned she expected to see a marked change in her appearance. She tried to picture herself swelling with Jess' child and wrinkled her nose. It wasn't exactly a thrilling notion. Still, it did have its rewards.

The bath was even more welcome than the food. It had been days since she'd bathed in a real tub and it felt delicious. Ariel could have fallen asleep in the warm tub, and nearly did. When Jess arrived a short time later she had just finished washing her hair.

Jess closed the door and leaned against it, a slow smile curving his lips. He paused, enjoying the entrancing sight of Ariel all rosy and glowing from her bath. She was even lovelier than he re-

membered. She was the tiniest woman he'd ever
seen, yet every inch of her was cleverly fashioned
and delicately molded into a perfect package of
femininity. She looked as if he could break her in
two with his bare hands but she was strong.
Strong, independent, and stubborn. Most women
would buckle under all the adversity she'd en-
dured since coming to Texas. Yet Ariel had survived and grown even more beautiful, if that were
possible. With fortitude and surprising strength
she had prevailed against everything fate had
placed in her path. And she was his, to love and
cherish the rest of his life.

"Are you going to stand there staring at me all
night?" Ariel asked saucily.

"Nope, I got other ideas how to spend the
night," Jess hinted brashly. "If you're not too
tired," he amended. He'd do nothing to hurt Ariel, no matter how badly he wanted to make love
to her. She had been through too much already.

Ariel's answer was to step out of the tub and
hold her arms out to him. Jess reacted swiftly,
pushing himself away from the door and moving
with the grace of a stalking panther. His arms
closed around her and Ariel felt her feet leave the
ground as he scooped her high in the air. She
squealed in delight as he swung her around then
set her back on her feet. Stepping back he slowly
began peeling off his clothes.

"No sense in wasting water," he said as he
stepped into the tub. "Wash my back, sweetheart."

Ariel eagerly complied, soaping the cloth and
scrubbing the broad expanse of his back. Jess
groaned in sheer pleasure. Suddenly he twisted
around and lifted her into the tub with him. The
water had grown cold but before long they were
generating enough heat to steam up the room.

"Jess, I just finished my bath!" Ariel laughingly protested as she landed atop Jess with a splash.

"Have you ever made love in a tub of water?"

"You know darn good and well I haven't."

"Then it's about time. Face me and straddle my legs."

"Jess, surely the bed is more comfortable."

"Perhaps," he allowed, "but how can you judge when you've never tried it? Relax, sweetheart, and let me show you."

His hands on her flesh were warm and persuasive, his silver eyes hypnotic and compelling. Ariel could refuse him nothing.

"Touch me," he urged, placing her hand on his swollen member. "Feel how much I want you."

Ariel's small hand closed around his erection, and she thrilled at the way it reacted to her caress. How could anything feel so soft, like velvet, yet pulse with strength and be so hard at the same time? she marveled. Her fingers tightened, drawing an agonized groan from Jess' throat. "Jesus, woman, you're killing me."

"Now you know how I feel when you torment me," Ariel teased, increasing the pressure and slowly moving her hand up and down along his magnificent length. Her words ended in a trembling sigh as Jess found the tip of her breast, drawing it into his mouth and sucking vigorously.

His hands moved ceaselessly over her slick flesh, sliding over her hips to her taut buttocks, molding and squeezing the taut mounds as he continued to torment her swollen nipples with his tongue and mouth. Ariel gasped when his fingers separated the velvet petals of her womanhood and slipped inside.

"You're so warm and tight, sweetheart," he moaned against her lips. "I want to love you all night long, in every way a man can love a woman.

But if you keep on doing that with your hand I'll spoil it for both of us.''

Ariel blushed and immediately released that part of him that had grown until her hand could no longer encompass him. Jess shuddered and began moving his fingers, still implanted deeply inside Ariel. Slowly at first, then faster, until she was panting and moaning and churning the water around them with her mindless thrashing. When her climax was only moments away he removed his fingers, lifted her buttocks, and slid into her with effortless ease. Then they were moving together, mouths fused, riding the crest of an incredible wave, bare flesh meshing with bare flesh.

Ariel went wild, clutching his shoulders fiercely. ''Jess, I feel as if I—I—oh, God!''

''I feel it too, sweetheart. Hang on tight, I'm right beside you.''

Then Ariel's mind shut down and her body took over, flinging her to the top of the highest mountain. She waited for Jess and he joined her for a blissful eternity until they came floating back to earth. Ariel hadn't yet recovered from Jess' loving when he lifted her from the tub and carried her to the bed. With utmost tenderness he dried her with the sheet. Then he dried himself and stretched out beside her.

''I'm the luckiest man alive.'' His voice was low and so filled with love that Ariel wanted to cry.

''You don't think me too bold or—or wanton for enjoying you like I do?''

''I think you're perfect. Few men find a woman who can satisfy them as completely as you do me. Your body is mine, just as mine is yours. Don't ever change. What we do is right and beautiful and magnificent. I love you, Ariel Leland.''

''I love you, Jess Wilder.''

They slept for a time. When Ariel awoke it was dark and she could see nothing but the silver gleam in Jess' eyes as he reclined on one elbow, staring at her. "It's about time you woke up," he said, his voice hinting that he knew of more pleasant things to do than sleep.

"Don't you ever tire?"

"Not when the woman I love is lying next to me in bed without a stitch of clothes on."

He rolled atop her, careful to keep the bulk of his weight from squashing her. He had been awake for a long time, watching Ariel, ready to love her again but loath to wake her out of so sound a sleep. He was ready—Jesus, he was ready, but he wanted to inflame Ariel's passion until it matched his own. He kissed and fondled and caressed, not one inch of her body immune from his erotic onslaught. When his lips found her soft woman's flesh, Ariel cried out. Desperately she clutched his head to her as the sensual agony of his gentle mouthing left her aching and trembling for more.

Raising her hips to his mouth, Jess teased and titillated with his tongue and lips until she was trembling with need. Then Jess drove her over the edge. As her climax seized her, Jess raised on his knees and pushed inside her. Then he was pumping furiously, driving Ariel even higher as he searched for his own reward. Ariel closed her eyes, lost in a maze of feelings so intense she wanted to explode. Jess' voice came to her as if from a great distance.

"Look at me, Ariel. Open your eyes and look at me. I want to see your face when you come to me. I want to see the passion burst into violet flame in your eyes. I want to hear the gasp on your lips and know that I pleased you."

Her eyes flew open, glazed with passion and overbright. Her voice was strained and taut with the onset of rapture. "You please me, Jess, oh— God—you—please—me."

Then words were no longer necessary as she showed him in the most basic way just how won-

derfully he pleased her. Jess waited until her cries
had turned to soft whimpers before driving himself to climax.

"What time is it?" Ariel asked later, much later.

"Can't be much past nine o'clock. You hungry?"

"No, the meal you sent up earlier was adequate
as well as delicious. It's time to answer my questions now. I want you to explain how you knew
I was with Dillon and what happened to the real
Mick Garner."

Jess got up and lit a lamp, then sat on the edge
of the bed. "I knew you needed me," Jess said,
astounding her. "I felt it in my bones. That's why
I went back to Waco without fulfilling my promise
to Judd. I finally realized that nothing in the world
is more important to me than you."

"You gave up on finding Dillon?" Ariel asked,
flabbergasted. As tenacious as Jess was she
wouldn't have expected him to abandon his
search or compromise his ideals. Not for her, not
for anyone.

"I told you, sweetheart, there's no competition
between you and Dillon. You win hands down.
When I reached Waco, Rosalie told me you were
missing. I was beside myself with worry and tried
to persuade the marshal to gather a posse to look
for you. But everyone in Waco seemed to believe
you are Tilly Cowles. Including lawyer Burns and
the marshal. The fools refused to believe the real
Tilly sold the ranch and took off with the money."

"Wasn't anyone suspicious when Tilly left?
That should have set them to thinking."

"She told them she didn't want to be around
when her kin arrived from St. Louis. She told
them she feared her stepfather would insist she
leave Texas and they believed her. Since there was
no reason to hold her, she left with Kirk Walters'
money. I'm afraid she cleaned out your bank account, sweetheart."

"I know." Ariel sighed. "They bragged about it to me. Surely the sale won't be binding once the law learns the truth, will it?"

"I don't rightly know; it's up to the judge to decide. But I'll do all in my power to see that all your property is restored to you. That's why I'm staying behind."

"We're not going back to Waco right away?" Ariel asked.

"You're going back to Waco. I'm staying here until this business with Dillon is resolved."

Ariel was stunned. Hadn't Jess just said he no longer felt driven to avenge Judd's death? "I don't understand, Jess. I thought you had a change of heart about Dillon."

"I talked to the marshal last night. Told him I'd take him to Dillon's hideout. He'd never find it without my help. He's gathering a posse right now; we ride out in the morning after—"

"I'll stay here, too," Ariel declared before he could finish his sentence. "We'll go back to Waco together."

"No, sweetheart, you're going to take the morning stage. It leaves at nine o'clock. I've already bought your ticket."

"What! You did that without consulting me?"

"I knew you wouldn't agree so I went ahead and did it anyway."

"Why, Jess, why must you go after Dillon when you just got through saying he was no longer important to you? Why can't you just tell the marshal how to get there?"

"I meant every word I said, sweetheart, but this doesn't involve just me anymore, it involves you."

Ariel scowled. "I wasn't harmed. They could have—raped me or killed me but they didn't."

"They were going to sell you into a life too vile to describe. You know what Mick Garner would have done with you."

"I know, but it didn't happen. Can't you let the law take care of Dillon?"

"Don't you understand? I have to be certain this time, Ariel. I know where he is, I know how to find him, and I want to be there when he's apprehended. They have your money, and for that reason alone I can't sit back and take the chance that Dillon will escape again."

"I don't care about the money. I'll admit the ranch is important to me, but so are you."

"Restoring the money to Walters might be the only hope you have of getting your ranch back. Nothing is gonna happen to me."

"Then why can't I wait here?"

Jess sighed. He knew this was going to be difficult and he didn't like it any more than Ariel did. "It's important that you get back to Waco as soon as possible. Your stepfather must be worried sick over you and the marshal there should know what happened. Perhaps lawyer Burns can straighten out this mess so you'll get your property back.

"Besides, I may be held up here for a few days once Dillon is captured. There will be questions that need answering and papers to sign before the marshal hands the money over to me. Marshal Smith and I have known each another for a long time and he's a good man, but Dillon's escaped too many times in the past for me to trust anyone but myself with his capture."

"So I'm to leave in the morning," Ariel repeated dully.

"I'll only be a day or two behind you," Jess promised.

"What if you're hurt—or—worse? There are three armed men in that cabin and a woman as capable of committing murder as they are."

"The marshal promised at least three men besides him and me. Dillon and his band don't stand a chance against the five of us. Look, sweetheart, I'm used to taking care of myself; been doing it for years."

"What if they escape? What if they somehow manage to get across the border?"

"That won't happen, but if it does, I promise I won't follow. Somehow I'll scrape the money together to repay Walters for the ranch. I've got some saved, maybe not enough, but it's all yours."

It was on the tip of Ariel's tongue to tell Jess about the baby, but after careful consideration she decided that now was not a good time. She didn't want his mind cluttered with thoughts that might distract him. He was obstinate and mule-stubborn but she could sympathize with his need to see an end to Dillon's career of murder and mayhem. If Jess accompanied her to Waco because of the baby he might regret it the rest of their lives. And blame her for forcing a decision on him.

Instead, she spoke the words that amounted to an unspoken blessing. "Love me again, Jess, love me with all the fury in your heart. It's going to have to last me until I see you again. Make it soon, my love, for I can't wait to be your wife."

The world was still gray with the faintest pink blush in the east when Jess awoke. There was still plenty of time before he put Ariel on the Waco stage, so he let her sleep. While she slumbered peacefully he gathered together his belongings—there wasn't much—and packed them in his saddlebags. When he finished he sat down on the edge of the bed and gazed at Ariel, thinking how lucky he was to have a woman like her love him. It frightened him to realize how close he'd come to marrying Ellie Lu Dodge, a superficial woman who couldn't have satisfied him half as well. Ariel might be tiny but she had more of everything most normal women possessed, including brains, beauty, and a dauntless spirit. They would produce wonderful children, he thought, already picturing dark-haired cherubs with violet eyes.

Ariel stirred and opened her eyes. "How long have you been staring at me?"

"Not long. I could sit here forever looking at you."

"Jess, you don't have to go with the marshal. We could go back to Waco together."

"It's not that easy, sweetheart. I explained it all to you last night."

"I know. How soon do you have to leave?"

"I'll join the marshal's posse right after I put you on the stage."

"We still have hours yet." Her voice was low and seductive and oh-so-enticing as she tossed aside the blanket and opened her arms.

Her body was flushed and warm from sleep; Jess couldn't help but reach out and caress her breasts. "Are you trying to change my mind?"

"I would if I could but I realize it would do no good," Ariel said. "I just want you to love me again before you leave."

"It's what I want too, but I thought you'd be too tired after last night."

For an answer she pulled his head down and kissed him. It wasn't long before their bodies were also joined and soaring aloft to pleasure's peak.

Three hours later Ariel was seated inside the Waco stage with four other passengers.

"I'll be just a few days behind you, sweetheart," Jess promised as he waved her off.

"Be careful," Ariel called back. "Please be careful."

The marshal and the posse were waiting when Jess arrived at the jailhouse.

"All set, Jess, let's go."

"I'm ready, Ted."

Marshal Ted Smith and Jess had known one another since the time Jess was U.S. marshal in

Fort Worth. They liked and respected each other and since Jess had turned bounty hunter Smith had helped him collect rewards for desperadoes he'd brought in.

They rode steadily. There were five of them; Smith, his deputy, two other men hastily deputized, and Jess. They passed the place where Jess had met and killed Mick Garner. On their return they would retrieve the body and take it into town. They were a half mile from the hideout when Jess called a halt.

"We'll go on foot from here," he said. "Secure your horses and check your ammunition. The only way Dillon will escape this time is if I'm dead."

Jess led the way and the others followed, crouching low as they neared the cabin. All looked quiet. Smith sent a man around to the back and he returned to report that all four horses were tethered behind the cabin. Those words were music to Jess' ears. He'd been worried that Dillon and his band might have decided to leave last night, or early this morning. Even if they had, he knew the posse would catch them but he felt much better knowing the four were still holed up in the cabin.

Ariel had been the reason the posse hadn't left at first light this morning. Jess had refused to leave until he put her on the stage himself. Ariel had a penchant for doing just as she pleased and getting into all kinds of trouble, and before he could concentrate on apprehending Dillon he wanted her safely on her way to join her stepfather in Waco. The marshal had agreed to delay their leaving to satisfy Jess.

Jess and the marshal were discussing how best to storm the cabin when the door opened and Gandy walked out. He went directly to the back and began saddling the horses.

"They're getting ready to leave," Jess hissed.

"That's Gandy, a mean son of a bitch if I ever saw one."

"If we go in now we'll catch them by surprise," Smith said, carefully weighing the situation. He raised his hand to give the signal, then lowered it when Pecos Pete came out the door. He also went around to the back, presumedly to help Gandy.

"Better yet." Jess chuckled. "Send your men around back to take care of Gandy and Pecos. You and I will go in together through the door and take Dillon and Tilly."

Smith whispered to his deputy and the man slipped away to alert the other two men. "No shootin' unless it's necessary," Smith warned. "I know how bad you want Dillon but unless he resists I want him alive to stand trial. Tilly, too. Don't much cotton to shootin' a woman."

"I don't care how we bring him in," Jess gritted out from between clenched teeth. "I just want him to pay for his crimes."

Slowly they edged toward the cabin, running the last few feet across the open yard that had neither tree nor bush to provide shelter. Jess stationed himself on one side of the door and Smith on the other. At Smith's signal they shoved the door open and stormed inside.

"It's the law, Dillon! Give up, you haven't got a chance," Jess shouted.

"What in the hell!" Dillon whirled, mouth agape, his eyes round with shock. "How did you get here?" Then he saw Jess, recognizing him immediately as the man he thought was Mick Garner. "You! How much did they pay ya ta bring them here?"

"Nothing, Dillon, I've been trailing you a long time," Jess snarled.

Suddenly Dillon's eyes narrowed and an incredulous look came over his face. "You ain't Mick Garner."

"Damn right I'm not. I'm Jess Wilder—recognize the name?"

"No, should I?"

Jess wanted to take the man by the neck and squeeze until the last breath left his body.

"You killed my brother in a bank robbery over two years ago in Fort Worth."

"Is that why you been doggin' me?"

"Isn't that reason enough? You took the only family I had. I loved my brother. He was young and had his whole life ahead of him until you snuffed it out with a single shot."

During this exchange neither Smith nor Jess paid much heed to Tilly, except to note that she was sitting on one of the cots fiddling with the carpetbags. At the time she didn't present much of a threat so they weren't prepared when she drew out a pistol from one of the bags. "Bart!" She tossed the gun to him and he caught it deftly, spinning around in the same breath and firing.

Then all hell broke lose as Tilly palmed another gun and joined the melee. Jess grunted and spun around when a wild shot slammed into his shoulder. When the shooting stopped Bart Dillon lay dead and Tilly had sustained a slight wound. Only Ted Smith remained standing, miraculously escaping injury. Moments later the other members of the posse stormed inside, having subdued Gandy and Pecos without firing a shot.

"Jess, are you all right?" Ted asked, dropping down to examine him.

"I've felt better," Jess said, wincing, "but I reckon I'll live. What about Dillon?"

"Dead. Tilly's wounded but she'll survive. Both Gandy and Pecos are tied up outside. Can you ride? We'll have you back to San Antone in no time where Doc Hadley can take care of you."

Grimacing from pain, Jess leaned heavily on Smith as he staggered outside. Someone had been sent to bring the horses around and somehow Jess found the spurt of adrenaline needed to mount Soldier. Staying conscious was the most difficult thing he had ever done.

Chapter 21

Ariel stepped off the stage four days later. She was exhausted; her clothes and skin were dusted with a fine layer of grime and she was looking forward with relish to a good soaking in a hot tub. It was much colder in Waco than it had been in San Antonio and she pulled her cloak more closely around her. With a pang of regret she realized she couldn't go out to the ranch—not yet, anyway, so she checked into the hotel, using the money Jess had given her before he put her on the stage. The clerk looked at her strangely, his eyes nearly popping out of his head. He couldn't wait to tell the marshal who'd just blown into town. He had to hand it to her, Tilly Cowles sure had guts!

After Ariel had the bath she craved, she prepared to call on the marshal and explain what had happened. Jess was adamant about her clearing this mess up as quickly as possible. Afterward she had to find her stepfather and face his anger. She could well imagine how Tom Brady felt about coming to Texas to bring home his wayward stepdaughter. He'd be even angrier when he learned she had no intention of leaving with him. Ariel had just donned her cloak and had her hand on the doorknob when a knock on the door startled her. She opened it instantly. It was the marshal.

"I didn't believe it when the hotel clerk told me

Tilly Cowles was back in town,'' he said without
offering a proper greeting. "There's a reward out
for your arrest, Tilly, so I suggest you come along
quietly.''

Ariel sighed wearily. It was starting again. Only
this time she would nip it in the bud. "I'm Ariel
Leland. I was kidnaped by Bart Dillon and taken
to San Antonio. Jess Wilder found me and sent
me ahead to explain things. He'll follow later, as
soon as Dillon and his band are apprehended. The
real Tilly is with Dillon; she arrived at Dillon's
hideout with my money and Kirk Walters'
money.''

"That's a wild story,'' the marshal said, shaking his head in disbelief. "But I reckon we'll find
out the truth soon enough. Your visitor from St.
Louis has arrived. I sent word for him to meet us
here; he'll soon clear up this mess.''

"Tom is here? Thank God. Even though I know
he intends to take me back to St. Louis I'll be glad
to see him. I've lived this nightmare long
enough.''

"Tom?'' the marshal repeated, eyeing Ariel
narrowly. "The name the man gave is—''

"I came as soon as I got your message, Marshal.''

He stood in the doorway, looking every bit the
dapper businessman. A very much annoyed one.
His sandy brows made a continuous slash across
his brow and his narrow face was drawn up in a
scowl as he glared at Ariel. His blue eyes, normally so clear, were stormy with disapproval. His
usual calm had deserted him and his thin shoulders shook with barely suppressed anger.

"It's about time you came back. You wouldn't
believe the trouble I've gone through for you.
How you get yourself into these messes, Ariel, is
beyond me. Your parents are fit to be tied over
this latest escapade.''

Ariel's jaw dropped open. She could do little

more than stare at the irate man. It had never occurred to her that her mother and Tom would send Denton Dobbs after her.

"Denton, where's Tom?" It sounded inane but it was all she could think of to say.

"He couldn't get away. And you know how your mother hates Texas. She appealed to me as your fiancé to come down to this godforsaken country and bring you home where you belong. After arriving I can well understand her hatred. It's a beastly place."

"My fiancé? Denton, I never said—"

"Hold on here. You know this woman?" the marshal asked, glaring at Denton.

"Of course. This is my fiancée, Ariel Leland. Just who did you think she was?"

"Well, now," the marshal blustered, "how in the hell was I to know who was Ariel Leland and who was Tilly Cowles? The other woman had everyone fooled."

"I told you the truth," Ariel grumbled bitterly, "but you all refused to listen."

"I'm sorry, Miss Leland," the marshal apologized, grinning sheepishly.

"You can't imagine how distraught I was when I arrived and was told you had already left," Denton remonstrated. "I hated to disappoint your parents so I waited around to see if you'd come back. I've put myself to a lot of trouble on your account, Ariel, and your poor parents are beside themselves."

"I was abducted, Denton," Ariel explained, growing angry. The man was impossible. Seeing him again brought to mind all the reasons she had rejected his proposal.

"Abducted! How dreadful. Were—you hurt? How did you escape? Your mother isn't going to like this, no indeed."

"It's a long story, but standing here in the

doorway is hardly the place to talk. I want to go home, to the ranch. I'll tell you all about it there.''

"But you no longer own the ranch," Denton reminded her.

"I never sold it. My impostor did.''

"How about it, Marshal?" Denton asked, turning to the lawman. "Who owns Leland Ranch?''

"I'm not qualified to answer that," the marshal hedged. "The judge will have to hear the case and decide.''

"Judge," Ariel repeated, annoyed. "It stands to reason that if I never sold the ranch it still belongs to me.''

"I think you had better come down to the office, Miss Leland, and tell me exactly what happened. Did Jess Wilder find you? He came to me and insisted I form a posse to look for you.''

"Yes, thank God Jess Wilder believed in me.''

"Who is Jess Wilder?" Denton asked, his eyebrows quirking upward.

"A—friend," Ariel replied. "He was my foreman for a while. He tracked Dillon, the man who abducted me, to San Antonio and rescued me.''

"I'd say he was more than a good friend to track you clear to San Antonio." Denton's voice was decidedly cool as he impaled Ariel with the intensity of his blue eyes.

"You two can hash this out later," the marshal interrupted. "All I need to know are the facts. Shall we leave? It's only a short distance to my office.''

Ariel had no choice but to accompany him and Denton Dobbs to the lawman's office. When she was seated across the desk from the marshal he asked her to begin. She related how she had been robbed of her valuables, the accident involving the stage, and being mistaken for Tilly Cowles when she was found with her hands shackled. He asked a few pertinent questions, which she answered before continuing, ending with the events of the past few weeks.

"That's an amazin' story, Miss Leland," the marshal said slowly. "And you say Jess Wilder and Marshal Smith are goin' after Dillon?"

"Not only is it amazing but rather improbable. Not that I'm questioning your integrity, my dear," Denton threw in. "I applaud your mother's decision not to allow you to come to Texas. Too bad you didn't heed her words. You always were headstrong and willful. Once we're married I'll expect you to settle down and lead an exemplary life. Big things are in store for me at the bank and I'll need a wife who is supportive and submissive to me in all things."

Ariel nearly laughed aloud. "Find someone else, Denton, I'm none of those things. I told you before I won't marry you."

"Your parents say otherwise. They are preparing to announce our engagement at this moment. By the time we arrive in St. Louis all the arrangements will have been made."

Ariel gritted her teeth in frustration. What would it take to discourage this man? She chose to ignore him. "Can I move back home, Marshal? Is Rosalie at the ranch?"

The marshal scratched his head in consternation. "Well, now, I don't know about that. You did say Wilder was bringin' back Walters' money, didn't you?" Ariel nodded. "Walters isn't gonna like this, but until the court decides what's to be done I reckon it won't hurt for you to move back to the ranch."

"Ariel—"

"I don't want to hear it, Denton. I'm going home."

"I'm going with you," Denton said firmly. "I fear if I let you out of my sight you'll disappear again. Beside, I don't think we'll be in town long. I'm taking you back to St. Louis in a few days."

"I'm not going."

"I hoped this wouldn't be necessary, Ariel. I hoped you'd come with me of your own free will."

"What are you talking about?"

"I have a court order obtained by your mother in St. Louis ordering your return. You're still underage and she has ever right to demand your return. It also gives me the power to act as your guardian. I'll do whatever is necessary to get you back to St. Louis."

He handed the document to the marshal with a flourish.

"Looks legal and bindin'," the marshal said, passing it to Ariel.

"I can't believe this! I never thought Mother would go so far!"

"She loves you, Ariel, and is thinking only of your future."

"My future is in Texas with—with—my friends," she finished lamely. Bringing Jess into the picture now would only complicate the issue.

"I'm taking you back home if I have to hog-tie you and drag you aboard the stage," Denton replied shortly. "I didn't come all this way to return home empty-handed."

"Can he do that?" Ariel asked the marshal.

"I reckon he can. That paper gives him the legal right to do just about what he pleases where you're concerned."

Denton smirked as if to say, *I told you so.*

Ariel burned in silent indignation, determined to go nowhere with Denton Dobbs except out to the ranch where she intended to remain until Jess arrived.

"If you plan to accompany me back to the ranch, I suggest we leave. I have only to pack my bag and send a telegram and I'll be ready."

"I'll pick you up in an hour," Denton said tersely. "But if you're thinking of sending a telegram to your mother, forget it. Nothing will change her mind."

"I'll ride out to Walters' place and explain all this to him," the marshal said. "Rosalie is still out at the ranch, by the way. Walters was lettin' her stay until he rented the place."

"How big of him," Ariel said dryly.

An hour later Denton arrived at the hotel with a rented buckboard. Ariel was waiting for him on the wide porch fronting the street. Her one bag joined three of Denton's in the bed of the buckboard and after a jerky start due to Denton's rather inept handling of the reins they rolled through town. Denton seemed to know exactly where he was going.

"How do you know the way?" Ariel asked curiously.

"I've had plenty of time to look over the spread after I arrived," he explained.

"Then you know what a wonderful place it is," Ariel said enthusiastically.

"It has possibilities," Denton admitted grudgingly. "But it's hardly what I'd call a booming enterprise."

"Father did very well at ranching. There's money in the bank to prove it."

"There *was* money in the bank," Denton corrected. "Obviously you are too young and inexperienced to handle these matters yourself for you were bilked out of thousands of dollars. I have spoken with Jason Burns several times and he agrees with me."

"How can you be so condemning when nothing that has happened was my fault?" Ariel exploded furiously.

"You're wrong, Ariel, everything that's happened thus far has been your fault. Leaving St. Louis without your parents' permission made it your fault. Your father was irresponsible for leaving his ranch to you. His will should have stipu-

lated that the property be sold and the money put
in trust for your future husband to administer as
he saw fit. Or that your mother act in your stead
and do as she saw fit. It's a pity it took a court
order to do what your father neglected to do."

"Don't you dare belittle my father's integrity!"
Ariel said angrily. "He knew what he was doing.
The ranch is mine and I intend to keep it."

"We'll see."

Ariel fell silent, refusing to be drawn into further conversation. When they rode into the yard
it looked deserted. Ariel glanced around, hoping
to see one of the hands, but the place had a neglected look about it, as if no one lived there. She
wondered if Rosalie had decided to leave and how
she would go about finding her. Ariel fretted unnecessarily for Rosalie came flying through the
front door.

"Ariel! Thank God you are safe! I prayed every
day to the Virgin Mary for your safe return." She
glanced briefly at Denton then promptly dismissed him. "Where is Señor Jess?"

Ariel flushed and Denton made a strangled
sound deep in his throat. "Jess will be along in a
day or two," Ariel replied.

"Come in, come in. I will get you something
hot to drink." The day had turned blustery and
Ariel had to admit she was chilled to the bone.

When Denton followed Ariel inside, Rosalie
frowned but said nothing. She had already met
the man and didn't think much of him. She supposed he was all right but was definitely not the
man for Ariel. She had been shocked to learn he
wasn't Ariel's stepfather but a man claiming to be
Ariel's intended husband. Rosalie thought that
highly unlikely for she knew of the love affair between Ariel and Jess and expected them to marry
one day and settle down on the ranch.

"Is there someone around to carry in our

bags?'' Denton asked with an air of superiority that set Ariel's teeth on edge.

"No one, señor, the hands left shortly after Señor Walters took over the ranch."

Denton looked annoyed. "I'll see to it myself."

The moment he left the room, Rosalie asked, "Is it true, Ariel? Is that man your intended husband?"

Ariel sighed wearily. "No, Rosalie, I am not going to marry Denton no matter what my mother and Tom plan to the contrary. You know how I feel about Jess."

"Sí." Rosalie grinned, vastly relieved. "Señor Jess is one *macho* hombre. I knew he would find you."

Just then Denton returned.

"I'll tell you all about it when we're alone," Ariel hissed. Rosalie left the room to prepare the coffee she'd promised, flashing Ariel a conspiratorial look on her way out.

Denton set the bags down and joined Ariel in the parlor. "I didn't want to air more personal business than was absolutely necessary in front of the marshal, Ariel, but there are some things we must discuss."

"I've told you everything there is to tell, Denton."

The intensity of his gaze gave her an uncomfortable sensation in the pit of her stomach.

"Then why do I get the feeling that you're holding something back?"

"It's your imagination, Denton," Ariel insisted, refusing to meet his eyes.

"I'm your friend as well as that of your parents, dear, and I want to help in any way I can. No matter what those desperadoes did to you, I'll understand. I'd never abandon you. There's already enough gossip circulating about you among your family's friends. Young women just don't leave home to go off on their own like you did.

We've heard all kinds of wild tales about Texas. Imagine how we felt when we heard you were mixed up with desperadoes and mistaken for an outlaw.''

"That's all over with now. I'm fine and unharmed. Did you hear that, Denton? Dillon didn't touch me nor did any of his men.''

"If you say so, dear," Denton said, not at all convinced. "What about this Jess Wilder? Why would he feel obligated to rescue you? Is there something going on between you two that I should know about?''

"My God, Denton, stop badgering me! Jess Wilder is a friend. One of the few I have here in Texas besides Rosalie. He came after me because he feels responsible after mistaking me for Tilly Cowles. Once you meet him you'll understand.''

"I doubt that," Denton returned sourly. "Kirk Walters said the man is tough and dangerous and hasn't a penny to his name. He even hinted that Wilder is a gunslinger who makes his living collecting bounty for criminals wanted by the law.''

"Jess *is* a bounty hunter, but he has good reason for doing what he does. He's a former U.S. marshal who turned bounty hunter in order to capture the man who killed his brother in a bank robbery. It may be true that Jess isn't rich but he's honest.''

"Perhaps *you* trust him to bring your money back but I don't. By now he's on his way to Mexico with the money from your bank account. Not to mention the considerable sum Walters paid for the ranch.''

"You wouldn't say that if you knew Jess," Ariel replied stoutly. "Everyone should have a friend like him.''

"I can see you're not going to listen to reason.'' Denton sighed in annoyance.

Suddenly Ariel rose to her feet. "I'm exhausted, Denton. I'm going to my room and rest.

I've said all I'm going to say on the subject. Have Rosalie show you to your room. I'm sorry but I won't be joining you for supper tonight, I feel a headache coming on.''

Denton Dobbs, always a gentleman, stood when Ariel left the room. Politeness had been drummed into him from the time he was a child, but he was no fool. He might be considered stuffy and dull by some but he knew when someone was telling the truth. And Ariel certainly wasn't telling the whole story. Not that it mattered a great deal. He was prepared to marry Ariel no matter what had happened. Not only was he truly fond of her but her stepfather had tremendous clout in St. Louis society. He knew all the right people and had promised Denton the sacrifice he was making in marrying his scandal-tainted stepdaughter wouldn't go unrewarded. Tom Brady owned the bank in which Denton Dobbs worked. What more needed to be said?

Both Willa and Tom Brady were fine people who loved Ariel and wanted a secure future for her. Especially in light of this latest fiasco of hers. She had always been headstrong but never had she caused as much gossip as when she left home alone and unprotected. Everyone knew what Texas was like. Denton realized he was taking a risk by marrying Ariel but he firmly believed that marriage and children would settle her down into a proper wife. Once she had several children hanging on her skirts she'd forget all about Leland Ranch. Besides, Tom Brady had hinted that the proceeds from the sale of the ranch would enhance Ariel's already impressive dowry.

Denton had agreed to come to Texas on Ariel's behalf even before the Bradys received the lawyer's telegram about the mixup. He had learned about the confusing situation when he stepped off the stage in Waco and called on Jason Burns to announce his presence and arrange to have the ranch sold. He couldn't believe that Ariel had taken off again and was damn angry over the whole situation. He was in a quandary over what to do and finally decided to stick around a while in case Ariel had second thoughts and returned. It was a good thing he did. But the amazing story she told sounded more like fiction than fact, something one would read in a dime novel. Now that she was back he intended to fulfill the Bradys' wishes in regard to their wayward daughter. The court order in his possession virtually assured him of her compliance.

When Rosalie brought her something to eat in the privacy of her room Ariel told her everything that had happened. ''I pray Jess and the posse capture Dillon, Tilly, and the others and that he returns safely.'' A tear slid down her cheek and she dashed it away with the back of her hand. ''I'm so frightened for him. What if he's hurt— or . . .''

''Nothing will happen to Señor Jess,'' Rosalie said soothingly. ''He can take care of himself.''

''That's just what Jess said.'' She smiled tremulously, picturing their reunion. ''I love him so. We're to be married when he returns.''

''Then he had better hurry,'' Rosalie said tersely, ''or Señor Dobbs will take you home to your mama. I find it hard to believe you would consent to marry a man like Señor Dobbs.''

''Denton isn't so bad, Rosalie, but I never agreed to marry him. It's what Mother and Tom wanted. They think I need the steadying influence of a husband. As long as Father was alive he wouldn't let them force me into a marriage with a man I didn't love. But when he died I lost my only support in the matter. I know Mama and Tom love me but they don't know what's best for me. Only I know what will make me happy.''

Denton ate a lonely meal by himself that night, grumbling over everything from the spiciness of the food to the lack of amenities at the ranch house. He knocked on Ariel's door before he retired to wish her good night and received no answer. He hoped she wasn't going to pout over this all the way to St. Louis. It made for damn hostile company.

The next day Ariel had a visitor. Kirk Walters arrived, angrier than she had ever seen him. Trudy was with him, no doubt to lend support.

"You're not getting away with this, Ariel," he declared. His voice shook from disappointment and disgust at the way things had turned out. "The marshal came out yesterday and told me everything. You do have a way of fouling up things."

"Why couldn't you have just disappeared? Why did you have to turn out to be the real Ariel Leland?" This from Trudy who hadn't forgiven Ariel for capturing the affection of Jess Wilder when nothing she herself did seemed to entice the handsome cowboy. "I find this entire mess strange and confusing."

"As do I, Miss Walters," Denton concurred. "But believe me when I say this is the real Ariel Leland—and my fiancée."

Trudy's eyes grew round. "You and Ariel are to marry?"

"No!" Ariel denied, sending Denton a quelling look.

"Yes," Denton contradicted. His voice was firm.

"I thought Wilder hightailed it after Ariel when the marshal refused to form a posse," Walters said, recalling how close Ariel and Jess had grown.

"Yes, well, as you can see, Wilder is not here. I'm here and I will decide what's best for my future bride."

Ariel gnashed her teeth in frustration. Denton was talking as if she hadn't a mind of her own.

"I'm capable of making my own decisions, Denton."

"The events of the past few months show that you are incapable of managing your own affairs. I'm thinking of your welfare, dear."

Trudy grinned delightedly. "What about Jess Wilder? Where is he now?"

"He had business in Waco," Ariel revealed to the gloating woman. "I expect him to show up in a day or two. With Kirk's money, I might add. And the money Tilly Cowles stole from my bank account."

"If you believe that, you're even more gullible than I thought," Kirk scoffed derisively. "A man like Jess Wilder probably never saw so much money in his life. I'm afraid we've seen the last of him. I bought this ranch in good faith and have no intention of relinquishing it to you or anyone else."

"Perhaps there is no need," Denton said smoothly. "Ariel and I will be leaving Waco in a day or two. No matter what the judge decides about the ranch, Ariel no longer has an interest in it."

"Now wait a minute . . ."

"If this Wilder fellow turns up with the money, Burns can forward it to us and the ranch is automatically yours," Denton continued, ignoring Ariel's gasp of protest.

"What happens if he never shows up?" Walters asked, unable to believe his good fortune.

"Something will be worked out. I'll leave the details to Jason Burns once the court decides on the matter. It certainly will expedite matters if Wilder returns with your money so the deal can be negotiated legally this time, but if he doesn't, which I believe to be the case, Ariel's legal guardian will no doubt deal with you fairly."

"Excellent, excellent," Walters said enthusiastically. "This matter has been too long in being settled. Am I to assume you speak for Ariel's guardian?''

"They will back everything I say," Denton assured him.

"Then I wish you a pleasant trip to St. Louis," Walters said, slanting Ariel a triumphant glance. "I know it won't be dull."

Ariel waited until the door closed on Kirk and Trudy before lighting into Denton with all the fury of a snarling wildcat. "How dare you! You have no right to speak for me. You don't own me! Nobody does. I have a mind and a will and I'll do as I damn well please!''

"The law is on my side, Ariel." Then his eyes narrowed in sudden inspiration. "Perhaps I should marry you before we leave Waco. I know your mother is planning a big wedding but I'm sure she'll understand our need for haste. A large ceremony could follow our simple marriage later.''

"You'll never get me to agree to that."

"The court order I have in my possession is quite impressive. I'm certain I can persuade a justice of the peace to forego the usual procedure and marry us without your consent after I explain the situation. So, my dear, which will it be? A marriage you've always dreamed of or a brief ceremony before a justice of the peace with only strangers in attendance?''

Ariel felt trapped. She wasn't certain that Denton could do what he threatened but she knew he was tenacious and determined and rarely gave up once he made up his mind. Evidently her mother and Tom trusted him implicitly and would condone whatever coercion he might employ in order to bring her back to St. Louis. Law in Texas was tenuous at best and a judge might very well be intimidated by Denton and his infernal court order. What would Jess do when he arrived and found her gone?

Thoughts of Jess brought a measure of calm to her rising panic. Jess wouldn't let Denton take her away; it was that simple. She had only to wait until he arrived and put Denton in his place.

When Ariel gave no voice to her preference, Denton made the decision for her. "I'll go into town later today and talk to the marshal, Jason Burns, and the justice of the peace. We'll be married tomorrow and leave for St. Louis on the next stage." Thinking he had everything all tied up in a neat little package and feeling quiet smug, Denton turned to leave.

"Denton wait!"

He stopped, frowning. He didn't like having his decisions questioned.

"You can't do this."

"Of course I can. It's the best thing for all concerned. We'll deal splendidly with one another, once you learn you can't do as you please."

Ariel's mind worked furiously. She couldn't marry Denton Dobbs. She loved Jess Wilder. She carried his child. Yet she didn't want to divulge such personal information to Denton Dobbs. If she told anyone it would be her mother. Once Willa Brady understood, Ariel felt certain her mother would no longer insist she marry a man she didn't love. But before she resorted to so drastic a measure she had to allow Jess the time he needed to reach Waco. According to her calculations he should be arriving any day now. He could ride much faster than the stage she'd traveled on and couldn't be too far behind her. Somehow she had to delay Denton a few more days.

"I—I don't want to get married before a justice of the peace," Ariel said slyly. "Mother will be disappointed if she's cheated out of the big wedding she's planning. I'll agree to accompany you back to St. Louis willingly if you agree to wait a week before leaving."

She offered a silent prayer that her ploy would

work. A week should be plenty of time for Jess to reach Waco.

"At least you're starting to talk sense," Denton said, thinking that he'd finally made Ariel see the light. "But how do I know you'll keep your word?"

"You have my solemn promise as long as you don't break yours. One week, seven days, is all I ask."

A slow smile curved Denton's thin lips. Surely seven days wasn't too much to ask for her compliance, was it? He could afford to be magnanimous. If he was going to be married to Ariel for the rest of his life he didn't want her animosity. Then suddenly his smile turned downward into a frown.

"If you're counting on Jess Wilder showing up with your money it just won't happen. Even if by some miracle he does, it won't do you a bit of good. I have been appointed your temporary guardian and the law will uphold any decision I make on your behalf."

Ariel smiled a secret smile. Denton wouldn't talk so bravely if he knew Jess Wilder!

Chapter 22

❧

J ess was burning. An inferno raged in his blood and set his body on fire. He struggled to open his eyes, knowing he had to, that there was something he must do. A bespectacled, elderly man was bending over him, his kindly eyes filled with concern. Jess tried to speak but his tongue was so dry it filled his mouth and blocked the words.

"Here, son, drink this, it will make you feel better."

With difficulty Jess focused on the voice and the figure wavering before his eyes, vaguely recalling that he had been brought here to be treated after he was shot by Dillon—or Tilly. He'd probably never know which one fired the bullet that had ripped into his flesh.

"Remember me? I'm Doc Hadley." He lifted Jess' head so he could drink from the tumbler he held in his hand. Jess drank thirstily then grimaced when the bitter liquid slid over his tongue. The doctor chuckled. "You'll sleep again and when you wake up you'll feel better."

"Can't sleep," Jess croaked, moistening his lips with the tip of his tongue. "Gotta get up to Waco."

"Not today, son, or for a long time. You been mighty sick. Got the bullet out with no problem and the wound isn't serious but there was nothing I could do about the fever."

Jess tried to rise; his world spun crazily and he fell back against the pillows. "Where is Marshal Smith?"

"He's out of town, chasing cattle rustlers. Should be back in a few days."

Jess groaned. There was something he had to do, something important, but his mind refused to release that vital piece of information as he began slipping over the edge into a black bottomless void. At the last moment before he began his downward plunge he recalled what it was that was so urgent. Ariel was waiting for him. Somehow he had to get word to her explaining his delay. By then it was far too late.

As Jess slipped into oblivion the doctor smiled and said, "Sleep is the best cure I know of, son."

"If your bags are packed I'll carry them down for you, Ariel."

Ariel gritted her teeth in frustration. There seemed to be no way out of her predicament. She had given her word. If Jess didn't arrive in Waco in seven days she'd agreed to willingly accompany Denton to St. Louis. She had no idea what was keeping Jess. As soon as she'd arrived in Waco she had sent a telegram to Marshal Smith in San Antonio but still hadn't received an answer. Jess said he'd only be a day or two behind her and already seven days had gone by with no word from him. She feared something terrible had happened to him and couldn't imagine why the marshal refused to answer her wire. With the passing of each day, Denton grew unbearable. He was so smugly certain that Jess would never return with her money he had purchased the stage tickets two days in advance.

"Can't we wait a few more days, Denton?" Ariel asked, knowing what his answer would be before he even gave it.

"A deal is a deal, Ariel. We're leaving today. I've had about all of Texas I can stand. Enough to last me a lifetime. I can't imagine what you find about Texas to like."

"I think we should wait long enough to hear what the judge decides about the ranch," Ariel persisted.

"It doesn't matter what he decides; the ranch will be sold to Kirk Walters, if it doesn't already belong to him. If you're thinking that Jess Wilder will show up, you might as well set your mind to the fact that he has fled across the border with your money. I've already asked the marshal here to check on it."

"Dammit, Denton, why do you always think the worst?"

"Watch your language, dear, it's unladylike," Denton said tranquilly. "It won't do once we're married."

"Don't think that just because I'm forced to return to St. Louis that I'll marry you," Ariel replied huffily. "No one can make me say yes, and no judge or preacher in St. Louis will marry us without my consent."

"Perhaps not," Denton agreed, "but at least I will have fulfilled my duty to your parents. I'll let them convince you that marriage to me is a vast improvement over your present circumstances."

While Denton hitched the buckboard Ariel found the time for a few private words with Rosalie.

"I'll be back, Rosalie, as soon as I convince Mama and Tom that I have no intention of marrying Denton and staying in St. Louis. In two months I'll be twenty-one and then no one can tell me how to live my life. Somehow, some way, I'll return to Texas and fight for what is mine."

"What about Señor Jess?"

"If only I knew what happened to him." Her voice caught on a sob. "I'm so frightened for him. What if he was wounded—or killed? I've wired Marshal Smith and received no word. I don't believe for a minute that Jess took the money and went to Mexico. He'll come, only I won't be here when he arrives."

"What should I tell him when he gets here?" Rosalie asked, commiserating with Ariel, aware of the problems she must overcome in order to return to Texas and Jess Wilder.

"Tell him about Denton and why I had to return to St. Louis," Ariel said earnestly. "And tell him also that I'm not going to marry anyone but him, that I—" Her words skidded to an abrupt halt. What earthly good would it do now to tell Jess she was carrying his child? She wanted him to desire her for herself, not for his child. Perhaps he didn't want children; they had never discussed it. In any event it was something she wanted to tell him in person.

"Ariel, is there something else you want to say to me before you leave?" Rosalie asked pointedly.

"It's uncanny how you know me so well," Ariel observed. "I didn't want to tell you but I think you already suspect that I'm carrying Jess' child."

"Sí, señorita," Rosalie replied solemnly. "I have known it for some time. That's why I was so worried when you were abducted. But I told no one. Not even Señor Jess."

"Thank you. I'd like to tell Jess myself. Being pregnant was a blessing in disguise. I might have been raped by one or all of those desperadoes if I hadn't blurted out that I was expecting a child. Who would have thought any of them had a shred of decency in their hearts? But strangely enough they were reluctant to kill or rape a woman carrying a child. Except for Gandy, and he was overruled."

"Do you want me to tell Señor Jess about the child when he arrives?" Rosalie asked.

"No," came Ariel's quick reply. "I—I want to tell him myself."

"You—you don't think that Señor Dobbs could be right when he said Señor Jess went to Mexico with the money, do you?"

"Absolutely not!" Ariel said with firm conviction. "I—I just didn't allow him enough time." Her mind refused to grasp the fact that something could have happened to prevent his leaving San Antonio. Jess had always seemed so invincible; almost bigger than life and impossible to defeat.

"It's time to leave, Ariel. Long good-byes serve no purpose except to upset you."

"I don't suppose you have a sentimental bone in your body, Denton," Ariel said crossly as she gave Rosalie one last hug.

Then he was hurrying her outside, handing her up on the upsprung seat, and settling a blanket around her knees. She turned and watched until she could no longer see the house or Rosalie standing on the porch waving good-bye.

The three weeks it took to reach St. Louis were the most miserable Ariel had ever spent. She was ill much of the time from the constant motion of the stage and the bad food they were served at the way stations and towns along the way. The blankets and rugs did little to dispel the cold and the crush of bodies inside the stage only added to her discomfort. She was in a foul mood during the whole time and Denton complained about her ill manners and grumpy disposition. To make matters worse her pregnancy made itself known to her in the most basic way. Her breasts were perpetually sore and the waist of her skirt became so tight she could not fasten the hooks. Fortunately it was too cold to remove her wrap so her unhooked skirt went unnoticed.

When the stage discharged its passengers in St.

Louis Ariel was ecstatic to set her feet on solid ground once more despite the fact that St. Louis was the last place in the world she wanted to be. She wanted to be with Jess. She worried ceaselessly over his failure to arrive in Waco in the time she had allotted him and fretted that he was hurt of dying or—God forbid—dead! The night they had spent together in San Antonio had been pure bliss. Denton Dobbs was badly mistaken if he thought he could fill Jess Wilder's shoes. Jess was twice the man Denton was and she'd bet her life on Jess' honesty. No, Ariel refuted her own doubts, Jess was merely delayed for reasons unknown to her. When she returned to Waco she was convinced he'd be waiting for her.

The thought entered her mind that Jess might decide to come to St. Louis, but she quickly dismissed it. It made more sense for him to wait at the ranch, assuming it was still hers, and see to the running of it. Once she told her mother and Tom about the baby there was no way they could keep her from returning to Texas. In fact, they would probably welcome her decision to leave, for remaining in St. Louis would only prove an embarrassment for everyone.

Denton hired a hack to take them to the Bradys' pretentious mansion located in the best part of town.

"I know you've been angry with me during this entire trip, Ariel, but it will pass," Denton said, patting her hand in a condescending manner. "We'll be married soon and people will forget how you ran off and got yourself in trouble. By this time next year you could be holding our first child in your arms."

Ariel giggled, the idea not only absurd but impossible. "That's highly unlikely, Denton."

"Don't you like children? I'm counting on having several."

"You may have all you please as long as you find another woman to bear them."

"Deliver me from a belligerent woman." Denton sighed wearily. "After three weeks in your company I'm beginning to appreciate the rewards of being single."

Ariel smirked, suppressing another giggle with difficulty.

The house hadn't change in the six months she'd been gone, Ariel thought as she walked into the foyer. It was still large, still tastefully furnished with expensive furniture and decorated in colors that suited her mother's tastes. Nothing had changed.

But she had. Changed drastically.

Since the moment she'd met Jess Wilder her entire life had taken a new direction. She'd fallen in love, conceived a child, and found a place where she actually felt she belonged.

"Ariel! Thank God you're finally home!" A tiny woman looking like an older version of Ariel ran down the stairs to enfold her daughter in her arms. The few strands of gray amidst her dark tresses only added to her charm. Her figure was still lithe and supple and her skin good despite the fine network of wrinkles fanning out around eyes a shade deeper than Ariel's true violet.

"Hello, Mama," Ariel greeted her, happy to see her mother despite all that she and Tom had done to force her back to St. Louis.

"How could you do this to us, Ariel?" Willa choked, wiping away a tear. "You've been deprived of nothing. Tom has been a good father to you all these years and how do you repay him? By leaving without a word to anyone. Do you realize the anguish you've put us through?"

"I'm sorry, Mama," Ariel said guiltily. She had never wanted to hurt anyone.

"You're as irresponsible as your father. I don't know what ever possessed him to leave you that ranch. I can't believe all the trouble you've gotten into over that worthless property.''

''It's not worthless,'' Ariel insisted stubbornly.

''Is Tom home?'' Denton asked, interrupting Willa's angry tirade. ''Perhaps we should all sit down so we can discuss calmly what happened while I was in Texas.''

''I'm right here, Denton.''

Ariel's stepfather strode down the stairs, his step light and springy despite his years. A big brash Irishman who had made it to the top by sheer guts and determination, Tom Brady was older than Willa's forty by fifteen years. He was still a handsome, vital man who loved life. He also loved Ariel like his own daughter, for he and Willa had been unable to produce a child of their own after she divorced Buck Leland. He was a stern parent who would have raised Ariel much more strictly, if Buck Leland hadn't interfered.

Tom Brady went immediately to Ariel, first embracing her then giving her a hard little shake. ''If I had had my way in your upbringing you wouldn't be so spoiled or selfish. Your mother nearly suffered apoplexy worrying about you, especially after that last telegram from Waco. Come into the parlor, young lady. You have much explaining to do.''

''I'm sorry, Tom, truly,'' Ariel said, ''but I had to live my life as I saw fit, not how you and Mama thought I should.''

''And see where it got you,'' Tom replied crossly. ''All right, now let's have it, every detail.''

They were seated in the parlor now, all except Tom who stood glaring down at Ariel while Willa wrung her hands nervously. She greatly feared Ariel's explanation would include something she didn't want to hear.

''It's a long story,'' Ariel warned.

''We've got plenty of time.''

One of the servants entered with a tray of coffee and Ariel helped herself, bolting down nearly two cups of the rich brew before beginning. She left little out except the part where she and Jess made love out on the prairie and later at the ranch.

Tom stopped her once to ask, "You were alone with the bounty hunter all those days and nights?" When Ariel nodded his face turned grim.

She continued, stumbling over the telling of Jess' showing up at the ranch and accepting the job of foreman during Pike's recuperation. "What reason did Jess Wilder have for coming back to the ranch?" Willa asked sharply. She wasn't naive enough to believe he'd simply stopped by to see how she was doing.

"That's a question I'd like answered myself," Denton interjected. "You seem to be obsessed with the man. According to you he's the only one who believed you were the real Ariel Leland. He's the one who rescued you."

"Rescued Ariel from whom?" Tom asked. "Obviously there are things I'm not yet aware of."

Denton launched into the story of Ariel's abduction and the confused mess he had blindly walked into when he arrived in Waco.

"My God, Ariel, you could have been killed or—" Tom regarded her keenly. "—abused."

"I wasn't harmed, Tom. Thank God Jess found me in time or I would have been sold into white slavery."

Willa gasped, ready to swoon.

"For God's sake, Willa, don't faint now," Tom berated her. Then he turned to Ariel. "This Jess Wilder has a way of showing up in your life at crucial moments. I'm grateful for all he's done on your behalf, but I don't like the way he keeps insinuating himself into your life."

"You no longer have to worry about the man,"

Denton said smugly. "I'm convinced he's taken Ariel's money and run for the border. We gave him plenty of time to return to Waco and when he failed to arrive Ariel finally realized the man was a scoundrel and agreed to come home."

"It wasn't exactly like that," Ariel said sourly. "Jess is a former U.S. marshal and wouldn't do anything dishonest."

"I thought you said he was a bounty hunter?" This from Willa who had recovered enough to grow curious about the relationship between Jess Wilder and Ariel.

Ariel explained about Jess' brother and his need to catch Bart Dillon.

"All this sounds like a plot from a dime novel," Tom said with a hint of disgust. "I hope you've had all the adventure you craved, for it's time now you settled down into a proper wife. I doubt St. Louis will ever forget this wild escapade of yours but marrying Denton will certainly lend you a measure of respectability."

"That's exactly what I told Ariel," Denton said, sounding much put upon. "I'm willing to forget her unwise antics if she is."

"How splendid of you," Willa trilled happily. "The wedding plans are nearly complete and the ceremony is set to take place in four weeks. I would have arranged for an earlier date but I feared you wouldn't arrive home in time."

"Four weeks will be just fine." Denton beamed. He glanced over at Ariel to see if she would protest.

She did.

"I have no intention of marrying Denton. The only reason I came home was because he threatened to force me into marriage before we left Waco with that damn court order he had in his possession. Really, Mama, was that necessary?"

"We felt it was," Tom answered for his wife.

"It was for your own good," Willa added.

"Marrying Denton will be the best thing you could do under the circumstances. It will put wagging tongues to rest and end speculation on what might have happened in Texas."

"I'm sorry, but I absolutely refuse to hear another word about marriage to Denton. He's a fine man, but he's not for me."

"I suppose Jess Wilder is more to your liking?" Willa blurted out.

Ariel thought of the normal run-of-the-mill dull, predictable life Denton was offering her and she shivered. Then she smiled as she thought, a Texas ranch and Jess Wilder. Those were the two things necessary to make her life complete. She would settle for nothing less.

"As a matter of fact," Ariel said slowly, "Jess Wilder *is* much more to my liking."

Absolute silence.

Her words struck everyone dumb.

But not for long.

"What! You prefer a crude gunslinger over me?" A mottled anger settled over Denton's face.

"Ariel didn't mean it the way it sounded," Tom blustered, sending Ariel a quelling glance.

"Oh, Ariel, how could you?" Willa sniffed, reaching for her smelling salts.

"You may as well know from the beginning," Ariel stated defiantly, "that I love Jess Wilder and he loves me."

"The man is a scoundrel, you'll never see him again," Denton scoffed. "You'll soon forget him and realize that I'm the best choice."

"I think it mighty big of Denton to still want you after all the fuss you've caused." Tom scowled, growing angry. "I'm still your guardian and I can force you to do what's best for you."

"I don't think you'd do that, Tom," Ariel said softly. "I loved my father dearly but I love you too. Don't force me to do something that will make me unhappy."

"It's because I love you that I'm forcing the issue," Tom asserted. "It would hurt me to hear your name slandered. The gossips will have a field day with this. If Jess Wilder loved you he'd be here now, meeting your family. I fear Denton is right, the money was simply too much of a temptation and you'll never see him again. I won't call off the wedding. Denton has proved his worth as a husband by going to Texas in my stead. Few men I know would want a woman as irresponsible and headstrong as you have been. You have a month to think about it. I truly believe you'll make the right decision."

"Tom, I—I'm sorry," Ariel said lamely. "I won't change my mind. I want to go back to Texas. I only came to St. Louis to explain my position in person."

"You have no reason to go back."

"The ranch . . ."

"Will be sold. I know you're tired, you may be excused. I'd like to speak to Denton in private. Willa, see that Ariel is settled in comfortably, we'll talk again later."

"What is your feeling about Jess Wilder?" Tom asked Denton once they were alone.

"From what I gather the man is dangerous. He's tough and hard and probably wants Ariel for her money. Now that he has it she's likely seen the last of him."

"What about the ranch? Does it still belong to her?"

"I promised Kirk Walters you would work something out if the judge decides in Ariel's favor. The man wants the ranch desperately. It has to do with the Brazos River and the fact that Walters' property has no access to the water except through Leland property. Jason Burns will apprise you of the outcome."

"You've done well, Denton. I couldn't ask for a better son-in-law."

Denton flushed with pleasure. "Glad to do it, Tom. I only hope Ariel comes to her senses."

They spoke a few more minutes, then Denton left for his own home, smugly certain that he'd soon be a bridegroom and the son-in-law of the influential Tom Brady.

Shaky and weak, his face wan and drawn, Jess saddled Soldier as he prepared to leave San Antonio. He was two weeks later than he had hoped but he hadn't counted on his festering wound or the fever that followed the shoot-out at Dillon's hideout. During the time Jess' injury kept him immobile, Marshal Smith had been out with a posse rounding up cattle rustlers. He returned just in time to bid Jess good-bye. He hadn't even had time yet to read the pile of correspondence that had arrived for him during his absence. The letters and telegrams still sat on his desk unopened.

"You look as if a good wind could blow you over, Jess, maybe you oughta stay in town for a few more days," Smith advised, his concern evident. "With all the money you're carryin' you gotta be in good shape in case you meet up with desperadoes. Are you sure you don't want me to send an escort along with you?"

"An escort will only drew attention to the fact that I'm carrying something valuable," Jess replied. "I'll be fine, Ted. By now Ariel must be beside herself with worry. I gotta get back to Waco with the money before Walters takes over the ranch again and Ariel is forced to leave with her guardian."

"You know what's best," Smith said, shaking his head skeptically. "Good luck to you. If you ever get down to San Antonio again look me up. We make a good team. Too bad Dillon didn't live long enough to have his neck stretched and Pecos was killed trying to escape. But at least Tilly and Gandy will be brought to trial for their crimes."

They shook hands and Jess mounted up, waving one last time before riding off.

Because of his weakness Jess' pace was deliberately slow, but he rode without excessive stops, forcing himself to maintain a steady pace. The money he carried could make a difference in Ariel's life. It would help decide if the ranch now belonged to her or to Kirk Walters. He wished he could think of some way to make Walters denounce his interest in Leland Ranch, but the man was utterly ruthless in his desire to own the land that Ariel's father had left her.

Ariel. He missed her with a fierceness that left him aching. Never again, he thought, never would he leave her again. He wanted to love and protect her forever. He recalled how she had looked their last time together, flushed and sated, her eyes glazed with spent passion. Hot curls of anticipation were unwinding in his stomach as he pictured their reunion. Jesus! Each time he made love to Ariel he swore it could never get better, but it did. Loving Ariel was all fire and heat and wildness and hot licks of savage rapture.

Jess tried to imagine the beautiful children they would make together. They would be imbued with her indomitable spirit and thirst for independence while inheriting his strength and oneness of purpose. He hoped Ariel could convince her mother and stepfather to sanction marriage between them but if they withheld their approval it wouldn't stop Jess from marrying the woman he loved. And he knew Ariel felt the same. He was tired of roaming, sick of chasing men for the bounty; he was ready to settle down and raise a family. If Ariel wanted to keep her ranch, for her sake he'd become the best damn rancher in Texas.

Jess crossed the Brazos River where it bordered on Leland property and rode straight for the ranch house. He dismounted in the yard and had reached the porch when the door flew open. Jess smiled, expecting Ariel to fly into his arms. He was stunned when Trudy Walters walked out to meet him.

"Jess Wilder, no one expected to see you again."

Jess scowled, looking past her into the house.

"If you're looking for Ariel, she's gone."

"Gone? Gone where? Where's Rosalie?"

"Ariel left with her fiancé, of course, and Rosalie decided to move to town."

"What in the hell are you talking about, Trudy? Ariel has no fiancé."

"Tell that to Ariel and Denton Dobbs. Ariel's mother sent Denton to Texas to clear up this mess with Ariel and bring her home in time for their wedding. I must admit I was rather surprised when Denton identified her as the real Ariel Leland. So was everyone else in town. The story Ariel told when she returned was rather wild."

"Ariel wouldn't leave of her own accord," Jess stated, his belief unshakable.

"How do you explain the fact that she boarded the stage over a week ago with Denton Dobbs?"

A foul oath left Jess' mouth. Trudy covered her ears.

"What about the ranch? And the money Tilly Cowles stole?"

"Jason Burns is to handle everything. For all practical purposes, the ranch belongs to Kirk. The judge has only to issue a decision for it to be legal. In any event, even if the judge rules that the ranch still belongs to Ariel, Denton has assured Kirk that a new deal will be forthcoming in Kirk's favor. Besides, no one expected you'd return with the money."

"You haven't made sense from the moment you opened your mouth," Jess said sourly. "Why in hell wouldn't I return with Ariel's money?"

Trudy shrugged her elegant shoulders. "Both Denton and Kirk thought you'd take the money and head for Mexico. Mr. Burns and the marshal weren't convinced but when you failed to arrive and their telegrams weren't answered they had to admit it looked suspiciously like you decided to take the money and run."

"Did Ariel think I'd stolen her money?"

"Well, I'm not sure, but she did leave Waco with her fiancé, didn't she?" Trudy hinted slyly.

Jess' mouth tightened and his silver eyes hardened into shards of cold steel. "If Ariel left the ranch it wasn't her own doing," he declared stoutly.

"You look so ruthless when you're angry." Trudy shuddered delicately. Her eyes grew fever-bright and her flesh tingled in a way that made her aware of the many reasons she had been drawn to Jess Wilder in the first place. She licked her lips, the pink tip of her tongue darting out like a small hungry bird. And she was hungry. Hungry for Jess Wilder.

She stepped closer, closer still, until the hardened nubs of her breasts brushed his broad chest. "Jess . . ." Her small hand fluttered to his chest, ending in a caress Jess had no difficulty interpreting.

"You're much more muscular than Kirk, did you know that? And more handsome, too. In fact, Kirk can't hold a candle to you. I'll bet you're even better in—" She paused, biting her bottom lip and looking at Jess to see if he realized what she'd almost let slip.

Jess' dark brows drew together in a puzzled frown. Why would Trudy compare him to her brother as if—as if—no, it was too preposterous. Besides, he had more important things to do than stand around listening to Trudy discuss Kirk Walters' attributes, or lack of them. Abruptly he turned and walked away.

"Jess, wait—where are you going? Won't you come in? I'll be here for several hours yet. You can—entertain me until Kirk comes for me. He wants me to decide where I want to live.''

''I gotta get to town pronto and turn in Ariel's money to Jason Burns, then talk to the marshal and Rosalie, if she's still there. I have no idea why people thought I'd steal Ariel's money but I intend to put everyone straight.''

Trudy watched Jess ride off, wishing she was the woman he wanted, the woman he loved. Her life had been anything but exemplary, and if she didn't have Kirk she'd have no one—but she'd gladly forsake everything and everyone for a man like Jess Wilder.

Chapter 23

J ess left the marshal's office after spending two hours relating the details of Bart Dillon and Pecos Pete's deaths and the capture of Tilly Cowles and Gandy. The marshal had already heard part of the story from Ariel but knew nothing of the deaths and apprehension of the other outlaws. He somewhat sheepishly explained that most people naturally assumed Jess had made off with Ariel's money, although he himself and Jason Burns had held grave doubts that Jess would do such a thing. But if he *had* it wouldn't be the first time a former lawman turned bad.

"I'm happy things turned out the way they did," the marshal said sincerely.

"Do you want the money Tilly Cowles stole? I'm hoping Walters will relinquish his claim on the ranch once his money is returned."

"I wouldn't count on that," the marshal warned. "Miss Leland's guardian expressed a desire to sell the ranch no matter what the outcome. As for the money, give it to Jason Burns. It belongs to Miss Leland and he's been instructed as to its disposal. Will you be stickin' around Waco? The town could use another good lawman."

"I'm going to St. Louis," Jess said grimly.

"St. Louis? I reckon Mr. Dobbs won't like that. I gathered from what he told me that he and Ariel are to be married soon."

"Over my dead body," Jess gritted out from between clenched teeth. "Ariel is going to marry me."

"Somehow that doesn't surprise me." The marshal grinned. "It was obvious Miss Leland wasn't happy to leave Waco. Nor thrilled at the prospect of marriage to Denton Dobbs. Good luck, Jess."

"Much obliged, Marshal, I'll need it."

Slinging the saddlebag full of money over his shoulder, Jess left the marshal's office, deep in thought. What if he arrived too late and Ariel had already married Denton Dobbs? That terrifying thought sobered him instantly. Surely Ariel knew he would come for her, didn't she? Or did she think like the others that he had made off with her money? Trudy had said that Ariel went along with Dobbs willingly yet the marshal hinted that Ariel wasn't happy about returning to St. Louis. He rather thought the marshal was more apt to tell the truth than Trudy. After he called on Jason Burns he hoped to find Rosalie, who was certain to know exactly why Ariel went to St. Louis instead of waiting for him to return with the money.

"Señor Jess! Señor Jess! Wait, I must talk with you!"

Rosalie was hurrying down the street toward him as fast as her legs could carry her. He waited, smiling in genuine welcome. Now maybe he could get to the bottom of this.

"I've watched and waited for you every day," Rosalie gasped, slightly out of breath. "Ariel is gone."

"I know," Jess said tightly. "I was out at the ranch. I hoped I'd be able to find you and learn the truth. Tell me what happened, Rosalie. Who is Denton Dobbs and why is he calling himself Ariel's intended husband?"

"Ariel's mother and stepfather sent Señor Dobbs here to bring Ariel home and clear up the trouble with Tilly Cowles. Ariel was surprised; she thought to see her stepfather instead of Señor Dobbs. When the man said he was her fiancé Ariel denied it and insisted she would not marry him."

"Then why did she return to St. Louis with him?" Jess asked, confused and hurt. "I told her I'd bring her money back for her. Didn't she believe me?"

"Oh, sí, she believed you, but Señor Dobbs had a legal paper appointing him temporary guardian and ordering her return to St. Louis. Why didn't you return when you were supposed to?"

"I was wounded in the shoot-out with the Dillon gang and then developed a fever that left me out of my head for days," Jess explained. "I came as soon as I could."

Rosalie regarded him keenly. "You look like you should still be in bed."

"I'm all right. Did Ariel leave a message for me?"

"Sí, she said she loves you and that she'll be back. She hopes to convince her parents not to sell the ranch to Señor Walters once the judge rules that the ranch still belongs to her. Señor Burns told her the ranch was sold illegally and if the money is returned to Señor Walters it will still be hers."

"I have the money right here." Jess grinned, patting the bulging saddlebags. "I'm on my way to the lawyer's office now."

"Then I pray Ariel will soon return."

"I'm not gonna wait, Rosalie. I'm going after her. If I wait too long I'm afraid her parents will force her to marry Denton Dobbs."

Rosalie grinned. "I knew you would say that."

"What about you, Rosalie, are you all right? Is there anything you need?"

"No, Señor Jess. I found work with a widower who hired me to care for his two children. They are twelve and fourteen and in dire need of guidance. Thanks to Buck Leland I am not desperate for work in order to survive but Lew Dancy has need of me.''

"I'll be sure and tell Ariel that you are well," Jess said, turning to leave.

In that instant Rosalie made a decision that she had been agonizing over ever since Ariel left. Despite her promise to Ariel that she would keep certain secrets to herself, Rosalie felt Jess had a right to know Ariel was carrying his child. As the father of Ariel's child Jess should know, just in case he might change his mind about traveling the long distance to St. Louis. Rosalie was leaving nothing to chance. Ariel and Jess belonged together.

"Señor Jess, wait."

"Is there something else?"

"Sí, but I promised Ariel I would say nothing. It is not easy to break a promise."

"If it concerns Ariel and I should know, then keeping it to yourself is even worse. What is it, Rosalie?"

"Ariel is . . ." She paused, choosing her words carefully.

"Is what, woman—what are you trying to tell me?"

"Ariel is expecting your child, señor."

The color drained from Jess's face. "H-how do you know?"

"She told me, señor, but I had already guessed."

"How far along is she?"

"Just over two months when she left here."

"Jesus H. Christ! Why didn't she tell me in San Antonio?"

"I do not know, señor."

"Much obliged, Rosalie, I'm beholden to you for telling me."

A baby! Jess thought gleefully as he strode pur-

posefully toward the office of Jason Burns. He was
going to be a father! A foolish grin stretched his
mouth and he couldn't help chuckling as he tried
to picture the son or daughter he would have.
Suddenly his steps faltered, recalling that Ariel
might be forced into marriage with Denton Dobbs
and his child would bear the name of another
man. "Like hell!" Jess said aloud, drawing the
attention of a passerby. "I'll kill the son of a bitch
and make Ariel a widow before I'll let another
man raise my child."

Jason Burns greeted Jess with more than a little
surprise. "Thought we'd seen the last of you,
Wilder. Ariel insisted you'd come back, and truth
to tell both the marshal and I kind of thought so
too. But when time passed and you failed to show
up we began to lose hope." They shook hands
and Jess slapped the saddlebag down on Burns'
desk.

"Here's Ariel's money. All of it," he empha-
sized. "You can return the amount Walters paid
for the ranch so Ariel can reclaim her property.
The rest goes in her bank account."

"Whoa, not so fast," Burns said. "In the first
place, I've been instructed by Ariel's guardian to
sell the ranch to Walters even if the money is returned. In the second place, I don't think Walters
will accept the money; he wants the ranch. In any
event, I just received a decision from the judge.
He ruled that the ranch still belongs to Ariel Leland because it was sold fraudulently. Not that it
will do her any good if her guardian still wants to
sell it to Walters."

"What if Walters decides he no longer wants
the ranch?" Jess asked curiously, exploring every
possible angle. He knew how much the ranch
meant to Ariel.

"Well now, that's highly unlikely," Burns said
slowly. "But if for some remote reason Walters

backs out of the deal I suppose I'd have to find
another buyer."

"That could take time," Jess mused thoughtfully.

Burns smiled deviously. "It could take a very
long time." He admired Ariel a great deal and
knew how badly she wanted to keep Buck Leland's ranch.

"Ariel will be twenty-one soon," Jess hinted
eagerly. "In a couple of months, if I'm not mistaken. Will that make a difference?"

"At age twenty-one Ariel will be able to make
her own decisions concerning her property, unless she has a husband who can make them for
her. But if you're thinking what I'm thinking,
you'll have a devil of a time convincing Walters
to back out of buying the property."

"Will you help?" Jess asked. "Will you come
with me to Walters' place and try to talk him out
of buying Leland Ranch?"

"What's your stake in this? Why are you so
interested in Ariel Leland's affairs?" Burns asked
suspiciously.

"The only stake I have is my concern over Ariel's welfare and protecting what belongs to her.
I'm gonna tell you straight out, Burns, I love Ariel. And she loves me. We were planning on getting married until Denton Dobbs showed up.
According to the marshal Ariel left town against
her will."

"I know for a fact Ariel wasn't anxious to leave
Waco and she did seem overly concerned about
you. She defended you fiercely when others tried
to accuse you of thievery. It's possible she loves
you."

"It's not only possible, it's the truth. Ask Rosalie, she'll verify my words."

"No need for that—I believe you. Ariel told me
you were a former lawman and I sent a wire to
Fort Worth to find out for myself. After I received

an answer I began to doubt Dobbs' theory that you took off with Ariel's money. Not that there aren't plenty of lawmen out there who have turned outlaw."

"Then you'll help me?" Jess pressed anxiously.

"I'll come with you to talk to Walters, but it won't do any good."

"All I ask is that you try. Will you ride out with me this evening? I want to eat and clean up first and a couple hours' sleep wouldn't hurt. I'll check in at the hotel and meet you out front at six o'clock."

"I'll be there," Burns agreed. "And I'll bring Walters' money. The rest I'll place in Ariel's bank account to do with as she pleases."

Kirk Walters paced his parlor, distraught and angry. He was astounded when Trudy told him that Jess Wilder was back in town and that he had in his possession the money Tilly Cowles had stolen. All of it, including what Kirk had paid for the ranch. He had hoped the man would disappear for good, that the ranch would be his by default. He hadn't heard yet from Jason Burns concerning the outcome of the judge's ruling, if one had been reached yet, but was counting on being declared the new owner of Leland Ranch. Now he feared the return of his money would make a difference in the judge's decision. He knew the sale had been fraudulent but since Ariel's guardian had renounced all interest in keeping the ranch Kirk hoped the judge would take that into consideration and rule in his favor.

"Will you stop that pacing?" Trudy complained. "How can I concentrate with you mumbling and acting as if the world has come to an end?"

"Dammit, Trudy, how can you remain so calm? You know how much I want that land. Don't you care at all about me and my problems?"

Trudy dropped the piece of embroidery she was working on and stared at her brother, thinking him quite handsome when he was angry, though not as handsome as Jess Wilder. "You know I care about you, Kirk," she said softly. "Haven't I proved it many times over?"

Abruptly Kirk stopped pacing, regarding Trudy with keen appreciation. He couldn't deny that she cared for him. They were so much alike, he reflected, both willing to take what they wanted without letting outside pressure or the dictates of society influence them. He recalled the day five years ago when he had found Trudy rutting in the stable with one of the common cowboys and how angry he had been. Even then Trudy was a ripe beauty with a body made for loving. He remembered clearly what he had said to her after he had nearly killed the cowboy and how Trudy had reacted.

His face grew heated and his breathing labored as the intervening years swept rapidly across his memory. He would have beaten Trudy too if she hadn't thrown herself on his mercy, groveling at his feet, begging him to keep her secret from their parents, both of whom were old and feeble. Trudy was a nubile eighteen and eager to drink deeply from love's bounty. He was twenty-seven and tempted beyond human endurance. His sister!

"What are you thinking?" Trudy asked, her eyes fastened to the front of Kirk's trousers. She licked her lips, suddenly gone dry, and swallowed reflexively as she saw him grow huge before her eyes. "God, Kirk!"

"You know what I'm thinking, Trudy. You're the only one who understands me. I know it's wrong but I need you right now than I've ever needed you before. That bastard Wilder has me tied in knots. He's thwarted me at every turn. Nothing has gone right since he rode into town."

"It's not wrong if it's what we both want, Kirk," Trudy said huskily.

"Remember what I said to you that day I caught you with the cowboy in the stable?"

"You said if I ever had the urge again to come to you and you'd take care of it. You didn't want me rutting with every cowboy on the spread."

"And I've kept my word, haven't I? I've always made sure you were satisfied."

Trudy nodded slowly.

"I'll find you a husband, Trudy, I swear it, only I still need you. You understand that, don't you?"

Trudy nodded again.

Kirk groaned and reached for her.

"Not here, Kirk!" Trudy gasped as he freed her of her bodice.

"Right here. On the floor, on the sofa, what does it matter? We're alone, the cook has gone for the night and no one will bother us. I can't wait."

Trudy's rapid breathing and Kirk's harsh panting mingled and stirred the silent air around them. A lamp burned on the table but Kirk didn't bother to dim it as he bared Trudy's breasts to his avid gaze. "Every time I look at you like this and fill you with myself I know why I've dragged my feet in finding you a husband. You're the best, Trudy. No one can compare with you."

"Not even Ariel Leland?"

He pulled her to the floor, sliding her beneath him. "Don't mention that bitch to me!" he growled, ripping her skirt in his eagerness to ram himself into her. "Open your legs, little sister, welcome me home."

He plunged.

She gasped and cried out.

Neither of them heard the knock on the front door.

"No one's home," Jason Burns said, ready to turn around and leave.

"There's a light in the parlor," Jess observed as he knocked again.

Still no answer.

"Perhaps they've gone to bed."

"It's not even seven o'clock, for Christ's sake," Jess growled. "They're in there all right." His hand drifted to the doorknob, surprised when it turned easily in his hand and the door swung open.

"A man could get shot for entering another man's house uninvited," Burns hissed as he glanced over Jess' shoulder. They looked into the foyer and saw nothing but a light shining from the parlor beyond.

Jess opened his mouth to call out a greeting when he heard it. Burns must have heard it too for he started violently. "Jesus, what's that?" Someone was whimpering and crying, a woman, he thought, while the other harsh noises that followed sounded as if they came from a man. "Sounds like someone needs help."

Jess' shoulders shook with suppressed laughter. He recognized the sounds immediately. He had made them himself many times in his life. "I reckon we're interrupting something," he said to Burns, who had just identified the noises and was blushing furiously. "Wonder if it's Trudy or Kirk?"

"Let's go," Burns urged, unwilling to intrude upon private moments. "We can come back tomorrow."

"I don't know about you but I'm not going anywhere until I see Walters. C'mon, follow me."

Ordinarily Jess wouldn't think of intruding at a time like this, but with Kirk Walters he'd dare anything. Something Trudy had said to him made him suspicious and he fully intended to satisfy his curiosity. He couldn't care less what Kirk and Trudy did in the privacy of their own home unless it was something he could use on Ariel's behalf. He had no scruples when it came to Kirk Walters for the man had shown himself to be ruthless in obtaining his own ends.

Reluctant but too curious to turn around and walk out the door, Burns followed close on Jess' heels. The parlor was at the end of the hall and they stood poised in the doorway. The room was well-lit and at first glance looked as if no one was there, until Trudy cried out in ecstasy and Kirk grunted as he strained to achieve his own reward.

They lay on the floor, naked, arms and legs entwined, their bodies slick with sweat and both panting heavily. The sight so sickened Burns that he gagged. Jess was shocked but had had a vague inkling of what he'd find. Besides, to a man like Kirk Walters, who put himself above the dictates of man and God, the taboo against incest was but another rule to be broken.

Trudy saw them first. Kirk was still bent over her, caressing her breasts, ready to begin again. She went still. Her mouth opened in a silent scream. Kirk was too intent upon licking her nipples to respond to her mute plea. When she stiffened, Kirk chuckled, thinking she was becoming aroused again. He certainly was.

"You always were a passionate little bitch, Trudy, that's why I love doing it to you. You're as horny as I am."

Trudy finally found her tongue. "Kirk! Please! Get off me! We're not alone."

"Of course we are. I'm not going to stop now. You promised to take my mind off Jess Wilder. I'd like to shoot that bastard."

"You've got your chance, Walters," Jess drawled lazily. "I'm right here and ready to face you in a showdown anytime you say."

Kirk lost his erection instantly. Trudy scooted from beneath him and grabbed her dress, holding it before her like a shield. Jess hardly spared her

a glance. Burns was too embarrassed to even look
at her.

"Who gave you permission to enter my
house?" Kirk demanded, sliding into his pants.
"You're trespassing."

"We came to give you back your money," Jess
replied, unperturbed by Kirk's anger. "And talk
you out of buying Leland Ranch."

"Fat chance," Kirk scoffed derisively. "Nothing you could say will change my mind."

Jess looked at Trudy who stood cowering in the
corner. His eyes narrowed, his face grew hard
with ruthless determination. He didn't like himself very much when he had to resort to such foul
methods of persuasion, but he'd go to any
lengths, use any methods, to restore Ariel's property to her.

"Your name won't be worth a damn once the
townspeople learn about this." He looked pur-
posefully at Trudy. "Your sister won't be able to
show her face in town. All her friends will shun
her like poison."

Trudy whimpered. "Kirk."

"Go upstairs, Trudy, this doesn't concern
you," Kirk ordered gruffly.

"This certainly does concern me. I'll tell everyone you forced me. Your own sister. They might
even put you in jail. Is that what you want? Do
you want to see me treated worse than a whore,
shunned and despised by all our friends? You
won't have any friends left once this leaks out."

"I'm a respected man. No one will take the
word of a drifter and gunslinger over mine."

Jason Burns gathered his wits and stepped forward. "Are you forgetting me, Kirk? I'm a respected citizen of Waco and my word is above
reproach. The townspeople will believe whatever
I say. And if Trudy wants to press charges I'll be
glad to represent her."

Humiliation, public ridicule, and defeat stared

Kirk Walters in the face and the sight of it frightened him. "What is it you want of me?"

"Denounce all interest in Leland Ranch, here and now, and let Jason Burns handle it from there. He'll wire Ariel's guardian something to the effect that you have your money back and no longer wish to purchase the property." Jess enunciated carefully so there was no misunderstanding of what he wanted.

"You bastard!" Kirk hissed. "You should have died in the fire."

"But I didn't. Your little games didn't work."

Jason Burns looked startled.

"I've known all along that Walters was behind all those 'accidents' at the ranch," Jess said. "I just couldn't prove it. It no longer matters, Walters, I want you out of Ariel's life once and for all. I promise to keep your little games with your sister from public knowledge as long as you stay out of our lives."

"And I strongly urge," Burns added sternly, still unable to look at Trudy, "that you send Trudy away to visit relatives out of state. I know you have an aunt in Nashville who would be more than happy to entertain Trudy, and possibly even find her a husband."

Jess grinned. "An excellent idea. Are you in agreement, Walters?"

"You can't prove I had anything to do with those accidents."

"But there are witnesses to what's going on out here with your sister."

"You win," Kirk said, reluctantly admitting defeat. "Trudy will leave within the week. And I no longer have any desire to purchase Leland land."

A strangled sob slipped past Trudy's lips as she turned and fled from the room. Jess almost felt sorry for her. For Kirk he felt nothing but contempt. In his opinion a man who abused his own sister was worse than the lowest animal. Obviously Jason Burns felt the same for he glared at Kirk, with disgust and condemnation.

The lawyer retrieved several packets of money from his pockets and laid them on the table beside Walters. "I believe you'll find the full amount you paid for Leland Ranch there in those packets. You no longer have any claim on the land. Even if Wilder hadn't returned the money the judge had just ruled in Ariel's favor, returning the land to her. The sale you participated in was fraudulent and couldn't be honored. Returning your money ties up all the loose ends."

"Ariel's guardian will sell it to someone else," Kirk predicted sourly.

Burns slanted a sly smile at Jess. "Perhaps not. Perhaps Ariel will find a way to keep her property."

"I'm sure of it," Jess concurred cryptically. "Shall we go, Burns? We've accomplished what we set out to do."

Jess suppressed a shudder as they rode away. Never had he witnessed anything so morally offensive, and he was no prude. He couldn't wait to shake the dust of Waco off his feet and head east toward St. Louis.

Ariel.

The name tasted sweet on his tongue. He couldn't wait to see her again, to take off her clothes and kiss the place where his baby grew. He wanted to love her, cherish her, protect and provide for her and his child. Come hell or high water Ariel Leland was going to be his wife, even if he had to make her a widow to do it.

Chapter 24

Ariel spent her first few days in St. Louis letting out the waistline of all her dresses. Thanks to the fuller styles and the shawl she nearly always wore, no one had noticed the slight increase in her girth. Just over three months along in her pregnancy, Ariel was still slim and looked lovelier than ever. Impending motherhood served only to enhance her beauty now that the period of morning illness was a thing of the past.

Ariel had been home two weeks but her adamant refusal to marry Denton seemed to have little effect on her mother and Tom. No matter how often she insisted she would not marry Denton, that she loved Jess, they merely smiled and went on with the plans. With the wedding less than two weeks away Ariel realized that she'd have to tell them she was expecting Jess' child. She hated to disappoint and disillusion them but something had to be done. She had hoped there would be no need to tell them, that she'd be on her way back to Texas by now. But it wasn't to be. As soon as Denton returned from his business trip to Chicago Ariel vowed to get them all together and tell them exactly why the wedding could not possibly take place.

"Ariel, are you awake? May I come in?"

It was early. Ariel hadn't yet gone down to breakfast when Willa rapped lightly on the door.

"Come in, Mama, I was just getting ready to go downstairs. I'm famished this morning."

"I'm glad your appetite is healthy—even though you mope about your room like a lost soul," Willa said with a hint of censure.

"I'm not moping, Mama, I miss Jess."

Willa chose to ignore the remark, as she did whenever Ariel mentioned Jess Wilder.

"Are you certain you won't accompany us to the Brooks' weekend party?" she asked hopefully. "I do hate to miss it but I don't like leaving you alone for two days. Especially with Denton out of town."

"I'll be just fine, Mama," Ariel assured her, just as she had done countless times during the past two weeks. "You and Tom go and have a good time."

"All your friends are anxious to see you and you've acknowledged none of their invitations."

"They're curious, is all. I won't give them the satisfaction of looking at me and speculating about what happened in Texas."

"You can't really blame them, dear, but they're still your friends. The same ones you'll come in contact with for years to come."

"Not if I can help it," Ariel said sourly.

"Ah, well, I suppose people can't blame you if you prefer not to attend a party without your fiancé. I'll just tell them you've too much to do before the wedding to attend parties."

Ariel gritted her teeth in frustration. Had her mother always been so featherheaded? She lived in a world of her own and listened to nothing Ariel said.

"When are you leaving?" Ariel asked, happy at the prospect of having the house to herself for an entire weekend.

"Right after breakfast. Don't forget that the dressmaker is coming for a fitting on your wedding gown tomorrow."

"I'll just send her away if she comes, Mama."

"Make sure the train is long enough," Willa continued blithely. "And do insist on a lace veil, I think it's so elegant. Hurry along, dear, we'll see you at breakfast."

Ariel suffered through a rather dismal breakfast, half-listening to her mother's inane chatter about the party, the wedding, and anything else that struck her fancy. Tom ate with gusto, every now and then answering one of Willa's silly questions. Occasionally his glance settled on Ariel, searching her face with a look of such utter bewilderment that Ariel actually felt sorry for him. She gave a heartfelt sigh of relief as she waved them off two hours later.

Around noon Ariel decided to go shopping for new clothes, something in a larger size, then abruptly changed her mind. Instead she chose a book from the library and curled up in a chair, enjoying the solitude. The cook had been given the weekend off as had the housekeeper, so Ariel was truly alone—not that she minded. The quiet allowed her to concentrate to her heart's content on Jess and the child she carried. She loved them both—desperately; she missed Jess—desperately. She'd half-expected him to send a telegram when he arrived in Waco but so far had heard nothing. The lack of communication sent an unnamed fear pounding through her veins.

What if something had happened to Jess?

The rapping at the door went on a long time before Ariel heard it. She frowned, wondering if Denton had returned a day early from Chicago or the dressmaker had decided to make an unscheduled appearance. She wanted to see neither of them and very nearly didn't answer the door.

He stood on the doorstep bigger than life and twice as handsome, dressed in brand-new pants, shirt, jacket, and shiny boots; the same battered Stetson was pushed to the back of his head. A lock of thick black hair fell down over his wide forehead and his silver eyes glittered like newly minted coins.

"Jess! I can't believe you came all the way to St. Louis!"

"I can't believe you'd think that I wouldn't."

Then they were in each other's arms, laughing, crying, wild kisses falling wherever they might. Jess lifted her off her feet and set her inside the door, banging it shut with his foot. They kissed passionately, and Ariel was shocked when she tasted tears. Men didn't cry, did they? It was a long time before either of them could speak.

"Are you ready to go home, sweetheart?" Jess asked, his voice ragged with emotion.

"Anytime you say, Jess." Ariel beamed, reluctant to move from his arms. "I should wait until Mama and Tom return, though. I've hurt them enough without taking off again without an explanation. Beside, I want them to meet the man I love."

"Your family isn't here?"

"No, they're away for the weekend. We have the whole house to ourselves."

Those were the sweetest words Jess had ever heard. Swinging her high in his arms, he growled, "Which way?"

Ariel giggled. "Aren't you hungry?"

"Famished, but not for food. Are you gonna tell me which room is yours or am I gonna make love to you right here in the parlor?"

The violet of Ariel's eyes deepened to dark, mysterious pools that spoke eloquently of her longing for him. She licked her lips as hot bolts of anticipation uncoiled inside her gut. "Up the stairs, second door on the left. Hurry!"

Jess leaped up the stairs, taking them two at a time as he hugged Ariel to his massive chest. He might have been carrying feathers instead of a one-hundred-pound woman. He flung the door open and slammed it shut, not bothering with the lock since they were the only two people in the huge house. He set her on her feet, then spent long moments just looking at her, his eyes missing nothing, not the slightest detail of her tiny, incredible form. Then she was in his arms again.

"I wanna hold you and never let you go, wildcat," he breathed against her lips. "But first I wanna look at you, every wonderful inch of you. I wanna see you naked and touch the place where my baby is growing."

Ariel went still. "You know? Rosalie told you!"

"Don't be angry at Rosalie, sweetheart. She felt bad about telling me but she did what she thought was right under the circumstances. She was afraid you might be forced to marry Denton Dobbs and wanted me to get to you before that happened."

"I'd never marry Denton!" Ariel replied. "How could you even think such a thing?"

"I knew you wouldn't do it willingly, but I didn't underestimate the power your parents hold over you. I'd kill Dobbs and make you a widow if I had to. No man is gonna raise my child."

It was spoken with such fierce conviction that Ariel shuddered, realizing that Jess Wilder would indeed kill for her if the need arose.

"I wanted to tell you myself." She pouted, annoyed that she hadn't been there to see Jess' face when he learned he was going to be a father. "You—you're happy about it, aren't you?" Lord, she never even considered what she'd do if he wasn't as thrilled about it as she was.

"I couldn't be more pleased," Jess said solemnly. "The first thing we gotta do is get married. Before we leave St. Louis, if that's possible." Suddenly he flashed a wicked grin that set Ariel's heart pounding. "I meant to say that getting married is the second thing we gotta do. We can do the first thing without leaving this room."

His eyes settled on the bed. Ariel felt herself grow warm all over.

With shaking hands Jess undressed her, removing her bodice and camisole. His breath caught painfully in his throat when he bared her breasts. Those perfect symmetrical globes were full and round, much larger than he remembered, with elongated, dark coral nipples thrusting impudently. "Jesus H. Christ! If being pregnant does *that* to you I'm gonna keep you this way forever."

He took her breast in his mouth, rolling his tongue over the tip, nipping it with his teeth then soothing it with the cool moistness of his mouth. He moved to the other breast, suckling gently, then harder, until Ariel cried out. Slowly he moved upward to her mouth, kissing her so thoroughly that Ariel began to tremble. Jess knew exactly how and where to touch her to create a need in her so potent nothing could assuage it but his body claiming hers in the most basic way.

Then Jess was removing the rest of her clothing, scattering the pieces wherever they fell until she stood gloriously nude before him. He dropped to his knees and rested his head against the slight rise of her abdomen, brushing tender kisses across the taut skin.

"Don't seem possible that my child is growing in there," he said reverently.

"It's still very small." Ariel smiled tenderly.

"It won't hurt him if we make love, will it?" If she said yes he wasn't certain what he would do except curl up and die right on the spot.

"It won't hurt either of us, Jess," Ariel assured him. "Not for months yet."

"Ah, sweetheart." It was a sigh and a plea and a prayer all at the same time.

Still on his knees, Jess rained kisses over her stomach, her hips, her thighs, careful to avoid that place where she ached for his touch.

"Jess, please!"

He knew what she was asking and obliged.

Grasping her buttocks, his tongue parted the hair at the juncture of her thighs, ruthlessly probing the shiny slick nub nestled there. Ariel groaned and nearly collapsed, but his hands held her in place as he continued to torment and tease with the hard tip of his tongue. Sliding one hand around her waist he used the other to separate the tender folds of her moist flesh and insert a thick finger deep inside. Ariel cried out, her body trembling violently as Jess' tongue and finger worked simultaneously. Jess caught her before she collapsed and carried her to the bed.

His clothes melted away like magic, joining hers on the floor as he settled down beside her. She looked down at him and smiled. His erection was enormous and she knew what it had cost him to bring her pleasure first. She wanted to pleasure him in the same way. Jess nearly lost it when she leaned over and took him in her mouth, but he gritted his teeth and persevered. Then suddenly Ariel was on her back, sprawled beneath Jess as he thrust into her, again and again, stroking her to another climax as he sought his own. They came together in a shattering explosion of bursting stars and colliding planets. It was a long time before either of them could talk. Jess was the first to express his feelings.

"I never thought it was possible to love someone as much as I love you."

"You're my whole world, Jess, I love you above everyone, except for our baby."

Jess grinned foolishly, pleased that Ariel wanted their child as much as he did. "You're still a wildcat in bed. Did I hurt you?"

"Not at all." Her eyes twinkled. "Maybe after we're married and do this more often it won't be so wild."

"Jesus H. Christ! I sure as hell hope you're wrong!"

Ariel giggled, then grew sober when she finally

noticed the still-raw scar on his shoulder. She traced it with her fingertip. "Tell me what happened in San Antonio. Is this what delayed you?"

"I was hit in a shoot-out at Dillon's hideout. The wound wasn't serious but I developed a fever and was out of my head for days."

"I wired Marshal Smith. Why didn't he answer my inquiry about you?"

"He was out of town, and didn't return until the day I left."

"Are the desperadoes in jail?"

"Tilly and Gandy are behind bars but Dillon and Pecos are dead. Dillon was killed in the shoot-out and Pecos got it trying to escape afterward."

"Pecos is dead?" Ariel asked, thinking of Rosalie. She hadn't told Rosalie about Pecos before because she felt it would serve no purpose. But now that he was dead Rosalie had a right to know she was free.

"Pecos and Dillon," Jess repeated. "Your money is in the bank and Walters' money has been returned to him. Walters no longer is interested in buying Leland Ranch."

"What! That's difficult to believe. What changed his mind?" She searched Jess' face, wondering what he had done to bring about such a miracle.

Jess shrugged. He'd decided before he left Waco not to tell Ariel the gruesome details concerning Trudy and her brother. He and Burns had made a pact to keep it to themselves as long as Walters kept to his end of the bargain. "Reckon Walters had a change of heart."

Ariel thought it highly unlikely, but from the implacable look on Jess' face knew it would do no good to probe. He could be as stubborn as he accused her of being. What really mattered was that she no longer had to worry about Kirk Walters. "Is the ranch still mine?"

"Yep. The judge ruled in your favor."

"Mama and Tom will just wire Mr. Burns to sell it to someone else," Ariel predicted.

"I wouldn't count on Burns finding another buyer anytime soon," Jess grinned. "Leastways not before your twenty-first birthday."

"Jess, you *are* a miracle worker!" Ariel cried, hugging him fiercely. "Once we marry it won't matter anyway. All the decisions concerning my property will fall to you."

"The property is yours, sweetheart, and it will stay yours. You're smart enough to make your own decisions. I just want you to know that if you decide to keep the ranch I'll try my damnedest to make it the best darn ranch in Texas. Something our children can be proud of. Now, what do you say we forget about the ranch for a while and think about how I'm gonna make love to you again. Got any preferences?"

"Hmmm, let me think," Ariel said, pretending to give the matter serious thought.

"Not too long, I hope. I don't know how long I can wait."

Suddenly Ariel twisted her body and flung herself atop him, straddling his hips so her sex was nestled snugly in his crotch. She felt him grow instantly erect and chuckled wickedly. "This time I'm going to do the tormenting."

She licked and nipped the hard little nubs of his breasts until he was grinding his pelvis against her in mindless fury. Then she kissed him passionately, sucking his tongue into her mouth then sliding hers into his mouth. She rotated her hips against his thick length but refused to allow him entrance. She touched and caressed him everywhere until Jess nearly went mad with need. Then he rebelled. Ariel knew he was at the end of his endurance and before he could flip her over on her back she raised her hips and with one hand guided him inside her.

Her flesh was hot and moist and tight and Jess

groaned, pushing himself deeper still, until she
had taken the thick incredible length of him into
her body.

"Jesus H. Christ, if it gets any better than this
I don't think I could stand it!"

Then he took her to paradise.

They dozed for a short time afterward and
when Jess awakened he surprised Ariel by saying, "Let's get married now—today. The next
time I bed you I want it to be legal."

"I don't think that's possible, although I'd like
nothing better." Ariel sighed wistfully. "There
are things to do, papers to fill out, all sorts of
details that must be attended to before we can be
married."

Jess frowned. "Can't we just find a preacher or
a justice of the peace?"

"This isn't Texas." She sighed again. Then
abruptly she sat up, her voice quivering with excitement as she went on. "I know someone who
might be willing to marry us on such short notice!
Judge Wyeth is an old family friend, he's known
me for years. If anyone could cut through the le-
galities he could."

"I knew you would think of something, sweetheart." Jess grinned, jumping out of bed and
pulling Ariel with him. "Put on your best dress,
we're gonna have a wedding. Hear that, little
one?" he said, rubbing Ariel's tummy. "Your
mama and I are gonna get hitched."

An hour later they entered Judge Harry
Wyeth's inner chambers. A small, thin man
somewhere in his late forties, his face was
wreathed in smiles when he saw Ariel. "Ariel Leland, how nice to see you. Are Tom and Willa
with you? I'm looking forward to attending your
wedding next week. How's the happy
bridegroom-to-be?"

"I'm not marrying Denton, Judge Wyeth, I
never agreed to the marriage. It was something

Mama and Tom wanted, as did Denton, I suppose." She turned to Jess who stood slightly behind her. "This is Jess Wilder, the man I'm going to marry. That's why we're here. We want you to marry us this afternoon."

"Ariel, this is highly irregular," Judge Wyeth blustered. "You know I can't marry you without your parents' consent, or without one of them present."

"I'm nearly twenty-one, Judge, old enough to make my own decisions. I met Jess in Texas and we fell in love. When Denton forced me to return to St. Louis with him Jess followed."

"What do your parents have to say about all this? And you, young man, why are you in such an all-fired hurry?"

"What Ariel said is true. I love her and would prefer to be married before I take her back to Texas."

"I think you ought to think about this, Ariel. Talk it over with your parents before making any decisions. There's plenty of time, no need to rush into anything."

"You're wrong, Judge, time is of the essence," Ariel said, flushing.

Realizing her embarrassment, Jess stepped forward, placing an arm around her shoulders and drawing her close. "What Ariel is trying to say, Judge," Jess explained bluntly, "is that she's carrying my child. Would you prefer that her child be born a bastard or are you gonna marry us and make it legal? I'm telling you straight out I won't stand by and let another man raise my child. Whether you marry us or not I'm taking Ariel back to Texas where she belongs."

Ariel sent Jess a quelling glance but he stood his ground. The truth might sting at first but it usually reaped rewards in the long run.

Judge Wyeth's jaw dropped open and it took several seconds for him to find his voice. Truth to tell, he liked the brash Texan who looked at Ariel with adoring eyes and spoke his mind. He knew Denton Dobbs and thought him a cold fish, much too dull for Ariel Leland, a young lady he'd known all her life. What an attractive pair Jess Wilder and Ariel made, he thought, and what magnificent children they would produce.

"Am I to assume Willa and Tom know nothing of your—er—condition?" he asked.

"Not yet," Ariel admitted sheepishly. "But I was going to tell them before the wedding so they wouldn't force me to go through with it. I hoped it wasn't going to be necessary but they have their hearts set on my marrying Denton."

Judge Wyeth rubbed his jaw, carefully weighing all the facts. And came to a decision. "I'll have the necessary papers drawn up immediately."

Less than an hour later Ariel and Jess walked out of the judge's chambers as man and wife. On the way home Jess stopped and bought her a plain gold band—they hadn't even thought of it earlier—and then they ate dinner at the best hotel in town. The house was dark and cold when they arrived back at the Brady mansion, but their bedroom was cozy and warm. They made love again, leisurely, driving each other to the limits then quickly withdrawing, only to begin again.

They slept.

Then loved again, and again, the last time at dawn. Then they fell into a deep sleep, having tasted lavishly of love's bounty and surfeit at last.

The scream brought Ariel out of a drugged sleep. She bolted upright, the sheet falling away from her nude body to reveal breasts still flushed from long hours of lovemaking, their coral nipples erect and lush.

Jess was slower to awaken, having performed with amazing stamina and magnificent gusto then plunging into thick slumber. But once having awakened he took stock of the situation much faster than Ariel, who could do little more than stare in confusion at the screaming woman standing just inside the door, hanging onto the doorknob for support.

"Your mother?" Jess asked. One black brow arched upward and it annoyed Ariel that he could remain so calm when she was shaking inside.

She nodded. Her words were little more than disjointed gasps and sputters. "Mama—and Tom aren't—supposed to be home—until tomorrow."

"Ariel, how could you!" Willa's screams finally ceased and those were the only words she managed to spit out before sliding gracefully to the floor in one of her more dramatic faints.

Then Tom arrived, wielding a cane in the event it was needed to defend his loved ones. Ariel lunged for the sheet, pulling it up to her chin as Tom appeared in the doorway. He looked at the prone figure of his wife first, then turned his startled gaze on Ariel and Jess.

Ariel cringed.

Jess had the gall to look amused.

Tom made a strangled noise deep in his throat.

"Who in hell is this man, Ariel? And what is he doing in your bed?"

"This is Jess Wilder, Tom. We got married yesterday."

"You what!" His face grew mottled and his hands shook with repressed rage. "I don't believe you."

"I have the marriage papers to prove it. Judge Wyeth married us. It's all legal and binding."

"Judge Wyeth, you say?" His voice trembled, his body went numb with disbelief. "He is our friend—why would he do such a thing?"

Jess decided it was time to get into the act. "The judge realized we loved each other and decided that making us man and wife was the best thing for all concerned."

"I wasn't talking to you," Tom bellowed.

"Tom, Jess is my husband," Ariel reminded him.

"Look what you did to your mother." He dropped to his knees, found Willa's smelling salts, and held the little vial to her nose. Willa stirred, coughed, and opened her eyes. She looked anywhere but at the bed.

"Tell me it isn't true, Tom," she said shakily. "Tell me I'm dreaming."

"It's true, Willa," Tom said tightly.

"Ohhh." Her eyes rolled back in her head.

"For God's sake, Willa, don't you dare faint again." He helped her to her feet. "You," he said, jabbing a finger at Jess, "I'll see you downstairs in ten minutes. Both of you. We'll get this settled."

"It's already settled. Ariel is my wife," Jess stated tranquilly.

"Ten minutes!" Tom barked.

Grasping Willa by the elbow he steered her from the room. Flustered and confused, the poor woman refused to look at the bed, keeping her eyes aimed straight ahead. Tom slammed the door behind them.

Jess burst out laughing.

"It's not funny," Ariel scolded. "I wasn't expecting them home until tomorrow. I wanted to break it to them gently, not like this." Her arm stretched out to encompass them both in bed, nude, their clothes strewn on the floor in the exact same place they had shed them.

Ariel started to get out of bed, but Jess pulled her back down beside him. "Where are you going, sweetheart?"

"You heard Tom, he said ten minutes."

"Let them wait. I haven't greeted my bride properly this morning."

"Jess!" Ariel squealed as his mouth found her breasts and his hands settled on more fertile ground.

An hour later they walked downstairs and entered the parlor where Tom paced back and forth in angry fury and Willa sat wringing her hands and sniffing back tears. Tom glared at them furiously, accusingly, well aware of what they had been up to.

"I sent for my lawyer. We're having this marriage annulled."

"Like hell!" Jess growled, facing him squarely. "No one is gonna take Ariel from me." They looked like two irate bulls ready to charge.

"Tom, Jess," Ariel pleaded, "can't we talk this over in a dignified manner?"

Unwilling to upset Ariel because of her condition, Jess backed off, but not down. "Sorry, sweetheart, it riles me when anyone even suggests breaking up our marriage." He glared at Tom and asserted evenly, "The marriage has been consummated."

"You've made that clear to us," Tom gritted from between clenched teeth.

"Oh my," Willa said, glancing at Jess from beneath lowered lids. Privately she thought he was the most appealing man she'd ever seen, next to Tom, of course, but so fierce he frightened her. She didn't know whether to feel pity for Ariel for having to submit to such a blatantly sexual creature or envy her.

"An annulment is still possible," Tom contended, standing nearly toe-to-toe with Jess. "You've taken advantage of my stepdaughter's innocence. We know nothing about you. Obviously your background leaves much to be desired."

"I love Jess, Tom, that's all that matters," Ariel said, smiling at Jess.

"And I love Ariel," Jess stated firmly. "What else is there to know?"

"I didn't want you to learn of our marriage like

this," Ariel said, biting her lip. "What brought
you home so early? Didn't you enjoy the party?"

"The party was fine," Willa interjected, finally
finding her tongue. "But I kept thinking about
you home alone and couldn't enjoy myself. I insisted Tom bring me home last night. It was late
so we didn't bother waking you."

Suddenly they became aware that someone was
rapping on the door. "I'll go," Tom said. "It's
probably the lawyer."

It wasn't the lawyer. Tom was gone a long time
and when he returned Denton Dobbs was with
him. "Ariel's *fiancé* is here," he announced in an
unnecessarily loud voice.

Jess scowled.

Ariel groaned.

Willa merely looked confused.

"What's this all about?" Denton asked. Obviously Tom had apprised him of this new development before they entered the room.

"Ariel and I are married," Jess said, more than
a little weary of this tiresome spectacle when obviously these people could do nothing to keep him
and Ariel apart. He and Ariel were man and wife
and he dared anyone to dispute it or try to change
the way things were. "I'm Jess Wilder." He
didn't offer his hand. Neither did Denton.

"Don't worry, Ariel, we'll have this whole ugly
business taken care of in no time," Denton promised, his voice laced with pity. "I'm sure the judge
will take into consideration the fact that you were
forced into this marriage and grant you an annulment. You have just to look at this man to know
he's dangerous and a well-bred young lady like
yourself had no defense against his kind of coercion."

"I married Jess of my own free will. Ask Judge
Wyeth, he'll tell you. Jess and I love each other."

"Our marriage will just be delayed a little

while," Denton continued in a confident manner, paying little heed to Ariel's words.

For Ariel's sake, Jess hung onto his temper, which had been dangling by a thread since Tom had demanded their presence in the parlor. He knew that Ariel loved both Willa and Tom Brady and didn't want to do anything that would destroy that love forever. Families were important. At one time he had Judd but now he had no one but Ariel, and he wasn't going to lose her. Yet he had to lay this matter to rest once and for all in a way that caused the fewest hard feelings. He could tell that Ariel was becoming more and more distraught by this and he wasn't going to allow it to continue, so he did what his conscience and pride demanded.

"Ariel is carrying my child. Do you want your first grandchild to be born a bastard? Or will you let Ariel and me live our lives as we see fit?"

"It's too soon, you couldn't possibly know that!" Denton blurted out before he had time to think about it.

"Ariel is over three months along," Jess said evenly.

Silence.

Ariel sent Jess a fulminating glance.

Jess grinned, amused but looking supremely satisfied.

Willa promptly fainted.

Tom rolled his eyes and acted as if he might join her.

Denton, his face a fiery red, swallowed convulsively and stammered, "I—I—can see this is a family matter. Perhaps I should leave. Under the circumstances, I think it best we cancel the wedding," he added before he left.

Suddenly Ariel giggled, finding his gross understatement hilarious.

Though he tried hard not to, Jess burst out in

uproarious laughter, the entire situation tickling his funny bone.

Tom found little mirth in the state of affairs as he tried to revive his wife.

It was some time before decorum was restored and all parties were able to sit down calmly and discuss the situation. When the smoke had cleared, Jess and Tom shook hands, Jess willingly, Tom with reservations. Willa had recovered enough to express her thrill over becoming a grandmother although she still viewed Jess with awe and a certain amount of trepidation. The man was just too *big*. Normal men didn't stand a chance in his intimidating presence. She didn't envy Ariel. Having to appease as well as please the huge Texan was a frightening prospect. Yet as she looked at Ariel she saw no fright in her daughter's violet eyes. Just love.

Later, in the privacy of their room, Jess and Ariel made plans to return to Texas.

"Are you sure you don't wanna stay in St. Louis longer? Until after the baby is born?" Jess asked as they discussed all that had happened earlier that day.

"I want to go home," Ariel said happily. "I want our baby born on the ranch, on my own land. Will you be happy ranching? It's an entirely different life than you're accustomed to."

"I'm ready to settle down, sweetheart," Jess told her. "I wanna spend the rest of my life making you happy and raising our children. Are you ready to go home?"

"Whenever you say. That piece of land is as close to heaven as I'll ever get in this life." Ariel sighed blissfully.

Jess looked properly affronted. "I thought heaven is where I take you every time we make love."

"Is it too much trouble to ask you to demonstrate again so I might make up my mind?" Ariel

asked, her eyes twinkling with feigned innocence.

"Heaven, here we come." Jess grinned, pulling
her into his arms.

Epilogue

Late summer, 1876

"Mail, sweetheart," Jess called as he walked into the house. He had just returned from a trip to town for supplies and picked up the mail while he was there. "Here's a letter from your mother."

Ariel greeted him with a kiss and when she would have snatched the letter from his hand, his arm snaked around her waist, refusing to let her go. "That's no kind of kiss. How about a proper greeting for your husband." He kissed her soundly, leisurely, as his hands slid around to her buttocks to hold her close. She felt his erection and giggled.

"Jess Wilder, you're incorrigible. Try to behave properly in front of your daughter."

"Jessica is far too young to know what we're doing, but it's about time she got used to it. She should know at an early age just how much her mother and father love one another. Besides," he growled, "I'm never gonna stop kissing and hugging you whenever the mood strikes me. I like it too much."

They both glanced over at the cradle in the corner of the room where six-month-old Jessica Wilder lay playing with her toes and cooing. Her hair was jet-black and her eyes violet like her mother's, but her engaging smile was all Jess'. Her other attributes were entirely her own and so en-chanting that few could resist her charm. Her parents were no exception. Jess adored his tiny daughter and spent as much time with her as possible without neglecting his duties. Besides Jess, Jessica was the most important person in Ariel's life.

With great reluctance Jess released Ariel. "Read your letter, sweetheart. I'll amuse Jessica while you see what your mother has to say."

"Did you see Rosalie in town?" Ariel asked as she ripped open the envelope.

Jess looked at her and grinned. "Sure did. She's as happy as a lark. She said to tell you she'll be out in a few days to see Jessica."

"I wish she was here with us." Ariel sighed wistfully.

After their return to Texas Ariel had tried to persuade Rosalie to return to the ranch with them but Rosalie refused, insisting that Lew Dancy's need for her was far greater than Ariel's. Once Ariel met Lew Dancy she could understand Rosalie's reluctance to leave; she wouldn't be too surprised to see a marriage between them soon. Lew appeared to adore Rosalie and the feeling was mutual. And the Dancy children were fond of her too, having been without a mother's influence for a long time.

When Ariel told Rosalie that she knew Pecos Pete was the man Rosalie had married years ago and that he was now dead, the Mexican woman had stared at her in disbelief. Then, when it had sunk in that she was finally free, she began to weep. But not for long; Rosalie wasn't the type to live in the past or brood over what once was. She hadn't loved Pecos for a long time. First Buck Leland and now Lew Dancy had filled her life with love.

"What does your mother say?" Jess asked as he scooped Jessica up from her cradle.

Ariel concentrated on her letter and her mother's cramped script. When she finished a wide smile brightened her pert features. "Mama and Tom are coming to Texas next month."

"What!" Jess gasped in disbelief. "Your mother is coming to Texas? What changed her mind?"

"Our daughter," Ariel said with a hint of pride. "Jessica managed to heal the rift that existed when we left St. Louis. Mama wants to see her grandchild and Tom wants to look over the ranch and see for himself what we've been bragging about. And," she added with a mischievous grin, "to make sure you're treating me all right."

"I'll be damned," Jess said slowly. "I never thought I'd live to see the day Willa and Tom Brady came willingly to Texas. If Jessica could do that, think what having *two* grandchildren could do. Maybe we oughta start practicing so we'll have some good news to tell them when they arrive."

"You're a horny varmint, Jess Wilder," Ariel teased. "I'll wager you do more practicing than any man in Texas."

"Every day of my life I thank the good Lord for giving me a woman who likes me this way," he returned, grinning with wicked delight.

"Behave, Jess. I want to discuss Mama and Tom's visit, not the frequency with which we make love. Let's have a party while they're here, show them real Texas hospitality. We've made some good friends in town and the family who bought Kirk Walters' ranch seem like lovely people. I'd like to get to know them better."

Jess' face turned somber when he thought of Kirk Walters and his sister Trudy. Trudy had already left town when they returned from St. Louis. Kirk told everyone she had gone to live with an aunt in Nashville. Then Kirk stunned his friends by putting his ranch up for sale. There was much speculation but no one seemed to know why he would just up and leave so abruptly. Jess thought he knew the answer but kept it to himself. No one need know Kirk's dark secret, but Jess strongly suspected that Kirk feared that gossip about him and his sister would somehow find its way to his friends. Rather than face severe censure, he simply left. It was also possible that Kirk couldn't stand the separation between him and Trudy and followed her to Nashville. The thought sickened Jess but didn't surprise him. Kirk Walters was a troubled man.

"Jess, did you hear me? I asked if we might have a party to celebrate my family's arrival."

"Sorry, sweetheart, my mind wandered. A party sounds wonderful. A barbecue, with lots of food and music and whiskey. We can show off our daughter."

"Jessica is sleeping," Ariel said, glancing at her daughter who lay peacefully in Jess' arm.

Jess kissed her fuzzy head and placed her gently in the cradle. Then he turned to Ariel, his silver eyes dark with desire. He held out his hand and waited until she placed hers in his huge palm.

"C'mon, sweetheart, since Jessica is sleeping there's something upstairs I wanna show you."

"I've seen it before, Jess," Ariel said, tossing her head and smiling saucily.

Jess frowned, then his face brightened, his eyes twinkling. "Have I ever shown you how to . . ." He lowered his voice and whispered in her ear.

Ariel's eyes grew round. The tip of her tongue flicked out to moisten her bottom lip as she slanted him a skeptical look. "Is that possible?"

"Come upstairs and find out."

She did.

Not only did she find out but she loved it.

Avon Romances—
the best in exceptional authors and unforgettable novels!

DEVIL'S MOON   Suzannah Davis
76127-0/$3.95 US/$4.95 Can

ROUGH AND TENDER   Selina MacPherson
76322-2/$3.95 US/$4.95 Can

CAPTIVE ROSE   Miriam Minger
76311-7/$3.95 US/$4.95 Can

RUGGED SPLENDOR   Robin Leigh
76318-4/$3.95 US/$4.95 Can

CHEROKEE NIGHTS   Genell Dellin
76014-2/$4.50 US/$5.50 Can

SCANDAL'S DARLING   Anne Caldwell
76110-6/$4.50 US/$5.50 Can

LAVENDER FLAME   Karen Stratford
76267-6/$4.50 US/$5.50 Can

FOOL FOR LOVE   DeLoras Scott
76342-7/$4.50 US/$5.50 Can

OUTLAW BRIDE   Katherine Compton
76411-3/$4.50 US/$5.50 Can

DEFIANT ANGEL   Stephanie Stevens
76449-0/$4.50 US/$5.50 Can

Buy these books at your local bookstore or use this coupon for ordering:

Mail to: Avon Books, Dept BP, Box 767, Rte 2, Dresden, TN 38225
Please send me the book(s) I have checked above.
☐ My check or money order—no cash or CODs please—for $_____ is enclosed
(please add $1.00 to cover postage and handling for each book ordered to a maximum of
three dollars—Canadian residents add 7% GST).
☐ Charge my VISA/MC Acct#_____Exp Date_____
Phone No _____ I am ordering a minimum of two books (please add
postage and handling charge of $2.00 plus 50 cents per title after the first two books to a
maximum of six dollars—Canadian residents add 7% GST). For faster service, call 1-800-
762-0779. Residents of Tennessee, please call 1-800-633-1607. Prices and numbers are
subject to change without notice. Please allow six to eight weeks for delivery.

Name_____

Address _____

City _____ State/Zip _____

ROM 0591

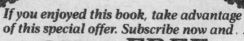

*If you enjoyed this book, take advantage
of this special offer. Subscribe now and . . .*

GET A *FREE*
HISTORICAL ROMANCE
——— NO OBLIGATION(a $3.95 value) ———

Each month the editors of True Value will select the four best historical romance novels from America's leading publishers. Preview them in your home Free for 10 days. And we'll send you a FREE book as our introductory gift. No obligation. If for any reason you decide not to keep them, just return them and owe nothing. But if you like them you'll pay *just* $3.50 each and save at least $.45 each off the cover price. (Your savings are a minimum of $1.80 a month.) There is no shipping and handling or other hidden charges. There are no minimum number of books to buy and you may cancel at any time.

send in the coupon below

Mail to:
True Value Home Subscription Services, Inc.
P.O. Box 5235
120 Brighton Road
Clifton, New Jersey 07015-1234

YES! I want to start previewing the very best historical romances being published today. Send me my FREE book along with the first month's selections. I understand that I may look them over FREE for 10 days. If I'm not absolutely delighted I may return them and owe nothing. Otherwise I will pay the low price of just $3.50 each; a total of $14.00 (at least a $15.80 value) and save at least $1.80. Then each month I will receive four brand new novels to preview as soon as they are published for the same low price. I can always return a shipment and I may cancel this subscription at any time with no obligation to buy even a single book. In any event the FREE book is mine to keep regardless.

Name _____

Address _____ Apt. _____

City _____ State _____ Zip _____

Signature _____
                    (if under 18 parent or guardian must sign)
Terms and prices subject to change.

76450-4